Claim Me

Capture Me: Book 3

Anna Zaires

♠ Mozaika Publications ♠

Copyright © 2016 Anna Zaires and Dima Zales
www.annazaires.com

Published by Mozaika Publications, an imprint of Mozaika LLC.
www.mozaikallc.com

Cover by Najla Qamber Designs
najlaqamberdesigns.com

Photo by Lindee Robinson Photography
Models: Sarah Stroven and Adam Stroven

Edited by Mella Baxter

e-ISBN: 978-1-63142-165-5
Print ISBN: 978-1-63142-166-2

PART I: THE ESCAPE

CHAPTER ONE

❖ LUCAS ❖

"Say that again?" I grip the phone tighter, nearly crushing it as my disbelief morphs into burning fury. "What the fuck do you mean she escaped?"

"I don't know how it happened." Eduardo's voice is tense. "We came back to your house a half hour ago and found her missing. The handcuffs were on the floor of your library, and the ropes were sawed through with something small and sharp. We had the guards scour every inch of the jungle, and they found Sanchez unconscious by the northern border. He has a hell of a concussion, but we got him to wake up a few minutes ago. He says he came across her in the forest, but she surprised him and knocked him out. That was over three hours ago. We're getting the drone feeds now, but it's not looking good."

My rage deepens with every sentence the guard speaks. "How did she get her hands on 'something small and sharp'? Or open the fucking handcuffs? You and Diego were supposed to watch her at all times—"

"We did." Eduardo sounds bewildered. "We checked her pockets after each meal, like you said, and we inspected the bathroom—the only place she's been alone and untied—several times. There was nothing there she could've used. She must've concealed the tools somehow, but I don't know how or when. Maybe she's had them for a while, or maybe—"

"Okay, let's suppose you didn't completely fuck up." I take a breath to control the explosive anger in my chest. The important thing now is to get answers and figure out where the holes in our security are. In a calmer tone, I say, "How could she have gotten out without triggering the alarms or any of the guard towers spotting her? We have eyes on every foot of that border."

There's a prolonged silence. Then Eduardo says quietly, "I don't know why none of the security alarms were triggered, but it's possible there were a couple of hours when we didn't have eyes on the border at all locations."

"What?" I can't hold back my anger this time. "What the fuck do you mean by that?"

"We did fuck up, Kent, but I swear to you, we had no idea the security software would let anything slide." The young guard is speaking quickly now, as if anxious to get the words out. "It was just a friendly poker game; we didn't know the computer wouldn't—"

"A poker game?" My voice goes deadly quiet. "You were playing poker while on duty?"

"I know." Eduardo sounds genuinely contrite. "It was stupid and irresponsible, and I'm sure Esguerra will have our hides. We just thought that with all the technology, it wouldn't be a big deal. Just a way to get out of the afternoon heat for a couple of hours, you know?"

If I could reach through the phone and crush Eduardo's windpipe, I would. "No, I don't know." I'm all but biting out the words. "Why don't you explain it to me, all nice and slow? Or better yet, put Diego on the line, so *he* can do it."

There's another bout of silence. Then I hear Diego say, "Lucas, listen, man . . . I don't even know what to say." The guard's normally upbeat voice is heavy with guilt. "I don't know why she decided to go past that tower, but I'm looking at the footage from the drones now, and that's exactly what she did. Just walked right by us, heading west, and then got on the bridge. It's like she knew where to go and when." A note of incredulity creeps into his tone. "Like she knew we'd be distracted."

I pinch the bridge of my nose. *Fuck.* If what he's saying is true, Yulia's escape is not dumb luck.

Someone gave my captive key security details— someone intimately familiar with the guards' schedule.

"Did she come in contact with anyone?" The most logical possibility is that the traitor is either Diego or Eduardo, but I know the young guards well, and they're both too loyal and too smart for this kind of double cross. "Did anyone talk to her besides the two of you?"

"No. At least, we didn't see anyone." Diego's voice tightens as he catches on to my suspicion. "Of course, she was by herself for a large portion of the day; someone could've come to the house when we weren't there."

"Right." Hell, the traitor could've even approached Yulia before I left for Chicago. "I want you to pull up the drone footage on any and all activity around my house in the past two weeks. If anyone so much as stepped a foot on my porch, I want to know."

"You got it."

"Good. Now get going and track down Yulia. She couldn't have gotten far."

Diego hangs up, clearly eager to make up for his and Eduardo's blunder, and I put the phone back in my pocket, forcing my fingers to unclench from around the object.

They'll catch her and bring her back.

I have to believe that, or I won't be able to function this evening.

* * *

While I wait for an update from Diego, I do the rounds with the guards, making sure they're all in position at Esguerra's new Chicago vacation home. The mansion is in the wealthy private community of Palos Park and well situated from a security standpoint, but I still check the newly installed cameras for blind spots and confirm the patrol schedules with the guards. I do this because it's my job, but also because I need something to keep my mind off Yulia and the suffocating anger burning in my chest.

She ran. The moment I was gone, she ran to her lover—to this Misha, whose life she begged me to spare.

She ran even though less than two days ago she told me she loved me.

The fury that fills me at the thought is both potent and irrational. I don't even know if Yulia's words had been meant for me; she mumbled them while half-asleep, and I didn't have a chance to confront her. Still, the possibility that she might love me had kept me tossing and turning the night before my departure.

For the first time in my life, I'd felt like I was close to something . . . close to some*one*.

I love you. I'm yours.

What a fucking liar. My ribcage tightens as I recall Yulia's attempts to manipulate me, to butter me up so

I'd agree to save her lover's life. From the very beginning, I've been just a means to an end for her. She slept with me in Moscow to get information, and she played the part of an obedient captive to facilitate her escape.

The time we spent together meant nothing to Yulia, and neither do I.

The buzzing of the phone in my pocket interrupts my bitter thoughts. Fishing it out, I see the encrypted number that's our relay from the compound.

"Yes?"

"We have a problem." Diego's tone is clipped. "It looks like your girl timed her escape perfectly in more ways than one. There was a delivery of groceries to the compound this afternoon, and the Miraflores police just found the driver walking on the side of the road, a few kilometers outside town. Apparently, he picked up a beautiful American hitchhiker just north of our compound. He had no idea she was anything other than a lost tourist—that is, until she pulled out a knife and made him get out of the van. That was over an hour ago."

"Fuck." If Yulia has wheels, her chances of eluding us go up exponentially. "Search all of Miraflores and find that van. Get the local police to help."

"We're already on it. I'll keep you posted."

I hang up and head back into the house. Esguerra's in-laws are already pulling into the driveway for their dinner with my boss and his wife, and Esguerra is likely not in the mood to be bothered right now. Still, I have to let him know what happened, so I send a one-line email:

Yulia Tzakova escaped.

CHAPTER TWO

❖ YULIA ❖

As soon as I'm in the city bounds of Miraflores, I pull into a gas station and ask the attendant to use the landline in the tiny store. He understands enough of my English to let me do so, and I dial the emergency number all UUR agents have memorized. As I wait for the call to connect, I watch the door, my palms slick with sweat.

Diego and Eduardo must know I'm missing by now, which means Esguerra's guards are looking for me. I felt bad threatening the van's driver and forcing him to get out of the car, but I needed the vehicle. As it is, I don't have long before Esguerra's men track me here—if they haven't already.

"Allo." The Russian greeting, spoken in a mellow female voice, brings my attention back to the phone.

"It's Yulia Tzakova," I say, giving my current identity. Like the operator, I'm speaking Russian. "I'm in Miraflores, Colombia, and need to speak to Vasiliy Obenko right away."

"Code?"

I rattle off a set of numbers, then answer the operator's questions designed to verify my identity.

"Please hold," she says, and there's a moment of silence before I hear a click signifying a new connection.

"Yulia?" Obenko's voice is filled with disbelief. "You're alive? The Russians' report said you died in prison. How did you—"

"The report was false. Esguerra's men took me." I keep my voice low, cognizant that the attendant is eyeing me with increasing suspicion. I told him I'm an American tourist, and my speaking Russian undoubtedly confuses him. "Listen, you're in danger. Everyone connected to UUR is in danger. You need to disappear and have Misha disappear—"

"Esguerra got you?" Obenko sounds horrified. "Then how are you—"

"There's no time to explain. I escaped from his compound, but they're looking for me. You need to disappear—you and everyone in your family. And Misha. They'll be coming for you."

"They cracked you?"

"Yes." Self-loathing is a thick knot in my throat, but I keep my voice even. "They don't know your current location, but they have the agency's initials and one former agent's real name. It's only a matter of time before they track you down."

"Fuck." Obenko goes silent for a moment, then says, "We need to get you out of there before you're recaptured." Before they have a chance to extract more information out of me, he means.

"Yes." The attendant is typing something on his cell phone while glancing at me, and I know I need to hurry. "I have a car, but I'll need help getting out of the country."

"All right. Can you get closer to Bogotá? We may be able to call in some favors with the Venezuelan government and smuggle you out across the border."

"I think so." The attendant puts down his phone and starts toward me, so I say quickly, "I'm on my way," and hang up.

The attendant is almost next to me, his forehead furrowed, but I hurry out of the store before he can grab me. Jumping into the van, I shut the door behind me and start the car. The attendant runs out behind me, but I'm already peeling out of the parking lot with a squeal of tires.

When I'm back on the road, I assess my situation. There's only a quarter tank of gas left in the van, and the attendant most likely reported me to the authorities—which means the vehicle became compromised faster than I expected.

I'll need a different set of wheels if I'm to make it out of Miraflores.

My heart hammers as I step on the gas, pushing the old van to its limits while keeping a careful eye on the road. One kilometer, one-point-five kilometers, two kilometers . . . My anxiety intensifies with every moment that passes. How long before Esguerra's men hear about the strange blonde at the gas station? How long until they start looking for the van via satellites? I can't have more than a half hour at this point.

Finally, after another kilometer, I see it: a small unpaved road that appears to lead to a farm of some kind. Praying that my hunch is correct, I turn onto it, leaving the main road.

A couple of hundred meters later, I spot a storage shed. It's a dozen meters to the right, and behind it is a thickly wooded area. I turn toward it and park the van behind the shed, under the cover of the trees. If I'm lucky, it won't be spotted for some time.

Now I need to locate another vehicle.

Leaving the shed, I walk until I come across a barn with an old, beaten-up tractor in front of it. I don't see any people, so I approach the barn and peek inside.

Jackpot.

Inside the barn is a small pick-up truck. It looks old and rusty, but its windows are clean. Someone uses it regularly.

Holding my breath, I slip into the barn and approach the truck. The first thing I do is search the nearby shelves for keys; sometimes people are stupid enough to leave them next to the vehicle.

Unfortunately, this particular farmer doesn't seem to be stupid. The keys are nowhere to be found. Oh, well. I glance around and see a rock holding down a piece of tarp. I grab the rock and use it to smash the truck's window. It's a brute-force solution, but it's faster than picking the locks.

Now comes the hard part.

Opening the driver's door, I climb onto the seat and remove the ignition cover under the wheel. Then I study the tangle of wires, hoping I remember enough of this to not disable the vehicle or electrocute myself. We covered hot-wiring in training, but I've never had to do it in the field, and I have no idea if it'll work. Every car is a little different; there's no universal color system for the wires, and older cars, like this pick-up truck, are particularly tricky. If I had any other option, I wouldn't risk it, but this is my best bet right now.

Here goes nothing. Steadying my breathing, I begin testing the different combinations of wires. On my third attempt, the truck's engine sputters to life.

I exhale a relieved breath, close the door, and drive out of the barn, heading back toward the main road.

With any luck, the truck's owner won't discover it missing for some time, and I'll make it to the next town before I have to get another vehicle.

* * *

As I drive, my thoughts turn to Lucas. Did the guards tell him about my escape? Is he angry? Does he feel like I betrayed him by leaving?

I love you. I'm yours. Even now, my cheeks flame as I remember those words, said in a dream that might not have been a dream. Until that night, I didn't know how I felt, didn't realize how attached I'd become to my jailer. There was so much wrongness between us, so much fear and anger and mistrust that it took me a while to understand this strange longing.

To make sense of something so irrational and senseless.

I'll miss you. Lucas said that to me as he cuddled me on his lap the next morning, and it was all I could do not to burst into tears. Did he know what he was doing to me with his confusing words of caring? Was that incongruous tenderness part of his diabolical revenge? An even more sadistic way to wreck me without inflicting so much as a bruise?

The road blurs in front of me, and I realize the tears I held back that day are rolling down my face, the adrenaline from my escape sharpening the remembered pain. I don't want to think about how Lucas broke me, how he promised me safety and tore my heart to pieces instead, but I can't help it. The memories loop through my mind, and I can't shut them off. Something about Lucas's behavior that last day keeps nagging at me, some discordant note I registered but didn't process fully at the time.

"Do not fucking beg for him," Lucas snapped when I pleaded for my brother to be spared. "I decide who lives, not you."

There were other things he said, too. Hurtful things. Yet when he took me that night, there hadn't been anger in his touch. Lust, yes. Insane possessiveness, definitely. But not anger—at least not the kind of anger I would've expected from a man who hates me enough to let my only family be murdered. And that "I'll miss you" the following morning. It just didn't fit.

None of it fit—unless that's how Lucas wanted it.

Maybe he wasn't done mind-fucking me yet.

My head begins to ache from the confusion, and I wipe the tears off my face before tightening my grip on the wheel. Whatever Lucas planned for me no longer matters. I escaped, and I can't keep looking back.

I have to keep moving forward.

CHAPTER THREE

❖ LUCAS ❖

I wake up Friday morning with a throbbing headache that adds to my fury. I've barely slept—Diego and Eduardo kept sending me hourly updates on their search for Yulia—and it takes two cups of coffee before I start feeling semi-human.

As I'm getting ready to leave the kitchen, Rosa walks in, dressed in jeans instead of her usual conservative maid's outfit.

"Oh, hi, Lucas," she says. "I was just looking for you."

"Oh?" I try not to glower at the girl. I still feel bad that I had to squash her little crush on me. It's not

Rosa's fault that my prisoner escaped, and I don't want to take out my shitty mood on the girl.

"Señor Esguerra said I can explore the city today if I take a guard with me," Rosa says, watching me warily. She must've picked up on my anger despite my attempts to look calm. "Is there anybody you could spare?"

I consider her request. Truthfully, the answer is no. I don't want to take any guards away from Nora's parents' house, and fifteen minutes ago, Esguerra texted me that he's taking Nora to a park, which means he'll need at least a dozen of our men to be in position there.

"I'm going to Chicago today," I say after a moment of deliberation. "I have a meeting there. You can come with me if you don't mind waiting for a bit. Afterwards, I'll take you wherever you want to go, and by lunchtime, one of the other guys will be available to replace me—assuming you want to stay in the city longer than a couple of hours, that is."

"Oh, I . . ." A flush darkens Rosa's bronzed skin, even as her eyes brighten with excitement. "Are you sure I wouldn't be imposing? I don't have to go today if—"

"It's all right." I remember what the girl told me on Wednesday about having never been to the United States before. "I'm sure you're eager to see the city, and I don't mind."

Maybe her company will get my mind off Yulia and the fact that my prisoner is still on the loose.

* * *

Rosa chatters nonstop as we drive to Chicago, telling me all about the various Chicago trivia she's read online.

"And did you know that it's named the Windy City because of politicians who were full of hot air?" she says as I turn onto West Adams Street in downtown Chicago and pull into the underground parking garage of a tall glass-and-steel building. "It has nothing to do with the actual wind coming off the lake. Isn't that crazy?"

"Yes, amazing," I say absentmindedly, checking my phone as I get out of the car. To my disappointment, there's no new update from Diego. Putting the phone away, I walk around the car and open the door for Rosa.

"Come," I say. "I'm already five minutes late."

Rosa hurries after me as I walk to the elevator. She takes two steps for every one of mine, and I can't help comparing her bouncy walk to Yulia's long-limbed, graceful stride. The maid is not quite as petite as Esguerra's wife, but she still looks short to me—especially since I've gotten used to Yulia's model-like height.

Fucking stop thinking of her. My hands clench in my pockets as I wait for the elevator to arrive, only half-listening to Rosa chattering about the Magnificent Mile. The spy is like a splinter under my skin. No matter what I do, I can't get her off my mind. Compulsively, I pull out my phone and check it again.

Still nothing.

"So what is your meeting about?" Rosa asks, and I realize she's staring up at me expectantly. "Is it something for Señor Esguerra?"

"No," I say, slipping the phone back into my pocket. "It's for me."

"Oh." She looks deflated at my curt reply, and I sigh, reminding myself that I shouldn't take out my frustration on the girl. She has nothing to do with Yulia and the whole fucked-up situation.

"I'm meeting with my portfolio manager," I say as the elevator doors slide open. "I just need to catch up on my investments."

"Oh, I see." Rosa grins as we step into the elevator. "You have investments, like Señor Esguerra."

"Yes." I press the button for the top floor. "This guy is his portfolio manager as well."

The elevator whooshes upward, all sleek steel and gleaming surfaces, and less than a minute later, we're stepping out into an equally sleek and modern reception area.

For a twenty-six-year-old guy born in the projects, Jared Winters certainly leads a good life.

His receptionist, a slim Japanese woman of indeterminate age, stands up as we approach.

"Mr. Kent," she says, giving me a polite smile. "Please, have a seat. Mr. Winters will be with you in a minute. May I offer you and your companion some refreshments?"

"None for me, thanks." I glance at Rosa. "Would you like anything?"

"Um, no, thank you." She's staring at the floor-to-ceiling window and the city spread out below. "I'm good."

Before I have a chance to sit down in one of the plush seats by the window, a tall, dark-haired man steps out of the corner office and approaches me.

"Sorry to keep you waiting," Winters says, reaching out to shake my hand. His green eyes gleam coolly behind his frameless glasses. "I was just finishing up a call."

"No worries. We're a bit late ourselves."

He smiles, and I see his gaze flick over to Rosa, who's still standing there, seemingly mesmerized by the view outside.

"Your girlfriend, I presume?" Winters says quietly, and I blink, surprised by the personal question.

"No," I say, following him as he walks back toward his office. "More like my assignment for the next couple of hours."

"Ah." Winters doesn't say anything else, but as we enter his office, I see him glance back at Rosa, as if unable to help himself.

CHAPTER FOUR

❖ YULIA ❖

"Yulia Tzakova?"

My heart leaps into my throat as I spin around, my hand automatically clutching the knife tucked into my jeans.

There is a dark-haired man standing in front of me. He looks average in every way; even his sunglasses and cap are standard issue. He could've been anyone in the busy Villavicencio marketplace, but he's not.

He's Obenko's Venezuelan contact.

"Yes," I say, keeping my hand on the knife. "Are you Contreras?"

He nods. "Please follow me," he says in Spanish-accented Russian.

I drop my hand from the knife handle and follow the man as he begins winding through the crowd. Like him, I'm wearing a cap and sunglasses—two items I stole at another gas station on the way here—but I still feel like someone might point at me and yell, "That's her. That's the spy Esguerra's men are looking for."

To my relief, nobody pays me much attention. In addition to the cap and sunglasses, I acquired a voluminous T-shirt and baggy jeans at that same gas station. With the shapeless clothes and my hair tucked into the cap, I look more like a teenage boy than a young woman.

Contreras leads me to a nondescript blue van parked on the street corner. "Where's the vehicle you used to get here?" he asks as I climb into the back.

"I left it a dozen blocks from here, like Obenko instructed," I say. I've spoken to my boss twice since my initial contact at Miraflores, and he gave me the location of this meeting and orders on how to proceed. "I don't think I was followed."

"Maybe not, but we need to get you out of the country in the next few hours," Contreras says, starting the van. "Esguerra is expanding the net. They already have your picture at all the border crossings."

"So how are you going to get me out?"

"There's a crate in the back," Contreras says as we pull out into the traffic. "And one of the border guards owes me a favor. With some luck, that will suffice."

I nod, feeling the cold air from the van's AC washing over my sweaty face. I drove all night, stopping only to steal another car and get the clothes, and I'm exhausted. I've been on the lookout for the sound of helicopter blades and the whine of sirens every minute I've been on the road. The fact that I've gotten this far without incident is nothing short of a miracle, and I know my luck could run out at any moment.

Still, even that fear is not enough to overcome my exhaustion. As Contreras's van gets on the highway, heading northeast, I feel my eyelids closing, and I don't fight the drugging pull of sleep.

I just need to nap for a few minutes, and then I'll be ready to face whatever comes next.

* * *

"Wake up, Yulia."

The hushed urgency of Contreras's tone yanks me out of a dream where I'm watching a movie with Lucas. My eyes snap open as I sit up and quickly take in the situation.

It's already twilight, and we appear stuck in some kind of traffic.

"Where are we? What is this?"

"Roadblock," Contreras says tersely. "They're checking all the cars. You need to get in the crate, now."

"Your border guard isn't—"

"No, we're still some twenty miles from the Venezuelan border. I don't know what this roadblock is about, but it can't be good."

Shit. I unbuckle my seatbelt and crawl through a small window into the back of the van. As Contreras said, there is a crate back there, but it looks far too small to fit a person. A child, maybe, but not a woman of my height.

Then again, in magic acts, they fit people into all kinds of seemingly too-small containers. That's how the cut-in-half trick is often done: one flexible girl is the "upper body" and a second one is "legs."

I'm not as flexible as a typical magician's assistant, but I'm far more motivated.

Opening the crate, I lie down on my back and try to fold my legs in such a way that I'd be able to close the lid over me. After a couple of frustrating minutes, I concede that it's an impossible task; my knees are at least five centimeters above the edge of the crate. Wʰ did Contreras get a crate this small? A few centiɱ deeper, and I would've been fine.

The van begins moving, and I realize w closer to the checkpoint. At any momer the back of the van will open, and I'll ʰ

I need to fit into this fucking crʳ

Gritting my teeth, I turn siᵈ my knees into the tiny spacʳ side of the crate. They dᵕ and try again, ignoring the burst of pain in my kneecap as it bumps against the metal edge. As I struggle, I hear raised voices speaking Spanish and feel the van come to a stop again.

We're at the checkpoint.

Frantic, I turn and grab the lid of the crate, pulling it over me with shaking hands.

There are footsteps, followed by voices at the back of the van.

They're going to open the doors.

My heart pounding, I flatten myself into an impossibly tiny ball, squashing my breasts with my knees. Even with the numbing effects of adrenaline, my body screams with pain at the unnatural position.

The lid meets the edge of the crate, and the van doors swing open.

CHAPTER FIVE

❖ LUCAS ❖

My meeting with Winters takes just under an hour. We go over the current state of my investments and discuss how to proceed given the recent froth in the market. In the time that Jared Winters has been managing my portfolio, he's tripled it to just over twelve million, so I'm not particularly concerned when he says he's liquidating most of my equity holdings and getting ready to short a popular tech stock.

"The CEO is about to get in some serious legal trouble," Winters explains, and I don't bother asking how he knows that. Trading on insider information may be a crime, but our contacts at the SEC ensure that Winters's fund is nowhere on their radar.

"How much are you putting behind the trade?" I ask.

"Seven million," Winters replies. "It's going to get ugly."

"All right," I say. "Go for it."

Seven million is a sizable sum, but if the tech stock is about to drop as much as Winters thinks, it could easily be another triple or more.

We go over a few more upcoming trades, and then Winters walks me out to the reception area, where Rosa is reading a magazine.

"Ready to go?" I ask, and she nods.

Getting up, she places the magazine back on the coffee table and beams at me and Winters. "Definitely ready."

"Thanks again," I say, turning to shake Winters's hand, but he's not looking at me.

He's staring at Rosa, his green gaze oddly intent.

"Winters?" I prod, amused.

He tears his eyes away from her. "Oh, yes. It was a pleasure," he mutters, shaking my hand, and before I can say another word, he strides back into his office and shuts the door behind him.

* * *

As I promised Rosa, after the meeting I take her shopping on the Magnificent Mile—also known as Michigan Avenue. As she tries on a bunch of dresses at a department store, I take a seat next to the fitting room and check my email again. This time, there's a short message from Diego:

Located the stolen pick-up truck at a gas station near Granada. No other cars reported stolen for now. Blockades up at all the major roads as per your instructions.

I put the phone away, frustrated anger churning in my gut. They still haven't found Yulia, and by now, she could be in another country. She has undoubtedly made contact with her agency, and depending on how resourceful they are, it's entirely possible that they've smuggled her out.

For all I know, she's already on a plane, flying to her lover.

"How do you like this?" Rosa asks, and I turn to see that she's come out of the fitting room in a short, form-fitting yellow dress.

"It's nice," I say on autopilot. "You should get it." Objectively, I can see that the dark-haired girl looks good in that dress, but all I can think about right now is the fact that Yulia may be on her way to Misha . . . to the man she truly loves.

"All right." Rosa gives me a huge smile. "I will."

She hurries back into the fitting room, and I pull out my phone to fire off an email to the hackers looking into UUR.

Even if Yulia managed to get away, she won't stay free for long.

No matter what it takes, I'll find her, and she'll never escape again.

CHAPTER SIX

❖ YULIA ❖

"Sorry about that," Contreras says, pulling the lid off my crate. "I didn't expect you to be this tall. I'm glad you were able to fit in there."

I groan as he pulls me out, my muscles cramping from being stuck in the tiny crate for the last hour. My knees feel like two giant bruises, and my spine is throbbing from being squashed against the side of the crate. I am, however, alive and across the Venezuelan border—which means it was all worth it.

"It's okay," I say, rotating my head in a semi-circle. My neck is painfully stiff, but it's nothing a good massage won't cure. "It fooled the police and border patrol. They didn't even try looking into the crate."

Contreras nods. "That's why I brought it. It looks too small to fit a person, but when one is determined . . ." He shrugs.

"Yeah." I rotate my head again and stretch, trying to get my muscles working. "So what's the plan now?"

"Now we get you to the plane. Obenko has already arranged everything. By tomorrow, you should be in Kiev, safe and sound."

* * *

Our drive to the small airstrip takes less than an hour, and then we're pulling up in front of an ancient-looking jet.

"Here we are," Contreras says. "Your people will take it from here."

"Thank you," I say, and he nods as I open the door.

"Good luck," he says in his Spanish-accented Russian, and I smile at him before jumping out of the van and hurrying to the plane.

As I walk up the ladder, a middle-aged man steps out, blocking the entrance. "Code?" he says, his hand resting on a gun at his side.

Eyeing the weapon warily, I tell him my identification number. Technically, eliminating me would accomplish the same thing as getting me away from Esguerra: I wouldn't be able to spill any more UUR secrets. In fact, it would be an even neater solution . . .

Before my mind can travel too far down that path, the man lowers his hand and steps aside, letting me enter the plane.

"Welcome, Yulia Borisovna," he says, using my real patronymic. "We're glad you made it."

CHAPTER SEVEN

❖ LUCAS ❖

By Saturday morning, I'm convinced that Yulia must be back in Ukraine. Diego and Eduardo were able to track her as far as Venezuela, but her trail seems to have gone cold there.

"I think she left the country," Diego says when I call him for an update. "A private plane registered to a shell corporation filed a flight plan to Mexico, but there's no record of it landing anywhere in that country. It must've been her people, and if that's the case, she's gone."

"That's not a fact. Keep looking," I say, even though I know he's most likely right.

Yulia got away, and if I'm to have any hope of recapturing her, I'll have to widen the net and call on some of our international contacts.

I consider bringing Esguerra up to speed on the whole situation, but decide to postpone it until Sunday. Today is his wife's twentieth birthday, and I know he's not in the mood to be bothered. All my boss cares about is giving Nora everything she wants—including a trip to a popular nightclub in downtown Chicago.

"You do realize guarding that place will be a nightmare, right?" I tell him when he brings up the outing at lunchtime. "It's too many people. And on a Saturday night—"

"Yes, I know," Esguerra says. "But this is what Nora requested, so let's figure out a way to make it happen."

We spend the next two hours going through the club schematics and deciding where to station all the guards. It's unlikely that any of Esguerra's enemies will catch wind of this, since it's such a spur-of-the-moment event, but we still decide to position snipers in the buildings nearby and have the other guards within a one-block radius of the club. My role will be to stay in the car and keep an eye on the club's entrance, in case there's any threat coming from that direction. We also work out a plan for securing the restaurant where Esguerra and his wife will have dinner before going to the club.

"Oh, I almost forgot," Esguerra says as we're wrapping up. "Nora wants Rosa to join us at the club. Can you have one of the guards drive her there?"

"Yes, I think so," I say after a moment of consideration. "Thomas can bring the girl to the club before taking his position at the end of the block."

"That would work." Esguerra rises to his feet. "I'll see you tonight."

He leaves the room, and I go outside to assign the guards their tasks.

* * *

Esguerra's dinner outing passes without an incident, and afterwards, I drive him and Nora to the club. Rosa is already waiting there, dressed in the yellow dress she bought on our shopping trip. The moment Nora steps out of the car, Rosa runs up to her, and I hear the two young women chattering excitedly as they head into the club. Esguerra follows them, looking mildly amused, and I stay in the car, settling in for what promises to be a long, boring night.

After about an hour, I eat a sandwich I packed earlier and check my email. To my relief, there's an update from our hackers.

Finally broke through the Ukrainian government's firewalls and deciphered some files, the email reads. UUR is an acronym for Ukrainskoye Upravleniye Razvedki, which roughly translates to "Ukrainian

Intelligence Bureau." It's an off-the-books spy group that was established in response to their main security agency's corruption and close ties to Russia. We're now working on decoding a message that may point to two UUR field operatives and a location in Kiev.

Smiling grimly, I write a reply and put away the phone. It's only a matter of time before we take down Yulia's organization. And once we do, she'll have nowhere to run, no one to help her.

No lover she could return to.

My teeth clench as violent jealousy spears through me. Yulia could be with him already, with this Misha of hers. He could be holding her at this very moment.

He could even be fucking her.

The thought fills me with blazing fury. If I had the man in front of me right now, I'd kill him with my bare hands and make Yulia watch. It would be her punishment for this latest betrayal.

A buzzing vibration from my phone cuts into my vengeful thoughts. Grabbing it, I read Esguerra's text, and my blood turns to ice.

Nora and Rosa attacked, the message says. *Rosa taken. I'm going after her. Alert the others.*

CHAPTER EIGHT

❖ YULIA ❖

The familiar smell of car exhaust and lilacs fills my nostrils as the car weaves through the busy Kiev streets. The man Obenko sent to pick me up at the airport is someone I've never seen before, and he doesn't talk much, leaving me free to take in the sights of the city where I lived and trained for five years.

"We're not going to the Institute?" I ask the driver when the car makes an unfamiliar turn.

"No," the man replies. "I'm taking you to a safe house."

"Is Obenko there?"

The driver nods. "He's waiting for you."

"Great." I take a steadying breath. I should be relieved to be here, but instead, I feel tense and anxious. And it's not just because I screwed up and compromised the organization. Obenko doesn't deal kindly with failure, but the fact that he extracted me from Colombia instead of killing me eases my worry in that regard.

No, the main source of my anxiety is the empty feeling inside me, an ache that's growing more acute with every hour without Lucas. I feel like I'm going through a withdrawal—except that would make Lucas my drug, and I refuse to accept that.

Whatever I had begun to feel for my captor will pass. It has to, because there's no other alternative.

Lucas and I are over for good.

"We're here," the driver says, stopping in front of an unassuming four-story apartment building. It looks just like every other building in this neighborhood: old and rundown, the outside covered with a dull yellowish plaster from the Soviet era. The scent of lilacs is stronger here; it's coming from a park across the street. Under any other circumstances, I would've enjoyed the fragrance that I associate with spring, but today it reminds me of the jungle I left behind—and, by extension, the man who held me there.

The driver leaves the car by the curb and leads me into the building. It's a walk-up, and the stairwell is as rundown as the building's exterior. When we walk past the first floor, I hear raised voices and catch a whiff of urine and vomit.

"Who are those people on the first floor?" I ask as we stop in front of an apartment on the second floor. "Are they civilians?"

"Yes." The driver knocks on the door. "They're too busy getting drunk to pay us much attention."

I don't have a chance to ask more questions because the door swings open, and I see a dark-haired man standing there. His wide forehead is creased, and lines of tension bracket his thin mouth.

"Come in, Yulia," Vasiliy Obenko says, stepping back to let me enter. "We have a lot to discuss."

* * *

Over the next two hours, I go through an interrogation as grueling as anything I'd experienced in the Russian prison. In addition to Obenko, there are two senior UUR agents, Sokov and Mateyenko. Like my boss, they're in their forties, their trim bodies honed into deadly weapons over decades of training. The three of them sit across from me at the kitchen table and take turns asking questions. They want to know everything from the details of my escape to the exact information I gave Lucas about UUR.

"I still don't understand how he broke you," Obenko says when I'm done recounting that story. "How did he know about that incident with Kirill?"

My face burns with shame. "He learned about it as a result of a nightmare I had." And because I had confided in Lucas afterwards, but I don't say that. I don't want my boss to know that he had been right about me all along—that when it mattered, I couldn't control my emotions.

"And in this nightmare, you what . . . spoke about your trainer?" It's Sokov who asks me this, his stern expression making it clear that he doubts my story. "Do you usually talk in your sleep, Yulia Borisovna?"

"No, but these weren't exactly *usual* circumstances." I do my best not to sound defensive. "I was held prisoner and placed in situations that were triggers for me—that would be triggers for any woman who'd undergone an assault."

"What exactly were those situations?" Mateyenko cuts in. "You don't look particularly maltreated."

I bite back an angry response. "I wasn't physically tortured or starved, I already told you that," I say evenly. "Kent's methods of interrogation were more psychological in nature. And yes, that was in large part due to the fact that he found me attractive. Hence the triggers."

The two agents exchange looks, and Obenko frowns at me. "So he raped you, and that triggered your nightmares?"

"He . . ." My throat tightens as I recall my body's helpless response to Lucas. "It was the overall situation. I didn't handle it well."

41

The agents look at each other again, and then Mateyenko says, "Tell us more about the woman who helped you escape. What did you say her name was?"

Calling on every bit of patience I possess, I recount my encounters with Rosa for the third time. After that, Sokov asks me to go through my escape again, minute by minute, and then Mateyenko interrogates me about the security logistics of Esguerra's compound.

"Look," I say after another hour of nonstop questions, "I've told you everything I know. Whatever you may think of me, the threat to the agency is real. Esguerra's organization has taken down entire terrorist networks, and they're coming after us. If you have any contingency measures in place, now is the time to implement them. Get yourselves and your families to safety."

Obenko studies me for a moment, then nods. "We're done for today," he says, turning toward the two agents. "Yulia is tired after her long journey. We'll resume this tomorrow."

The two men depart, and I slump in my chair, feeling even emptier than before.

CHAPTER NINE

❖ LUCAS ❖

As soon as I read Esguerra's message, I radio the guards and order half of them to head to the club. None of them had noticed any suspicious activity, which means that the threat, whatever it was, had come from within the club, not outside as we'd expected. I'm about to rush into the club myself when I get another text from Esguerra:

Recovered Rosa. Follow the white SUV.

I instantly radio the guards to do so, and at that moment, another message comes in:

Bring the car to the alley out back.

I start the car and zoom around the block, nearly running over a couple of pedestrians in the process.

The alley at the back of the club is dark and stinks of garbage mixed with piss, but I barely register the ambience. Stepping out of the car, I wait, my hand on the gun at my side. A few seconds later, the men radio me that they located the white SUV and are following it. I'm about to give them further instructions when the door to the club swings open, and Nora comes out, her arms wrapped around Rosa. Esguerra follows them, his face twisted with rage. As the light from the car illuminates their figures, I realize why.

Both women are shaking, their faces pale and streaked with tears. However, it's Rosa's state that sends my blood pressure through the roof. Her bright yellow dress is torn and stained with blood, and one side of her face is grotesquely swollen.

The girl had been violently assaulted, just like Yulia seven years ago.

A crimson fog fills my vision. I know my reaction is disproportional—Rosa is little more than a stranger to me—but I can't help it. The images in my mind are of a fragile fifteen-year-old, her slender body torn and bleeding. I can see the shame and devastation on Rosa's face, and the knowledge that Yulia went through this makes my guts churn.

"Those fuckers." My voice is thick with rage as I step around the car to open the door. "Those motherfucking fuckers. They're going to fucking die."

"Yes, they will," Esguerra says grimly, but I'm not listening. Reaching for Rosa, I carefully pull her away from Nora. Esguerra's wife doesn't appear to be hurt as badly, but she's still clearly shaken. Rosa sobs as I shepherd her into the car, and I do my best to be gentle with her, to comfort her as I couldn't comfort Yulia all those years ago.

As I buckle her in, I hear Esguerra say his wife's name, his voice strangely tense, and I turn to see Nora double over next to the car.

The baby, I realize in an instant, remembering her pregnancy, but Esguerra is already bundling her into the car and yelling for me to drive to the hospital, now.

* * *

We get to the hospital in record time, but long before Esguerra comes out into the waiting room, I know that the baby didn't make it. There was too much blood in the car.

"I'm sorry," I say, taking in my boss's shattered expression. "How's Nora?"

"They stopped the bleeding." Esguerra's voice is hoarse. "She wants to go home, so that's what we'll do. We'll take Rosa, too."

I nod. I told the hospital I'm Rosa's boyfriend, so I've been getting regular updates on her condition. As expected, the girl has refused to talk to the police, and since none of her injuries are life-threatening, she doesn't need to stay overnight.

"All right," I say. "You take care of your wife, and I'll get Rosa."

Esguerra goes back to Nora, and I follow up with our cleanup crew, giving them instructions on what to do with the guy they found knocked out at the club. From the little I pieced together via Rosa's hysterical explanations, the maid had been attacked in the back room of the club by two men she'd danced with earlier. Nora came to her rescue, knocking out a third guy who had been guarding the room. Esguerra made it there in the nick of time, killing one of the assailants, but the other one dragged Rosa outside and would've taken his turn in the car if Esguerra hadn't saved her. It was that man who got away in the white SUV—the SUV whose license plate I'm tracking now.

Once we know his identity, the driver of that SUV is as good as dead.

Putting the phone away, I go to get Rosa. When I walk into her room, I find her sitting on the bed in nurse's scrubs; the hospital staff must've given them to her to replace her torn dress. Her knees are drawn up to her chest, and her face is bruised and pale. An image of Yulia flashes through my mind again, and I have to take a deep breath to suppress a swell of rage.

Keeping my movements slow and gentle, I approach the bed. "I'm sorry," I say quietly, clasping Rosa's elbow to help her to her feet. "I really am. Can you walk, or would you like me to carry you?"

"I can walk." Her voice is thin, high-pitched with anxiety, and I drop my hand when I realize my touch is upsetting her. "I'm fine."

It's an obvious lie, but I don't call her out on it. I just match my pace to her slower one, and lead her out to the car.

* * *

An hour after we get back to Esguerra's mansion, my boss comes down to the living room, where I'm waiting to fill him in on the developing situation.

"Where's Rosa?" he asks. His voice is calm, betraying nothing of the hollow agony I see in his gaze. He's compartmentalizing to cope with what happened, choosing to focus on what needs to be done rather than dwelling on what can't be fixed.

"She's asleep," I answer, rising from the couch. "I gave her Ambien and made sure she took a shower."

"Good. Thank you." Esguerra crosses the room to stand in front of me. "Now tell me everything."

"The cleanup crew took care of the body and captured the kid Nora knocked out in the hallway," I say. "They're holding him in a warehouse I rented on the South Side."

"Good. What about the white car?"

"The men were able to follow it to one of the residential high-rises downtown. At that point, it disappeared into a parking garage, and they decided against pursuing it there. I've already run the license plate number."

"And?"

"And it seems like we might have a problem," I say. "Does the name Patrick Sullivan mean anything to you?"

Esguerra frowns. "It's familiar, but I can't place it."

"The Sullivans own half of this town," I say, recounting what I just learned about our newest enemy. "Prostitution, drugs, weapons—you name it, they have their fingers in it. Patrick Sullivan heads up the family, and he's got just about every local politician and police chief in his pocket."

"Ah." There's a flicker of recognition on Esguerra's face. "What does Patrick Sullivan have to do with this?"

"He has two sons," I explain. "Or rather, he *had* two sons. Brian and Sean. Brian is currently marinating in lye at our rented warehouse, and Sean is the owner of the white SUV."

"I see," Esguerra says, and I know he's thinking the same thing I am.

The rapists' connection complicates matters, but it also explains why they attacked Rosa in such a public place. They're used to their mobster father getting them out of trouble, and it never occurred to them that they might be crossing someone just as dangerous.

"Also," I say while Esguerra is digesting everything, "the kid we've got strung up in that warehouse is their seventeen-year-old cousin, Sullivan's nephew. His name is Jimmy. Apparently, he and the two brothers are close. Or *were* close, I should say."

Esguerra's blue eyes narrow. "Do they have any idea who we are? Could they have singled out Rosa to get at me?"

"No, I don't think so." A fresh wave of anger makes my jaw clench. "The Sullivan brothers have a nasty history with women. Date-rape drugs, sexual assault, gang bangs of sorority girls—the list goes on and on. If it weren't for their father, they'd be rotting in prison right now."

"I see." Esguerra's mouth twists coldly. "Well, by the time we're done with them, they'll wish they were."

I nod. The minute I learned about Patrick Sullivan, I knew we'd be going to war. "Should I organize a strike team?" I ask, gripped by familiar anticipation. I haven't been in a good battle in a while.

"No, not yet," Esguerra says. He turns away and walks over to stand by the window. I don't know what he's looking at, but he's silent for well over a minute before he turns back to face me.

"I want Nora and her parents taken to the estate before we do anything," he says, and I see the harsh resolve on his face. "Sean Sullivan will have to wait. For now, we'll focus on the nephew."

"All right." I incline my head. "I'll begin making the arrangements."

CHAPTER TEN

❖ YULIA ❖

I sleep fitfully my first night at the safe house, waking up every couple of hours from nightmares. I don't remember the exact details of those dreams, but I know Lucas is in them, and so is my brother. The scenes are a blur in my mind, but I recall bits and pieces involving trains, lizards, gunfire, and underneath it all, the delicate scent of lilacs.

Around five in the morning, I give up trying to fall back asleep. Getting up, I put on a robe and wander into the kitchen to make myself some tea. Obenko is there, reading a newspaper, and as I enter, he looks up, his hazel eyes sharp and clear despite the early hour.

"Jet-lagged?" he asks, and I nod. It's as good of an explanation for my state as any.

"Want some tea?" I offer, pouring water into a tea kettle and setting it on the stove.

"No, thanks." He studies me, and I wonder what he's seeing. A traitor? A failure? Someone who's now more of a liability than an asset? I used to care what my boss thought, craving his approval as I once craved my parents', but right now, I can't work up any interest in his opinion.

There's only one thing I care about this morning.

"My brother," I say, sitting down after I make myself a cup of Earl Grey. "How is he? Where's your sister's family now?"

"They're safe." Obenko folds his newspaper. "We've relocated them to a different location."

"Do you have any new pictures for me?" I ask, trying not to sound too eager.

"No." Obenko sighs. "We thought you were gone, and when you contacted us, I'm afraid taking photos wasn't our main priority."

I take a scalding sip of tea to mask my disappointment. "I see."

Obenko lets out another sigh. "Yulia . . . It's been eleven years. You need to let go of Misha. Your brother has a life that doesn't involve you."

"I know that, but I don't think a few pictures every now and then is too much to ask." My tone is sharper than I intended. "It's not like I'm asking to see him . . ."

I pause as the idea takes hold of me. "Well, actually, since you don't have the pictures, maybe I can just view him from a distance," I say, my pulse accelerating in excitement. "I could use binoculars or a telescope. He would never know."

Obenko's gaze hardens. "We've talked about this, Yulia. You know why you can't see him."

"Because it would deepen my irrational attachment," I say, parroting his words to me. "Yes, I know you said that, but I disagree. I could've died in that Russian prison, or been tortured to death by Esguerra. The fact that I'm sitting here today—"

"Has nothing to do with Misha and the agreement we made eleven years ago," Obenko says. "You fucked up on this assignment. Because of you, your brother has already been uprooted, forced to change schools and give up his friends. You don't get to make demands today."

My fingers tighten on the tea cup. "I'm not demanding," I say evenly. "I'm asking. I know it was my mistake that led to this situation, and I'm sorry. But I don't see how that's relevant to the matter at hand. I spent six years in Moscow doing exactly what you wanted me to do. I sent you a lot of valuable intel. All I want in return is to see my brother from a distance. I wouldn't approach him, wouldn't speak to him—I would just look at him. Why is that a problem?"

Obenko stands up. "Drink your tea, Yulia," he says, ignoring my question. "There will be another debriefing at eleven."

CHAPTER ELEVEN

❖ LUCAS ❖

I spend the night coordinating with the cleanup crew and preparing for our departure. If there's any silver lining to this disaster, it's that we're going home early, and I will soon be able to hunt down Yulia with no distractions.

First, though, I need to take care of the situation here.

I begin by making breakfast for Rosa, who hasn't come out of her room this morning. At first, I'm tempted to slap together a sandwich, but then I decide to try my hand at one of the omelets I've watched Yulia make. It takes me two attempts, but I succeed at producing something that resembles one of Yulia's delicious confections. It doesn't taste half-bad either, I decide, trying a bite before putting half of the omelet on a plate for Rosa.

Holding the plate with one hand, I knock on the door of Rosa's bedroom. After a couple of minutes, I hear footsteps, and she opens the door. She's dressed in a long, shapeless T-shirt, and to my relief, her eyes are dry, though the bruising on her face looks even worse.

"Hi," I say, forcing a smile. "I made an omelet. Would you like some?"

The maid blinks, looking surprised. "Oh ... Sure, thanks." She accepts the plate and glances at it. "That looks great, thank you, Lucas."

"You're welcome." I study her injuries, my stomach tightening at the sight. "How are you feeling?"

Her face flushes, and she looks away. "I'm fine."

"Okay." I can tell she doesn't want company, so I say, "If you need anything, just let me know," and then I head back into the kitchen.

I need to eat my own breakfast before tackling the next task.

* * *

By the time Esguerra comes out of the house, everything is ready for him.

"I brought the cousin here," I say when my boss steps out onto the driveway. "I figured you might not want to go all the way to Chicago today."

"Excellent." Esguerra's eyes gleam darkly. "Where is he?"

"In that van over there." I point at a black van I parked behind the trees farthest from the neighbors.

We walk toward it together, and Esguerra asks, "Has he given us any info yet?"

"He gave us access codes to his cousin's parking garage and building elevators," I say. "It wasn't difficult to get him to talk. I figured I'd leave the rest of the interrogation to you, in case you wanted to speak to him in person."

"That's good thinking. I definitely do." Approaching the van, Esguerra opens the back doors and peers into the dark interior.

I know what he's seeing: a skinny teenager, gagged and with his ankles tied to his wrists behind his back. He's the third guy, the one Nora knocked out at the club yesterday. I've already had a couple of guards work him over, and now he's ready for Esguerra.

My boss doesn't waste time. Climbing into the van, he turns around and asks, "Are the walls soundproof?"

I nod. "About ninety percent." I can smell the urine and sweat inside the van, and I know these odors will soon be overwhelmed by the coppery stench of blood.

"Good," Esguerra says. "That should suffice."

He closes the van doors, locking himself in with the boy, and a minute later, the sound of his victim's pleas and screams fills the air. I tune them out, letting Esguerra have his fun while I read the latest update from Diego and Eduardo. They found a record of the private plane landing in Kiev, so Yulia is definitely out of Colombia.

I forward Diego's findings to the hackers, and when Esguerra is done, I wrap the teenager's body in a plastic sheet and message the cleaning crew to come in.

* * *

Half an hour later, I'm walking back toward the house when my phone vibrates with another text from Esguerra.

New development. Need to expedite the departure.

My adrenaline spikes. Entering the house, I intercept Esguerra in the hallway. "What happened?"

"Frank, our CIA contact, emailed me," Esguerra says, pushing back his wet hair. He must've taken a shower to get rid of the Sullivan kid's blood. "An artist's sketch of myself, Nora, and Rosa is being circulated in the local FBI's office. It had to have come from the Sullivan brother who got away in that white SUV. I'm guessing it won't be long before the Sullivans find out who we are, and given what I did to the other Sullivan brother in the club and the cousin just now . . ." He doesn't finish, but he doesn't have to.

Esguerra and I both know Patrick Sullivan will be out for blood.

"I'll send Thomas to prepare the plane," I say. "Do you think Nora's parents can be ready to go in the next hour?"

"They'll have to be ready," Esguerra says. "I want them and the women away before we do anything."

"How many guards should we send on the plane with them?"

"Four, just in case," Esguerra says after a moment of deliberation. "The rest can stay to be part of our strike team."

"All right. I'll go tell the others and make sure Rosa is ready to go."

* * *

We arrive at Esguerra's in-laws' house in full force, our limo followed by seven armored SUVs transporting twenty-three guards. The neighbors gape at us, and I feel a twinge of amusement at the thought of Nora's parents trying to explain this to their suburban acquaintances. I'm sure the good people of Oak Lawn have heard rumors about Nora's arms dealer husband, but hearing and seeing are two different things.

Predictably, the parents aren't ready yet, so Esguerra and his wife go in to round them up. Rosa stays in the car, explaining to Nora that she doesn't want to be in the way.

When we're alone, I turn around and look at Rosa through the limo partition.

"Would you like some music?" I ask, but she shakes her head. She's not speaking, just staring out the window, and I'm sure she's thinking about what happened yesterday.

Not wanting to discomfit her, I roll up the partition and use the time to check on the plane. Thomas assures me that it's ready to go, so I double-check my weapons—an M16 slung across my chest and a Glock 26 strapped to my leg. I'd like to be even better armed, but I'm driving. Fortunately, Esguerra has an entire arsenal in the back under one of the seats. I'm hoping we won't need it, but we're prepared in case we do.

Some forty minutes later, Esguerra comes out of the house, hauling a huge suitcase. He's followed by Nora's father with another suitcase, and finally, Nora and her mother.

Though there's plenty of room in the back, Rosa comes to sit at the front with me, explaining that she wants to give the four of them more room.

"You don't mind, do you?" she asks, glancing at me, and I give her a reassuring smile.

"No, please have a seat." I roll up the partition again, separating us from the main cabin, and start the car. "How are you doing?"

"Fine." Her voice is quiet but steady. I don't press her for more, and we drive in comfortable silence for some time. It's not until we pull off the interstate onto a two-lane highway that Rosa speaks again. "Lucas," she says quietly. "I'd like to ask you for a favor."

Surprised, I glance at her before directing my attention back to the road. "What is it?"

"If there's ever a chance—" Her voice breaks. "If you ever get them, I want to be there. Okay? I just want to be there."

She doesn't spell it out, but I understand. "You got it," I promise. "I'll make sure you see justice served."

"Thank you—" she begins, but at that moment, I catch a glimpse of movement in the side mirror, and my pulse leaps.

On the narrow highway behind our SUVs is an entire cavalcade of cars, and they're gaining on us quickly.

I floor the gas pedal with a surge of adrenaline. The limo jerks forward, accelerating at a mad pace, and I lower the partition to meet Esguerra's gaze in the rearview mirror.

"We have a tail," I say tersely. "They're onto us, and they're coming with everything they've got."

CHAPTER TWELVE

❖ YULIA ❖

"Bayu-bayushki-bayu, ne lozhisya na krayu . . ." My mom is singing a Russian lullaby to me, her voice soft and sweet as I snuggle deeper into the blanket. *"Pridyot seren'kiy volchok, i ukusit za bochok . . ."*

Her crooning is off-key and the words are about a gray wolf that will bite my side if I lie too close to the edge of the bed, but the melody is warm and comforting, like my mom's smile. I bask in it, savoring it for as long as I can, but with each word, my mom's voice gets fainter and softer, until there's only silence.

Silence and cold, empty darkness.

"Don't go, Mom," I whisper. "Stay home. Don't go to Grandpa tonight. Please, stay home."

But there's no response. There's never a response. There's only darkness and the sound of Misha crying. He's feverish and wants our parents. I pick him up and rock him back and forth, the sturdy weight of his toddler's body anchoring me in the sea of darkness. "It's okay, Mishen'ka. It's okay. We'll be okay. I'll take care of you. We'll be okay, I promise."

But he doesn't stop crying. He cries all through the night. His screams get hysterical when the headmistress comes for him in the morning, and I know she did something to him. I saw the bruises on his legs when he came out of her office last evening. She hurt him somehow, traumatized him. He hasn't stopped crying since.

"No, don't take him." I struggle to hold on to Misha, but she pushes me away, taking my brother with her. I come after her, but two older boys block my way, forming a human wall in front of me.

"Don't do it," one of the boys says. "It won't help."

His eyes are pitch black, like the darkness around me, and I feel myself spinning. I'm lost, so lost in that darkness.

"I have a proposition for you, Yulia." A man dressed in a suit smiles at me, his hazel eyes cold and calculating. "A deal, if you will. You're not too young to make a deal, are you?"

I lift my chin, meeting his gaze. "I'm eleven. I can do anything."

"Bayu-bayushki-bayu, ne lozhisya na krayu . . ."

"It's your fault, bitch." Cruel hands seize me, dragging me into the darkness. "It's all your fault."

Pridyot seren'kiy volchok, i ukusit za bochok . . ."

The melody trails off again, and I'm crying, crying and fighting as I fall deeper into the darkness.

"Tell me about the program." Strong arms catch me, imprisoning me against a muscular male body. I know I should be terrified, but when I look up and meet the man's pale gaze, I'm suffused with heat. His face is hard, every feature carved from stone, but his blue-gray eyes hold the kind of warmth I haven't felt in years. There's a promise of safety there, and something else.

Something I crave with all my soul.

"Lucas . . ." I'm filled with desperation as I reach for him. "Please fuck me. Please."

He drives into me, his thick cock stretching me, spearing me, and the heat of him dispels the lingering coldness. I'm burning, and it's not enough. I need more. "I love you," I whisper, my nails digging into his muscled back. "I love you, Lucas."

"Yulia." His voice is cold and distant as he says my name. "Yulia, it's time."

"Please," I beg, reaching for Lucas, but he's already fading away. "Please don't go. Stay with me."

"Yulia." A hand lands on my shoulder. "Wake up."

Gasping, I sit up in bed and stare into Obenko's cool hazel gaze. My heart is drumming in my throat, and I'm covered in a thin layer of sweat. Turning my head, I take in the sight of peeling wallpaper and gray light seeping through a dirty window. There's no Lucas here, nobody to catch me in the darkness.

I'm in my bedroom at the safe house, where I must've fallen asleep before the debriefing.

"Was I . . . Did I say anything?" I ask, trying to get my shaky breathing under control. The dream is already fading from my memory, but the bits and pieces I recall are enough to knot my insides.

"No." Obenko's face is expressionless. "Should you have?"

"No, of course not." My frantic heartbeat is beginning to slow. "Give me a minute to freshen up, and I'll be right out."

"All right." Obenko walks out of my room, and I pull the blanket tighter around myself, desperate for what little comfort I can find.

CHAPTER THIRTEEN

❖ LUCAS ❖

At the explosion of gunfire, I glance at the side mirror and see our guards in the SUVs shooting at the pursuing vehicles. A bullet dings against the side of our car, and I swerve, making the limo a more difficult target. In the back, Nora's parents scream in panic, and Esguerra jumps off the seat to get to his weapons stash.

Fucking hell. My hands tighten on the wheel. This shouldn't be happening. Not while we have civilians with us. Esguerra and I can handle this, but not Rosa and Nora—and certainly not Nora's parents. If anything were to happen to them . . . I press harder on the gas pedal, pushing the speedometer past 100 miles per hour.

More gunfire. In the side mirror, I see our men exchanging fire with the pursuers. All the way in the back, one of Sullivan's cars careens into one of ours, trying to force it off the road, and there's another burst of gunfire before the pursuers' SUV skids off the road and flips over.

Another car gains on one of our SUVs, smashing into its side. Behind it are at least a dozen vehicles—a mix of SUVs, vans, and Hummers with grenade launchers mounted on their roofs.

No, not a dozen.

They have as many as fifteen or sixteen cars versus eight of ours.

Motherfucking fuck. I push the gas pedal again, and the speedometer climbs to 110. We need to go faster, but the armored limo is too heavy. It's built for protection, not speed.

One of our SUVs in the back flies up, exploding in mid-air. The blast is deafening, but I ignore it, all my attention on the road ahead. I can't think about the men we just lost or their families.

If we're to survive, I can't afford the distraction.

"Lucas." Rosa sounds panicked. "Lucas, that's—"

"A police blockade, yes." I have to raise my voice to be heard over the din of gunfire and explosions. There are four police cars blocking our way, and they're surrounded by SWAT teams. They're here for us—which means they must be in Sullivan's pocket.

In the back, Julian is shouting something at Nora, and in the rearview mirror, I see him dragging out bulletproof vests and a handheld grenade launcher.

"We have to go through them," I yell, keeping my foot on the gas. We're seconds away now, rocketing toward the blockade at full speed. I aim the limo at the narrow gap between two police cars. For this, the heavy weight of the armored limo is an advantage.

"Hold on!" I shout at Rosa, and then we're crashing into the cars, the impact of the collision throwing me forward. I feel the seatbelt cutting into me, hear the SWAT team's bullets hitting the side and windows of our car, and then we're through, the limo barreling ahead as two more cars behind us collide and explode.

Sullivan's cars, I determine with relief a moment later. From what I can see in the side mirror, our SUVs are still intact. Beside me, Rosa is white with fear but seemingly uninjured.

Before I can catch my breath, I hear a deafening *boom* and see the police cruiser behind us fly up, exploding in the air. It lands on its side, burning, and one of Sullivan's Hummers slams into it. There's another explosion, followed by a Sullivan van careering off the road. I grin savagely as I catch sight of Esguerra standing in the middle of the limo, his head and shoulders sticking out of the opening in the roof.

My boss must be using the handheld grenade launcher from our stash.

There's another explosive *boom* as he fires the next shot, but no enemy vehicle goes belly-up this time. Instead, one of the Hummers swerves, ramming into one of our SUVs, and I see the guards' car flip over, rolling off the road.

Shit. My elation dissipates. Esguerra better get his aim straight, or we're fucked.

As if in response to my thoughts, there's another boom, followed by a Sullivan van exploding behind us. Two Sullivan SUVs crash into it, but my satisfaction is short-lived as I hear the ding of bullets against the side of our car. Swearing, I yank the wheel and begin zigzagging from side to side.

Unlike the limo, Esguerra's head is not bulletproof.

"Come on, Esguerra," I mutter, squeezing the wheel. "Fucking shoot them."

Boom! Another Sullivan SUV explodes, taking out the one behind it in the process.

"He's doing it," Rosa says in a shaking voice. "They have only six cars left now."

I steal a glance in the mirror and verify that she's right. Six enemy vehicles versus five of ours.

We might make it yet.

Suddenly, I see a flash of fire in the mirror. Two of our SUVs fly up in the air, and I realize the Hummers took them out. *Fuck. Fuck, fuck, fuck.*

"Come on, Esguerra." My knuckles turn white on the steering wheel. "Just fucking do it."

Boom! One of the Hummers veers off the road, smoke rising from its hood.

"Señor Esguerra did it!" Rosa's voice is filled with hysterical glee. "Lucas, he got it!"

I don't have a chance to reply before one of the enemy cars swerves and crashes into another. Our men must've shot the driver.

"Three of them left, Lucas. Only three!" Rosa is all but jumping in her seat, and I realize she's high on adrenaline. Past a certain point, one stops feeling fear, and it all becomes a game, a rush unlike any other. It's what makes danger so addictive—for me, at least.

I feel most alive when I'm close to death.

Except that's not true anymore, I realize with a jolt. The buzz is muted today, dulled by my worry for our civilians and my fury over our men's deaths. Instead of excitement, there's only a grim determination to survive.

To live so I can catch Yulia and feel alive in a whole different way.

"Lucas." Rosa sounds tense all of a sudden. "Lucas, are you seeing that?"

"What?" I say, but then the sound reaches my ears.

It's the faint but unmistakable roar of chopper blades.

"It's a police helicopter," Rosa says, her voice shaking again. "Lucas, why is there a helicopter?"

I floor the gas pedal instead of answering her. There are only two possibilities: either the authorities heard about what's happening, or it's more dirty cops. My money's on the last one, which means we're beyond fucked. By my calculations, Esguerra only has one shot left in that grenade launcher of his, and there's no way he can take down that chopper.

"What are we going to do?" Rosa's panic is evident. "Lucas, what are we—"

"Quiet." I floor the pedal, focusing on the structure looming ahead of us. We're almost to the private airport now, and if we can get inside, we stand a chance.

"I'm going for the hangar!" I yell to Esguerra, and take a sharp right turn toward the structure. At the same time, I floor the gas pedal, pushing the limo to its limits. We're all but rocketing toward the hangar now, but the roar of the helicopter is getting inexorably louder.

Boom! My ears ring from an explosion, and I swerve instinctively before righting the car and pressing on the gas again. Behind us, one of our SUVs careens into another, and they collide with a squeal of tires before rolling off the road.

"They shot it." Rosa sounds dazed. "Oh my God, Lucas, the helicopter shot it."

I shake my head, trying to get rid of the ringing in my ears, but before the noise dies down, there's another deafening explosion.

The Hummer behind us goes up in flames, leaving two enemy SUVs and the helicopter.

Esguerra came through with one last shot.

Before I can take a breath, a blast rocks the limo. My vision goes dark and my head spins, the ringing in my ears turning into a high-pitched, dizzying whine. Only decades of training enable me to keep my hands on the wheel, and as my vision clears, I register what Rosa is screaming.

"We're hit, Lucas! We're hit!"

Fuck, she's right. There's smoke rising from the back of the car, and the rear window is shattered.

"Are Esguerra and his family—" I begin hoarsely, but then I see Esguerra pop up in the rearview mirror. He's covered in blood but clearly alive. Pulling Nora up from the floor, he hands her an AK-47. Behind them, her parents look dazed and bloody, but conscious.

We're almost to the hangar now, so I take my foot off the gas. I can hear Esguerra giving his wife instructions in the back. He wants her to take her parents and run for the plane as soon as we stop.

"You run with them too, Rosa, you hear me?" I say, not taking my eyes off the road. "You get out, and you run."

"O-okay." She sounds like she's on the verge of hyperventilating.

We plow through the open gates of the hangar, and I slam on the brakes, bringing the limo to a screeching holt.

"Run, Rosa!" I yell, unbuckling my seatbelt, and as she scrambles out of the car, I jump out on my side, grabbing my M16.

"Now, Nora!" Esguerra yells behind me, throwing open the passenger door. "Go now!"

Out of the corner of my eye, I see Rosa running after Nora and her parents, but before I can verify they got to the plane, a Sullivan SUV squeals into the building.

I open fire, and Esguerra joins in.

The SUV's windshield shatters as it screeches to a stop in front of us and armed men pour out.

"Get back! Behind the limo!" I yell at Esguerra, covering his retreat. Then he covers me as I dive behind the limo myself.

"Ready?" I say, and he nods. Synchronizing our movements, we pop up on each side of the limo and unleash a volley of shots before ducking back.

"Four down," Esguerra says, reloading his own M16. "I think there's only one left."

"Cover me," I say and crawl around the limo. I can feel the sweat dripping into my eyes as I slither on my stomach while Esguerra fires at the SUV to distract the guy. It takes almost a minute before I see an opening and fire at the shooter.

My bullets hit him in the neck, setting off a geyser of blood.

Breathing hard, I climb to my feet. After the nonstop racket of the battle, the silence feels like I've gone deaf.

"Good job," Esguerra says, coming out from behind the limo. "Now if our remaining men got the—"

"Julian!" On the other side of the hangar, Nora is waving her AK-47 above her head. She looks overjoyed. "Over here! Come, let's go!"

A huge smile lights up Esguerra's face as she begins running toward him—and then a blast of searing heat sends me flying.

CHAPTER FOURTEEN

❖ YULIA ❖

The second "debriefing" is even more grueling than the first. Obenko and the two agents want me to go over every conversation with Lucas and describe each of our encounters in detail. They want to know how he kept me tied up, at what point he gave me clothes, what kind of meals I cooked, and what his sexual preferences are. I cooperate at first, but after a while, I begin stonewalling them. I can't bear to have my relationship with my former captor dissected by these men. I don't want them knowing about my feelings for Lucas or my fantasies about him. Those softer moments between us and the things he promised me—those are mine alone.

74

What happened during my captivity was wrong and twisted, but it also meant something—to me, at least.

"Yulia," Obenko says after I evade yet another one of his questions. "This is important. The man with whom you spent two weeks is Esguerra's second-in-command. From what you're telling us, it sounds like he, not Esguerra, is the driving force behind them coming after us. It's crucial that we understand exactly what he wants and how he thinks."

"I've already told you everything I know." I try not to let my frustration bleed into my voice. "What more do you want from me?"

"How about the truth, Yulia Borisovna?" Mateyenko gives me a penetrating look. "Did Kent send you here? Are you working for him now?"

"What?" My jaw falls open. "Are you serious? I'm the one who warned you. Do you honestly think I would betray my brother's adoptive family?"

"I don't know, Yulia Borisovna." Mateyenko's expression doesn't change. "Would you?"

I rise to my feet. "If I were working for him, why would I tell you that he got this information from me? A double agent wouldn't warn you that she'd cracked—she'd come to you as a hero, not a failure."

Next to Mateyenko, Sokov crosses his arms. "That would depend on how clever the double agent is, Yulia Borisovna. The best ones always have a story."

I turn to Obenko. "Is that what you believe as well? That I betrayed you?"

"No, Yulia." My boss doesn't blink. "If I did, you'd already be dead. But I do think you're hiding something. Aren't you?"

"No." I hold his gaze. "I've told you everything. I don't know anything else that could help us."

Obenko's mouth tightens, but he nods. "All right, then. We're done for the day."

* * *

When Mateyenko and Sokov leave, I go back to my room, a tension headache throbbing in my temples. I have no doubt Obenko meant what he said: if he thought I was a double agent, he would've killed me.

After surviving Russian prison and Esguerra's compound, I might die at the hands of my colleagues.

Strangely, the thought doesn't upset me much. The hollow chill that has settled in my chest numbs everything, even fear. Now that I'm here—now that I've done everything I can to ensure my brother's safety—I can't work up more than a smidgeon of interest in my own fate. Even the memory of Lucas's cruelty feels distant and muted, as if it happened years ago instead of days.

When I'm back in my room, I lie down and pull the blanket around me, but I can't get warm.

Only one thing could chase away this cold—and he's thousands of miles away.

CHAPTER FIFTEEN

❖ LUCAS ❖

Rat-tat-tat!

The sharp crackle of gunfire cuts through the darkness, bringing me back to my senses. My brain feels like it's swimming in a thick, viscous fog.

Groaning, I roll over onto my stomach, almost puking from the agony in my skull. Where's Jackson? What happened? We were out on patrol and then . . . *Fuck!*

Ignoring the throbbing in my head, I begin crawling on the sand, away from the gunfire. My whole body hurts, the sand particles pelting my eyes and filling my lungs. I feel like I'm made of sand, my skin ready to dissolve and blow away in the harsh, stinging wind.

More gunfire, then a pained cry.

Fear squeezes my chest. "Jackson?"

"I'm hit." Jackson's voice is filled with shock. "Oh, fuck, Kent, they got me."

"Hang on." I crawl back toward the gunfire, dragging my useless rifle. I ran out of ammo five minutes after we were ambushed, but I don't want to leave the weapon for the hostiles. "I called it in. They're coming for us."

Jackson coughs, but the sound turns into a gurgle. "Too late, Kent. It's too fucking late. Get back."

"Shut up." I crawl faster, the dim light of the moon illuminating a small mound next to our overturned Humvee. Jackson's voice is coming from that direction, so I know it must be him. "Just hang on."

"They're not . . . They're not coming, Kent." Jackson is wheezing now. The bullet must've hit his lungs. "Roberts . . . He wanted this. He ordered this."

"What are you talking about?" I finally reach him, but when I touch him, all I feel is wet meat and fractured bone. I yank my hand away. "Fuck, Jackson, your leg—"

"You have to"—Jackson sucks in a gurgling breath—"go. They'll blow this place if they come. Roberts, he . . . I caught him. I was going to expose him. This isn't Taliban. Roberts knew"—he coughs wetly—"knew we'd be here. This is his doing."

"Stop. We're going to get through this." I can't think about what Jackson is saying, can't process the implications of his words. Our commanding officer couldn't have betrayed us like that. It's impossible. "Just hang on, buddy."

"Too late." Jackson gurgle-wheezes as I reach for him again. "Roberts..." He chokes, and I feel hot liquid coating my hands as I press them over his stomach.

"Jackson, stay with me." My heart beats in a sick, erratic rhythm. Not Jackson. This can't be happening to Jackson. I increase the pressure on his wound, trying to stop the bleeding. "Come on, buddy, just stay with me. Help will be here soon."

"Run," Jackson mumbles inaudibly. "He'll kill..." He shudders, and I feel the moment it happens. His body goes limp, and the stench of evacuated bowels fills the air.

"Jackson!" Keeping my hand on his stomach, I reach for his neck, but there's no pulse.

It's over. My best friend is dead.

Rat-tat-tat!

The gunfire is back, and so is the syrupy fog in my brain. It's also hot—far hotter than it should be at night in the desert. The heat is consuming me, eating away at me like—

Fucking hell, I'm burning!

Throwing myself to the side, I roll, not stopping until the burning heat recedes. My ribs scream in pain and my head spins, but the flames licking at my skin are gone.

Panting, I open my eyes and stare at the tall ceiling above me.

Ceiling, not night sky.

My brain synapses finally connect and begin firing.

Afghanistan was eight years ago.

I'm in Chicago, not Afghanistan, and whatever took me down has nothing to do with my old commander.

Rat-tat-tat!

I turn my head to see a small figure running on the other side of the hangar. Four men in SWAT gear are running after her. As I watch in disbelief, Esguerra's wife turns and fires her AK-47 at the pursuers before darting behind one of the planes.

Shit. I have to help Nora. Groaning, I roll over onto my side. There's burning rubble all around me, and the limo is on fire. In the hangar wall behind the limo is a gaping hole through which I can see the police chopper. It's sitting on the grass outside, its blades no longer turning.

Sullivan's henchmen must've taken out the guards in our last SUV before coming for us.

As I struggle to my feet, I see Esguerra leap toward the burning limo. He survived, I realize with relief. Fighting a wave of dizziness, I take a step toward the car, ignoring the agonizing pain in my ribs.

Before I can get there, Esguerra jumps out of the limo, holding two machine guns, and sprints after Nora's pursuers. I'm about to go help him when I spot movement near the helicopter.

Two men are climbing out, clearly intent on getting away.

I react even before I consciously realize who they are. Lifting my weapon, I pepper them with bullets, purposefully aiming my shots away from critical organs. When I stop, the hangar is silent again, and I look back to see Esguerra embracing Nora, both of them seemingly unhurt.

A vicious smile curves my lips as I turn and make my way to the two men I injured.

It's time for the Sullivans to get their due.

* * *

"Is that who I think it is?" Esguerra asks hoarsely, nodding toward the older man, and my smile widens.

"Yes. Patrick Sullivan himself, along with his favorite—and last remaining—son Sean."

I shot Patrick through the leg and his son through the arm, and both men are rolling on the ground, blubbering in agony. Their pain helps soothe some of my raging fury. For what they did to Rosa and Nora, and for the guards who died today, these men will pay.

"I'm guessing they came in the chopper to observe the action and swoop in at the right time," I say, holding my aching ribs. "Except the right time never came. They must've learned who you were and called in all the cops who owed them favors."

"The men we killed were cops?" Nora asks, visibly trembling. She must be coming down from an adrenaline high. "The ones in the Hummers and the SUVs, too?"

"Judging by their gear, many of them were." Esguerra wraps a supportive arm around her waist. "Some were probably dirty, but others just blindly following orders from their higher-ups. I have no doubt they were told we were highly dangerous criminals. Maybe even terrorists."

"Oh." Nora leans against her husband, her face suddenly turning gray.

"Fuck," Esguerra mutters, picking her up. Holding her against his chest, he says, "I'm going to take her to the plane."

To my surprise, Nora shakes her head. "No, I'm fine. Please let me down." She pushes at him with such determination that Esguerra complies, carefully setting her on her feet.

Keeping one arm around her back, he gives her a concerned look. "What is it, baby?"

Nora gestures toward our captives. "What are you going to do with them? Are you going to kill them?"

"Yes," Esguerra answers with no hesitation. "I will."

Nora doesn't say anything, and I remember my promise to her friend. "I think Rosa should be here for this," I say. "She'll want to see justice served."

Esguerra looks at his wife, and she nods.

"Bring her here," Esguerra says, and despite the grimness of the situation, I feel a twinge of amusement as I walk back to the plane.

Esguerra's delicate little wife has acclimated to our world quite well.

When I get to the plane, Rosa steps out to meet me, her face pale. "Lucas, are they—"

"Yes, come." Carefully taking her arm, I lead her out of the hangar. As we step outside, I see that Patrick Sullivan has passed out on the ground, but his son is still conscious and pleading for his life.

I glance at Rosa, and I'm pleased to see that her cheeks have regained some color. Approaching Sean Sullivan, she stares down at him for a couple of seconds before looking up at me and Esguerra.

"May I?" she asks, holding out her hand, and I smile coldly as I hand her my rifle. Rosa's hands are steady as she aims at her attacker.

"Do it," Esguerra says, and she pulls the trigger. Sean Sullivan's face explodes, blood and bits of brain matter flying everywhere, but Rosa doesn't flinch or look away.

Before the sound of her shot fades, Esguerra steps toward unconscious Patrick Sullivan and releases a round of bullets into the older man's chest.

"We're done here," Esguerra says, turning away from the dead body, and the four of us return to the plane.

PART II: THE LEAD

CHAPTER SIXTEEN

❖ LUCAS ❖

I spend the week after our return from Chicago dealing with the aftermath of the trip and recuperating from my injuries. According to Goldberg, our estate doctor, I have cracked ribs and a few first-degree burns on my back and arms—injuries that are beyond minor in light of the battle we survived.

"You're one lucky son of a bitch," Diego says when I finally sit down with him and Eduardo to catch up on the Yulia situation. "All those guys . . ."

"Yeah." My teeth ache from clenching my jaw all day long. The faces of our dead men haunt me, just like those of the guards who died in the plane crash. Over the past couple of months, we've lost more than

ANNA ZAIRES

seventy of our people, and the mood on the compound is grim, to say the least.

Between organizing funerals, finding new recruits, and cleaning up the mess in Chicago, I've been running on nothing but adrenaline fumes.

"I hope you made the fuckers pay," Eduardo says, his voice vibrating with fury. "If I'd been there—"

"You'd be dead just like the others," I say wearily. I'm in no mood to indulge the young guard's bluster; my burns are mostly healed at this point, but my ribs hurt with every movement. "Tell me what you've learned thus far. Did you figure out if anyone had contact with my prisoner prior to the escape?"

Diego and Eduardo exchange an odd look. Then Diego says, "Yes, but I don't think it's her."

I frown. "Her?"

"Rosa Martinez, the maid from the main house," Eduardo says hesitantly. "She ... Well, the drone footage showed her coming to your house a couple of times during those two weeks."

"Oh, yeah." I chuckle humorlessly. "She had some kind of strange curiosity about Yulia." I'm not about to tell the guards about Rosa's possible crush on me. The girl seems to be past that now, and I don't think she'd appreciate the others knowing about her feelings.

She's been through enough.

"Oh, good. I'm glad you know about that." Diego blows out a relieved breath. "We figured it's unlikely to be her, but I wanted to let you know just in case. She's the only one who came by your house on Tuesday, so . . ." He shrugs.

"Wait, Tuesday? As in, the day before we left?" I'd warned Rosa away long before that, and I thought she'd listened. "She came to my house on Tuesday?"

"That's what the footage shows," Eduardo says cautiously. "But it can't be her. I know Rosa—we dated for some time. She's not . . . she wouldn't—"

I hold up my hand, cutting him off. "I'm sure she's not the one to blame," I say, even as a hard knot forms in my chest. If Rosa came to my house after I warned her away, that changes things.

My assumptions about the girl were wrong.

"You did well telling me about this," I say to the two guards. "But I'd appreciate it if you kept quiet about it for now. We don't want anyone getting the wrong idea—Rosa herself included."

If there's something more to her actions than a misplaced crush, I don't want anyone to tip her off.

Diego and Eduardo both nod, looking relieved as I dismiss them. When they're gone, I pick up the phone and call the men we sent to Chicago.

Esguerra's CIA contacts did their best to cover up our high-speed battle, but it was impossible to conceal it all, and now every news outlet in Chicago is blaring with speculation about the clandestine operation to apprehend a dangerous arms dealer. The "arms dealer" story originated with the police chief, who had been in cahoots with Sullivan. The man used the information that Sullivan uncovered about us to come up with the tale of an arms dealer smuggling explosives into Chicago. Under that pretext, he assembled the SWAT team that helped Sullivan, and told everyone that Sullivan's men were reinforcements from another division. The operation was kept secret from other law enforcement agencies—which is why we didn't have advance warning of the attack. So now there's a shitload of work to be done. The police chief and any remaining Sullivan moles have to be taken care of, and the remnants of Sullivan's organization must be wiped out before Nora's parents can return home.

As much as I'd like to tackle Rosa's betrayal, I have more pressing matters to deal with first.

* * *

It's not until I'm lying in my bed late that night that I have a chance to think about Rosa again. Could she have done it? Could she have helped Yulia escape? If so, why? Out of jealousy or because someone got to the maid?

Could Yulia's agency have bribed or threatened Rosa?

I mull over that possibility for a few minutes before deciding that it's unlikely. The compound is isolated, and all emails and phone calls with the outside world are monitored. Esguerra is the only one whose communications are private, which means there's no way UUR could've contacted Rosa without raising alarms in the system.

Whatever Rosa did, she did of her own initiative.

The knot in my chest tightens, the bitterness of betrayal mixing with the ever-present anger. Rage has been my companion since I learned of Yulia's escape, and now I have a new target for my fury. If it weren't for the fact that the maid has just been through an ordeal, I'd drag her in for questioning tomorrow. As it is, I'm going to give Rosa another week to heal and use the time to keep a close eye on her, just in case I'm wrong about her motivations.

If she *is* on someone's payroll, I'm going to find that out. In the meantime, I have to finish the cleanup in Chicago and locate Yulia, and I have to do it soon. Not having Yulia is messing with my head. Despite working to exhaustion, I can't sleep at night. There are dozens of urgent business matters that should occupy my thoughts, but it's not worry over finding new guards or containing media leaks that keeps me awake. No, what I think about when I lie in bed is her.

Yulia.

My beautiful, treacherous obsession.

The moment I close my eyes, I see her—her eyes, her smile, her graceful walk. I remember her laughter and her tears, and I ache for her in a way that goes beyond my cock's craving for her silky flesh. As much as I'd like to fuck her, I also want to hold her, to hear her breathing next to me and smell the warm peach scent of her skin.

I fucking miss her, and I hate her for it.

Does she think about me at all, or is she too busy with the man she loves? I picture her lying in his arms, drowsy and replete after sex, and my fury edges into agony, tightening my chest until I can't breathe. I'd take a dozen broken ribs, suffer a hundred burns to avoid this sensation.

I'd do anything to have her back with me.

I love you. I'm yours.

Motherfucker.

I turn on the bedside lamp and sit up, wincing at the pain in my ribs. Getting up, I walk to my library and grab a random book.

It's only when I return to my bed that I realize the book I took was the last one I saw Yulia reading.

The tightness in my chest returns.

I have to get her back.

I simply have to.

CHAPTER SEVENTEEN

❖ YULIA ❖

"I have a new assignment for you," Obenko says, walking into the kitchen of the safe house apartment.

Startled, I look up from my plate of cream-of-wheat kasha. "An assignment?"

Over the past week, my boss has been busy erasing all traces of UUR's existence from the net and reassigning key agents to lower-profile operations whenever possible. He's also been studiously ignoring me—which is why I'm surprised to see him here this morning.

Obenko takes a seat across from me at the table. "It's in Istanbul," he says. "As you know, the situation with

Turkey and Russia is beginning to heat up, and we need someone on the ground."

I consume another spoonful of kasha to give myself time to think. "What do you want me to do in Istanbul?" I ask after I swallow. I have no appetite—I haven't had one all week—but I force myself to eat to keep up appearances.

I don't want Obenko to know how listless I feel and speculate about the cause of my malaise.

"Your assignment is to get close to a key Turkish official. To do that, you'll matriculate at Istanbul University as part of a graduate student exchange program with the United States. We have already prepared your documents." Obenko slides a thick folder toward me. "Your name is Mary Becker, and you're from Washington D.C. You're working on your Master's in Political Science at the University of Maryland, and though your undergraduate degree is in Economics, you minored in Near Eastern Studies— hence your interest in a study abroad program in Turkey."

The kasha I've eaten turns into a rock in my stomach. "So it's another long-term play."

"Yes." Obenko gives me a hard look. "Is that a problem?"

"No, of course not." I do my best to sound nonchalant. "But what about my brother? You said you'd get me the pictures."

Obenko's mouth thins. "They're in that folder as well. Take a look and let me know if you have any questions."

He gets up and walks out of the kitchen to make a call, and I flip open the folder, my hands shaking. I'm trying not to think about what this assignment will entail, but I can't help it. My throat is cinched tight, and my insides churn with nausea.

Not now, Yulia. Just focus on Misha.

Ignoring the papers in the file, I find the photos clipped to the back of the folder. They're of my brother—I recognize the color of his hair and the tilt of his head. The pictures were clearly taken in a rush; the photographer captured him mostly from the side and the back, with only one photo showing his face. In that picture, Misha is frowning, his youthful face looking unusually mature. Is he upset because his family had to relocate, or is something else behind his tense expression?

I study the pictures for several minutes, my heart aching, and then I force myself to set them aside so I can look at my assignment.

Ahmet Demir, a member of Turkish Parliament, is forty-seven years old and known to have a weakness for blond American women. Objectively speaking, he's not a bad-looking man—a little balding, a little chubby, but with symmetrical features and a charismatic smile. Looking at his photo shouldn't make me want to throw up, but that's precisely how I feel at the prospect of getting close to him.

I can't imagine sleeping with this man—or any man who's not Lucas.

Feeling increasingly sick, I push the papers away and take several deep breaths. The last time I felt a dread this strong was before my first assignment, when I feared a man's touch in the wake of Kirill's attack. It was a phobia I battled through in order to do my job, and I'm determined to overcome whatever it is I'm feeling now.

For Misha, I tell myself, picking up his pictures again. *I'm doing it for Misha.* Except this time, the words ring hollow in my mind. My brother is no longer a child, no longer a helpless toddler abused in an orphanage. The face in the photo is that of a young man, not a boy. Because of my mistake, his life has already been disrupted. I don't know what reason his adoptive parents gave him for changing their identities, but I have no doubt he's stressed and upset. The carefree, stable life I wanted for him is no longer a possibility, and despite the black guilt gnawing at my chest, I'm aware of a sense of relief.

What I feared has come to pass, and I can't undo it.

For the first time, I consider what would happen if I left UUR—if I simply walked away. Would they let me go, or would they kill me? If I disappeared, would Obenko's sister and her husband continue treating my brother well? I can't imagine that they wouldn't; he's been their adopted son for eleven years. Only monsters would throw him out at this point, and by all indications, Misha's adoptive parents are decent people.

They love Misha, and they wouldn't harm him.

I pick up the documents in the folder and study them. They look authentic—a passport, a driver's license, a birth certificate, and a social security card. If I accept this assignment, I'll start over as Mary Becker, an American grad student. I'll live in Istanbul, attend classes, and eventually become Ahmet Demir's girlfriend. My interlude with Lucas Kent will fade into the past, and I'll move on.

I'll survive, like I always have.

"Do you have any questions for me?" Obenko asks, and I look up to see him walk back into the kitchen. "Did you have a chance to look through the file?"

"Yes." My voice sounds hoarse, and I have to clear my throat before continuing. "I'll need to brush up on a number of subjects before I go to Istanbul."

"Of course," Obenko says. "You have a week before the start of the summer semester. I suggest you get busy."

He leaves the kitchen, and I pick up my half-full plate with unsteady hands. Carrying it over to the garbage, I dump the remnants of my breakfast, wash the plate, and walk to my room, a ghost of a plan forming in my mind.

For the first time in my life, I may have a choice about my future, and I intend to seize the opportunity with both hands.

* * *

Over the next week, I learn the basics of Turkish language and culture. I don't need to know a lot, just enough to pass for an American graduate student interested in the subject. I also memorize Mary Becker's background and brush up on American college life. I prepare stories about my roommates and frat parties, read Economics textbooks, and come up with Mary's interests and hobbies. Obenko and Mateyenko quiz me daily, and when they're satisfied that I make a convincing Mary Becker, they buy me a plane ticket to Berlin.

"You'll travel as Elena Depeshkova to Berlin," Obenko explains. "And as Claudia Schreider from Berlin to New York. Once you're in the United States, your identity as Mary Becker will go into effect, and you'll fly from there to Istanbul. This way, nobody will be able to connect you to Ukraine. Yulia Tzakova will disappear for good."

"Got it," I say, slicking on a bright red lipstick in front of a mirror. I'll be wearing a dark wig for Elena's role, so I'll need bolder makeup for that. "Elena, Claudia, then Mary."

Obenko nods and makes me repeat the names of all of Mary's relatives, beginning with distant cousins and ending with parents. I don't make a single mistake, and when he leaves that day, I know my hard work has paid off.

My boss believes I'll make an excellent Mary Becker.

The next morning, Obenko drives me to the airport, dropping me off at the Departures area. I'm Elena now, so I'm wearing the wig and high-heeled boots that go well with my dark jeans and stylish jacket. Obenko helps me load my suitcases onto a cart before driving away, and I wave him goodbye as he disappears into the airport traffic.

The minute his car is out of sight, I spring into action. Leaving my suitcases on the cart, I run to the Arrivals area and grab a cab.

"Head toward the city," I tell the driver. "I need to pull up the exact address."

He starts driving, and I take out my phone. Opening the tracking app I installed a couple of days ago, I locate a small red dot heading toward the city a kilometer or two ahead of us. It's the tiny GPS chip I surreptitiously placed in Obenko's phone back at the safe house.

I may have no intention of carrying out the Istanbul mission, but I certainly found use for the surveillance equipment UUR gave me.

"Take a left here," I instruct the driver when I see the red dot turning left off the highway. "Then keep going straight."

I give him directions like this until I see Obenko's dot come to a stop in the center of Kiev. Telling the driver to stop a block away, I take out my wallet and pay him; then I jump out and walk the rest of the way, keeping a close eye on my app to make sure Obenko doesn't go anywhere.

I find Obenko's car in front of a tall building. It looks like some kind of office space, with an international corporation's logo blazing at the top and the first floor occupied by businesses ranging from a trendy coffee shop to a high-end clothing boutique.

Slowly, I approach the building, scanning my surrounding every few seconds to make sure I'm not being watched.

What I'm doing is a long shot: there's zero guarantee Obenko will visit his sister any time soon. However, this is the only way I can think of to find Misha. Given their recent relocation, my brother's adoptive parents are still getting settled into their new lives, and there's a chance they might need something from Obenko, something that will necessitate him to visit them personally.

If I follow my boss long enough, he might lead me to my brother.

I know my plan is both desperate and borderline insane. Since I'm walking away from UUR, my best bet is to disappear somewhere in Berlin, or better yet, go all the way to New York. And I'm planning to do exactly that—*after* I see my brother with my own eyes.

I can't leave Ukraine without making sure Misha is okay.

Two days, I tell myself. *I will do this for a maximum of two days.* If I still haven't found my brother by then, I'll leave. They won't realize I didn't board the plane until I don't meet my handler in Istanbul in three days—which gives me a little over forty-eight hours to tail Obenko before getting out of the country.

The dot on my phone indicates that Obenko is on the second floor of the building. I'm curious what he's doing there, but I don't want to expose myself by following him in. I doubt my brother's family is here; Obenko would've relocated them out of the city—assuming they'd lived in the city before. My boss never disclosed their location to me for security reasons, but from the backgrounds in my brother's pictures, I gathered that they'd lived in an urban environment, like Kiev.

Entering the coffee shop, I order a pastry and a cup of Earl Grey and wait for Obenko's dot to start moving again. When it does, I grab another cab and follow him to his next destination: our safe house.

He stays at the apartment for several hours before the dot starts moving again. By then, I've had lunch at a nearby restaurant and swapped my dark wig for a red one I brought with me for this purpose. I've also changed my jeans for a long-sleeved gray dress, and the high-heeled boots for flat booties—the most comfortable option "Elena" had in her carry-on bag.

Obenko's next destination appears to be another office building downtown. He stays there for a couple of hours before heading back to the safe house. I follow him again, feeling increasingly discouraged.

This is clearly not the way to find my brother.

My phone is beginning to run low on batteries, so I go to another coffee shop to charge it while Obenko is at the safe house. I also get online and buy a plane ticket to Berlin for the next morning to replace the one that has gone unused today.

It's time to admit defeat and disappear for good.

Sighing, I order myself another tea and drink it as I read the news on my phone. Obenko seems to be settled in for the night, his dot sitting firmly in the safe house every time I check the app. Finishing my tea, I get up, deciding to go to a hotel and get some rest before the long journey tomorrow. Just as I step outside, however, my phone beeps in my bag, signifying movement on the app.

My heart leaps. Fishing out the phone, I glance at the screen and see that Obenko's dot is going north— possibly out of the city.

This could be it.

Instantly energized, I jump into a cab and follow Obenko. I know there's a 99.9 percent chance this has nothing to do with my brother, but I can't help the irrational hope that grips me as I watch Obenko's dot heading farther north.

"Are you sure you know where you're going, young lady?" the cab driver says when we're out of the city. "You said you were going to get directions from your boyfriend."

"Yes, he's texting me as we speak," I assure him. "It's not much farther."

I'm lying through my teeth—I have no idea how far we're going—but I'm hoping it's not far. With all my cab rides, I'm running low on cash, and I'll need whatever I still have to get to the airport tomorrow morning.

"Fine," the driver mutters. "But you better tell me soon, else I'm dropping you off at the nearest bus stop."

"Just another fifteen minutes," I say, seeing the dot turn left and stop a half-kilometer later. "Turn left at the next intersection."

The driver shoots me a dirty look in the rearview mirror but does as I ask. The road we end up on is dark and full of potholes, and I hear him curse as he swerves to avoid a hole wide enough to swallow our whole car.

"Stop here," I tell him when the tracker app says we're two hundred meters away. Exiting the car, I approach the driver's window and hand him a stack of bills, saying, "Here's half of what I owe you. Please wait for me, and I'll give you the rest when you bring me back to the city."

"What?" He glares at me. "Fuck, no. Give me the full amount, bitch."

I ignore him, turning to walk away, but he leaps out of the car and grabs my arm. Instinctively, I whirl around, my fist catching the underside of his chin as my knee hits him in the balls. He collapses to the ground, wheezing and clutching at his groin, and I bring my foot down on his temple, knocking him out.

I feel awful hurting this civilian, but I can't let him drive off in this cab. If he leaves, I'll have no way of getting back to the city and I'll miss my flight tomorrow morning.

Pushing aside my guilt, I check the driver's pulse to verify that he's alive, grab the keys from the car in case he wakes up, and then head toward the blinking red dot on my phone map.

A couple of minutes later, I come across what looks like an abandoned warehouse. Disappointed, I stare at it, debating whether I should even approach. Whatever Obenko is doing here is unlikely to involve my brother's adoptive parents; my boss wouldn't ask his sister to meet him in the middle of nowhere just to give her some documents. It's far more probable that he's in the middle of an operation, and the last thing I want is to stand in his way.

Despite that, I take a step closer. Then another and another. My legs seem to be carrying me of their own accord. I've come this far, I reason to justify my compulsion. What's another few minutes to confirm that I've wasted my time?

There is a faint glow of light visible on one side of the warehouse, so I make my way there and crouch in front of a small, dirty window. Inside, I hear voices, and I hold my breath, trying to understand what they're saying.

"—getting good," a man says in Russian. There's something familiar about his voice, but I can't place it. The wall is muffling the sound. "Really good. I think another couple of years, and they'll be ready."

"Good," another man replies, and this time, I recognize the speaker as Obenko. "We'll need all the help we can get."

"Would you like a demonstration?" the original speaker says. "They'll be happy to show you what they've learned thus far."

"Of course," Obenko says, and then I hear a grunt, followed by the *thump* of something falling. The noises repeat again and again, and I realize I'm listening to a fight. Two or more people are engaged in hand-to-hand combat, which, combined with the bits I overheard, means only one thing.

I've stumbled upon a UUR training facility.

That's it. I need to leave before I'm caught.

I turn around, about to head back, when the original speaker laughs loudly and exclaims, "Good job!"

I freeze in place, a sick feeling spreading through me. *That voice.* I know that voice. I've heard it in my nightmares over and over again.

Cold sweat breaks over my skin as I turn, drawn to the window despite myself.

It can't be.

It just can't be.

My pulse is a violent drumbeat, and my hands tremble as I place them on the wall next to the window.

I'm imagining this.

I'm hallucinating.

I have to be.

Sinking my teeth into my lower lip, I edge to the left until I can see through the window. I know I'm taking a terrible risk, but I have to know the truth.

I have to know if they lied to me.

The scene that greets my eyes is straight out of my own training sessions. There are several teenagers of both genders standing in a semi-circle. Their backs are to me, and in front of them is a wide mat on which two men—or, rather, a man and a boy—are wrestling. Obenko is standing to the side, watching them with an approving smile.

I notice all of this only briefly because my eyes are glued to the wrestling pair. With the two of them twisting and rolling on the mat, I can't get a good look at either of them—at least until they stop, with the man pinning his younger opponent to the mat.

"Good job," the man says, rising to his feet. Laughing, he extends his hand to help his defeated opponent. "You were excellent today, Zhenya."

The boy gets up as well, brushing the dirt off his clothes, but I'm not looking at him.

All I see is the man standing next to him.

He hasn't changed much. His brown hair is thinner and has more gray in it, but his body is as strong and broad as I remember. His shoulders strain the seams of his sweat-soaked T-shirt, and his arms are as thick as drain pipes.

Nobody could best Kirill in hand-to-hand combat seven years ago, and it seems he's still undefeated.

Alive and undefeated.

Obenko lied to me. They all lied to me.

My rapist wasn't killed for what he did to me.

He wasn't even removed from his role as a trainer.

A metallic taste fills my mouth, and I realize I bit through my lip.

"It's your fault, bitch. It's all your fault." Kirill's massive body presses me into the floor, his hands cruelly tearing at my clothes. "You're going to pay for what you did."

Acid rises in my throat, mixing with the bitterness of bile. I feel like I'm going to choke on my terror and hatred, but before the memories can suffocate me, someone else enters my field of vision.

"It's my turn," a blond-haired boy says, approaching the mat. "Uncle Vasya, I want you to watch this." He assumes a fighter's stance opposite Kirill, and the fluorescent lights illuminate his face.

It's a face I know as well as my own—because I've spent hours staring at it in photos.

Because every feature on that face is a masculine version of what I see in the mirror.

My brother is standing in front of me, ready to spar with Kirill.

CHAPTER EIGHTEEN

❖ LUCAS ❖

"It's done," I say, entering Esguerra's office. "Your in-laws can go home tomorrow if they're so inclined."

Over the past week, we've exterminated the remnants of Sullivan's crime family, and the CIA has finally agreed to let Nora's parents return to their home. After the media nightmare we caused, it took promises of major favors, but Esguerra's contacts came through for us.

"You got the police chief as well?" Esguerra asks.

I nod, approaching his desk. "His body is dissolving in lye as we speak. He was the last of the moles—Chicago PD is now squeaky clean and vermin-free.

Other than a few CIA higher-ups, nobody knows your in-laws were involved in this mess."

"Excellent." Esguerra rubs his temples, and I see that he looks unusually tired. Like me, he's been working nonstop since our return from Chicago. He doesn't have to put in these hours—I'm overseeing most of the logistics of the cleanup—but work seems to be his way of coping with the miscarriage. "I'll tell Nora. In the meantime, I want you to assign another dozen men to watch over her parents for the next few months. I'm not expecting any trouble, but it's best to be safe."

"Got it," I say. "You might also want to tell them to stay away from crowded places for a while, just in case."

"That's a good idea." Esguerra gives an approving nod. "As long as they're able to return to work and resume their social lives, they shouldn't mind the restrictions too much."

"I'm sure you'll miss them," I say drily. Nora's parents have been our reluctant guests for the last two weeks, and I imagine Esguerra must've found their disapproving presence wearing.

To my surprise, my boss chuckles. "They're not so bad. You know, family and all that."

"Right." I try not to stare at him but fail. Esguerra's changed; it's obvious to me now. When I first met him, the word "family" would've never passed his lips. And now he's putting up with in-laws who can't stand his guts and bending over backward to keep his young wife happy.

It's both amusing and unsettling to observe, like seeing a jaguar playing with a house kitten.

"You'll understand someday," Esguerra says, and I realize my expression must've given me away. "There's more to life than this." He waves at the flatscreen monitors behind him and the stack of papers on his desk.

"Are you going to give it up then? Walk the straight and narrow?" I say, only half-kidding. Esguerra is certainly wealthy enough to do so. His net worth is in the billions; even if he never sold another weapon, he could live like a king for the rest of his life.

Still, I'm not surprised when Esguerra shakes his head and says, "You know I can't do that. Once in this life, always in this life. Besides"—he bares his teeth in a sharp smile—"I'd miss it. Wouldn't you?"

"Definitely," I say, and we share a moment of grim understanding.

The jaguar may play with the kitten, and even love said kitten, but he'll always be a jaguar.

* * *

As I leave Esguerra's office, my phone vibrates with an incoming message. I open my email, and my lips curl in savage anticipation.

Message decoded, the email from the hackers reads. A confirmed UUR black site is located twenty-five kilometers north of Kiev. They seem to be in the process of covering up their tracks, but they're not fast enough. We're getting closer to the two field operatives. Hope to have more news soon.

At the bottom of the email is an attachment. It's a grainy satellite photo with an X marking a spot on the map where, I presume, the black site facility is located.

We have a place to start.

"Hi, Lucas," a softly accented female voice says, and I turn to see Rosa approaching from the direction of the main house. She's dressed in her usual maid's outfit, with her dark hair pinned in a sleek knot. "How are you?"

Rage surges through me, but I manage to say calmly, "I'm fine." Her casual friendliness grates on me like chalk on glass. I'm tempted to string her up in the shed and interrogate her this very moment, but it would be smart to wait a little longer. Taking a steadying breath, I mimic her friendly tone and ask, "How's everything with you?"

She shrugs, her eyes dropping lower for a moment. "You know. Day by day."

"Right." Despite everything, I feel a swell of pity. Though the bruises on Rosa's face have faded, I remember how the girl looked after the club, and some of my anger cools.

If I believed in karma, I'd be inclined to think she's already been punished.

"How are your ribs doing?" she asks, looking up at me again. There appears to be genuine concern in her gaze. "Are they still hurting?"

"No, not as much as before," I say, my anger easing a little. "It'll be at least another month before I can resume training normally, but I've gotten to the point where I can breathe without pain."

"Oh, good." Rosa smiles, then asks nonchalantly, "Any news on your escapee?"

My fury returns in full force; it's all I can do not to wring the girl's neck. "Why, yes," I say silkily. "I have just found her." It's a lie—I have no idea if the location the hackers uncovered will lead me to Yulia—but if Rosa is working with UUR, I want her to panic and reach out to them. "In fact," I add, deciding to really frighten the maid, "I'll be going after Yulia as soon as I drop off Nora's parents."

"Oh." Rosa blinks, and I see a shadow pass over her face. "That's good."

"Yes, it is, isn't it?" I give her my blandest smile. "I can't wait. Now if you'll excuse me, I have to check up on our new recruits."

And before she can respond, I turn away and head toward the training field.

If I stay in Rosa's presence a moment longer, I'll kill the girl with my bare hands.

CHAPTER NINETEEN

❖ YULIA ❖

My brother.

Kirill is training my brother.

I feel like I stepped into one of my nightmares. I need to back away, to leave before I'm seen, but I can't move. My feet have grown roots, and my lungs scream for suddenly scarce air.

Misha and Kirill.

Student and teacher.

I taste vomit and my vision darkens, fading at the edges.

Run, Yulia. Go before it's too late.

I want to obey the voice in my head, but I'm paralyzed, frozen in place.

Obenko didn't just lie to me about Kirill's death. He deceived me about everything.

I try to suck in oxygen, but my throat is too tight. The window wavers in front of me, like the lens of a shaking camera, and I realize it's because I'm trembling violently, my fingers icy and numb as my palms press against the wall.

Run, Yulia. Now.

The voice gets more insistent, and I force myself to take a tiny step back. But I still can't look away from the horror in front of me.

Go, Yulia! Run!

Before I can take another step, Misha glances at the window and freezes, staring straight at me.

I see his blue eyes widen, and then he shouts, "Intruder!" and leaps toward the window.

My paralysis finally breaks, and I turn and run.

My legs are like wooden sticks, stiff and clumsy, and I can't get enough air. It's as if I'm moving through quicksand, every step requiring desperate effort. I know it's shock weighing me down, but the knowledge doesn't help. My muscles feel like they belong to a stranger, and my feet are numb as they touch the ground.

The car. I need to get back to the car.

I focus on that one goal, on putting one foot in front of the other and not thinking. As I run, I feel the stiffness in my muscles fading, and I know adrenaline is finally kicking in, overpowering my shock.

"Yulia! Stop!"

It's Obenko. Hearing him fills me with such rage that all remnants of my sluggishness fade. Gritting my teeth, I pick up my pace, my legs pumping with increasing desperation. If they catch me, I'm dead, and then nobody will make Obenko pay for his monstrous betrayal.

I will rot in a nameless grave while Kirill turns my brother into a conscienceless killing machine.

"Yulia!"

It's a different voice calling my name. I recognize Kirill's deeper tones, and sick terror explodes in my veins. The memories snake around me like poisonous vines. I try to push them away, but bits and pieces slip through, flashing through my brain in a disjointed reel.

Entering my room in the dorm. A large hand closing over my mouth as I'm grabbed from behind.

I run faster, the ground blurring in front of my eyes. My breath is coming in wheezing gasps, and my lungs are about to burst.

Struggling. Falling to the floor. A man on top of me. Immobilized, helpless.

I'm a dozen meters from the car, and I grip the keys in my pocket, preparing to jump in.

Pop! Pop! The car window shatters, and I zigzag to avoid the next bullet.

"Do not shoot to kill!" Kirill roars behind me. His voice sounds closer; he's gaining on me. "I repeat, do not shoot to kill!"

The knowledge that he wants me alive is more terrifying than the idea of dying. Putting on another burst of speed, I leap for the car. The cab driver is on the ground, still unconscious, and I desperately hope none of the bullets hit him. I don't have time to worry about it, though, because as I'm about to jam the keys into the door, a hand grips my shoulder.

I whirl around, gripping the keys like a weapon, and jab upward, aiming at my attacker's eye. He jerks back, and I drop down and roll under the car, registering only dimly the smaller frame and light hair of my opponent.

It wasn't Kirill who caught up with me; it was Misha.

I scramble to my feet on the other side of the car and begin running again. Even through my terror, I'm aware of an illogical flash of pride. My brother is a fast runner. Obenko had never mentioned that.

I hear him sprinting behind me, and I wonder if he knows who I am, if he realizes he's killing his own sister. Is he in on Obenko's deception, or did they lie to him too?

"Grab her!" Kirill shouts, and a hard body hits me in the back, knocking me to the ground. I manage to twist in the air, so I land on top of Misha, and before he has a chance to act, I punch him in the jaw and jump up to resume running.

Only it's too late. As I turn, another body hits me, knocking me off my feet, and this time, I don't have a chance to land a punch.

In a flash, my arm is twisted behind my back, and my face is pressed into the gritty dirt as a massive weight presses me down.

"Hello, Yulia," my trainer whispers in my ear. "It's good to see you again."

CHAPTER TWENTY

❖ LUCAS ❖

Esguerra notifies me that Nora's parents wish to fly out first thing in the morning, and I decide to do exactly what I told Rosa: go to Ukraine directly after taking them home. I'm still not fully recovered, but the workload from the Chicago disaster is easing up, and my ribs can heal in Ukraine just as well as here.

Now I need to break the news to Esguerra and fill him in on everything I've learned about UUR.

"So let me get this straight," Esguerra says when I stop by his office and explain about the black site. "You want to take a dozen of our best-trained men to conduct an operation in Ukraine when we're still trying to recover from all the losses? What's the urgency on this?"

"They're in the process of covering their tracks," I say. "If we wait much longer, they'll be much harder to track down."

I keep silent about the fact that every day that passes without Yulia is fucking torture, and I can't sleep without her by my side.

"So what?" Esguerra says, frowning. "We'll get them eventually—when we're stronger and have rebuilt our security team. We can't spare a dozen guards right now. UUR is not an immediate threat to us the way Al-Quadar were. We're going to make the Ukrainians pay for the crash, but we'll do it when the time is right."

I take a deep breath. I know Esguerra has a point, but I can't stay on the estate while Yulia is out there with this Misha of hers.

"All right," I say. "How about I go to Ukraine by myself, with just a couple of guards? I could take Diego and Eduardo—surely you can spare the three of us."

Esguerra's gaze sharpens. "Why? Is it because of the girl who escaped?"

I hesitate for a moment, then decide to tell the truth. "Yes," I say, watching Esguerra's reaction. "I want her back."

"I thought you were just amusing yourself with her."

"I was—but I'm not done."

Esguerra stares at me. "I see."

"She's mine," I say, deciding it's time to lay it out there. "I'm going to get her back, and I'm going to keep her."

"Keep her?" Esguerra's expression doesn't change, but I see a muscle twitch in his jaw as he leans forward in his seat. "What exactly do you mean by that?"

I plant my feet wider apart and give him a level look. "It means I'm going to put trackers on her and keep her for as long as it suits me. I'm sure you won't object to that."

The twitch in Esguerra's jaw intensifies as we stare at each other, neither one backing down. The air thickens with tension, and I know that this is it: this is when I find out if my boss truly values my loyalty.

Esguerra breaks the silence first. "So that's it? You're ready to forget about the crash?"

"She was following orders," I say. "And besides, who said she's getting off scot-free?"

For this new betrayal—for running to her lover—Yulia *will* pay.

Esguerra holds my gaze for a few more seconds before getting up and walking around his desk. Stopping in front of me, he says quietly, "You and I both know I owe you for Thailand, and if this is what you want—if *she* is what you want—then I won't stand in your way. But she's bad news, Lucas. Do what you must to get her out of your system, but don't forget what she is and what she's done."

"Oh, don't worry." I give him a humorless smile. "I won't."

I haven't yet decided how I'm going to punish Yulia when I get her back, but I do know one thing.

Her lover's days are numbered.

* * *

That evening, I make arrangements to have Thomas—another guard I trust—keep an eye on Rosa. I don't tell him why; I just ask him to follow her discreetly and to monitor all her emails and calls. My top priority right now is finding Yulia, but I haven't forgotten about the potential danger Rosa poses to us.

When I'm back from Ukraine, I'm going to deal with her. First, though, I need to get Nora's parents home and figure out how to get into Ukraine undetected.

I start by reaching out to Buschekov, the Russian official we met with in Moscow. I don't mention Yulia's escape, but I do give him the information I've uncovered so far about UUR. The more pressure I can bring to bear on Yulia's agency, the better.

Unfortunately, Buschekov claims to be unable to help me with discreet entry into Ukraine, explaining that tensions are running too high between the two countries. I suspect he just doesn't want to risk whatever agents he has in place there, but I don't press him on this. If I had a firm lock on Yulia's location, it would be different, but this black site is just a lead, and I need to preserve whatever goodwill we have with the Russians. That means there's only one thing left to do.

I contact Peter Sokolov, Esguerra's former security consultant, and ask him for help.

Peter saved Esguerra's ass after the crash, but to do so, he let the terrorists take Nora, and my boss has sworn to kill him if he ever lays eyes on him again. I, however, do not share Esguerra's feelings. In fact, I'm grateful that Esguerra is alive and well. I haven't kept in touch with Peter, but I do have his email from before, so I send him a message explaining the situation. The Russian's contacts in Eastern Europe are unparalleled; he's the one who introduced us to Buschekov in the first place.

He doesn't respond right away, but I don't expect him to. I know he's busy with his vendetta against the people on his list. Still, I'm hoping he'll spare a moment to check his email. All I need is to have a couple of air control officials in Ukraine look the other way when I land in Kiev.

As one final step, I brief Diego and Eduardo on our upcoming mission.

"It's going to be just the three of us," I explain, "so we're going to keep a low profile. We don't want anyone catching wind of our presence there until we're gone. The goal is to find out what we can and get out of the county in one piece. Is that clear?"

They both nod, and early the next morning, we load the plane with weapons, body armor, falsified documents, and everything else we'd need in case things don't go according to plan.

Now I just need Peter to come through.

* * *

By the time we land in Chicago, there's still no answering email from Sokolov, so I hand Esguerra's in-laws off to our Chicago security crew and instruct the guards to see them safely home. Both of Nora's parents seem relieved to be back on US soil, and I suspect we won't be seeing them in Colombia again any time soon.

"So what's the plan?" Diego asks when I return to the plane. "Are we flying to Kiev right away?"

"We might stop over in London for a day or two," I say. "I'm waiting on a lead." As I speak, my phone vibrates with an incoming message. Opening my email, I read the response from Peter, and a smile spreads across my face.

"Never mind," I say, turning toward the pilot's cabin. "We're heading to Ukraine."

CHAPTER TWENTY-ONE

❖ YULIA ❖

"So, tell us, Yulia," Obenko says, leaning on the table. "Why didn't you get on that plane?"

I remain silent and focus on taking small, even breaths. One inhale, one exhale. Then again and again. That's all I can do at the moment. Anything else is beyond me. Somewhere out there, lurking at the edge of my consciousness, is the pain of betrayal, the kind of monstrous pain that will destroy me if I let it, and so I focus on the mundane, like my breathing and the flickering fluorescent lights above my head.

My hands are handcuffed behind me, and my ankles are secured to my wrists with a long chain. I'm still wearing the dress they captured me in, but they took off my wig at some point. I have no idea when that happened or where I am, since I have only a vague recollection of the hours that followed my capture. I know this is an interrogation chamber of some kind, with a wall-sized mirror and hard metal furniture, but I don't know if we're still in Kiev. I think I was driven somewhere from the warehouse, so perhaps not, but either way, it doesn't matter.

I'm not getting out of here alive.

"Answer me, Yulia," Obenko says in a harsher tone. "Why didn't you fly out as you were supposed to, and how did you find the training facility? Are you working for Esguerra now?"

I don't respond, and Obenko's eyes narrow. "I see. Well, if you don't want to talk to me, perhaps you'll talk to Kirill Ivanovich." He rises to his feet and gives the mirror a small nod before stepping out of the room.

A minute later, my former trainer walks in, his thin lips curved in a hard smile. Despite my best efforts to remain calm, my throat closes and cold sweat dampens my armpits as he approaches the table and sits down across from me.

"Why are you being so stubborn?" His knee brushes across my bare leg under the table, and I have to swallow to contain the vomit rising in my throat. "Are you a double agent, like they think you are?"

I try to move my leg, to shift away from his touch, but the chain keeps me in place. From this distance, I can smell his cologne, and my breathing speeds up until I'm almost hyperventilating. Desperate to control myself, I look down at the table, focusing on the oily stains marring the metal surface. *Inhale. Exhale. Inhale. Exhale.*

"Yulia..." Kirill's hand grips my knee under the table, his fingers digging into my thigh. "Are you working for Esguerra?"

Inhale. Exhale. Inhale. Exhale. I can survive this. I can keep the pain at bay. *Inhale. Exhale.*

His hand moves higher up my thigh. "Answer me, Yulia."

Inhale. Exhale. I feel the darkness approaching, the blankness that shielded me during my capture, and I embrace it for once, letting my mind flit away from this room, away from the encroaching agony. It's not me chained to this chair—it's just my body. It's just bones and flesh that will soon cease to be animate. There's nothing they can do to hurt me because I'm not here.

I don't exist in this place.

* * *

"—catatonic," a man says. His voice sounds like it's coming through a thick wall of water. I have trouble making out the words, and I struggle to push away the darkness as he says, "You're not going to get any answers from her this way. Just end it. It's obvious she's gone rogue."

"We need to find out what she knows," another man replies, and I recognize this voice as Obenko's. "Besides, if she's not a double agent, maybe this can still be fixed."

"You're deluding yourself," the original voice responds, and this time, I recognize it as belonging to Mateyenko, one of the senior agents who interrogated me after my return. "She'll never forgive you for this."

"Maybe not, but I have an idea," Obenko says, and I hear the sound of retreating footsteps. My mind slowly begins to clear, and I open my eyes a sliver, peeking through my eyelashes.

I'm still in the interrogation room, but I'm no longer chained at the table. Instead, I'm lying on my side on the cold cement floor next to the chair, my wrists still handcuffed behind my back.

There are two men standing by the door—Kirill and Mateyenko. They're speaking in low tones, occasionally glancing in my direction, and nausea twists my insides as darkness presses in again. Did Kirill touch me while I was out? Was he the one who unchained me and put me here?

"She's awake," Mateyenko exclaims, striding toward me, and I stop fighting off the darkness.

I'm not here.

I don't exist.

* * *

"Yulia." A cool hand brushes over my forehead. "Yulia, are you awake?"

The wall of water is back, messing with my hearing, but something about that voice catches my attention. The darkness dissipates, the wall of water thinning, and I open my eyes.

A blond boy is crouching over me, his eyes piercingly blue in his handsome face.

We stare at each other for a second; then my brother jumps to his feet. "Uncle Vasya," he yells. "She woke up."

I hear footsteps, and then strong hands drag me off the floor and place me back in the chair. My pulse jumps, but before my panic spirals out of control, I realize that Kirill is nowhere in sight.

It's just Obenko and me.

"Where's Misha?" I ask hoarsely. My throat feels coated with sand, and my mouth is woolly and dry. I must've been out for a while.

"He stepped out so we could talk," Obenko says. "So, Yulia, let's talk."

"All right." I become aware that I'm shivering and the tips of my fingers are numb and frozen. Despite that, my voice is steady as I say, "What do you want to talk about? The fact that you lied to me for eleven years?" My voice strengthens as the residual fog in my brain clears. "That you stole my brother and are having him trained by a monster?"

Obenko lets out a weary sigh. "There's no need to be so dramatic. I didn't lie to you—not about Misha, at least. I just didn't tell you everything."

"What's 'everything'?"

"Up until two years ago, Misha led exactly the kind of life we showed you in those pictures. He was a normal, happy, well-adjusted boy. Then things began to change. He started skipping school, getting into fights, shoplifting cigarettes..." Obenko grimaces. "My sister didn't know what to do, so she reached out to me to see if I could talk some sense into him. But when I tried, I could see it wouldn't work. Misha was too restless, too bored with his life." Obenko looks at me. "Kind of like how I felt at his age."

"So you what?" My frozen hands clench behind my back. "Decided he should be a spy?"

Obenko doesn't blink. "He needed direction, Yulia. He needed a sense of purpose, and we could provide that. There are so many youths like him in our disillusioned country—boys who lose their way and never find it again. They don't know what they're doing with their lives, don't care about anything but a momentary thrill. I didn't want your brother to be like that."

"Right." I feel like I'm about to choke. "You wanted him to be like you and Kirill."

"Yulia, listen, about Kirill..." Something resembling guilt shadows Obenko's gaze. "You have to understand that we're a small covert organization. We couldn't afford to lose someone as skilled and experienced as Kirill. Not over one mistake."

"One mistake?" My voice cracks. "Is that what they're calling brutal assault now?"

Obenko sighs again, like I'm being unreasonable. "What happened with you was an isolated incident," he says patiently. "It was the one and only time he lost control like that. I understand that it was a traumatic experience for you, but he's an asset to our agency and our country. The best we could do was relocate him away from you—and make sure you could move past it."

"By telling me that he was dead? That you had him assassinated?"

Obenko nods. "It was for your own good. That way you could forget him and move forward."

"You mean, be of use to UUR."

Obenko doesn't respond, and I know that's exactly what he means. In his mind, I'm not a person. I'm a pawn on a chessboard—one that could function either as an asset or a liability.

"Does Misha know?" I ask, staring at the man I'd once looked up to. "Does he know I'm his sister?"

Obenko hesitates, then says, "Yes, Misha knows. He remembered you from the orphanage, so we had no choice but to tell him about you. He also knows that you turned on us—that whatever happened to you at Esguerra's compound made you betray your own country."

My nails dig into my palms. "That's a lie. I didn't betray you."

"Then why did you follow me? Why did you slip me this?" Obenko places his hand on the table and uncurls his fist to show me the GPS chip I planted in his phone.

After a moment of consideration, I decide I have nothing to lose by telling the truth. I'm already a liability in Obenko's eyes. "Because I wanted to see Misha one last time," I say evenly. "Because I couldn't do this anymore."

"So you were going to walk away." Obenko gives me an assessing look. "You know, I suspected that might be the case. You weren't the same after you came back."

I shrug, not about to explain about my complex relationship with Lucas and my inability to take on another "assignment." Whatever guilt I'd felt at abandoning UUR is gone, vaporized by the crushing blow of Obenko's betrayal and Misha's eager abandonment of the life I fought so hard to give him.

I've spent eleven years protecting my brother, only to find out he's going to end up like me.

I suppose I should be devastated, but the pain is still distant, held at bay by a cold numbness that overpowers everything, even my fury.

"I want to talk to him," I say to Obenko. "I want to talk to Misha."

He studies me for a moment, then slowly shakes his head. "No, Yulia. You'll only confuse the boy. He's where he needs to be, mentally and emotionally, and

I walk over to the cot and lie down, staring at the ceiling. I know I won't be able to fall asleep, so I don't even try. My mind spins and whirls, cycling between bitter rage and numb despair. Three facts repeat over and over:

Kirill is alive and training my brother to be a spy.

My brother has been fed a bunch of lies about me.

I will die tomorrow unless I agree to work for UUR.

There's nothing I can do about the first two problems, but the third one is within my control—if Obenko is to be believed, at least. Theoretically, I could agree to carry out my assignment, and if I prove myself, all will be forgiven.

I could also promise to carry out the assignment, but run instead.

It's a tantalizing idea, except it won't be easy. I admitted to wanting to disappear, so if they do decide to let me out into the field, I'll be kept under close observation. They might even put some kind of trackers on me, the way Lucas planned to.

My despair gives way to bitter amusement. It seems I'm destined to be a prisoner one way or another.

A shiver rattles my body, and I realize I'm cold again, my hands and feet frozen and stiff. Rolling up into a small ball, I pull the blanket over my head and pretend I'm in a cocoon where nothing bad can ever touch me, where I can sleep and dream of a different life—a life where Lucas looks at me the way he did that last morning before his trip, and I don't have to leave.

A familiar pain pierces my chest, and I close my eyes, letting the memories come. Our relationship had been wrong in so many ways, yet there had been so much right about it too. And now . . . now none of the wrongness matters.

All I'm left with are the memories and a potent, impossible longing to see him one last time before I die.

* * *

The blanket is pulled off me, and strong hands tug at my underwear, tearing it off as my dress is flipped up. A heavy male body presses me down, and my wrists are pinned above my head. At first, I think I'm dreaming of Lucas, but then I smell it.

Cologne.

Lucas never wears cologne.

My eyes snap open on a surge of panic, and a hoarse scream bursts from my throat—a scream that's instantly muffled by a large palm over my mouth.

"Quiet now," Kirill whispers as I writhe hysterically, trying to throw him off. "We don't want to disturb anyone, do we?"

His hand over my mouth is crushing my jaw, and his other hand is squeezing my wrists so hard I feel my bones grinding against one another. With his legs pinning mine to the bed, I can't move or kick, and nauseating terror rips through me as I feel his erection rubbing against my bare leg.

"We're going to have a little fun," he says, his dark eyes gleaming with cruel excitement. "For old times' sake."

And forcing his knee between my legs, he lowers his head.

CHAPTER TWENTY-TWO

❖ LUCAS ❖

I raise my fist, signaling for Diego and Eduardo to stop as I peer through my night vision goggles at the building in front of us. For a black site, it's surprisingly small—just a ramshackle one-story house in a heavily wooded rural area.

"Are you sure this is the place?" Diego whispers, crouching next to me. "It doesn't look like much."

"I'm guessing most of it is underground," I say, keeping my voice low. "I see two SUVs in the shed in the back, and I don't think Ukrainian villagers drive SUVs."

We left our own car in the woods a half-mile away to scope out the location and figure out our plan of action. Whatever we do, we need to be quick and discreet, so we can be out of the country before UUR realizes we were here. Thanks to Peter Sokolov's contacts, we landed at a private airport undetected, and we have to be able to leave the same way.

"Go around the back and keep an eye on the place from there," I tell Eduardo, who has come up behind Diego. "I'm going to try to hack into their computers remotely."

He nods and disappears into the bushes, and I take out the device I brought with me. One of the benefits of working with Esguerra is having access to cutting-edge military intelligence technology—like this remote data skimmer.

Opening my laptop, I sync it with the device and tell Diego, "Good news: we're within range. Now we just need to let the hacking program do its magic."

It takes more than an hour to break through the firewalls, but gradually, my screen fills with all kinds of data, including blueprints of the house and a live video feed of a dimly lit hallway.

"Is that from inside their building?" Diego asks, looking over my shoulder.

"You bet," I say, watching as two men walk past the camera. One of them looks unusually young, barely a teenager, which throws me for a moment—until I remember that UUR is in the habit of recruiting children.

I click on the next video feed and see what looks like an interrogation room. It's empty except for a metal table and two chairs. Next, I access a camera in what must be a security room. There's one heavily armed man sitting there in front of a row of computers. I click to the next feed, which shows yet another hallway, and several more feeds that reveal cell-like rooms. To my disappointment, all those rooms are empty.

This facility must not be heavily used.

I click through a few more camera feeds, comparing the rooms I see to the blueprints on my screen, and jot down notes on how everything is positioned. In the process, I come across two more men—one that's built like a heavyweight wrestling champion and a leaner one who appears to be in his forties.

"Only five agents so far, and one of them is a kid," Diego says over my shoulder. "If that's all, we might be able to take them."

"Right." I click through a few more feeds, making notes on the interior of each room, and pause when I come back to one of the empty cells—or at least a cell I'd thought empty before. Now I see I was wrong: there's a small mound on a cot covered by a blanket.

"Is that—"

"Yes, looks like they have a prisoner there," I say, peering at the grainy feed. It's definitely a person-sized mound; I should've noticed it the first time. "Hold on, let me see if I can get a clearer image."

Activating the hacking program's remote control feature, I isolate the portion of surveillance mechanism that controls the camera in that room. Carefully, I angle it so it's pointed directly at the cot. The person, whoever it is, is unmoving, as if passed out or asleep.

"Okay, so six people," Diego says, "if we count this prisoner as a threat. Pretty decent odds, especially if we catch them by surprise."

"Yes, I think so," I say, clicking over to the next image. Originally, I planned for us to just gather data and leave, but I can't pass up this opportunity. It's possible that one of these agents knows Yulia's whereabouts. My ribs choose that moment to twinge with pain, but I ignore the dull ache.

Even with me injured, we should be able to take five or six opponents.

Turning on my earpiece, I say, "Eduardo, I need you to plant some explosives on the northwest and southwest corners of the house. Use enough to take down the walls but not destroy the whole house. We want to capture as many of them alive as we can."

"Got it," Eduardo replies, and I turn to glance at Diego.

"We're going in right after the first blast," I say. "Get ready."

He nods, taking out his M16, and I turn my attention back to the computer. Within a minute, the hacking program takes control of the surveillance feeds outside, replacing the image of Eduardo stealthily approaching the house with a nonthreatening view of night-darkened trees and bushes.

Now we just need Eduardo to set the charges.

As we wait for that, I check all the internal video feeds again. On the hallway feed, I see one of the men walk toward the cell with the prisoner. It's the agent who's built like a wrestler, alone this time. With mild interest, I watch him enter the cell, place his gun in the sink on the other side of the room, and step toward the covered figure on the cot. He bends over it and, to my surprise, unzips his jeans.

What the fuck? My attention sharpens as he pulls the blanket off the figure—which I now see is female—and flips up her dress. With the way he's standing, the camera doesn't allow me to see much of the prisoner, yet my chest tightens with anxious premonition.

"Kent?" Diego says, but I'm not listening to him. All my attention is on the computer screen as I frantically work to angle the camera.

The man straddles the prisoner and grabs her wrists—thin, delicate wrists that look impossibly breakable in his bear-like grasp. The camera tilts, angling to the left, and I see tangled blond hair and a beautiful pale face.

My heart stops for a split second; then feral fury blasts through me.

Yulia.

She's here—and she's being attacked.

CHAPTER TWENTY-THREE

❖ YULIA ❖

Kirill's breath is hot and fetid on my face, and his massive bulk is like a mountain on top of me, crushing me into the cot. My insides heave with horror and disgust, and I feel my mind sliding toward the dark place where I don't exist and can't feel this.

No. With stark clarity, I know that if I go there, I'm lost. I'll never emerge from that darkness. I have to stay conscious. I have to fight.

I can't let him destroy me again.

Suppressing my instinctive inclination to struggle, I let myself go limp, my wrists relaxing in Kirill's brutal grip. I don't react as he drags his tongue over my cheek, and I don't tense as he parts my legs, settling heavily between them. He needs to think me dazed and tamed.

It's my only chance.

I feel his cock, hard against my bare thigh, and nausea rises in my throat, my long-ago meal threatening to come up. *Just a second longer*, I tell myself, keeping my muscles relaxed. *Don't rush it. Wait for the right moment.*

The right moment arrives when he shifts on top of me and his face ends up directly over mine. I peer at him through a tiny crack between my eyelids, and when he lowers one hand to grab my breast, I strike.

With all my strength, I jerk my head up, smashing my forehead straight into his nose.

Blood spurts everywhere as Kirill recoils with a startled shout. Any other man would've clutched his broken nose, but he just rears up, snarling, "Bitch!" and smashes his fist into my jaw.

My head whips to the side, the blast of pain stunning me for a second. I see stars at the edge of my vision and taste coppery blood. But Kirill is not done with me yet.

"Fucking bitch!" The next blow is to my stomach, his fist like a wrecking ball hitting my kidney. "Always thought yourself too good for me, did you?"

I can't reply; I can only wheeze through the agony as I curl up to protect myself. He let go of my wrists to hit me, I realize dazedly, and as he raises his fist again, I twist my upper body to the side. His fist grazes my cheekbone instead of shattering it as he'd likely intended, but my ears still ring from the blow. I twist again, trying to throw him off, but his lower body is like a boulder on top of me.

Fight, Yulia, fight. The words are like a desperate chant in my mind. I strike upward with my fist and manage to hit his jaw, but his eyes just glitter brighter as he catches my wrists again. I can see the rage and madness in their dark depths, and I know I won't walk away from this alive.

"You're going to pay for that," he says in a low, guttural hiss, and I feel his hairy balls on my thigh as he forces my legs wider, his fingers cutting off all blood flow to my hands. His cock presses against my entrance, and I scream, bracing for the inevitable horror of violation.

Boom!

For a moment, I'm sure that he hit me again, that the deafening noise is my facial bones cracking, but the dust and plaster raining down on me dispel that impression. Kirill jumps off me with a curse, his cock sticking out of his unzipped pants, and staggers back a couple of feet as another explosion shakes the room.

Seizing the chance, I roll off the cot and scramble to my feet, ignoring the throbbing pain in my face and side. There is a sharp crackle of gunfire above us. Kirill freezes in place, his gaze swinging madly between me and the door. He has to realize the facility is being attacked, and I feel his hatred for me warring with his sense of duty. He should be out there, defending his colleagues, but what he really wants is to make me suffer.

The latter impulse seems to win out.

"You fucking traitor," he grits out, the veins in his forehead bulging, and then he steps toward me, his fist raised for a blow.

Reflexively, I duck, and at that moment, another blast rattles the room, throwing Kirill off-balance and causing more plaster to rain down on us. A creaking, groaning sound seems to emanate from the depths of the building itself, and one corner of the room suddenly crumbles, bricks and plaster falling in an avalanche less than a meter from me.

Gasping, I jump to the side—and then I see it.

A brick with a rusted metal rod embedded in it.

I leap for it, sliding on my stomach across the debris-littered floor. Bits of rock and plaster scrape my bare legs and belly, but my hands close around the metal rod, and I jump up just in time to smash the brick across Kirill's face as he rushes at me.

He staggers back, catching himself on the sink, and I again hear the furious staccato of automatic gunfire above us. This time, though, the deafening noise doesn't stop. Whoever the attackers are, they have serious firepower. I don't get a chance to wonder about their identity, though, because I see Kirill reach into the sink and pull out a gun.

Reacting in an instant, I let go of the heavy brick and throw myself to the side, rolling across the floor toward my attacker. I hear the shot, feel the burning sting of the bullet as it grazes my arm, and then I'm smashing into Kirill's knees at full speed.

He must not have fully recovered from my earlier hit, because he staggers back again, and his next shot goes wide. I scramble to my feet, my ears ringing from the shot and the gunfire above, and grab his right wrist, twisting it sideways in an effort to break his hold on the gun.

In the next instant, I'm flying across the room. He backhanded me with his other hand, I comprehend hazily as I slam into a wall. Air whooshes from my lungs, and I wheeze in paralyzed agony as Kirill points the gun at me, his face twisted with manic rage.

He's going to kill me.

The knowledge injects adrenaline straight into my brain. Without further thought, I throw myself at Kirill, my arms extended in a desperate grab, and my hand closes around the cold metal of the barrel. I feel it buck under my fingers, hear the deadly whine of the bullet, and then I'm falling.

I'm falling, but I'm not dead.

I land on top of Kirill, stunned, my hand still convulsively grasping the barrel. I can't believe I'm alive. Instinctively, I yank at the gun, trying to pull it out of his grasp, and to my shock, I succeed. Clutching the weapon, I crawl backward off Kirill's massive body, and it's only when I'm a couple of feet away that I understand what happened.

A portion of the ceiling collapsed on top of him, knocking him out. There's a thin trickle of blood on his temple, and plaster all around him.

Kirill is unconscious, maybe even dead.

Dizzily, I climb to my feet and point the weapon at him, trying to steady my violently shaking hand. My vision is blurry, and every thought seems to require inordinate effort. All I'm aware of is hatred. Black and potent, it pulses through my veins, taking away all rational thought. My finger tightens on the trigger, almost of its own volition, and I watch as the first shot rips a bloody hole in my rapist's side.

His body jerks, and I shoot again, pointing the gun between his legs. His deflated cock and balls explode in a spray of bloody meat. My dizziness intensifies, my head swimming with pain, and I clench my teeth, determined to remain conscious long enough to finish him off.

A fresh burst of gunfire above draws my attention, and I realize suddenly that I still have no idea what's happening or who the attackers are. Almost immediately, I recall something else.

Misha.

My brother was here earlier.

Icy terror cuts through my haze. Could Misha still be here? Could he be *upstairs*, in that war zone with the unknown enemies?

Before I can even process the thought, I'm already out the door, sprinting down the basement hallway.

I have to get to Misha.

If he's still alive, I have to save him.

As I round the corner to the stairs, I collide with a person running toward me. We crash into each other, and as we tumble to the floor, I realize with shock that it's Misha—that my brother was sprinting toward me. He lands on top of me, and before I can catch my breath, he climbs to his feet, breathing heavily.

"Misha!" Fighting my dizziness, I scramble to my feet. I'm still holding Kirill's gun, but I manage to grab Misha's arm before he can step away. "Are you hurt? Are you injured? What's happening?" My questions come out in a frantic mix of Russian and Ukrainian, but Misha just shakes his head, his eyes wide and uncomprehending. He seems to be in shock; under the dirt and blood covering his face, his cheeks look sickly pale.

My heart hammers as I run my free hand over him, looking for gunshot wounds or broken bones, but other than a few scratches, he seems to be in one piece. Relieved, I grab his arm again and tug him into one of the rooms off the hallway. "Come on. We have to get out of here."

"You ... they ..." He seems to have trouble speaking. "They just—"

"Yes, I know, come on." I drag him into a small cell that resembles the one I was just in and look for a place to hide. There isn't one, and my stomach sinks as the gunfire upstairs stops, and then resumes with even greater violence.

"Misha." Gripping my gun tightly in my right hand, I raise my left hand and gently touch his cheek. My baby brother is already a couple of inches taller than me, and if his lanky frame is anything to go by, he still has quite a bit of growing to do. He's also shaking uncontrollably, his skin icy under my touch. "Mishen'ka, do you know a way out of here?"

He swallows. "No."

"Okay." I'm shaking myself, but I keep my voice calm so as not to add to his terror. "Do you know what's going on upstairs? Who's attacking?"

"I don't know." His shaking intensifies. "They just . . . They killed Uncle Vasya and—"

"Obenko is dead?" Despite everything, I feel a slight pang in my chest. Pushing the illogical emotion aside, I lower my hand and ask, "How many are there? Did any of them say anything?"

Misha shakes his head again, his eyes brimming with tears. "They killed Uncle Vasya," he whispers, as if unable to believe it. "And Agent Mateyenko." His face crumples, just like it did when he was a toddler.

"Oh, Misha . . ." I step closer, swallowing my own tears. "I'm sorry." More than anything, I want to hug and console him, but there's no time, so I say, "We have to figure out a way out. There must be—"

I'm interrupted by the sound of heavy footsteps pounding down the stairs. Misha tenses, and I see terror flash in his eyes. "They're coming for us. They're going to—"

"Shh." I hold up my finger to my lips as I step back and cast a desperate look around the room. I don't know if Kirill's gun was fully loaded when he got to my cell, but even if it was, there can't be more than a couple of bullets left. Still, I could potentially use those bullets as a distraction so Misha can get away.

"Come," I whisper, grabbing his arm. "The minute you see a chance to run, you run. Understand?"

"But they're—"

"Quiet," I hiss, towing him down the hallway. When we reach the next room, I shove my brother in there and whisper, "Don't make a sound."

And gripping the gun with both hands, I turn back toward the stairs, ready to meet my fate.

CHAPTER TWENTY-FOUR

❖ LUCAS ❖

Yulia.

I have to get to Yulia.

The thought hammers in my brain as I run down the stairs, ignoring the blood dripping down my arm. A bullet had grazed my shoulder and my ribs ache from all the movement, but I'm barely cognizant of the pain. The fight turned out to be lengthy and brutal; even caught off-guard and dazed by the bombs we set, the UUR operatives weren't easy to take down. Being forced to exchange fire with them while Yulia was getting assaulted downstairs nearly drove me mad. As soon as we took out two of the three agents defending the house on the first floor, I sprinted to the basement stairs, leaving Diego and Eduardo to deal with the remaining shooter. I hope they're able to capture him instead of killing him like we did the other two, but either way, it's not worth me sticking around.

Saving Yulia beats gathering intelligence any day.

When I get to the bottom of the stairs, I force myself to slow down. The young agent ran this way after we killed the second shooter, and Yulia's assailant could be lying in wait for me here too. He couldn't have missed the shots and explosions upstairs. Or so I'm hoping, at least. I gave the order to detonate the bombs before we were optimally positioned for that exact reason: I figured the man was unlikely to continue with Yulia once he realized they were under attack.

Gripping my M16, I stop as I reach the corner. The hallway with all the rooms is to my right. If my recollection is correct, Yulia's cell should be the fourth one on the left.

This is going to be tricky. I can't shoot indiscriminately, like I did upstairs—not without risking Yulia's life.

Crouching, I risk a quick look around the corner.

The hallway is empty.

I risk a second glance, this time eyeballing the distance to the nearest cell with an open door.

Ten feet. I can make it.

Tightening my grip on the gun, I dive for the cell, rolling across the floor. I half-expect to feel the bite of bullets, but nothing happens as I throw myself through the open door and leap to my feet, scanning the room for danger.

Empty. No sign of anyone.

I inhale to steady my racing heartbeat. The knowledge that Yulia is only a few rooms away from me is like a fire in my blood, but I know I need to be patient. Somewhere down here are two potentially dangerous opponents, and I have to be cautious if I'm to survive and get her back.

Plastering myself against the wall next to the door, I study the hallway, all my senses on alert. I have no doubt they know I'm here, which means it's just a matter of time before someone gets impatient and tries to take me out. To combat my own urge to act, I mentally count to ten, then do so again.

By my third count, I hear a faint scrape and catch a flash of movement. It's almost nothing—just a shadow changing shape inside one of the other doorways—but I know.

This is the enemy.

The safest move would be to pepper that doorway with bullets, but I can't risk shooting Yulia by accident. As is, I can see that the bombs we set off did some damage down here. The floor is covered with plaster, and the ceiling lights are flickering madly. The idea of Yulia hurt in any way is intolerable, so I push the thought aside, along with the fear and rage clawing at my chest. I can't focus on any of that, not until I have Yulia safely with me.

Taking another breath, I mentally measure the distance to the other doorway.

Seven feet, give or take a few inches.

I allow myself one more steadying breath, and then I spring for it, covering the distance in three long strides. A shot rings out, but I'm already there, knocking the gun out of the shooter's hand as I tackle him to the floor and pin him with my assault rifle across his throat.

No, I realize a split second later.

Across *her* throat.

Yulia is on her back underneath me, her blue eyes huge with shock. Her pale face is dirty and bruised, marred with blood and bits of plaster, but there's no doubt that it's her.

"Lucas?" she chokes out, and I see her gaze suddenly flick to the right.

I react instinctively. Clutching Yulia with one hand and the M16 with the other, I throw myself to the side and roll, pulling her with me. My ribs hurt like hell, but the brick that was about to connect with my head crashes into the floor instead, and I jump up to meet the new threat—the young agent I saw in the video feed.

The boy has clearly had some training, and he's fast. As I swing my weapon at his head, he ducks and simultaneously kicks out with his right leg. I jump back, causing his foot to miss my side, and before he can regroup, I thrust the gun forward, ramming the barrel into his solar plexus.

His face turns ghostly white, and his knees buckle. He collapses to the floor, gasping for air, and I raise the gun to knock him out. But before I can bring the handle down on his head, I spot a flicker of movement at my side.

It's Yulia leaping at me, teeth bared.

"Get away! Don't hurt him!" Her scream verges on hysterical as I catch her mid-leap and twist to pin her against the wall. Her fist lands in my side, causing my ribs to scream in agony as I struggle to contain her without dropping my weapon. She grabs for the gun, trying to wrestle it away from me, and I grunt in pain as her elbow hits me in the ribs again.

"Fucking hell, Yulia, stop!" I don't want to hurt her, but I can't let her get that weapon. She's already shot at me once; there's no telling what she'd do with a fully loaded M16. As I'm wrestling with her, in my peripheral vision I see a shadow move across the hallway.

If it's the other agent joining the fight, I'm screwed.

Steeling myself, I twist and slam my elbow into Yulia's ribcage. It's a carefully controlled blow—I use just enough force to knock the air out of her—and then I jump back and turn to face the boy, who's still on the floor but beginning to recover from my hit.

His eyes widen as I raise the gun, pointing it straight at him, and for the first time, I get a good look at his features.

Features that are oddly familiar.

"No!"

Before I have a chance to process what I'm seeing, Yulia slams into me, tackling me with such force that I stagger back before I can catch myself. Her face is twisted with terrified anger as she wrestles with me for the weapon, and I begin to get an inkling of what's happening.

"Misha!" she yells at the top of her lungs, followed by some Russian word, and my suspicion crystallizes into certainty as I see the boy struggle to his feet and rush at me, his teeth bared in a grimace that's nearly identical to the one on Yulia's face.

Motherfucker.

"Stop," I snarl, yanking the gun out of Yulia's hands with one hard pull. "I'm not going to fucking hurt him!"

The boy crashes into me before I finish speaking, and I hit him in the throat, tempering the force of my blow to avoid crushing his trachea. Even with my light tap, he collapses, choking and gasping for air, and I'm left to deal with Yulia's attack.

She flies at me like a feral creature, all teeth and claws, her eyes wild with terror. She clearly didn't believe my promise not to hurt the boy, whoever he is to her, and is fighting like a mama bear protecting her cub. Cursing, I block her attempt to knee me in the balls, and duck to avoid her swinging fist. Before she can lash out again, I catch her and pin her arms to her sides, squeezing her tightly. The M16 is still in my hand, but I don't use it. I just hold Yulia against me, letting her tire herself out with her desperate struggles.

She weakens faster than I expected, likely because she's injured. Within a couple of minutes, she goes limp in my arms, her breathing fast and shaky. I feel her muscles quivering in exhaustion as I hold her, and despite the violent ache in my ribs, a familiar mix of lust and tenderness spreads through me, warming my chest and stiffening my cock.

Yulia.

I finally have my Yulia.

Her breasts are soft against me, her body slim and delicate in my embrace. She smells of fear, sweat, and blood, but underneath it all is the faint scent of peaches—a fragrance I'll forever associate with her. I breathe it in, indulging myself for a moment, but then I recall the shadow I saw moving earlier.

The other agent—Yulia's attacker—is still on the loose.

"Did he hurt you?" My voice thickens with spiking rage. "Did that bastard touch you?"

Yulia's whole body goes rigid, and then she starts struggling again. "Let me go." Her words are muffled against my shirt. "Let me go, Lucas!"

I tighten my arms around her, ignoring the pain the move causes me. "Answer me."

She stills, breathing rapidly, and I see the boy trying to get to his feet. I clench my jaw and turn Yulia so I have my M16 pointed at him. He freezes immediately, and I try to figure out how to proceed next. Everything in me demands that I rush into the hallway to capture the agent who assaulted her, but if I let go of Yulia, she'll attack me again, and I don't want to have to hurt her.

Also, there's the fucking kid.

As I wrestle with my dilemma, I realize that I'm no longer hearing any gunfire—that, in fact, it's been quiet for a couple of minutes. Just as the thought occurs to me, I hear running footsteps on the stairs, and a minute later, Eduardo bursts into the room, ready to take down our remaining opponents.

"Wait," I order as he points his weapon at the kid. "Don't shoot him."

Yulia begins to struggle again, so I squeeze her tighter and whisper in her ear, "Calm down. We're not going to hurt him. If I wanted him dead, he'd already be dead."

That seems to get through to her. She stops fighting, and I risk loosening my grip on her. When I see that she's still not attacking, I release her and step back. At the last moment, I change my mind and grab her wrist with my left hand, anchoring her to me.

There's no way I'm chancing her escaping me ever again.

"There's one more down here somewhere," I tell Eduardo in a hard voice. The thought of Yulia's attacker on the loose is intolerable. "Find him and bring him to me."

Eduardo nods and disappears, and Yulia stares at me, trembling all over. She looks like she's on the verge of either fainting or bolting. "You're not—" Her voice breaks. "You're not going to hurt Misha?"

I glance down at the boy, who's wisely remaining motionless on the floor. "If that's Misha, then no." I take a calming breath, trying not to wince at the pain in my ribs. "Who is he to you?"

Yulia's eyes widen. "You don't know? But you said—"

"I think it's possible I misunderstood," I say, keeping my voice even. "Who is he? Your cousin?"

She blinks. "My brother."

Now it's my turn to be taken aback. "You said you were an only child."

"I lied," she says. Then her forehead wrinkles in confusion. "But you said you knew. When I asked you not to kill him, you said you knew. What did you mean? Why did you—"

"I thought he was your lover, okay?" Anger—at myself this time—clips my words. "Why did you lie about being an only child?"

Yulia moistens her lips. "Because I didn't trust you."

Of course—and apparently, with good reason. I force myself to take another breath. In a calmer tone, I ask, "Are you hurt? Did that fucker hurt you?"

She stiffens again. "How do you—"

"I hacked into this facility's video feed," I say. Releasing her wrist, I raise my hand to run my fingertips over the swelling on the left side of her face. "Did he do this?" I ask, trying to suppress my fury. "Did he hit you?"

"He . . ." Yulia swallows. "I fought, so he hit me. Then you—" She stops. "How did you find this place?"

I narrow my eyes, refusing to be distracted. "Did he rape you?"

"He tried, but no." Her gaze drifts down. "Not this time."

"This time?" I all but explode on the spot. "He hurt you before?"

She looks up, seemingly startled. "I told you about that. You don't remember?"

"That was—"

"Kirill, yes." Her bruised lips flatten. "They lied to me about him. He was alive. Alive and training Misha . . ." She glances down at the boy, who's been utterly silent during our conversation. I don't know how much English he understands, but judging from the stunned look on his face, he must've gotten at least some of it.

I can see Yulia is about to start talking to him, so I grip her chin firmly to bring her attention back to me.

"We're going to get him," I promise grimly. "He won't get away this time."

To my surprise, Yulia's mouth curves in a small smile as I lower my hand. "It's okay. I took care of him."

"What?"

"He's dead—or will be shortly, if he's not already." Yulia's smile sharpens. "He's in my cell. Or at least his body should be there."

I'm about to tell her to take me there when Eduardo enters the room. "He's gone," the guard says with evident disgust. "The bastard somehow made it to one of the SUVs in the backyard and squealed out of here. There must've been another exit down here. He bled the whole way to the car, though, so he's hurt pretty badly. Maybe he'll bleed out on his own."

Yulia's eyebrows draw together. "Who are you—"

"He's talking about Kirill." I fight to keep my voice level. "I saw a shadow move in the hallway earlier, when you and Misha were doing your best to bash my head in. He must not have been hurt as badly as you thought, or else—"

"I shot his cock and balls off." Yulia's curt statement makes me—and all the other males in the room—flinch instinctively. "Also, I put a bullet in his side," she says, and before anyone can respond, she rushes out of the room, running down the hallway toward her cell.

"Keep an eye on him," I tell Eduardo, nodding at Yulia's brother, and then I take off after her, determined not to let her out of my sight ever again.

CHAPTER TWENTY-FIVE

❖ YULIA ❖

Lucas is here. He promised not to hurt my brother. Kirill might have escaped.

I can't process any of it, so I don't even try. As I burst into the cell where Kirill attacked me, I see right away that Eduardo was right.

Kirill is gone.

There's blood all over the place. I turn to follow the trail leading out of the room, but Lucas is already there, looming in the doorway like a human mountain. His hard jaw is shadowed with blond stubble, and his eyes are the color of an iced-over lake. With his SWAT-like gear and machine gun, he looks like the ultimate merciless soldier.

I want to flee from him and jump into his arms at the same time.

I do neither. Instead, I say dully, "He's gone." I know I'm stating the obvious, but all forms of higher thinking seem to be beyond me at the moment. My head is throbbing with pain, and my knees feel like they might buckle at any moment. The adrenaline that sustained me during my fight with Lucas is gone, leaving me trembling in the aftermath.

Kirill almost raped me again. Lucas saved me. Lucas had thought Misha was my lover.

I shake my head, a hysterical laugh escaping my throat.

"Yulia . . ." Lucas reaches for me, frowning, and my laughter intensifies. I can't stop laughing, not when he pulls me into his embrace, his M16 digging into my back, and not when he rocks me against him, whispering soothing nothings into my ear. He promises that he'll find Kirill for me, that he'll make sure the fucker suffers, but I'm not listening to him. My mind is like a ping-pong ball, leaping from one insane fact to the next.

Lucas is in Ukraine. My brother is here with me. Lucas doesn't intend to kill him—though he did when he thought Misha was my lover.

My hysterical laughter turns into equally hysterical sobbing. I know it's pathetic, but I can't stop. All the heartache and stress of the past few hours coalesce into an expanding ball in my throat, and no matter how much air I draw in, I can't stop feeling like I'm suffocating.

Misha could've been killed. He could still be killed if Lucas changes his mind. I want to plead for my brother's life again, but all I can manage is a choked sound that devolves into another sob.

"Hush, sweetheart, it'll be all right . . ." Lucas's voice is a soft rumble in my ear. "I'll protect you from him, I promise."

Bending down, he picks me up, cradling me against his chest, and I wind my arms around his neck, pressing my face into his throat. Almost instantly, I feel calmer, my sobs easing as he carries me down the hallway.

When we pass by the room where I left my brother, however, I see that it's empty, and the choking sensation returns. "Where is he?" My voice takes on a higher pitch as I push at Lucas's shoulders. "Where's Misha?"

"I assume Eduardo brought him upstairs, which is where I'm taking you now," Lucas says, pressing me tighter against him. "Don't worry, baby. He's going to be fine, and so will you."

His words reassure me somewhat. I still don't trust Lucas, but I don't see what he has to gain by lying to me in this instance. As he told me, if he wanted Misha dead, he would've already killed him.

"What are you going to do with him?" My tone is a tiny bit calmer as I pull back to look at my captor. "With us, I mean?"

"You're coming with me, and so is your brother." Lucas's eyes glitter as he takes the stairs two at a time. "Now relax—we'll sort all the rest of it soon."

And before I can ask anything else, he steps out into the ruins of the first floor of the house.

* * *

The next several hours are hazy in my mind. I recall seeing Obenko's bloodied corpse as Lucas carried me out of the wreckage, but I must've passed out soon after that because I don't remember the drive to the airport or the plane taking off. My last semi-clear recollection is of my brother sitting in the car next to me, his eyes red and swollen and his hands handcuffed behind his back.

A few times during the flight, Diego shakes me awake and makes me tell him my name and how many fingers he's holding up. The first time that happens, I ask about my brother, and Diego points to a blanket-covered bundle on the couch across the cabin.

"We gave him a sedative so he wouldn't keep fighting us," the guard explains. "Your brother didn't take the other agents' deaths well."

I try to get up to make sure Misha is all right, but my whole body lodges a violent protest, beginning with my skull, and I fall back into my plush seat with a pained groan, fighting a wave of nauseating dizziness.

"Don't try to move," Diego says, buckling me in with the seatbelt. "Lucas thinks you might have a concussion. He said I'm to watch over you while he's flying the plane."

"But Misha—"

"He's fine." Diego walks over and pokes Misha's shoulder. My brother makes an incoherent noise, and the guard says, "See? He's sleeping. Now relax. We're already over the Atlantic and should be home soon."

"Home?" I try to think through the throbbing pain in my temples.

"Our compound." The young Mexican grins. "The wind is at our back, so we'll be landing in no time."

I want to argue that Esguerra's compound is not *my* home, but the pain in my head intensifies, and I fade into unconsciousness again.

* * *

"—a lot of bruising on her back, face, and stomach, and yes, a mild concussion. I'm going to give her some pain medication, so she can rest comfortably. There's no need to wake her up; it's not that severe of a head injury. Her body's just been through a trauma and needs to heal. The more she sleeps, the better. I suggest you take it easy as well; you're not doing your ribs any favors with all this activity."

The voice is somewhat familiar. Prying open my eyelids, I see Lucas standing next to a short, balding man—the doctor who inspected me when I was first brought to the estate. What was his name? Stifling a groan, I turn my head to take in my surroundings and realize I'm in Lucas's bedroom, lying on his large comfortable bed.

I'm also clean and naked under the blanket. Lucas must've undressed and washed me while I was passed out.

"Where's Misha?" My words come out in a barely audible croak. Clearing my throat, I try again. "Where's my brother?" Judging by drawn shades and bedroom lights being on, it's already evening or maybe even night.

Lucas and the doctor turn to face me at the same time. Lucas's mouth is set in a hard line, but the moment I try to sit up, he crosses the room in a couple of strides and sits down on the edge of the bed. "You are to rest." His tone is harsh, but his touch is gentle as he pushes me back down. "Don't move."

He starts to get up again, and I grab his hand in desperation. "I need to see Misha."

Lucas hesitates for a moment, then says gruffly, "Fine. I'll have him brought here. But you rest, understand?"

I tighten my grip on Lucas's hand. "Where are you holding him?" Now that we're out of immediate danger, a new fear takes hold of me. My brother is here, in Esguerra's compound, in the hands of men who can snuff out his life as easily as squashing a bug. If I hadn't stopped Lucas in that basement, he would've likely killed Misha—just as he'd killed Obenko and the other agents.

My captor is dangerous, and I can't forget that.

"Misha—or Michael, as he told us he prefers to be called—is staying in the guards' barracks," Lucas says, his jaw muscle flexing. He seems angry about something, but I have no idea what. "Diego and Eduardo are keeping an eye on him. Now if you'll excuse me, I'll call Diego and have your brother brought here."

I release Lucas's hand, and he gets up. "Give her the pain meds," he instructs the doctor. "I'll be back in a minute."

The man nods, and Lucas walks out after giving me one last hard look. Even with the pain squeezing my temples, I understand his silent warning:

Behave or else.

If he'd asked me, I could've told him that his caution is unwarranted. Not only am I feeling like a truck ran me over, but Lucas has my brother. Even if I wanted to run, I wouldn't go anywhere without Misha—which must be why Lucas had him brought here, I realize with a shudder.

"Here you go," the doctor says, extending his hand toward me, and I automatically accept the two pills he gives me.

"Thank you, Dr. Goldberg," I say, finally recalling his name.

The short man gives me a kind smile and helps me sit up, putting two pillows under my back as I clutch the blanket to my chest. He also gives me a bottle of water, which I use to wash down the pills. There's no point in resisting; the pills might cloud my mind, but the headache is doing that already. Even after sleeping the whole trip, I feel sluggish and exhausted, my body aching all over.

"You should rest," Dr. Goldberg says, then turns away to rummage in his bag as I tuck the blanket tighter around my naked chest, pinning it in place with my arms.

As if obeying his instruction, my eyelids get progressively heavier, my thoughts beginning to drift as the doctor stands there, quietly humming under his breath. I'm almost asleep when I suddenly remember something he said earlier.

"Is Lucas hurt?" I sit up straighter, my sleepiness fading in a rush of worry. "You mentioned his ribs."

Dr. Goldberg turns around, eyebrows arched in surprise. "Oh, that. Yes, cracked ribs take time to heal. He's supposed to abstain from physical activity, not run around like Rambo."

I frown. "When did he crack his ribs?" From the way the doctor is talking, it sounds like an older injury.

Dr. Goldberg gives me an owlish look. "You don't know?" Then his face clears, and he shakes his head. "Of course you don't know. What am I thinking?"

"Did something happen here?"

He hesitates, then says, "I think it's best if Kent fills you in."

"Fills her in on what?" Lucas asks, walking into the room, and I see my brother come in after him, his hands handcuffed in front of his body.

"Misha!" I almost jump from the bed, injuries be damned, but at the last moment, I remember that I'm naked under the blanket. Flushing, I tighten my arms at my sides and give my brother a smile instead. "How are you doing?" I ask in Russian. "Are you okay?"

Misha stares at me, and I see color creep up his neck as he glances from me to Lucas and then to Dr. Goldberg.

I turn to my captor. "Lucas, would it be possible—"

"You have five minutes," he growls and strides out of the room. The doctor follows him out, closing the door behind him, and I find myself alone with my brother for the first time in eleven years.

CHAPTER TWENTY-SIX

❖ LUCAS ❖

The moment the door to the bedroom closes, I turn to Goldberg and say, "Prepare the trackers. I want them implanted before you leave."

The doctor blinks at me. "Tonight? But—"

"She's already on pain meds, and as banged up as she is, she'll hardly feel the discomfort." I fold my arms across my chest. "You can use a local anesthetic to make sure there's no pain when they go in." Pausing, I frown at Goldberg. "Unless you think this will impede her recovery?"

"No, but . . ." He gives me a wary look. "Don't you think she's been through enough?"

"Excuse me?"

Goldberg sighs and says, "Never mind. I can see you're set on this. I'll prepare for the procedure."

He walks over to the couch and sits, opening his doctor's bag to take out a syringe with a thick needle and the sterilized implants I gave him earlier. The trackers are tiny, about the size of a grain of rice, but capable of transmitting a signal from anywhere in the globe. I watch him for a few moments, then walk over to the window and stare blindly outside, trying to contain the fury simmering in me.

Kirill escaped.

He hurt Yulia, and then he fucking escaped. I don't know how he managed it—if Yulia was right about the damage she inflicted, he should've been at death's door—but the fucker drove away in the SUV, and we couldn't give chase without alerting the authorities to our presence in their country. As is, given all the explosions and gunfire, it was bound to be only a matter of time before we got in trouble. Our safest bet had been to hightail it out of the country as fast as we could, and that's exactly what we did.

Of course, we only did that because Yulia had been injured, and I wanted to get her home as quickly as possible. Otherwise, I would've chased down the bastard and worried about getting out of the country later.

Thinking about that—about Yulia beaten and nearly raped—sends fresh rage surging through me. I don't know which one of us I'm angrier at: Yulia for lying about being an only child and running away, or myself for not doing proper due diligence before jumping to conclusions.

Misha is her brother, not her lover.

Her fucking teenage brother.

During the flight, I had time to think about everything, and in hindsight, it's obvious how my jealousy had blinded me to the truth. The idea of Yulia in love with another man had been so intolerable I refused to listen to her pleas.

My obsession with her nearly got her killed.

"Lucas?" Goldberg's voice cuts into my thoughts. When I spin around to glare at him, the doctor says cautiously, "I think their five minutes are up. If you want me to do the procedure, I'm ready."

"All right." I force my tone to even out. "Let's go."

Misunderstanding or not, Yulia won't escape from me ever again.

CHAPTER TWENTY-SEVEN

❖ YULIA ❖

The second the door closes behind the doctor, I scoot closer to the edge of the bed, making sure the blanket covers my chest. My head pounds with the movement, but I say, "Mishen'ka—"

"It's Mikhail—or Michael, since you're so fond of the English language," my brother snaps, his light-colored eyebrows drawing together in a ferocious frown. "I'm not a child."

"No, I can see that." Ignoring the throbbing in my temples, I study his features, noticing the changes brought about by adolescence. At fourteen, he's already begun the transition into manhood, his face leaner and harder than I recall seeing in pictures as recent as from a few months ago.

Suppressing an irrational urge to cry, I begin again. "Michael"—the formal American version of his name feels foreign on my tongue—"I want to talk to you about . . . well, about everything."

He just stands there, looking tense and angry, so I plow on. "I'm sorry about Obenko—your uncle, that is. I know he meant a lot to you. And Mateyenko . . . They were good agents. They truly cared about their country, and I know Obenko cared about you . . ." I realize I'm rambling, so I take a breath and say, "Listen, I know the men holding us seem scary, but I promise you, I'll do everything in my power to protect you. Lucas said he won't hurt you, and I—"

"Is he your lover?" Misha's cheeks redden as he asks the question, but he doesn't look away, his gaze locked on me accusingly.

I feel my own face heat up. This is not a conversation I want to be having with my young brother. "He's . . . It's complicated. But you don't need to worry about that. I'll make sure you're safe, okay?"

"Yeah, like you made sure Uncle Vasya was safe." Misha's tone is harsh, but I sense the fear and grief underneath. The training he received in the last two years wouldn't have prepared him for this. My baby brother might know how to fight and shoot a gun, but I doubt he'd seen death up close before yesterday.

That part doesn't come until later in the training program.

"Michael . . ." I bite my lip, wondering how to best tackle Obenko's lies. "I know your uncle has told you some things about me, and—"

"Are you going to accuse him of being a liar too? Isn't it enough that he's dead because of you?" Misha's face tightens, and his eyes gleam a shade too brightly. "These killers, they came after *you*. This all happened because of you."

"No, Misha—Michael—that's not true." My heart aches at his pain. "I escaped so I could warn Obenko about—" I cut myself off, realizing I'm about to scare my brother further. In a calmer tone, I say, "Look, I know how it must seem to you, but I swear, I came with the best intentions. Everything I've done since leaving the orphanage was so that—"

"Oh, please." Misha steps toward me, his handcuffed hands stiff in front of his body. "You left me there to rot. One day you were promising you'd always be there for me, and the next you were gone."

Shocked, I open my mouth, but he doesn't give me a chance to reply. "You think I don't remember?" His voice rises as he takes another step toward me. "Well, I do. I remember everything. You lied to me. You said we'd always be together, and then you left!"

"That's enough." Lucas's voice freezes us both in place as the door opens and my captor steps in. He's followed by Dr. Goldberg, who's wearing latex gloves and carrying a surgical tray with various-sized syringes and needles.

My heart skips a beat, then leaps into overdrive. "What is this?" I can't hide my panic as I look at Lucas. "You said—"

"It's the trackers I mentioned to you before," Lucas says, crossing the room. Stopping in front of my bed, he glances at my brother, whose horrified gaze is locked on the tray. "She'll be fine," Lucas says, grabbing Misha's arm and dragging him away from the bed.

"No, wait." Cold sweat breaks out all over my body as Dr. Goldberg picks up a small syringe and comes toward me. I'm not ready for this battle. "Lucas, please, you don't need these," I plead as he tows my brother across the room, ignoring Misha's attempt to drop to the floor and kick out his knees. "I won't run, I promise. I'll do anything you want . . ."

Lucas stops in the doorway and pulls Misha against him in a chokehold. His muscled forearm is thicker than Misha's neck. "I know," he says, his arctic gaze pinning me in place. "You will. And right now, I want you to be a good girl and let the doctor give you some local anesthetic to make the insertion easier."

"But—"

Misha's face turns purple as Lucas tightens his arm, and I nod quickly, my eyes burning with helpless tears. "Okay, yes. I'll do it. Just let him go."

"I will—when the implants are in." Releasing Misha's throat, Lucas grabs his shirt and drags him out of the room, shutting the door on the way.

"I'm sorry," the doctor says, leaning over me. His brown eyes are filled with sympathy. "I know this isn't easy for you. If you could please lie down on your stomach . . ."

My bruises ache dully as I obey, stretching out and turning over onto my stomach. The doctor pulls the blanket off me, and I feel a small pinch between my shoulder blades as the needle sinks into my skin. It's followed by another pinch at my nape and a prick near my underarm. My skin grows numb, and I close my eyes, my tears dampening the sheets under my face.

My captor is as cruel as ever, and this time, there's no escape.

CHAPTER TWENTY-EIGHT

❖ LUCAS ❖

"What do you want from us?" the boy asks in English, rubbing his throat with his handcuffed hands. His gaze swings between me and the bedroom door, and I know he's deciding whether he should attack me to try to save his sister. "Are you going to kill us?"

His English is good, nearly as good as Yulia's, which makes sense. UUR must've also taught him from an early age.

"No, Michael," I say. "Not if your sister does what she's told." I wouldn't kill him—and I certainly wouldn't kill Yulia—but it's best if the kid doesn't know that yet. He may be young, but he's strong and skilled for his age.

I'll need leverage to keep him in line.

Sure enough, the boy's chin juts out belligerently. "If you're not going to kill us, why did you bring us here? I'm not going to betray my country, so if you think you can get me to talk—"

"I doubt a trainee would know anything worthwhile, so you can relax. Torture is not on the agenda today."

He glares at me, and I see him weighing the odds of winning against me in a fight.

"I wouldn't if I were you." I step to the right so that I'm between him and the bedroom door. "I promised Yulia I wouldn't hurt you, but if you keep attacking me . . ." I leave the threat unsaid, but the boy blanches and takes a step back.

Satisfied, I gesture toward the couch. "Sit. You can watch some TV until Diego returns."

The kid doesn't move. "Why are you doing this to Yulia? What do you want from her?"

"That's none of your business." My words come out harsher than I intended. I overheard the two siblings talking when I came in, and though I don't understand Russian, it was obvious to me that Michael accused his sister of something. She'd looked hurt, devastated by whatever the boy said to her. It almost made me change my mind about forcing the implants on her today.

Almost, but not really.

The need to lock Yulia down, to chain her to me, is a compulsion I can't fight. Not having her with me these last couple of weeks has been the worst form of torture, and I won't put myself through it ever again. Esguerra definitely had the right idea when he used the implants on his wife. The trackers will keep me informed of Yulia's whereabouts at all times. With the devices embedded in her neck and back, only a highly skilled surgeon would be able to remove them safely.

"She's my sister," the boy snaps, his blue eyes—eerily like Yulia's—burning with fury. "If you hurt her—"

"You won't be able to do anything about it," I say, figuring it's best to establish that right away. "The only reason you're alive and well is because I'm keeping you that way. A lot of people on this compound died because of your agency, and my boss was nearly killed. Do you understand?"

The kid stares at me for a few moments, then walks over to the couch and sits down, his shoulders rigid with tension.

He gets it now.

If something were to happen to me, he and Yulia would be goners.

I suppose I should feel bad scaring the boy, but he needs to know the reality of his situation. So far, the kid has been nothing but trouble. He attacked Eduardo on the plane, landing a kick to his groin, and when Diego dropped him off at my house, the guard told me the boy tried to grab his weapon in the car on the way here.

For his own safety, Yulia's brother needs to accept his new circumstances.

"Listen, Michael . . ." I approach the couch and pick up the remote control. "I don't intend to harm Yulia— or you, for that matter. But you need to cooperate and stop fighting us."

The kid gives me a sullen look. "Fuck you."

I should probably castigate him for his language, but I've said worse when I was his age. "What do you want to watch?" I ask, waving the remote at the TV.

He doesn't reply for a moment, then says in a low voice, "You killed my uncle."

I turn toward him in surprise. "Your uncle?"

"Yeah." The boy jumps to his feet, his hands clenched. "You know, the man whose head you shot off yesterday?"

I frown. The story is more complicated than I thought. "He was one of the agents at the black site?"

"Fuck you." The kid plops down on the couch and stares straight ahead. "I hope you eat shit and die."

"*Modern Family* it is, then," I say, turning on the TV and selecting the popular comedy. "Diego should be here any minute, but for now, I think that should hit the spot."

The show starts playing, and I walk over to the bedroom door and lean against the wall, keeping an eye on the boy while listening for sounds from the bedroom. Everything is quiet in there, and a few minutes later, Diego shows up.

"Watch him carefully," I tell the guard, lowering my voice to just above a whisper. "It seems we might've killed some of his family. I have to talk to Yulia to make sense of it all, but for now, keep an eye on him. The kid wants blood."

Diego nods, his face set in grim lines, and I know he understands.

Nothing motivates quite like revenge.

I walk them to the door, making sure the boy doesn't try anything along the way, and then I return to the bedroom, where Goldberg is already packing up his bag.

Yulia is lying on her stomach, stiff and silent, with square bandages marking the insertion sites. The blanket is folded down to her waist, exposing her slim back and the elegant line of her spine. Her face is turned away from me, her hair spread in a tangled blond cloud across the sheets, and my chest aches as I see the scrapes and bruises marring her smooth skin.

Maybe I should've waited with the trackers after all.

No. Shaking off the uncharacteristic self-doubt, I look at the doctor. "Did it go okay?" I ask, and Goldberg nods, picking up his bag.

"Everything went fine," he says, heading for the door. "The bleeding should stop in about an hour, and you can replace the bandages with regular Band-Aids at that point if you want. If you keep the insertion points clean, there won't be any scarring."

"Good. Thank you." I approach the bed and sit down, waiting for the doctor to leave. As soon as I hear the front door close, I extend my hand and run my fingers over Yulia's naked back, avoiding the bruised areas. Her skin is cool and silky, and I feel her quiver under my touch. Instantly, my body comes to life, my hunger for her awakening with savage fury.

Cursing silently, I withdraw my hand, curling it into a fist to keep myself from reaching for her again. I can't take her yet. She's traumatized and hurt, too weak to handle my pent-up desire.

I have to let her heal.

To my surprise, Yulia rolls over onto her back and stretches her arms above her head—a move that draws my gaze to the soft, round globes of her breasts. "Aren't you going to fuck me?" she murmurs, and I see her nipples hardening, as if from arousal.

My cock turns into a metal spike in my jeans. I know her nipples are most likely reacting to the cool air from the AC, but my mouth still waters with the urge to suck them, to lick the pale flesh around the pink aureolas and sink my teeth into the soft underside of her breasts. Only the black-and-blue marks on her face and stomach keep me from grabbing her then and there.

With effort, I tear my gaze away from her breasts. "No," I say hoarsely. I know I should get up, get away from the temptation, but I can't move. I want her, and not just for sex. The longing that consumes me emanates from deep within my being. We've only been apart for two weeks, but it felt like years. "I'm not going to touch you today."

Yulia's cracked lips twist, her eyes unnaturally bright, and I notice wet streaks on her cheeks. "No? I'm no longer pretty enough for you?" There's a dark taunt in her voice, and I realize that she's punishing me for the trackers, that this is her way of reclaiming control.

Even knowing that, I rise to her bait. "You're gorgeous, and you fucking know it," I say harshly. If tormenting me like this makes Yulia feel better, I'll allow it—if only to alleviate the uncomfortable prickling of guilt the sight of her tears generates.

I should've fucking waited.

"So do it. Fuck me," Yulia says, kicking off the rest of her blanket. She's naked underneath—I undressed and bathed her when we arrived an hour ago—and my body tightens at the sight of her flat stomach and slim, shapely legs that seem to go on forever. And between those legs . . . Heat rises in me, my breathing turning fast and heavy as I look at the glistening pink folds between her thighs.

"I'm not touching you," I repeat, but even to my own ears, my words lack conviction. She'd been unconscious when I bathed her, and even that simple act had brought me to painful arousal.

Yulia fully awake and taunting me with her body is like a defenseless mouse parading in front of a starved cat.

"Why not?" She arches her back, thrusting her breasts upward in a porn star pose, and I bite back a tortured groan as her nipples draw my attention once more. "Isn't this why you chased me down? So you could fuck me?"

She's right, except fucking is only part of it now. I want what we had before and more.

I want all of her.

Giving in to the vicious hunger riding me, I climb onto the bed and straddle her on all fours, caging her with my body without touching her. Her eyes widen, and I catch a glimmer of fear in her gaze.

She didn't expect me to take her up on her offer.

A dark smile forms on my lips. Leaning down, I whisper in her ear, "Yes, beautiful. I brought you here to fuck you—and I will. Soon. For now, we're going to do something different."

A shudder runs through her as my breath warms her neck, and she lets out a quiet moan as I kiss the tender spot under her ear, then nibble on her delicate earlobe. Her hair tickles my face, and her peach-like fragrance fills my nostrils, making me burn with the need to possess her, to slide down my zipper and thrust inside her, sheathing myself in her soft, wet heat.

The urge is almost unbearable, but I make myself move down her body, ignoring the insistent throbbing of my cock. I lick her neck, kiss her collarbone, and suck each erect nipple before tasting her flat, trembling belly. When my face is parallel to the V between her thighs, I bend my head and inhale deeply, breathing in her warm female scent. Yulia tenses, her thighs tightening to restrict my access to her sex, and I gently but firmly grasp her inner thighs, pulling her legs wide apart.

"Relax, I won't hurt you," I murmur, looking up at her. Her blue eyes are wide and uncertain, the porn-star act gone without a trace. I can sense her growing anxiety, and the image of Kirill attacking her flashes through my mind, cooling my lust by a small degree.

For all her bravado, my beautiful spy is nowhere near ready to play these games.

Keeping my gaze locked on her face, I press my mouth to her pussy, tasting her slick pink flesh. Yulia quivers, her slender hands knotting into fists at her sides, and I nibble on the soft folds around her clit, teasing and licking the sensitive area before swiping my tongue along her slit. She moans, closing her eyes, and I taste her growing arousal as her inner muscles clench helplessly under my tongue.

"Yes, sweetheart, that's it . . ." I breathe in her intoxicating scent again, then close my lips around her clit and lave the underside of it with my tongue before sucking on it with strong, pulling motions. She cries out, her hips lifting off the bed, and I feel the tension in her rising. My own body responds with a fresh surge of blood to my cock, and my balls tighten as I feel her contractions begin.

I lick her until she's limp and panting in the aftermath of her orgasm, and then I finally give in to my own need. Rising up on my knees, I unzip my jeans and close my fist around my swollen cock.

A few hard jerks of my hand, and I'm coming too, my seed splattering all over her white belly and breasts. It's not a particularly satisfying release—I'd much rather be inside her—but the sight of my cum on her body is erotic in its own way.

On some primitive level, it marks her as my property.

Yulia doesn't move or speak as I climb off the bed and walk to the bathroom. She just watches me, her eyes half-closed, and when I return with a warm, wet towel a minute later, she remains silent, her expression unreadable as I clean her off.

When I'm done, I undress and climb into bed next to her. Carefully, I draw her against me, trying not to put pressure on her injuries as I curve my body around hers from the back. My ribs ache, but I ignore the nagging pain. It feels too good to have her in my arms, to hold her and know that she's mine.

Yulia is stiff at first, but after a few moments, I feel the tension in her muscles slowly ebbing. In another minute, her breathing evens out, and I know healing sleep has claimed her again.

My own eyelids grow heavy, and I brush my lips across her temple before closing my eyes. "Good night, beautiful," I whisper, euphoric contentment spreading through me as she snuggles closer with a sleepy mumble.

I have my Yulia back, and I'm never losing her again.

PART III: THE CARETAKER

CHAPTER TWENTY-NINE

❖ LUCAS ❖

The sun is impossibly bright in the sky as I walk toward Esguerra's office, the humid air making me sweat despite the early hour. Still, I feel lighter than I have in weeks, the knowledge that Yulia is sleeping in my bed filling me with an incandescent mix of satisfaction and relief.

I found her. I have her.

Even the knowledge that Kirill escaped is not enough to spoil my mood this morning. I left Diego to watch over sleeping Yulia so I could start the process of hunting Kirill, but I feel infinitely calmer after eight hours of sleep.

So calm, in fact, that my pulse barely increases when I see Rosa walking across the lawn toward me. As she approaches, I see that she looks uneasy, her hands twisting fistfuls of her skirt at her sides.

"I heard you were in another shootout in Ukraine," she says, studying me with worried curiosity. "And that you found her. Is it true? Are you all right?"

I nod, my good mood slipping away with every word she speaks. Before leaving the house, I skimmed Thomas's report on Rosa and found that it contained no new information. The maid hasn't reached out to anyone outside the compound, nor has anyone tried to contact her. If the girl is working with UUR or any of our enemies, she's either really good at concealing it, or my original guess about jealousy was right.

It's time to deal with this problem once and for all.

"Rosa," I say softly, stepping closer to her. "Why did you help Yulia escape?"

The maid's bronzed face turns pale. "Wh-what do you mean?"

"Did someone pay you?"

She takes a step back, her eyes huge. "No, of course not! I—" She makes a visible effort to compose herself. "I don't know what you're talking about," she says in an almost steady voice. "Whatever she's told you is a lie. I had nothing to do with her escape."

I smile coldly. "Yulia didn't say a word, but I find it interesting that you think she would have."

Rosa pales even more, and I see her hands tighten convulsively as she continues to back away. "Please, Lucas, it's not what you think."

"No?" I close the distance between us and grab her upper arm before she can turn and run. "What is it then?"

"It's—" She clamps her lips shut and shakes her head, staring up at me. "I had nothing to do with her escape," she repeats, lifting her chin, and I see that she has no intention of admitting anything to me.

"All right," I say, tightening my grip on her arm. "Since you're Esguerra's maid, let's see what he has to say about all this."

And ignoring her terrified expression, I resume walking toward Esguerra's office, dragging Rosa along at my side.

* * *

Esguerra's face is rigid with fury as I present the drone footage. The videos are low resolution and obscured by trees in a few places, but there's no mistaking Rosa's curvy figure in her maid's outfit as she approaches my house. Rosa sits quietly, trembling from head to toe while Esguerra watches the videos on his computer. It's not until he turns toward her that she begins crying.

"Why?" His voice is like ice as he rises to his feet. "What did you hope to gain by this? You know what we do to traitors."

Rosa shakes her head, crying harder as Esguerra approaches her, and despite my own anger, I feel a flicker of pity for the girl. In the next second, however, I remember what almost happened to Yulia because of Rosa, and my pity disappears without a trace.

Whatever my boss chooses to do to the maid will be no less than she deserves.

"Please, Señor Esguerra," she begs as he grips her elbow and drags her off the chair where she was huddling. "Please, it wasn't like that . . ."

"What was it like, then?" I ask, fishing my Swiss knife out of my pocket and opening the blade. Stepping toward the maid, I twist my fist in her hair, pulling her head back as Esguerra holds her upright by her upper arms. "Why did you help my prisoner escape?"

Tears streak down Rosa's face and her mouth quivers as I press the blade against her throat, nicking her neck just enough for her to feel the first bite. "Don't, please . . ." Her terror washes over me, but this time, it leaves me cold. I'm in my interrogation mode, and so is Esguerra. I see it in the hard gleam of his eyes.

If the girl doesn't talk in the next couple of minutes, the tiny wound I left on her neck will be the least of her worries.

"Julian, did you see—" Nora freezes as she enters the office, her eyes widening as she takes in the scene.

"Fuck," Esguerra mutters, releasing Rosa abruptly. I barely catch her as she stumbles backward, crashing into me. Before she can get away, I secure the sobbing maid with my forearm across her throat and lower my knife. At the same time, Esguerra steps toward his wife, saying, "Nora, baby, go home. This is a security matter."

"A security matter?" Nora's voice is thin as her gaze swings wildly between me and her husband. "What are you talking about?"

"Rosa helped Lucas's prisoner escape," Esguerra explains tersely, taking Nora's arm and putting his hand on her back to guide her out of the room. She digs in her heels, but her petite frame is no match for his strength, and he gently but firmly steers her toward the exit. "We're interrogating her to find out more. It's nothing you need to worry about, my pet."

"Are you insane?" Nora's voice rises as she begins to struggle, and Esguerra stops, wrapping his arms around her from the back as she tries to kick, then headbutt him. "She's my friend. Don't touch her!"

Esguerra's only response is to lift his tiny wife against his chest and hold her tightly to restrain her flailing. Nora screams, bucking in his arms, and Rosa's sobbing intensifies as Esguerra begins carrying Nora out. He's almost at the door when Nora yells, "Stop, Julian! She didn't do it. It was me—all me!"

Rosa's sobs cut off as suddenly as if she'd been muted, and Esguerra stops, lowering Nora to her feet.

"What?" His expression is thunderous as he grips his wife's narrow shoulders. "What the hell are you talking about?"

I very nearly ask the same question, but at the last moment, I keep my mouth shut. Given Nora's unexpected involvement, it's best if Esguerra handles it from here on.

He'd gut me for so much as looking at his wife the wrong way.

"I did it." Nora raises her chin to meet her husband's furious gaze. "I helped Yulia escape. So if you're going to interrogate anyone, it should be me. She had nothing to do with it."

"You're lying." Esguerra's voice is lethally soft. "I saw the drone footage. She went to Lucas's house right before our departure."

Nora doesn't miss a beat. "Right. Because I asked her to."

Rosa makes a choking sound, her hands clawing at my forearm, and I realize I inadvertently tightened my arm across her throat. Cursing silently, I lower my arm and push Rosa away from me, letting her collapse on the chair she was sitting on earlier. Esguerra's wife is lying—I'm almost certain she's lying—but I have no idea how to prove it. There was no reason for Nora to help Yulia; she doesn't know the Ukrainian spy, and she certainly doesn't have any feelings for me.

"Why would you do this?" Esguerra demands. He's clearly thinking along the same lines. "You despise this girl. You hate her for the crash, remember?" His eyes drill into Nora, but she doesn't back down.

"So what?" She twists out of Esguerra's hold and steps back, her small chest heaving. "You know I had a problem with Lucas torturing a woman at his house—even *that* woman."

Recognition flickers across Esguerra's face before his jaw tightens further, and I realize to my shock that Nora might've done it after all. Esguerra did mention that she and Rosa had been to my house the day Yulia arrived. If so, Nora might've seen Yulia sitting in my living room, naked and bound to a chair. It's not inconceivable that the sight bothered the girl; for all her newfound toughness, Nora is a product of her upbringing—her soft American middle-class background.

Most people new to this way of life would've objected to me torturing Yulia, and it's possible Nora did too.

Fucking hell. If Nora weren't Esguerra's wife . . .

Esguerra himself looks on the verge of murder as he catches Nora's arm and drags her closer to him. "Walk me through this." His blue eyes gleam with rage. "You instructed Rosa to do what, exactly?"

Rosa begins crying again, and I spare her a glance before turning my attention back to the drama playing out in front of me. I've never seen Esguerra so mad at his wife before. If I were Nora, I'd be backpedaling right about now; the things I've seen her husband do would make serial killers squirm.

Nora's face is white as she stares up at Esguerra, but her voice barely shakes as she says, "I asked her to help Yulia escape. I didn't tell her how to do it—she knows this place better than me, so I left the exact method up to her. Rosa didn't want to do it, but I told her how much it bothered me, and with the baby and everything, she gave in to my request."

Manipulative little witch. I want to wring Nora's neck and applaud in admiration at the same time. Mentioning the baby they just lost was a low blow, but it had the desired effect. Esguerra's grip on Nora's arm slackens, and pain flits across his face before he composes himself. When he speaks again, some of the lethal bite is gone from his voice.

"Why didn't you talk to me about it? If it bothered you that much, why didn't you say something?"

"I didn't think it would've helped," Nora says, and I see her big dark eyes fill with tears. "I'm sorry, Julian. I wanted the girl gone by the time we returned, and I told Rosa to make it happen. I was sure you wouldn't go along with it." Her chin quivers as the tears spill over and roll down her cheeks. "Please, if you have to punish someone, it should be me, not Rosa. She was just being a good friend to me. Please, Julian." She reaches up to touch his face with her free hand, and I avert my gaze as Esguerra catches her wrist and pulls her flush against him, his nostrils flaring. The tension between them turns thickly sexual, and I suddenly feel like an intruder, a peeping tom observing an intimate moment.

Clearing my throat, I step toward Rosa and grab her upper arm, pulling her to her feet. "I'll let you two figure this out," I say, marching the maid toward the door. "In the meanwhile, I'll have Rosa watched by the guards."

Neither Esguerra nor his wife justify my statement with a response, and as I exit the building, I hear the sound of something falling, followed by Nora's choked cry. Rosa sucks in her breath—she must've heard it too—and her shoulders shake with a fresh bout of tears.

"Don't worry," I say, giving the girl an icy look as I lead her away from the building. "Esguerra may be a sadist, but he won't hurt her—much. You, on the other hand, are still a question mark. If Nora lied to protect you . . ."

I don't complete my statement, but I don't have to.

We both know what Esguerra will do to Rosa if she allowed Nora to take the fall for her.

CHAPTER THIRTY

❖ YULIA ❖

I wake up groggy and confused, hurting from head to toe. Groaning, I stumble out of bed and make my way to the bathroom. Still half-asleep, I take care of business, and it's only when I'm washing my face that it dawns on me that I'm alone—and untied.

A soreness at the back of my neck reminds me of the reason for that: the tracker implants. Lucas must be certain I won't be able to run away again.

I lift my hand and touch the bandage on my nape, then turn to peer at my back in the mirror. Besides the spot I'm touching—and amidst a mottled canvas of bruises—there are two more areas where the trackers went in. The bandages on the wounds are simple Band-

Aids now; Lucas must've changed them while I was sleeping. I vaguely recall the doctor giving instructions about that.

I also remember what happened afterwards, and a violent blush sears my face, chasing away the remnants of my sleepiness. I'm not sure why I egged Lucas on like that, but at the time, it seemed to make sense. He clearly cares little about me as a person, and I wanted him to admit it. I wanted him to prove to me once and for all that I'm nothing more than a convenient body for him to fuck, a sexual object that he can and will hurt at will.

Except he didn't hurt me. He gave me pleasure, and then he took his own with his fist, leaving me covered with his seed.

"Yulia?" A knock on the door startles me, and I turn, my pulse jumping into the stratosphere. The voice is not Lucas's, and I'm completely naked.

"Yes?" I call out, grabbing a big fluffy towel off the rack and wrapping it around myself.

"Lucas asked me to watch you this morning," the man says, and I exhale in relief as I recognize Diego's voice. "I hope I didn't scare you. He said you might be sleeping for a while, and I was in the kitchen, grabbing myself a snack, when I heard the water running. You okay? Do you need anything?"

"No, I'm fine, thanks," I say, my heartbeat slowing a bit. "I'll just, um . . . I'll be right out."

"No problem. Take your time. I'll be in the kitchen." I hear retreating footsteps.

On autopilot, I brush my teeth and run a comb through my hair, untangling the wild blond mess. Honestly, I don't know why I'm even trying to look presentable. The face staring at me from the mirror is like something out of a nightmare. My lips are already beginning to heal, but the left side of my face, where Kirill hit me, is one giant ugly bruise. Smaller scrapes and bruises decorate the rest of my face and body— except for my back, which looks even worse than my face.

No wonder I'm still in pain.

Carefully, I rotate my neck from side to side, trying to ease the stiffness in my muscles. My head aches with the movement, but not as much as yesterday. The doctor had been right about the mildness of my concussion; I had passed out on the plane as much from shock and exhaustion as the head injury itself.

Feeling marginally better, I tighten the towel around myself and walk to the bedroom to change. All the skimpy outfits that Lucas got for me are still there, and I select a pair of shorts and a T-shirt at random, grimacing in pain as I put the clothes on.

When I finally make my way to the kitchen, I find Diego there, spreading cream cheese on a toasted bagel.

"Hey," he says, giving me his usual charming grin. "Are you hungry?"

My stomach chooses that moment to rumble, and the young guard's smile widens. "I'll take that as a yes," he says, putting his bagel down on his plate and getting up. "What would you like? Cereal, toast, fruit? Here, sit." He gestures toward the table. "I'm under strict orders to make sure you don't do anything strenuous today."

"Um, cereal would work." I walk over to the table and sit down, feeling disoriented. It seems like only minutes ago, I was in Ukraine amidst gunfire and explosions, and now I'm in Lucas's kitchen, talking about cereal with one of the mercenaries who killed my UUR colleagues.

My *former* UUR colleagues, I mentally correct myself. I ceased being part of the organization when I made the choice to disappear instead of carrying out my assignment.

"Where's my brother?" I ask, remembering what Lucas told me about the guards watching him.

Diego gives me another grin. "He's with Eduardo. The poor guy drew the short straw."

I blink. "Oh?"

"Let's just say your brother is not very happy to be here." Diego walks over to the fridge and takes out a carton of milk. Pouring cereal into a bowl, he adds the milk, grabs a spoon, and brings the bowl to me. Before I can ask, he says, "But he's okay, so don't worry. Nobody's going to hurt him."

I pick up my spoon, though I no longer feel hungry. My stomach is tight with anxiety. Of course Misha is not happy to be here. How could he be? His uncle was killed in front of his eyes, and he must be terrified out of his mind. And if Obenko didn't lie about Misha's relationship with his adoptive parents, they must be worried sick about him. Unless he lives at the UUR dorms, like other trainees? If that's the case, they might not be aware of what happened yet, though I'm sure someone is bound to notify them soon.

What a disaster—and it's all my fault. If I hadn't been so weak, Lucas wouldn't have known anything about UUR. I let my captor break me, and then I inadvertently led him to my brother—the very person I was trying to protect. I remember yesterday's argument with Misha, the accusations he threw at me, and I want to curl up and cry.

"Are you all right?" Diego sits down across from me and picks up his bagel. "You look really pale."

"I'm fine," I say automatically, dipping my spoon into the cereal and bringing the soggy corn flakes to my lips. "Just a bit out of it."

"Of course." Diego gives me a sympathetic grin. "Jet lag is a bitch, plus you got it pretty rough yesterday."

He focuses on his bagel, and I choke down a few bites of cereal before putting down my spoon. I didn't lie about being out of it; my thoughts are all over the place, my mind jumping from one question to another. The future—especially my brother's future—is like a terrifying black hole looming in the distance, so I try to focus on the present and the near past.

"How did you know where to find me?" I ask Diego when he's done with his bagel. "In general, how did you locate that facility?"

"Oh, yeah, that . . ." The guard gets up and takes his plate over to the sink. "I'm afraid your rescue was more or less luck on our end, but I'll let Kent fill you in on that."

Great. Another person stonewalling me. Does every person on this compound regard me as Lucas's property to such an extent that they can't answer my questions on their own?

Suppressing my frustration, I force myself to eat another spoonful of cereal before getting up to dump the rest of it in the garbage.

"What are you doing? Here, I got it." Diego intercepts me before I can get to the sink, grabbing the bowl out of my hands. "You need to rest today."

"I'm fine," I say, then lean against the counter, the weakness in my knees belying my statement. "I want to see Misha—Michael, I mean. Can you bring him here or take me to him?"

"Nope," Diego says cheerfully. "Eduardo took him to the training gym an hour ago. Why don't you rest for now, and then we'll see what Kent says later?" The guard is smiling, but I can sense the steel underneath his easygoing facade. He's not about to let me do anything other than rest and wait for Lucas to come home.

I want to argue, but I know it'll be useless. Besides, getting back in bed doesn't sound all that unappealing.

"All right," I say. "Thank you for the breakfast."

Making my way back to the bedroom, I lie down, feeling as exhausted as if I just ran ten kilometers. My head is throbbing again, and my bruises ache. Even my throat is sore, and my skin feels tight and achy all over. On the nightstand next to the bed, I see the pain pills from yesterday, and after a moment of indecision, I reach for the bottle and extract two pills. Picking up a water bottle that someone thoughtfully left on the nightstand, I swallow the pills and wash them down with water before lying back and closing my eyes.

There's no point in fighting Lucas's orders today. I need to save my strength for when it matters.

CHAPTER THIRTY-ONE

❖ LUCAS ❖

After being away for several days, I have a shitload of work to catch up on, and I don't make it home until dinnertime. When I finally walk in, I see Diego watching TV on my couch.

"How is she?" I ask, glancing at the bedroom. "Still sleeping?"

Diego nods, rising to his feet. "Yeah. Like I told you in my texts, she slept through lunch, then woke up for an hour or so, read in bed, and then fell asleep again. I made a sandwich for her, but she left most of it untouched. Oh, and she kept asking to see her brother, but I said you have to authorize that."

"I see. Thank you for watching her. I'll let you know if I need you tomorrow."

Diego grins. "No problem, man."

He leaves, and I enter the bedroom to check on Yulia. Excessive sleeping is not an uncommon reaction to physical trauma and extreme emotional stress—it's the body's way of letting itself heal—but her lack of appetite worries me.

It's dark in the room, so I make my way over to the bed and turn on a bedside lamp. Yulia doesn't so much as twitch at the soft light. She's lying on her back, the blanket pulled up to her chest and her face turned toward me. My chest tightens at the sight of her swollen jaw and darkened eye. With her slender hand lying palm-up on the pillow, she looks achingly young and defenseless, a hurt child instead of a grown woman.

If Kirill is still alive, he'll wish he were dead ten times over by the time I'm done with him.

This morning, I sent out feelers to all our contacts in Europe and gave our hackers a new assignment: tracking down Kirill Luchenko. I also reached out to Peter Sokolov again to see if he knows anyone in Ukraine who can help. He responded right away, promising to look into it, so now it's just a matter of time before we locate the fucker.

Assuming he didn't croak from his wounds, that is. Since Yulia shot his dick off, it might be touch and go for a while.

Sitting down on the edge of the bed, I reach over and stroke her upturned palm with the tip of my finger, feeling the warm softness of her skin. Like the girl herself, her hand is deceptively delicate, an embodiment of elegant femininity. But I know how dangerous it can be—and now Kirill does too.

The fucking bastard will die a dickless eunuch. I really like that.

Yulia's fingers curl in response to my touch, and a small moan escapes her throat. She still doesn't wake up, though, and some instinct makes me reach over and touch her forehead with the back of my hand.

Fuck.

She's hot—much too hot. Her forehead is burning.

In the next instant, I'm on my feet, pulling out my phone. Goldberg doesn't pick up at first, so I call him again. Then again.

On the third attempt, he picks up the phone. "What is it?"

"Yulia is sick," I say without preamble. "Something's really wrong with her. I need you here. Now."

"On my way."

He hangs up, and I sit down on the bed and pick up Yulia's hand, noticing the dry heat coming off her skin. My heart thuds with a dull, heavy rhythm as I lift her wrist up to my face and press my lips against her palm.

"You'll be all right," I whisper, ignoring the sharp fear clawing at my insides. "You'll be all right, baby. You have to be."

* * *

"Looks like a type of flu," Goldberg says after examining Yulia. "It hit her hard, probably because her immune system was already under stress from her injuries and everything. I'll get her started on an antiviral and give her Tylenol to bring down the fever. Other than that, you just keep her comfortable and make sure she gets enough fluids."

As he speaks, Yulia's eyelids flutter open, and she stares at me in confusion. "Lucas?" Her voice is weak and raspy as she rolls over onto her side. "What—"

"It's okay, sweetheart. You're just feverish from the flu," I say, sitting down on the bed next to her. Picking up the water bottle from the nightstand, I slide my arm under her upper back and help her sit up, propping her up on the pillows. Handing her the bottle and the pills Goldberg gives me, I murmur, "Here, drink this. It'll make you feel better."

I can feel the doctor's amused gaze on me as he packs his bag, but I no longer give a fuck what he thinks or whom he tells about my weakness for Yulia.

She's mine, and it's time everyone knew that fact.

Yulia obediently swallows the pills and washes them down with all the water remaining in the bottle. "Where's Misha?" she asks when she's done, and I sigh, realizing this is going to be an ongoing battle.

"Your brother had a very nice day with Eduardo," I say, putting the empty bottle back on the nightstand as Goldberg discreetly slips out of the room. "They had a lengthy workout session where Michael worked off quite a bit of his aggression toward the guard, and now they're eating dinner, I believe—which is what we should be doing. Are you hungry? I can heat up some chicken noodle soup. It's canned, but—"

"I'm not hungry," she says, shaking her head. "I just want to see Misha."

"How about this: you take a shower, eat a little soup and drink some tea, and I'll see what I can do about getting Misha over here again?" I want her to eat so she can recover, and this seems like the best way to go about it.

"Okay." Yulia pushes the blanket off her legs and starts to get up, but I catch her and lift her against my chest before she can do more than take a couple of shaky steps. She gives me a startled look, but winds her arms around my neck, holding on to me as I carry her to the bathroom.

When I reach my destination, I carefully lower Yulia to her feet and begin to undress her, pulling off her T-shirt and shorts while she stands there mutely, her eyes glazed with fever. For some reason, I'm reminded of when she was first brought here, bedraggled and malnourished after the Russian prison. It seems impossible that only a month has passed since then— that I met her just three months ago.

It feels like I've been obsessed with my captive for a lifetime.

"Do you need a moment?" I ask, and Yulia nods, the unbruised parts of her face reddening with a flush.

"Okay. I'll be right outside. Call out if you feel dizzy or anything."

I step out to let her use the restroom, and when I hear the shower turn on, I come back in. She's already standing inside the glass stall, her hand shaking as she reaches for shampoo.

"Here, let me help you," I say, swiftly stripping off my own clothes and joining her in the shower. "I don't want you to strain yourself."

"I'm okay," she protests, but I take the shampoo from her hand and pour a small amount into my palm, then step under the spray to keep the water from hitting her in the face. As I lather her hair, she leans against me, closing her eyes, and I suppress a groan as her firm, curvy ass presses against my groin, taking me from semi-erect state to full-blown hardness. Up until then, I'd managed to keep my eyes off her naked body, my libido taking a back seat to my concern for her health, but this is too much.

Even sick and hurt, she turns me on unbearably.

Down. Fucking go down, I will my cock. My blood feels like molten lava in my veins as I turn Yulia toward the spray and rinse the shampoo from her hair before applying conditioner to the long blond strands.

"Lucas . . ." Her voice is a shaky whisper as she turns to face me, her fever-bright eyes locking on my face. Water droplets cling to her brown lashes, emphasizing their length, and my lungs feel like I can't get enough air as she reaches for me, her hand brushing over my abs before traveling downward to curl around my hard, aching cock.

It takes all my strength to step out of her reach. "What are you doing?" I ask hoarsely, my stiff cock bobbing up to my navel as the water spray hits her in the chest. "You have the fucking flu."

She follows me, blinking the water out of her eyes. "Let me take care of you, at least like this." Her fingers brush against my erection again, but I catch her wrist before she can wrap her hand around the shaft.

"What the fuck, Yulia?" I stare down at her in disbelief, seeing the dark circles under her eyes and the unnatural pallor of her skin. She's about to collapse, and she wants to give me a handjob?

At my rejection, Yulia's lips tremble, and she drops her gaze, her wrist going limp in my grasp. She looks utterly dejected, and as I stare at her bent head, a dark possibility occurs to me.

"Are you doing this because you think you have to?" I ask, my voice roughening. "Are you afraid I'll hurt your brother if you don't have sex with me?"

She looks up, her eyes swimming with tears, and I realize that's exactly what she fears, that she thinks me capable of this. She's not entirely wrong—I would use her brother to control her if I had to—but not for this.

Not while she's in this condition.

"Yulia . . ." I gently cup her jaw, making sure I touch only the uninjured side of her face. "I'm not going to punish you for being sick, okay? I'm not that much of a monster. Your brother is safe. You can rest and recover without worrying about him."

"But—"

"Shh." I press the tips of my fingers to her lips. "He'll be fine on one condition: that you stop stressing and let yourself heal. Do you think you can do that?"

She nods slowly, and I lower my hand. "Good. Now, let's wash the rest of you and get you into bed. Tonight, I'm taking care of you, okay?"

Yulia nods again, and I rinse off her conditioner, then carefully wash her all over, ignoring my persistent arousal. I tell myself that I'm a doctor caring for a patient, that this is no different than washing a child, but my cock doesn't buy it. Nonetheless, I manage to get through the shower without jumping her, and by the time I towel her off and bring her back to bed, I'm almost back in control.

"Now soup and tea," I say, propping her up on the pillows again, and she gives me a listless look, her pallor even more pronounced.

"Okay," she murmurs. "And then my brother, right?"

"Yes," I say, but by the time I return with the soup and tea, she's already asleep, her skin burning even hotter.

CHAPTER THIRTY-TWO

❖ YULIA ❖

The next several days pass in a fog of fever and pain. My bones ache, and my throat feels like I swallowed a ball of fire. Even the roots of my hair hurt, the heat of the fever consuming from within. The illness takes everything out of me, leaving me weak and shaking, and the simplest activities—like going to the bathroom and showering—require Lucas's help.

I sleep for what feels like twenty hours a day, and if it weren't for Lucas forcing water, tea, and soup on me at regular intervals, I'd sleep even more. But he keeps waking me up to spoon-feed me various liquids, and I'm too drained to resist his gentle but insistent brand of caregiving. He's with me at night, his big body curved protectively around mine as we sleep, and he's next to me during the day—all day.

"Don't you have someplace to be?" I croak out the first time I see my captor at my bedside, working on a laptop in an uncomfortable-looking chair. "You're usually gone at this time."

Lucas's hard mouth curves in a smile. "I'm taking a sick day. How are you feeling? Hungry? Thirsty?"

"I'm okay," I murmur, closing my eyes. "Just really, really tired." The exhaustion seems to have settled deep in my bones, weighing me down like an anchor. Even this brief exchange has depleted my nonexistent energy, and I'm already almost asleep again when Lucas makes me sit up and drink room-temperature water from a cup with a curved straw.

Swallowing hurts my throat, but the liquid invigorates me enough that I ask about my brother. Lucas assures me that he's fine, but when I continue to insist that I see Misha, Lucas makes Eduardo take an impromptu two-minute video of my brother and email it to us. On the video, my brother is eating a burger and arguing with Diego about the merits of Krav Maga versus Tae Kwan Do. He looks neither afraid nor abused, which reassures me quite a bit.

"I'll bring him by when you're a little stronger," Lucas promises. "Goldberg said you should be through the worst of it by tomorrow."

But I'm not. The next day is even worse, my fever spiking uncontrollably, and I wake up mid-day to hear

Lucas arguing with the doctor about whether I need to be hospitalized.

Blearily, I open my eyes to see my captor pacing around the room, a thermometer clutched in his powerful fist. "Her fever is almost a hundred and four. What if it's pneumonia or something like that?"

"I told you, her lungs are clear," Dr. Goldberg says with a hint of exasperation. "As long as you keep giving her enough liquids, she'll be fine. You just need to let this illness run its course. The human body doesn't handle extreme stress well, and from what you've told me, she's been through more in the past three months than most people survive in a lifetime. She's traumatized physically and mentally, and she needs rest and sleep to heal. In a way, this flu is her body's way of telling her to slow down and take care of herself."

Lucas stops in front of the bed, his hands clenched. "If anything happens to her . . ."

"Yes, I know, you'll tear me limb from limb," the doctor says wearily. "So you've said. Now if you don't mind, I have a guard with a bullet in his leg who needs my attention. Call me if her fever goes higher, and for now, alternate her Tylenol with Advil."

He departs, and I close my eyes, sinking back into sleep.

* * *

The fever continues for three more days, spiking and falling in an unpredictable manner. Every time I wake up, feeling like I'm dying, Lucas is by my side, ready to feed me liquids, put a wet towel on my forehead, or carry me to the bathroom.

"Are you sure you don't have a nursing degree?" I joke weakly when he places me back in bed, having changed the sheets and fluffed up my pillows. "Because you're really good at this."

Lucas smiles and tucks the blanket around me. "Maybe I'll look into it if this gig with Esguerra doesn't work out."

I manage a tiny smile in return, and then I'm out again, too exhausted to cling to wakefulness for long.

That night, the fever torments me nonstop, defying Lucas's efforts to bring it down with Tylenol and cool towels. I toss and turn, alternately shivering and sweating as troubled dreams invade my mind. The wolf of the children's lullaby comes to me, gnawing at my side, and I scream as his snout transforms into Kirill's face—a face that explodes into bits as I shoot him, over and over again. Lucas shakes me awake, holding me on his lap until my hysterical sobbing subsides, but as soon as I fall asleep again, I see a variation of the same dream, only this time, my bullets miss Kirill and hit my brother while Kirill laughs, holding his bloodied cock.

"Yulia, hush, sweetheart, don't. He's okay. Misha is okay." The assurance, delivered in Lucas's deep voice, calms me down until I'm swept into yet another twisted dream-memory, and the vicious cycle continues until my fever breaks in the morning.

"I'm sorry," I whisper when I wake up and see Lucas sitting next to me, his eyes ringed with dark circles and his hard jaw unshaven as he frowns at something on his laptop. "Did I keep you up all night?"

He looks up from the computer. "No, of course not." Despite his tired appearance, his pale eyes are sharply alert as he reaches over to the nightstand and hands me the cup with the straw. "How are you feeling?"

"Like I couldn't swat a fly," I say hoarsely after sucking down the full cup of water. "But overall, better." For the first time in days, my head doesn't ache, and my skin feels like it actually wants to stay attached to my body. Even my throat is almost back to normal, and there's a hollow sensation in my stomach that feels suspiciously like hunger.

Lucas's tense look eases as he places his laptop on the nightstand and gets up. "I'm glad. Another few hours like that, and I was flying you to a hospital, no matter what Goldberg said." Leaning over me, he carefully picks me up and brings me to the bathroom, where he runs a bath for me since I'm too weak to stand in a shower stall.

"Why are you doing this?" I ask when he's done washing me from head to toe. Now that I'm feeling marginally more human, it dawns on me just how extraordinary Lucas's actions over the past several days have been. I don't know many husbands who would've cared for their wives with such dedication.

"What do you mean?" Lucas frowns as he wraps me in a thick towel and picks me up. "You needed a bath."

"I know, but you didn't need to be the one to give it to me," I say as he carries me back to the bedroom. "You could've had one of the guards help or—" I stop as his expression darkens.

"If you think I'm letting another man touch you . . ." His voice is pure lethal ice, and despite myself, I shiver as he lays me back on the bed, stuffing two pillows under my back to prop me up to a half-sitting position. Leaning in, he growls, "You're mine and mine alone, understand?"

I nod warily. I'd let myself forget for a moment how dangerous—and insanely possessive—my captor can be.

Straightening, Lucas makes a visible effort to get himself under control. His chest expands with a deep breath, and he asks in a calmer tone, "Are you hungry? Do you want some chicken broth?"

I lick my cracked lips. "Yes. And maybe something like a sandwich?"

His eyebrows lift. "Really? A sandwich? You must be on the mend. How about eggs? I tried making an omelet recently, and it didn't come out awful."

"You did?" I stare at him. "Okay, sure, I'll gladly have some eggs."

Lucas smiles and disappears through the doorway. Twenty minutes later, he comes back carrying a tray with a delicious-smelling omelet and a steaming cup of Earl Grey.

"Here we are," he says, placing the tray on the nightstand and picking up the plate with the fork. Spearing a piece of omelet, he holds up the fork and commands, "Open up."

"I can feed myself," I begin, reaching for the plate, but he moves it out of my reach.

"Too weak to swat a fly, remember?" He gives me a steely look. "Now sit back and open your mouth."

Sighing, I obey, feeling uncomfortably like a two-year-old as Lucas sits on the edge of the bed and feeds me with the nonchalant efficiency of a nurse. However, the glint in his eyes is distinctly un-nurselike, and to my shock, I realize he's enjoying this on some level.

He likes me helpless and dependent on him.

To test my theory, I watch him closely the next time he brings the fork to my mouth. And there it is: the moment my lips close around the fork, his gaze dips to my mouth and lingers there, his hand tightening on the handle of the utensil. The blanket bunched around my lap is blocking his lower body from my view, but I suspect that if I checked, I'd find him hard, his thick cock bursting out of the confines of his jeans.

A spiral of heat snakes down my spine, and my nipples tighten under the blanket. My body's reaction catches me off-guard. I'm hardly in shape to be thinking about sex. Nonetheless, I'm cognizant of a growing slickness between my thighs as Lucas continues feeding me, leaning over me each time he brings the food to my lips.

The omelet is good—Lucas really did learn how to make it—but I barely register the rich, savory flavor, all my focus on the twisted eroticism of the situation. In a way, Lucas's insistence on taking care of me is an extension of his desire to possess me, to control me completely. Weak and ill, I'm at his mercy more than ever, and for some perverse reason, the knowledge turns both of us on.

Before long, the omelet is gone, and I slump back against the pillows, equal parts stuffed and exhausted by the simple act of eating. Arousal or not, I'm still not well. Lucas puts a straw in my tea and lets me drink down half a cup, and then I fade out again, my body demanding yet more rest.

* * *

When I wake up again, I feel moderately stronger, and I remember some of the nightmares I had during the night.

"Can I please see my brother?" I ask Lucas when he brings me a sandwich and a bowl of soup. "I'd really like to talk to him."

Lucas shakes his head. "You're not well enough yet."

"I'm fine. Please, I really need to talk to him." I put my hand on Lucas's thigh, feeling the hard muscle through the rough material of his jeans. "I just want to see him with my own eyes."

"I don't want you to tire yourself out," Lucas says, but I can tell he's wavering.

"How about this?" I push myself up to a straighter sitting position. "I'll eat, and then if I don't fall back asleep, you'll let him come by. Just for a little while. Please, Lucas."

His eyes narrow. "You'll eat, and I'll think about it."

I nod eagerly and dig into my sandwich, consuming it in several big bites. Lucas insists on feeding me the soup himself, his pale eyes heavy-lidded as he brings the spoon to my mouth. I don't object; I'm too excited by the idea of seeing Misha, and I don't mind this weird kink my captor seems to have developed. Also, I don't want Lucas to realize that I'm not as recovered as I thought. Once again, eating has tired me out, and I'm beginning to feel uncomfortably warm, as though the fever is returning.

Fortunately, Lucas doesn't catch on to that, so when I don't fall asleep immediately after my meal, he messages Diego to bring Misha to see me.

"I'm going to give you ten minutes with him," Lucas says, dressing me in one of his T-shirts. "But the second you feel tired—"

"I'll end it and rest," I say, curving my lips in what I hope is a bright, healthy smile. "Don't worry. It's going to be fine."

Lucas frowns as he feels my forehead, but at that moment, there is a knock on the door.

My brother and Diego are here.

"Ten minutes," Lucas warns, tucking the blankets around me. "I'll be right outside, okay?"

I nod. "Can you please put a chair a few feet away from the bed? I don't want Misha to catch this bug."

Lucas does as I ask before leaving the room, and a few moments later, my brother walks in.

"How are you feeling?" he asks in Russian as soon as he enters the bedroom, and I put my hand up, not wanting him to get too close. Though I suspect I'm past the contagious stage of this illness, I still feel more like a germ-infested rag than a person.

"I've been better," I say, waving Misha toward the chair Lucas prepared for him. My skin is hurting again, but my brother doesn't need to know that. "How are you? How are they treating you?"

Misha hesitates, then shrugs. "All right, I guess." He sits down in the chair, and I notice that his hands are not handcuffed this time.

"They let you walk around untied?" I ask, surprised, and my brother nods.

"They don't leave me alone with weapons, and I'm handcuffed at night, but yeah, I have some freedom."

"Good." I rack my brain for a good place to start, then decide to just come out with it. "Michael," I say quietly, "where are your adoptive parents? How did you end up with UUR?"

He gives me a stony look. "Uncle Vasya said he told you everything."

"He told me . . . some things. But I'd like to hear it from you." After Obenko's betrayal, I have zero trust in my former boss's version of the story. "Do your parents know what you were doing? Did they agree to your training?"

Misha looks at me silently.

"Mishen'ka . . ." My bones ache as I sit up straighter. "All I want is to know a little bit about your life. You have no reason to believe me, but eleven years ago, I made a bargain with Vasiliy Obenko—your Uncle Vasya. I promised him I'd join UUR in exchange for his sister adopting you and providing you with a good life. That's why I left: because I wanted you to have the kind of life we had before our parents were killed, the kind of life I couldn't provide for you in the orphanage . . ."

As I speak, Misha shakes his head. "You're lying," he says, jumping to his feet. "You left. Uncle Vasya told me you joined the program because you didn't want the responsibility of a baby brother . . . because you were tired of being in the orphanage. He felt bad that you left me behind, and he told Mom about me and then . . ." He stops, his chest heaving. "He wouldn't have lied to me about this. He wouldn't have." He repeats that as if trying to convince himself, and I realize that my brother is not as sure of Obenko as he appears. Has he already had a chance to witness the man's ruthlessness?

"I'm sorry," I say, lying back against the pillows as my brief burst of energy wanes. "I wish that were true, but for your uncle, his country always came first. You know that, don't you?"

Misha's lips flatten, and he shakes his head again. "No. He said you're good at twisting things."

"Misha . . ."

"It's Michael." He folds his arms across his chest. "And I don't want to talk about this anymore."

"Okay." I'm still too sick to argue with a traumatized teenager. "Just tell me one thing . . . Are they good people, those adoptive parents of yours? Did they treat you well?"

After a moment's hesitation, Misha nods and sits down in the chair. "They did—they are." His gaze softens a little. "Mom makes potato pancakes on the weekends, and Dad plays table tennis. He's really good at it. I used to play with him every evening when I was little."

Tears of relief fill my eyes at the genuine emotion in his voice. Whatever caused him to end up in UUR, Misha loves his adoptive parents—loves them like I loved our Mom and Dad.

"Do you see them often?" Now that my brother is actually speaking to me, I find myself desperate to hear more about his life. "Since you started training, I mean? Are you staying at the dorms, or do you still live at home? What do your parents think of you doing this?"

Misha blinks at my rapid-fire questions. "I . . . I see them once a month now," he answers slowly. "And yes, I'm staying at the dorms. Mom didn't want that, but Uncle Vasya said it would be best, said it would help me with the transition and everything."

I nod encouragingly, and he continues after a brief pause. "They're mostly okay with me joining the agency. I mean, they understand that we serve our country." His gaze slides away as he fidgets in the chair, and I read between the words.

His parents might've understood, but they were less than happy to have their adolescent son recruited to the cause.

"Do you think they're worried about you?" Ignoring my growing exhaustion, I push myself to an upright sitting position again. "Would they have heard about what happened?"

"They—" His voice cracks as he looks back at me, blinking rapidly. "Yeah, I think they must know by now. Someone would've notified Mom about Uncle Vasya."

"I'm sorry, Michael." I bite my lip. "I'm really sorry that it happened like that. Believe me, if I could undo it—"

"Don't." Misha stands up, his hands clenched. "Don't pretend."

"I'm not—"

"That's enough." Lucas's voice is knife sharp as he enters the room, approaching my brother with furious strides. "I told you, you're not allowed to upset her." Grabbing Misha by the back of his shirt, he drags him toward the door, growling, "She's sick. Which part of that don't you understand?"

"Lucas, stop." I throw off my blanket, my pulse leaping in sudden fear. "Please, he didn't do anything."

Lucas instantly lets go of Misha and crosses the room toward me as I swing my feet to the floor, about to get up despite a wave of dizziness.

"What are you doing?" Glaring at me, he grabs my legs and places them back on the bed, forcing me back into the half-sitting position on the pillows before caging me between his arms. His eyes gleam with fury as he leans in, his face centimeters from mine. "You are to rest, understand?"

"Yes." I swallow the knot in my throat. "I'm sorry."

Apparently that satisfies Lucas, because he straightens and turns toward my brother. "Let's go," he says, jerking his thumb toward the door, and Misha shoots me an apologetic look before exiting the room ahead of Lucas.

Exhausted, I slide down the pillows and close my eyes.

My brother is all right for now, but this is no place for him. I need to get him back to his parents.

He has to go home.

CHAPTER THIRTY-THREE

❖ LUCAS ❖

After I escort Michael out of the house and hand him over to Diego, I return to the bedroom to find Yulia asleep again. Though the bruises from Kirill's assault are barely visible now, deep blue shadows lie under her eyes, and her face is pale and thin. She lost weight during the illness, and she once again looks disturbingly fragile, like a glass figurine that could shatter at the slightest touch.

I must be a pervert, because I want her anyway.

Taking a deep breath, I undress and climb into bed beside her. The pillows are all bunched up, so I arrange them more comfortably and lie down, pulling her against me. She's still wearing the T-shirt, but I don't mind the barrier between our bodies.

It keeps my lust for Yulia under control, helps me maintain the illusion that I'm a dispassionate caretaker rather than a man who's had to jerk off twice a day for the past week.

Last night, I didn't sleep, so I should be out like a light, but I'm wide awake as I feel the heat rising off her skin again. The fucking fever is back. I knew I shouldn't have listened to Yulia, but I couldn't resist the plea in her big blue eyes. I still don't know the full story with her brother—the boy refuses to answer any questions— but I know she loves him.

She ran away to save him from me.

Closing my eyes, I berate myself for the hundredth time for not listening to her. Over the past several days, I've had a chance to replay our pre-escape conversations in my mind, and I see that I have no one but myself to blame for the misunderstanding. If I'd let Yulia speak, I would've known who Misha was, and I would've promised not to harm him.

Even *I* have limits.

Yulia mumbles something in her sleep, burrowing closer to me, and I kiss the delicate shell of her ear, my chest tightening as I feel her burning skin. She's not nearly as sick as last night, but she's still far from well.

Carefully disentangling myself from her, I go to the bathroom and return with a cool wet towel. When I remove the T-shirt and run the towel over her body,

Yulia wakes up, blinking at me with dazed blue eyes, but before I'm done wiping her down, she falls asleep again.

I turn off the light and get in bed beside her again, pulling her into my arms. My body heat is not optimal right now, but I've noticed she sleeps better when I'm holding her. She's less prone to nightmares that way.

Closing my eyes again, I try not to think about the source of her nightmares, but it's impossible. Yulia's illness has derailed my normal work routine, but I've made sure that the search for Kirill is proceeding uninterrupted. Unfortunately, other than some vague rumors and a few false leads, there's been nothing in the past few days. It's like the bastard just vanished. It's feasible he didn't survive his wounds, but in that case, we should've found a body or heard something about a funeral.

No, my gut instinct tells me Yulia's former trainer is alive—likely in horrendous pain, but alive. I'll have to step up my efforts to find him when Yulia is well.

First, though, I need to get her well.

Kissing her temple, I snuggle her closer, ignoring the lust stiffening my cock. With any luck, Yulia's improved appetite means she's on the mend, and I will soon have her strong and healthy again.

If not, Goldberg will wish he'd never been born.

* * *

To my relief, over the next two days, Yulia's recovery continues with no further relapses. Her appetite returns with a vengeance, and I find myself scouring the Internet for simple but nutritious recipes. I'm still pretty terrible in the kitchen, but I've discovered that with enough focus and concentration, I can make basic dishes by following instructions and watching online videos—something I've never been motivated to do before. But with Yulia completely dependent on me, it feels wrong to feed her only sandwiches and cereal.

I want her to eat well so she regains her health.

"What are you doing, man?" Diego asks when he enters my kitchen and sees me chopping up vegetables for stew. "I've never seen you cook before."

"Yeah, well, I'm expanding my skill set," I say, depositing all the vegetables into a large pot before glancing at my open laptop for the next step in the process. "It's never to late to learn, right?"

"Uh-huh, sure." Diego gives me a dubious look. "Why didn't you just ask Esguerra's housekeeper to make some extra food for you? She usually doesn't mind."

"I'm not Ana's favorite person right now," I say, carefully measuring out a teaspoon of salt. "You know, with Rosa and all."

"Oh, right." Diego sits down at the table and watches me with evident fascination. "She's pretty upset about the whole thing, huh?"

"You could say that again."

Though Nora's intervention saved Rosa from our interrogation and subsequent punishment, the maid has been under house arrest for the past week while Esguerra is deciding what to do with her. If it weren't for Nora's friendship with the girl, it would've been easy, but Esguerra doesn't want to upset his wife by executing her close friend.

Besides, neither one of us is completely certain that Nora told the truth, which means there's still a chance the maid could've been working for someone else.

Now that Yulia is feeling better, I'm going to question her about that—and about everything else.

"So that's it? You're a master chef now?" Diego says as I pour the suggested amount of water into the pot and cover it before turning on the stove. "Does that mean Eduardo and I can come over for dinner?"

"Fuck, no. Make your own damned stew."

Diego bursts out laughing, but quickly sobers up when I turn to face him.

"Enough chitchat," I say, wiping my hands on a paper towel. "Fill me in on the new trainees and where we are with the recruiting efforts."

The guard launches into his daily report, and I sit down at the table, keeping an eye on the pot to make sure it doesn't boil over.

* * *

When the stew is done, I check on Yulia and find her napping in the armchair in the library, dressed in another one of my T-shirts. I brought her here after lunch when she insisted on getting up, claiming she was tired of lying in bed all day. Judging by the book on her lap, she fell asleep while reading.

Frowning, I brush my hand over her forehead to check for fever. To my relief, her skin feels normal to the touch. She's still not fully recovered, but Goldberg was right not to let me panic.

I glance at the clock.

Four p.m. Plenty of time before dinner.

Making a decision, I quietly exit the room and head outside. I need to do my rounds with the guards and catch up with Esguerra. With any luck, Yulia will nap for the next couple of hours while I do some work, and then we'll have a nice meal together—our first normal meal since her return.

I can't fucking wait.

CHAPTER THIRTY-FOUR

❖ YULIA ❖

An unnerving sensation wakes me up. It's almost like someone's watching me, or—

Gasping, I sit up in the armchair and gape at the petite, golden-skinned girl standing in the middle of Lucas's library. She's wearing a light blue sundress, and her shiny dark hair streams over her slim bare shoulders. I'm pretty sure I've never seen her before, though something about her delicate features is familiar.

"Who are you?" I try to keep my voice level—not an easy feat with my heart pounding in my throat. I'm still weak from my illness, and though the doll-like creature in front of me doesn't seem like much of a threat, I know looks can be deceiving. "What are you doing here?"

"I'm Nora Esguerra," she says in unaccented American English. Her dark, thickly lashed eyes regard me with cool derision. "You've met my husband, Julian."

I blink. That explains how she got into the house—she must have the same master keys as Rosa—and why she looks familiar. Her picture was in the files Obenko gave me in Moscow.

Also, I've seen those dark eyes once before.

"You were looking in the window the first day I was brought here," I say, tugging Lucas's T-shirt down to cover more of my thighs. Had I known I'd have visitors, I would've put on some real clothes. "With Rosa, right?"

The girl nods. "Yes, we looked in on you." She doesn't apologize or explain, just studies me, her eyes slightly narrowed.

"Okay, and you're here today because . . ." I let my voice trail off.

"Because I've been waiting for a chance to talk to you, and this is the first time Lucas has left the house in several days," she says, and approaches my armchair.

Feeling uneasy, I stand up. Though my legs still feel like cooked noodles, I'll be better able to protect myself on my feet—if the need arises.

"What did you want to talk about?" I ask, keeping a careful eye on the girl's hands. She doesn't appear armed, but something about her posture tells me she might not need weapons to inflict harm.

She's had some fighting training, I can tell.

"Rosa," the girl says. Her small chin lifts as she gives me a hard look. "Specifically, what you're going to tell Lucas and Julian about her."

I frown in confusion. "What do you mean?"

"They're going to want to know how you escaped and who helped you," Nora says evenly. "And you're going to say that it was Rosa acting on my instructions. Do you understand?"

"What?" That's the last thing I expected to hear. "You want me to blame you?"

"I want you to tell the truth," she says coolly. "And yes, that means telling everyone that Rosa was helping you on my request."

"She didn't say anything about it being your request," I say, my mind racing. It sounds like the maid is in trouble, and Esguerra's wife is trying to protect her by admitting her own involvement. Except—

"It doesn't matter what Rosa said or didn't say." Nora's voice tightens. "I'm telling you now that Rosa was acting on my orders, and that's what you will say when Lucas and Julian ask you about it. Understand?"

"Or what?" I can hear the threat in the girl's tone, but I want to see how far she'd go. "Or what, Mrs. Esguerra?"

"Or I will personally ensure that Julian flays every bit of flesh from your bones." She gives me a cool smile. "In fact, I may do it myself."

I stare at her, trying to recall what I know about the girl. She's young—a couple of years younger than me, according to Esguerra's file—and recently married to the arms dealer. Before that, she was supposedly kidnapped by him; there was an FBI investigation that lasted more than a year. But regardless of her background, it's obvious to me that she's not all that different from her husband now.

She's not making an idle threat.

"All right," I say slowly. "Let's presume you did suggest to Rosa that she help me. Why? What would've been your motivation? Lucas will want to know."

"He'll understand my motivation. All you need to do is tell the truth—the full truth, including my involvement."

My lips twist. "Right. And I assume the full truth doesn't include your visit to me today."

"Correct." Her dark gaze is unblinking. "There's no reason for Rosa to pay for my actions. I'm sure you agree with that."

"I do." If Esguerra's wife wants her notoriously ruthless husband to think the whole thing was her idea, I have no intention of standing in her way—especially given this little chat. "Now, is that all, or can I help you with something else?"

"That's all," she says, then turns and starts walking away. But before I can exhale in relief, she stops in the doorway and looks back at me. "Just one more thing, Yulia . . ."

I lift my eyebrows, waiting.

"From what Julian's said, Lucas seems . . . unusually enamored with you." Her voice is oddly flat. "It's fortunate for you, given what's occurred."

She's talking about the plane crash, I realize. Esguerra's wife would naturally blame me for that. At least I didn't succeed in seducing her husband; I have a feeling if Nora knew Esguerra was my initial assignment, I might've woken up with my throat slit.

"I'm sure you were just doing your job," she continues in that same flat tone. "Carrying out your superiors' orders."

I nod warily. I have no idea what she wants me to say. I didn't know that my intel would be used to bring down her husband's plane, but even if I did, I'm not sure that would've changed anything. I might've tried to get Lucas to stay off that plane, though he had still been a stranger to me at the time, but I wouldn't have lifted a finger to save Esguerra. I still wouldn't.

Given everything I know about the man, the world would be better off without him—and so would his wife.

"Good. That's what Lucas told Julian," Nora says. "It wasn't personal, so to speak."

I nod again, hoping she gets to the point soon. The lingering tiredness from the illness is making my legs tremble, and I'm sweating from the exertion of standing for so long. I don't want to show vulnerability in front of Esguerra's wife, though. It would be like baring one's throat to a small but deadly she-wolf.

"Okay, Yulia . . ." The she-wolf's eyes gleam with a peculiar light. "I guess what I'm trying to say is, for your sake, I hope you share Lucas's feelings. Because if he ever withdraws his protection . . ." She doesn't complete her sentence, but I understand her perfectly.

My brother is not the only one who doesn't belong on this estate.

"Understood," I manage to say calmly. "Anything else?"

She gives me a tight smile. "No. That's all. Hope you feel better soon."

She turns and disappears through the doorway, and I collapse back into the armchair, as exhausted as if I'd just fought a war.

CHAPTER THIRTY-FIVE

❖ LUCAS ❖

It takes me longer than expected to catch up on everything I've neglected over the past several days, and by the time I get home, it's almost seven-thirty.

The first thing I do upon entering the house is go to the library. To my surprise, Yulia is not there.

"Lucas?" she calls out, and I realize her voice is coming from the kitchen. Frowning, I backtrack and go there.

"What are you doing?" I say when I see her carrying two spoons to the kitchen table. Approaching her in two long strides, I grab the utensils from her hand and clasp her elbow. "You need to be resting."

"I'm all right," she protests as I guide her to the table. "Really, Lucas, I'm much better. I got tired of sitting on my butt all day and wanted to set the table for dinner."

"Tough shit." I pull out her chair. "Sit, and I'll take care of that. Your only job right now is to recover, got it?"

Yulia gives me an exasperated look but obeys. For the first time since her illness began, she's wearing her normal clothes—a pair of jean shorts and a tank top—but the skimpy outfit only emphasizes the severity of her weight loss. Her stomach is concave, and her arms are reed thin. I don't know why she's pushing herself so hard, but I don't like it.

"You are not to move a muscle," I say as I wash my hands and take out a pair of bowls. Yulia must've already turned on the stove to warm up the stew, because when I check, I find it simmering on a low setting. I pour each of us a generous portion and bring the bowls over to the table. "I don't want you to have another relapse," I say, sitting down across from her.

She sniffs at the stew instead of replying. "You made it?" she asks, looking up, and I nod, curious to see what she'll think. I tasted it earlier and liked it, though I still have far to go before I can rival Yulia in the cooking department.

She dips her spoon in and tries a little of the broth surrounding the veggies. "It's good, Lucas," she says, and I can't suppress a smile at the surprise in her voice.

"I'm glad you like it," I say, digging into my own portion. "It wasn't difficult to make, so I should be able to repeat it."

Yulia begins eating with evident enthusiasm, and I watch her, pleased to see her enjoying my efforts. There's something oddly satisfying about seeing her at my kitchen table, eating the food I made and wearing the clothes I got for her. I never thought of myself as the nurturing type, never considered that I might want to take care of someone, but that's precisely what I want to do with her. It's particularly strange because, this illness aside, Yulia is one of the most capable women I've met.

She's quiet as we make quick work of the stew, and I let her eat in peace, worried that even this meal might be too taxing for her. When we're done, I clean up and make Yulia a cup of her favorite Earl Grey.

"How are you feeling?" I ask when I bring it to the table, and she smiles, patting her flat belly.

"Extremely full. The stew was amazing. Thank you for making it."

"My pleasure." I grin as she stifles a yawn before sipping her tea. "Sleepy?"

"Just food coma, I think," she says with another almost-yawn. "I can't possibly want to sleep. I've slept enough for a lifetime."

"Your body needed it," I say, my amusement fading as I recall her near-catatonic state after Kirill's attack. "You've been through a lot."

She looks down at her cup. "Yeah, I guess."

"Yulia . . ." I sit down and reach across the table to cover her hand with mine. "What happened? How did you end up with Kirill?"

Her slender fingers twitch under my palm, but she doesn't look up.

"Yulia." I squeeze her hand lightly. "Look at me."

She reluctantly meets my gaze.

"Do you have any other siblings you're hiding from me?"

She shakes her head.

"Anyone else you're trying to protect?"

She blinks. "No."

"Then tell me what happened. Why were you in that cell? Did they think you double-crossed them?"

"They . . . it . . . It's complicated, Lucas." Her lips tremble for a second before she presses them together.

"I see." I get up and walk around the table. Yulia gives me a startled look when I pull her to her feet, but I just pick her up and walk to the living room, carrying her cradled against my chest.

"What are you doing?" she asks when I sit down on the couch, holding her on my lap. She's disturbingly light in my arms, as breakable as after her stint at the Russian prison.

"I'm getting comfortable so you can tell me your complicated story," I say, settling her more securely on my lap. Even after her weight loss, her ass is soft and curvy, and her hair smells sweet, like peaches mixed with vanilla. My body reacts instantly, but I ignore the spike of lust. Keeping one arm around her back, I tuck a strand of hair behind her ear with my free hand and say softly, "Talk to me, sweetheart. I won't hurt you or your brother, I promise."

Yulia looks at me for a few moments, and I know she's debating how much to trust me. I wait patiently, and finally, she murmurs, "Where do you want me to start?"

"How about at the beginning? Tell me about Michael. When did you both get recruited by the agency?"

Yulia takes a deep breath and launches into her story. I listen, my chest aching as she tells me about a ten-year-old girl whose parents left her to watch her two-year-old brother on an icy winter night and never returned, about the police visit the next morning and the horrors of the orphanage that followed.

"Nobody paid much attention to me—like I told you, I was skinny and awkward at that age, a real ugly duckling. But Misha was beautiful," she says in a raw voice. "He could've starred in baby-product commercials. And I wasn't the only one who thought so. The headmistress kept bringing him to her office, and I'd see men, different men each time, go in. I don't know what they did to him, but there would be bruises on him, and blood occasionally. And he wouldn't stop crying for days afterwards. I tried to report it, but nobody would listen. The country was in disarray—it still is—and nobody cared about the orphans. We were out of the way, and that was all that mattered." Her eyes glitter fiercely as she says, "I would've done anything to get Misha out of there. Anything."

Fury is a pulsing beat in my skull, but I keep quiet and continue listening as Yulia tells me about a visit from a well-dressed man whose cold hazel eyes both scared her and gave her hope.

"Vasiliy Obenko offered me a deal, and I took it," she says. "It was the only way I could save Misha. We'd been at the orphanage for less than a year, and he was already a mess: acting out, crying at random times, disobeying his teachers . . . Even if a good family had come along, they wouldn't have wanted to adopt a child with those kinds of behavioral issues, no matter how beautiful he was. I was so desperate I considered taking Misha and running away, but we would've starved on the streets or worse. The world isn't kind to homeless children." She draws in a shuddering breath, and I stroke her back, trying to keep my own hands from trembling with rage.

I'm going to find the headmistress of that orphanage and make the child-pimping bitch pay.

"So yeah," Yulia continues after a moment, "when Obenko came to recruit me in exchange for his sister and brother-in-law adopting Misha and providing him with a good home, I jumped at the opportunity. I knew there was a chance I was making a deal with the devil, but I didn't care. I just wanted Misha to have a shot at a better life."

Of course. That explains so fucking much: her bizarre loyalty to an organization that abused her, her willingness to carry out "assignments" after what happened with Kirill. It was never about patriotism; all along, she'd been doing it for her brother.

"And did Obenko uphold his part of the bargain?" My tone is relatively calm.

"Sort of—well, I don't know." She bites her lip. "I'm still trying to untangle the truth from the lies. Misha was supposed to have a normal life, and it seems like he did—at least until a couple of years ago. His adoptive parents have nothing to do with the agency; Obenko's sister is a nurse, and her husband is an electrical engineer. Part of the bargain was that I stay away from Misha and his new family, so I only saw him in pictures. I didn't realize my brother had been recruited by UUR until I followed Obenko to a warehouse on the outskirts of Kiev and saw Misha there, being trained by Kirill along with the other youths."

"The Kirill you thought was dead?" My rage intensifies as I picture her reaction to this double blow—to a betrayal so cruel even I can't fathom it.

Yulia nods, her gaze hardening as she tells me about her capture and subsequent interrogation at the hands of her own agency. "They thought I'd been turned, you see," she says. "That I betrayed *them*."

"I don't understand something." I slide my hand under her hair and rest it on her nape, managing to keep my fury under control. "What prompted you to follow Obenko to that warehouse? Did you suspect something?"

"No, not at all." Her blue eyes are shadowed. "I started following Obenko in the hopes that he might eventually lead me to his sister's family—to my brother. I wanted to see Misha just this once before—" She stops, her teeth sinking into her bottom lip.

"Before what?"

Yulia doesn't respond.

"Before what, beautiful?"

"Before I left for another assignment," she whispers, blinking rapidly.

Her words fill me with such violent jealousy that I almost miss it when she adds, almost inaudibly, "And disappeared for good."

"What?" My hand tightens on the back of her neck. "What the fuck do you mean by that?"

She winces, and I gentle my grip, massaging the area I just abused. She still doesn't say anything, however, and the seconds tick by, each one adding to my fury.

"Yulia . . ." Only the knowledge of what happened the last time I let jealousy blind me stops me from exploding on the spot. "What the fuck do you mean by that?"

"Nothing. I was just—" She closes her eyes for a second before opening them to meet my gaze. "I was going to walk away, okay?" Her voice shakes. "I couldn't do it anymore, couldn't carry out another assignment for them. I was going to use the plane tickets and the identities they gave me to disappear and start over fresh."

"You were?" I lower my hand to the small of her back, some of my anger cooling. "Why? Why after all these years?"

She gives a tiny shrug and looks down, avoiding my gaze. "I figured my brother was safe at this point—it's not like his adoptive parents would put him back in the orphanage after eleven years."

"I'm sure they wouldn't have put him back after five years either." I grip her chin to force her to look at me. I can feel her discomfort with the topic, and it makes me even more determined to unravel this mystery. "You didn't know about Kirill and your brother yet. So why did you decide to run?"

She remains silent.

"Yulia . . ." I lean forward until our noses are almost touching. This close, her sweet scent is intoxicating. I breathe it in, feeling like I'm on the verge of losing control. My heart pounds heavily in my chest, and when I speak, the words come out rough and strained. "Why did you decide to run, beautiful? What changed?"

Her lips part as she stares at me, and the temptation to kiss her, to taste the pink, lush softness of her mouth is unbearable. I'm hyperaware of her, of everything about her. The shallow, uneven rhythm of her breathing, the warmth of her soft, smooth skin, the way her long brown lashes tangle with one another at the far corners of her eyes—it all lures me in, intensifying the hunger burning in my veins. Only the conviction that I must have this answer—that it's something truly important—keeps me from giving in to my need.

"Tell me, baby," I whisper, moving my hand to stroke her cheek. "Why couldn't you do it anymore?"

Yulia's breath hitches, her eyes filling with tears as she pushes at my shoulders, trying to twist away. Her distress is such that I almost let her go, but some instinct makes me hold on.

"Shh," I soothe, tightening my arm around her back to hold her still. "It's okay. You're okay. Just tell me, sweetheart. Tell me why you were going to leave."

"Lucas, please . . ." Her tears overflow, spilling down her cheeks as she stops pushing at me. "Please, don't."

"Don't what?" I feel like I'm tormenting a helpless kitten, but I can't stop. Leaning closer, I kiss away the salty moisture on her cheeks and murmur, "Don't ask? Why not? What don't you want to tell me? What are you hiding?"

Yulia closes her eyes, and I brush my lips across her trembling eyelids. "Come on, sweetheart," I whisper, pulling back. "Just tell me. What changed for you? Why didn't you want to do this?"

"Because I couldn't." Opening her eyes, she gazes at me, her eyes swimming with fresh tears. "I just couldn't do it anymore, okay?"

"Why?"

She tries to pull away, but I tighten my arm again, keeping her in place.

"Why, Yulia?" I press. "Tell me."

"Because I fell in love with you!" With shocking strength, she pushes at my chest, and I'm so stunned that I loosen my grip, letting her scramble off my lap. The momentum propels her backward, nearly causing her to fall, but before I can grab at her, she catches her balance and sprints into the bedroom, slamming the door behind her.

CHAPTER THIRTY-SIX

❖ YULIA ❖

Dura! Idiotka! Imbecile! Debilka!

Sobbing, I shove a chair against the bedroom door, wedging the back under the doorknob to keep it jammed. My arms shake from overexertion and adrenaline, and regret is like a sledgehammer beating against my skull. How could I have been so stupid? How could I have admitted my feelings to Lucas *again*? The last time, at least, I thought I was dreaming, but I have no such excuse today.

Fully awake and conscious, I gave in to Lucas's relentless tenderness, crumpled under the merciless pull of his gentle demands.

"Yulia!" The doorknob rattles as he pushes against the door. "What the fuck are you doing? Let me in."

My chest heaving, I back away from the door, pressing my fist against my mouth to muffle my sobs. Why did I do this again? Am I some kind of masochist? I know what I am to him: a sex toy, someone he wants to own and possess. If I had any doubts on that front, the trackers would've dispelled them. What he's done is the closest thing to putting a dog leash on a human being, and no amount of sickroom care can make up for his intention to keep me prisoner until he tires of me.

Love and captivity don't mix—for most sane people, at least.

"Yulia." Lucas bangs his fist on the door. "Fucking let me in!" He kicks at it, and the chair makes a creaking sound as it moves a couple of centimeters across the carpet, letting the door open a crack.

I cast a desperate glance around the room. I don't know what I'm looking for, but there's nothing, so I continue edging backward as Lucas starts kicking at the door in earnest. The crack widens with each violent blow, and just as my trembling legs touch the bed behind me, the chair breaks and the door flies open.

"Lucas, I—" I'm not sure what I'm planning to say, but he doesn't give me a chance. Before I can gather my scattered thoughts, he's on me, and my world goes topsy-turvy as I tumble backward onto the bed. He lands on top of me, and in a blink of an eye, he grabs my wrists, stretching my arms above my head. His pale eyes burn into mine as he presses me into the mattress, his muscular body hot and heavy on top of me. He's already aroused—I can feel the hard swelling in his jeans— and I know there's only one way this evening will end.

My flu-induced respite is over.

His hands tighten around my wrists, and dark anxiety beats at me, mixing with perverse excitement. I'm viscerally aware of my captor's strength, of the power of his large male body. When Kirill had been on top of me like this, all I'd felt was terror and revulsion, but with Lucas, it's infinitely more complicated. Underneath the instinctive fear and distrust, there's a potent animal attraction mixed with a deeper longing, a desire for connection that makes no sense in the context of who and what we are.

I'm in love with a man who has every reason to despise me—a man who scares me to my very soul.

"Yulia . . ." he murmurs, staring down at me, and I draw in a shaking breath, feeling like I can't get enough air. I feel torn in two: a part of me wants to run and hide, pretend this isn't happening, but another part, the weaker part, wants to give in to him again, tell him how much he means to me and beg him to keep me forever.

Beg him to love me like I love him—like I will always love him.

"Yulia, sweetheart . . ." His gaze softens, and I realize I'm crying again, my entire body shaking with gasping sobs. "Hush, baby, it's not that bad . . . You're okay. Everything is going to be okay."

But I can't stop crying—not even when he kisses me, his tongue sweeping over my lips, and not when he releases my wrists and rolls off me to strip off my clothes. I can't stop crying because he's wrong. It won't be okay. There's no future for us, no hope for anything resembling a normal life. He's an arms dealer's second-in-command, a man with no conscience, and I'm his prisoner.

There are no happily-ever-afters for people like us.

The pain of that knowledge is so consuming that I barely feel it when Lucas tears off my thong and climbs on top of me after taking off his own clothes. My chest is agonizingly tight, my vision blurred with tears. It's only when he settles between my legs, his powerful thighs spreading mine apart, that the animal awareness returns, my body responding to him despite my distress. The tip of his cock nudges against my dampening folds, but instead of pushing forward, he stills, holding himself propped up on his elbows as he cradles my face between his large palms.

"Yulia . . ." His eyes burn with dark hunger, his sun-bronzed skin stretched tight over his sharp cheekbones. "You're mine," he says, his voice low and guttural. "Nothing and no one will take you from me. No more lies, no more running, no more hiding. I'm going to take care of you and protect you. You and your brother both, do you understand?"

I manage a small nod, my hands moving up to clutch at his sides. His hard body is vibrating like a string, his muscles coiled as if for a fight, and I know he's struggling to control himself. On any other night, he would've already been inside me, but he's trying to hold back, to go slowly because of my recent illness.

Something about that loosens the tight knot in my chest, chases away the panic I was feeling. Maybe I'm not just a toy to him.

He wouldn't hold back if he didn't care.

"It's okay, Lucas," I whisper, blinking to clear away the tears. Given what he's promising, letting him have my body is the least I can do. "I'm okay."

His pupils expand, darkening his blue-gray eyes, and then he lowers his head, capturing my lips in a deep, feral kiss. His tongue sweeps into my mouth, conquering and caressing at the same time, and my lower belly tightens as I feel the hard, insistent pressure of his cock. Heat builds inside me, centering between my legs, but a flutter of panic returns too. Despite my reassurances, I'm far from ready for this—emotionally, at least.

Sex with my captor is never casual and easy.

But it's too late to express my hesitations. Lucas's lips and tongue devour me, taking away my breath, and one of his hands moves down my body, kneading my breasts before traveling lower to touch my sex. His fingers find my clit, playing with it until I'm slick and throbbing, and then he grips his cock and guides it to my entrance, lifting his head to look at me at the same time.

His eyes glitter as he holds my gaze, and we both inhale sharply as the smooth, broad head of his cock breaches me, stretching my tight flesh. I'd forgotten how thick he is, how large all around. Despite my arousal, my inner muscles need to adjust to the feel of him inside me, and my breathing turns shallow as he presses deeper, his penetration slow and controlled but inexorable. When he's all the way in, he pauses, holding himself still above me, and I see sweat droplets forming on his forehead. He's still trying to rein himself in, to be as gentle as someone like him can be.

"I love you," I whisper, unable to hold back the words. At this moment, it doesn't matter that he might not return my feelings, that the odds are stacked against us in every way. "I love you, Lucas, so much."

His gaze fills with volcanic heat, his powerful muscles bunching even tighter, and I see the last of his self-control disintegrate. "Yulia," he groans, and then he withdraws and surges into me, thrusting so hard that air whooshes out of my lungs. It should've been too much, too overwhelming, but somehow it's just right, and I wrap my legs and arms around him, holding on tight as he starts hammering into me, claiming me with feral intensity.

"Lucas . . ." His name comes out on a ragged moan as the heat inside me coils and grows, transforming into an unbearable tension. "Oh God, Lucas . . ." Every muscle in my body vibrates from the agonizing pleasure, my heartbeat pounding audibly in my ears. The moment seems to stretch on forever, and then I climax with startling violence, my muscles clamping down on his shaft as every nerve ending in my body explodes with sensations.

Lucas lowers his head, swallowing my cry with his mouth, and continues thrusting into me, riding me through the orgasm. He fucks me like a man possessed, his hand sliding into my hair to hold me in place for his voracious kiss, and I feel another orgasm building, each merciless stroke of his cock bringing me closer to the edge. But before I can go over, he stops and raises his head to look at me.

"Say it again," he rasps out, his eyes boring into mine. His skin glistens with sweat, his chest heaving with harsh breathing as his cock throbs deep inside me. "Tell me you love me."

"I love you," I gasp, lifting my hips in a desperate attempt to reach the peak. "Please, Lucas, I love you!"

He sucks in an audible breath, and I feel him swell inside me, growing even thicker and harder as he thrusts in one last time before throwing back his head with a savage groan. His cock jerks inside me, his seed spurting out in several warm bursts, and then he rolls his hips in a circular motion, grinding his pelvis against my sex. To my shock, his movements push me over the edge, and I cry out, my nails digging into his back as a shattering wave of pleasure sweeps through me again, leaving me limp and shaking in its wake.

"Fuck, baby," Lucas groans, and I feel his cock spasm one last time before he withdraws and rolls off me. Like me, he's covered in sweat and breathing hard, but somehow he finds the strength to pull me toward him, embracing me from behind.

As my heartbeat slows and the post-orgasmic bliss begins to fade, I close my eyes, trying not to think about what I've done.

Trying to ignore the terrifying power Lucas holds over me now.

ANNA ZAIRES

CHAPTER THIRTY-SEVEN

❖ LUCAS ❖

When my breathing slows and my muscles start obeying my instructions, I get up and carry Yulia to the bathroom for a quick rinse. She's silent and withdrawn, all but swaying on her feet as I wash her, and I know I pushed too hard, took her too roughly too soon. I should've given her at least a couple more days to regain her strength, but instead, I attacked her like a rampaging caveman, making no allowances for her fragile state.

Regret gnaws at me, mixing with worry for her health, but underneath the heavy press of guilt is a glow of hot, dark satisfaction. Beyond the aftermath of stunning pleasure, beyond the physical relief of sex, it's a feeling that warms me from the inside out, making me feel like I'm on top of the world.

Yulia loves me. There's no doubt of that now. She loves *me*, not some dream phantom or lover I'd made up.

It's ridiculous, but I feel like I won a fucking lottery.

When we're both clean, I help Yulia out of the shower and towel her off before picking her up again. Taking care of her this way feels like the most natural thing now, and the glowing sensation intensifies when she wraps her arms around my neck and trustingly lays her head on my shoulder as I carry her back to the bedroom.

"How are you feeling?" I ask, stopping next to the bed. Bending down, I place her gently on the sheets and clarify, "I didn't hurt you, did I?"

"No," Yulia whispers, closing her eyes. She looks exhausted, and worry spears through me again. What if this causes her to relapse? I should've held back, should've controlled myself better. Hell, I should've waited to get answers until she was completely well instead of giving in to my impatience.

Pushing the guilt away, I turn off the light and climb into bed beside her, pulling her into my arms. The feel of her warm, slim curves turns me on again, but this time, I'm able to ignore my body's reaction.

"Goodnight, beautiful," I whisper, reaching down to pull the blanket over us. "Sleep well."

Within a minute, Yulia's breathing takes on the steady rhythm of sleep, and I close my eyes, the glow returning as I hold her tight.

She loves me, and she's mine.

Life couldn't get any better.

* * *

To my relief, the next morning Yulia wakes up with no signs of a relapse. I'm in the kitchen making breakfast when she walks in, already dressed in a pair of shorts and a T-shirt, her hair brushed and her eyes bright and alert.

"Hi," she says softly, stopping in the doorway. A delicate flush colors her cheeks as she looks at me. "Are you home again today?"

"Just for a bit," I say, smiling at her. "How are you feeling?"

"I'm okay." She gives me a tentative smile in return. "Just a little hungry."

"Good. The omelet's almost ready."

"Do you want some help?" she asks, coming up to the stove. "I can—"

"Thank you, but I got it." I wave her away. "If you want, make us both some tea, and I'll have this on the table in no time."

Yulia does as I suggest, and five minutes later, we're sitting down to eat.

"I want to see Misha today," she says after consuming half of her portion in record time. "Since I'm well and everything."

"I'm sure that can be arranged," I say. "I'll ask Diego to bring him over this afternoon." I'm still mad at the little punk for upsetting her the other day, but I know I can't keep her from him—not after what she told me last night.

Yulia puts down her fork, her expression unreadable. "Lucas . . ." She reaches up to brush her fingers over the back of her neck. "Am I still a prisoner in this house, even with the trackers?"

I frown. "No, you're not." I'd already decided that I would give her freedom to roam around the estate once the trackers were in. "I told you that."

"Then why does Diego need to bring my brother over? Can't I go see him on my own?"

I hesitate, looking at her. Though in theory, I like the idea of granting Yulia some independence, now that the moment is here, I feel uneasy at the thought of her walking around the estate by herself.

"You can," I say finally. "But not today. I need to introduce you to more people here first. They need to know who you are and what you mean to me."

"Because of my connection to the crash," she says, and I nod, relieved she understands. Though some of my unease stems from irrational possessiveness, there's a reason to be cautious.

The guards who died in the plane crash had friends and families, some of whom reside on the compound. And though Esguerra and I have done our best to keep the details of the crash under wraps, I know there are rumors about Yulia's involvement.

Until I publicly claim her as mine, she's not safe on her own.

"What about my brother?" she asks, picking up her tea, and I notice that she stopped eating, her blue eyes trained on me intently. "Is he in danger?"

"No," I reassure her. "Diego or Eduardo are with him at all times."

"So *he* is a prisoner?"

I sigh. "Yulia, your brother is ... well, it's a fluid situation. Once we're sure he won't shoot anyone or try to run away, we'll give him more freedom as well, okay? It'll just take some time."

She takes a few sips of her tea and resumes eating, but I see a small frown etched into her forehead. She's worried about Michael—the brother who doesn't seem to appreciate the sacrifices she made for him.

"What were you two arguing about?" I ask when we're done with our food. "Your brother seemed angry with you for some reason."

Yulia finishes her tea, then says quietly, "He's confused. Obenko fed him a bunch of lies about me when he recruited him, and he was his uncle, so ..." She shrugs, as if it doesn't matter, but I see the shadow of pain in her eyes.

UUR's betrayal goes deeper that I thought.

"So Michael doesn't know what you did for him?" My hand tightens around my cup as I picture all the things I'm going to do to Yulia's former colleagues.

"I don't think so, but it doesn't matter." She attempts a smile. "Misha's here now, so I just need to talk to him, straighten it all out."

"All right," I say, coming to a decision. Rage beats in my chest, but I keep my voice level as I say, "Let's go. I'll take you to see him myself."

Yulia's eyes widen. "Now? Don't you have work?"

"It'll wait." Putting down my cup, I stand up and walk around the table. "Do you feel up for a walk?"

She immediately jumps to her feet. "Definitely," she says, beaming. "Let's go."

* * *

We leave the house through the front door. As we step outside, I take Yulia's hand, squeezing her fingers lightly, and she gives me a wry look.

"I'm not going to run, you know," she says, and I smile, some of my anger fading.

"It's not to prevent you from running," I say, tightening my grip on her hand. Yulia is mine now, and nobody's going to hurt her again—not without answering to me, at least.

"Ah." She looks around at the guards and other passersby, most of whom are surreptitiously staring at us. "So this is strategic?"

"Partially." I'm holding Yulia's hand because I want to, but broadcasting our relationship to others is a definite bonus, especially since a few of the guards are eyeing her long, slender legs with obvious appreciation.

I glare at them, and they swiftly turn away.

Fuckers.

Yulia glances up at me and steps closer, all but pressing herself against my side as we walk. I give her an approving nod. She's smart to publicly accept my protection. As soon as everyone on the estate knows she's mine, she'll be safe.

We pass by the guards' barracks, and Yulia looks up at me again. "Where are we going?" she asks. "I thought Michael was staying here."

"He is, but Diego told me he's at the training field with him this morning. So that's where we're heading."

"Oh, I see." Yulia falls silent as we walk past a small group of guards. As soon as we're out of earshot, she slows down and turns her head to look at me. "Lucas . . ." she says quietly. "There's something I've been meaning to ask you."

"What is it?"

"When we first returned, Dr. Goldberg mentioned you'd been injured recently. What happened? Was there some trouble on your trip?"

"Trouble?" With my free hand, I absentmindedly touch my ribs, which bother me less each day. "Yeah, you could say that." And as we walk, I tell Yulia about the events in Chicago, from the nightclub assault on Rosa to the chase and its aftermath. I try to gloss over the more gruesome details, but even so, by the time I'm done, Yulia is ghost white, her hand icy in my grasp.

"You could've been killed," she whispers in horror. "And Rosa . . . Oh God, poor Rosa . . ."

"Yes, about that . . ." We're not far from the training field, so I stop and turn to face Yulia. "Why don't you tell me about Rosa? I want to know how she helped you escape."

Yulia's hand stiffens in my hold before she relaxes it again. "What do you mean?" she says, her eyebrows pulling together in seeming confusion. Her expression is the perfect imitation of sincere cluelessness; if I hadn't felt her hand twitch, I would've never known that my question gave her pause. "She didn't—"

"No more lies, remember?" I interrupt. "We had an agreement."

Yulia licks her lips. "Lucas, I . . ."

"You won't be ratting her out, if that's what worries you," I say, releasing her hand. Stepping closer, I grasp Yulia's chin, tilting her head up to meet my gaze. "We know what Rosa did, and we have the video to prove it."

"You do?" Yulia's slim throat works. "Did you— Is she okay?"

"For now." I drop my hand but don't bother elaborating further. "Now tell me exactly what happened. How did you escape?"

She stares at me, and I know she's deciding whether she can believe me about the video. Finally, she says quietly, "On the day before your departure, Rosa came by and gave me a razor blade and a hair pin. She also told me a little bit about the guards' schedules, including the fact that the ones at North Tower Two play poker on Thursday afternoons."

"I see." That explains why Yulia walked by that tower at that exact time. "And why was she helping you? Did your agency get to her?"

"No, of course not." Yulia seems surprised. "How could they have?"

"I don't know. But then why would she do this?"

Yulia hesitates again, then says slowly, "It was strange. She acted like she didn't like me, so I didn't understand at first, but then . . ."

"Then what?" I prompt when she doesn't continue.

"Then she mentioned something about Nora," she says, staring at me with wide, unblinking eyes. "It sounded like she asked her to do this. Rosa wouldn't tell me why, though."

Well, fuck. I want to punch someone.

Esguerra's wife didn't lie after all.

"Do *you* know why this Nora helped me?" Yulia asks, and I realize I'm just standing there, seething with silent rage. "She's Esguerra's wife, right?"

"She is," I say grimly, turning to resume walking. "Unfortunately, she is."

If she weren't, she'd already be dead. But as things stand, unless Esguerra chooses to punish Nora, she's untouchable, and if Rosa acted on her orders, the maid might be too.

CHAPTER THIRTY-EIGHT

❖ YULIA ❖

As we resume walking toward the training field, I sneak a cautious glance at Lucas, trying to see if he bought my story. So far, it looks like he has. His square jaw is taut with anger, his mouth set in a hard, thin line. He looks like he's ready to murder someone, and to my surprise, I feel a tiny spurt of guilt for lying to him about Nora.

It's as if I'm betraying his trust.

No. I shake off that ridiculous feeling. There's never been trust between us. Lust, yes, and even some incongruous tenderness, but not trust. I may no longer be handcuffed, but with the trackers embedded in my body, I'm still Lucas's captive, and falling for him didn't make me blind. I know what kind of man he is and what he's capable of. If Lucas knew that Nora told me to implicate her in my escape, it's highly probable that the maid would be killed—which, I'm guessing, is why Esguerra's wife took the fall for her. *If* she took the fall, that is. It's possible the petite girl simply owned up to the truth, and if that's the case, I didn't lie to Lucas. I just didn't mention Nora's visit, which is a completely different matter.

Besides, when I think about what happened to Rosa, I feel sick inside. I know how horrible she must be feeling. The last thing I want is for her to be hurt more.

Thankfully, as we walk, Lucas's anger seems to dissipate, and by the time we approach a large, grass-covered field, he appears to have gotten over it completely.

"Is this it?" I ask, looking around the field. It's divided equally between a shooting range and an obstacle course. There's also a flat-roofed building—an indoor gym, maybe?—on one side and what looks like a supply shed in the corner.

"Yes, this is the training area," Lucas says as we walk past a few guards practicing mixed martial arts. "And I think that's your brother over there." He points toward a small cluster of men on the obstacle course.

Sure enough, my brother's bright blond hair stands out like a beacon among the mostly Latino guards. He's doing pushups on the grass next to a slim, brown-haired guard who looks to be only a few years older than him.

As we get closer, I realize they're having a competition. The other men are standing in a semi-circle, cheering them on and placing bets in a colorful mixture of Spanish and English. Both Misha and the guy he's competing against are shirtless and dripping with sweat, and I wonder how long they've been at it. Not that it takes much exertion to sweat in this weather; my own shirt is sticking to my back just from walking here.

"Looks like Michael is ahead," Lucas comments, and I hear a note of dark amusement in his voice. "I'll have to boost the new recruits' training regimen. This simply won't do."

I shush him, not wanting to interrupt my brother's concentration. Misha's face is red, and his arms are shaking as if they're going to give out. The other guard, however, is in even worse shape, and as I watch, the young man collapses on his stomach, unable to do another pushup.

"Go, Michael!" someone shouts, and I turn to see Diego clapping. He's grinning from ear to ear. Turning to the other guards, he holds out his hand and says smugly, "Told you the kid could do it. Now pay up."

While he speaks, my brother collapses on the grass as well. Panting, he rolls over onto his back, and I see a huge, bright smile on his face. He looks as happy as in those photos.

I hurry toward him, my own face split in a joyous smile. "Good job, Michael," I call out, feeling like I might burst from pride. "That was amazing."

He sits up, his eyes widening as he sees me approach. "Yulia?" he says in Russian. "How are you feeling?"

"I'm much better, thank you," I respond in the same language. Then, cognizant that some of the other guards have started frowning, I say in English, "Glad to see you boys are having fun."

Misha climbs to his feet, brushing off bits of dirt and grass from his shorts. "Um, yeah," he says in English, casting an embarrassed glance at the others. "We were just, you know . . ."

"Yeah, she knows," Lucas says, coming up behind me. Crossing his arms in front of his chest, he looks at the guards, and they quickly scatter, mumbling something about having a job to do.

Only Diego stays behind, a big grin lighting up his face. "We should hire him," he says. "He's already better than some of these new guys, and with a bit more training—"

Lucas holds up his hand, interrupting Diego. "Michael's going to come with us for a bit," he says. "I'll call you when I need you."

"All right," Diego agrees easily. "I'll be around."

He lopes off to join the others, and Lucas turns to Misha, who's watching him warily.

"I have to speak to a few guards," Lucas says. "Can I trust you to stay on this field and not get into trouble if I leave you alone with your sister?"

Misha's face is stony, but he nods.

"Good." Lucas clasps my elbow and pulls me to him. Lowering his head, he presses a quick, hard kiss to my lips before stepping back. "I'll see you both soon. Stay within sight. Got it?"

"Yes," I say, trying to ignore the burn in my cheeks. "We'll be here."

Lucas walks away, and I turn to face Misha, my embarrassment intensifying when I see an identical flush on his face. I know why Lucas kissed me like that—it's all about claiming me in public today—but that doesn't mean I wanted my fourteen-year-old brother to witness it.

Misha already thinks poorly of me.

"Do you want to take a walk?" I offer, trying to pretend the kiss didn't happen. "I haven't seen this area before. Maybe you can show me around?"

"Sure." Misha seems glad to have something to do. Grabbing his shirt from the grass, he pulls it on and says, "Here, let's go this way."

He leads me toward the obstacle course, and I follow, ignoring the mix of hostile and curious looks coming our way from the guards.

"How are you?" I ask in English. I want to get used to speaking with Misha this way, so that Lucas and the others don't think we're trying to hide something from them. "Are they still treating you well?"

He nods. "They watch me all the time," he responds in English, "but other than that, it's okay."

"Good." I give him a relieved smile. "How are your accommodations?"

He shrugs as we walk around a pair of guards practicing scaling a barbed-wire fence. "They're fine. A little better than the dorms, I guess."

"That's good. And what about—"

"How long are they going to keep us here?" he interrupts, giving me a sidelong look. "The guards wouldn't tell me anything."

"Right. About that . . ." I take a deep breath. "I'm going to talk to Lucas, but before I do, I need to know a little bit more about your situation."

Misha frowns. "What do you mean?"

This is going to be tricky. "How did you end up in UUR, Michael?" I ask carefully, using his preferred name. "Did your uncle ask you to join?"

"No." Misha doesn't blink. "It was my idea."

I stop, staring at him in shock. "Yours?"

My brother gives me a level look. "I was in some trouble in school, and Uncle Vasya came to talk to me. He told me how stupid I was being, how many kids would've killed for a chance at my kind of life. And I told him that's not what I wanted. I didn't want to be an accountant or a lawyer or a nurse. I wanted to be an agent, like him."

I frown in confusion. "This was openly discussed in your family? UUR and everything?"

"No, of course not. My parents were very secretive about Uncle Vasya's job, but I kept overhearing things. Also, I knew I had a sister who was working for our country. My parents told me about that because I kept asking them why you left me." I wince, but he's already plowing ahead. "Anyways," he says, "I put two and two together, and on that visit, I confronted Uncle Vasya about it. He admitted that you'd joined his program, and then he told me how I came to be adopted by my parents."

"Michael, that's not—"

"Don't lie. He said you'd lie about it." Misha's tone sharpens. "He was a good man. He died for Ukraine."

"I know that, but ..." I draw in a steadying breath. "Listen to me, Michael. Your uncle and I had a deal. Your adoption was part of it. You were supposed to be safe, not recruited into this life. It was only supposed to be me. I joined the agency because I wanted to protect you, and I couldn't do it at the orphanage. Obenko promised me—"

"Stop. I don't want to hear it." Misha steps back, shaking his head. "You're lying. I know you are."

"No, Mishen'ka." My heart squeezes at the anger and confusion in his gaze. "Your uncle didn't tell you everything. I didn't leave because I was tired of the orphanage. I left because that was the only way to keep you safe."

Misha keeps shaking his head, but he's no longer interrupting, so I tell him about the visit by the man in the suit and the bargain he offered me, including how I was supposed to stay away from Misha and the pictures I received every few months. As I speak, I see uncertainty replace some of the anger in my brother's eyes.

He doesn't know whom to believe, and I can't blame him.

"I still have all those pictures," I say when he remains silent. "I uploaded them to a secure cloud service a few months ago. I could show them to you one day, if you want."

Misha stares at me. "You kept them?"

"Of course." My chest is painfully tight, but I attempt a smile. "You're my only family, Michael. I kept every single one."

He swallows and looks away before resuming walking. I catch up with him, and we walk without speaking for a few minutes. There are a million things I want to tell him, a billion questions I want to ask, but I don't want to push us into another argument.

It's nice to just have my brother's company for now.

To my surprise, Misha breaks the silence first. "I didn't know it was you that day," he says quietly as we stop to observe two guards throwing knives.

"What?" I turn to look at him. "What are you talking about?"

"That day at the warehouse, when I helped them catch you. I didn't know that was you." Misha's forehead is creased with tension. "I only found out later."

"Oh, of course." It hadn't even occurred to me that he could've known. "You hadn't seen me since you were three, and I was wearing a wig. Besides, why would you ever expect your sister to be lurking outside your training facility?"

"Right." He folds his arms across his chest. "So why *were* you there? Uncle Vasya said that you'd turned on us, that you were no longer loyal to UUR."

"I never turned on the agency, but I *was* going to walk away," I say, deciding to be completely honest. "I was following Obenko because I was hoping he'd lead me to you, so I could see you one last time before I left."

Misha blinks. "You followed him to see me? But why were you going to walk away?"

"It's a long story, Michael."

"Is it because of him?" Misha glances toward the other side of the field, where Lucas is talking to a group of guards. "Because"—his cheeks redden—"you two are lovers?"

"It's . . ." God, why is this so difficult? It's not like *I'm* fourteen. "It's complicated between us," I finally manage to say. "His boss has been at odds with Ukraine for a while, and—"

"Is Kent forcing you?" Misha's eyes flash with blue fire. "Because I'll kill him if he is—"

"No, of course not," I interrupt, my pulse jumping. The last thing I need is Misha in defender mode. "I want to be with Lucas," I say firmly. "It's just a complicated situation because of UUR and everything."

My brother doesn't look convinced, so I add quickly, "And yes, us being lovers was a big part of why I was going to walk away."

Misha flushes again and looks away. "Okay," he mutters. "That's what I thought."

"Yes, and you were right." Pushing aside my discomfort, I give him a rueful smile. "You're very smart, and pretty much an adult now. I'll have to get used to that. The last time I saw you, your biggest achievement was going on the potty, so it's a bit of an adjustment for me, seeing you all grown up like this."

Misha grins, as pleased by that praise as any boy of fourteen, and I realize how mature my brother acts most of the time. I don't have much experience with teenagers, but I doubt many of them could've handled this situation as well as he has.

In fact, few *adults* could've kept their cool while being kidnapped, taken halfway around the world, and kept captive on an arms dealer's jungle compound.

As I ponder that, a flicker of motion from across the field catches my gaze.

"We should head back," I say, realizing Lucas is waving at me. "I think Lucas is calling us."

Misha nods, falling into step beside me, and as we walk back, I try to think of the best way to approach my captor about sending my brother home.

CHAPTER THIRTY-NINE

❖ LUCAS ❖

After I talk to the new recruits on the field, I catch Yulia's eye and wave at her, motioning for her to return. She grabs her brother and starts walking back, and I head over to the pull-up bar, figuring I'd get some quick exercise in while I wait.

I'm midway through my first set of wide-grip pull-ups when I see Esguerra approach.

"What's up?" I ask, letting go of the bar to land on the grass. The sun is unbearably hot, and I use the bottom of my shirt to wipe the sweat off my face. "Were you looking for me?"

"We need to figure out the Rosa situation," he says without preamble. "Nora is after me to lift her house arrest, but we still don't know if—"

"We do, actually," I interrupt. "I was going to talk to you this afternoon. I just got confirmation from Yulia that Nora *was* involved."

Esguerra's face darkens. "What did your spy say, exactly?"

I convey my conversation with Yulia almost word for word. "So yeah," I conclude, "looks like it wasn't Rosa's own initiative—not that it means she should get away with it." Nor should Nora, in my opinion, but I know better than to say that.

"Fuck." Esguerra spins around, his posture rigid with fury, and I see the moment he spots the approaching figures. Turning back toward me, he says incredulously, "Is that—"

"Yes." I meet his gaze coolly. "That's Yulia and her brother, Michael. I told you we grabbed him during the trip to Ukraine, remember?"

The corner of his real eye begins to twitch. "Grabbed him, yes. Gave him free run of the compound alongside his treacherous sister, no. What the fuck are you doing, Lucas? You said she's not getting off scot-free."

"And I said I'm keeping her." The steel in my voice matches the iciness of his expression. "She's mine to punish or not. Just as Nora is yours."

For a moment, I'm sure Esguerra's going to hit me, and I tense, ready to strike back. But he takes a breath instead and steps back, his hands hanging loose at his sides. Turning, he looks at Yulia and her brother, who are now less than fifty feet away.

Yulia must've spotted him because she's moving slower now, her face white with anxiety. Her brother is walking next to her, but as they get closer, she grabs his wrist and steps in front of him, as if trying to hide him from Esguerra's view.

"She's mine," I repeat in a low, hard voice as Yulia comes to a complete stop some thirty feet away, her gaze flitting from me to Esguerra and back again. "If you do anything to them . . ."

Esguerra turns his head to look at me. "I won't." His eyes gleam coldly. "But, Lucas, do us both a favor. Keep her as far away from me as you can."

I incline my head, but he's already walking away, heading in the opposite direction from where Yulia and her brother are standing.

* * *

On our walk home, Yulia is silent, and I know she's worrying about Esguerra. Diego came back to get Michael shortly after my confrontation with Esguerra, and Yulia smiled and gave her brother a parting hug. Since then, however, she's barely said a word, her gaze distant and her shoulders tense as she walks next to me.

I want to reassure her, tell her that she's stressing over nothing, but the words stick in my throat. Esguerra's estate is large in terms of acreage, but population-wise, it's more like a small village. Everybody runs into each other on a regular basis, and keeping Yulia out of Esguerra's hair won't be easy—at least if I do as I promised and let her roam on her own.

Esguerra might not harm her in the near term, but he won't forgive her either.

As we get closer to the house, Yulia's gait slows, and I realize the long walk must've tired her out, depleting her body's all-too-recently replenished strength reserves. Without a second thought, I bend down and swing her up into my arms, ignoring her startled squeak and my ribs' faint twinge of pain.

"What are you doing?" she exclaims as I resume walking. "Lucas, you don't need to carry me—"

"Hush." I press her tighter against my chest, ignoring her half-hearted attempts to push me away. "I'm carrying you home."

She stops struggling, and after a moment, she winds her arms around my neck and lays her head on my shoulder. "Lucas . . ." Her voice is as weary as I've ever heard it. "It's not going to work, you know."

"What are you talking about?"

"You and I." She lifts her head to look up at me, and I see the dark shadow of despair in her gaze. "It's not going to work."

"Bullshit." I pick up my pace, a burst of fury propelling me forward. "It's going to work if I want it to."

Yulia slowly shakes her head. "No. Maybe in another life—"

"In another life, our paths would've never crossed, beautiful. This is the only way you could've been mine."

If her parents hadn't been killed in that car crash, if I hadn't been working for Esguerra, if UUR hadn't given her that assignment . . . The number of ways I could've *not* met her is endless, but I did meet her, and there's no fucking way I'm giving her up.

Yulia sighs and places her head back on my shoulder, letting me carry her without further protests. I know she's not convinced, however.

Like me, she's seen too much of this world to believe in happy endings.

* * *

"Lucas, I think Misha should go home."

I pause with the spoon halfway to my mouth. "Home?"

"To his parents," Yulia clarifies, putting down her own utensil. Her bowl of soup steams in front of her, mostly eaten. "His adoptive parents."

"I thought he was with your agency." I put down my spoon and wipe my mouth with my napkin.

I've been expecting something like this since the incident this morning, and I'm not looking forward to this conversation.

"He was with UUR of his own free will, yes, but by all indications, he's also close to his parents." Yulia's gaze is unflinching. "They let him join against their better judgement, and I'm sure they're going crazy with worry for him now."

I drum my fingers on the table. "So you want me to what, bring him back to them? What about the fact that you haven't seen him in eleven years? Don't you want to spend some time with your brother?"

Yulia's face tightens. "Of course I do, but I can't be that selfish. Misha doesn't belong here, and he's not safe. I saw the way Esguerra was looking at him . . . at us both. He hates us, Lucas. I know you said you'll protect us, but—"

"He won't lay a finger on either one of you," I say, and mean every word. As much as I respect Esguerra, I'll kill him before I let him harm Yulia. "You're safe, and so is your brother."

"But for how long?" She leans forward. "Until you get tired of me? And then what? We're at Esguerra's mercy?"

"I won't get tired of you." I can't picture a day I wouldn't want her. I've lusted after women before, but never like this. My craving for Yulia feels like a part of me now, like something imprinted on my DNA. "You don't have to worry about that."

"You can't expect me to believe that, but okay, let's assume for a moment that it's true." She pushes her bowl aside. "That still leaves us with the fact that your job is dangerous, Lucas. Your *life* is dangerous. Just look at what happened when you went to Chicago. If there's a bullet coming at Esguerra, it's more than likely to hit you first."

I look at her silently, knowing she's right. I'd said as much to Michael. If something were to happen to me, Yulia and her brother would be on their own, in a place where nobody will raise a finger to help them.

No, it's worse than that. If I were gone, they'd likely be killed on the spot.

"I can't send Michael back right now," I say after a couple of moments. Leaning back, I lace my fingers behind my head and give Yulia an even look. "Not if you want him to remain safe, at least."

All color drains from her cheeks. "Why?"

"Because Operation UUR is in full swing." The hacking program we used during our raid on the black site downloaded and transmitted a lot of confidential data from the agency's computers. We now have names and cover identities of just about every UUR operative, and we're systematically taking them out. I don't explain that to Yulia, though. All I say is, "It would be too dangerous for your brother."

She understands, and her face turns impossibly paler. "What about his parents? Are they—"

I lower my arms and lean forward. "I already put out word that Obenko's sister's family is not to be touched." I did that as soon as I realized Michael's connection to them. "However, their names *are* in our files," I continue before Yulia can say anything, "and given your brother's very direct involvement with the agency, it's best if he stays here for now."

"Oh God." She pushes her chair back and stands up, her hand pressed to her mouth. She's visibly shaking. "You're murdering them all, aren't you?"

My eyebrows snap together. "You asked me to spare Michael, and that's exactly what I'm doing." I rise to my feet and walk around the table. Reaching Yulia, I curl my fingers around her wrist and pull her hand down, away from her trembling lips. "That's what you wanted, isn't it?" I tug her closer to me. "Your brother left unharmed, even though he's connected with the agency? And I'm even extending the courtesy to his adoptive parents. So you see, it's all going to work out."

Tears glisten in Yulia's eyes as she shakes her head, but she doesn't move away as I let go of her wrist and grasp her hips, molding her lower body against mine. My growing erection presses against her belly, and my breathing picks up as molten heat moves through my veins. Our unfinished dinner, UUR, her brother—none of that matters right now.

All I can focus on is the beautiful girl in my arms and the pain in her big blue eyes.

"Yulia . . ." I breathe in her scent, my hunger intensifying as her tongue flicks out to moisten her lips. I'm leaning in to taste the glossy softness of those lips when she presses her palms against my chest, pushing with all her strength to keep me at bay.

"Lucas, please, listen to me . . ." Her chest rises and falls in a shallow rhythm. "Most of the agents had nothing to do with the crash. It was Obenko's idea, and he's now dead. You don't need to—"

"Forget about them," I growl, my hands tightening on Yulia's hips when she tries to pull away. My frustrated lust adds to my anger, and my tone sharpens as I say, "The agency is not your problem anymore. You're with me now, understand?"

"But, Lucas, they're—"

"Living on borrowed time," I say harshly. "Those who are still living, that is. Your agency killed dozens of our men, and they're going to pay for that. The only ones who'll be spared are your brother and you."

The tears are streaking down her cheeks now, but the sight doesn't sway me. There's nothing she can say that would convince me to forgive our enemies. They chose to strike at us, and now they're reaping the consequences of their actions. It's just that simple.

Still, I don't like seeing Yulia upset.

Letting go of her hips, I raise my hand to brush away her tears. "Don't cry for them," I say in a slightly softer tone. "They don't deserve it. You know that."

"That's not true." Her voice is strained. "Some of them might not deserve it, but many are guilty of nothing more than wanting to serve their country and—"

"And the forty-five men who died on that plane were guilty of nothing more than working for Esguerra." I drop my hand, my anger returning in full force. "Nobody is innocent in this business, beautiful—not even you."

Yulia takes a step back, but I catch her arm before she can back away.

"You haven't asked about Kirill," I say coldly. My cock throbs in my jeans, but I push the lust aside, knowing I need to deal with this once and for all. "Don't you want to know what measures we're taking to find him?"

She blinks. "I assumed he died. His wounds—"

"There's no body and no burial record of any sort. No sign of him, period. Dead men aren't that good at covering up their tracks."

Yulia draws in an unsteady breath. "So what are you saying?"

"I'm saying the bastard is most likely alive—and hiding with help from others in your agency." I pause, trying to rein in my rage. When I speak again, my voice is moderately calmer. "The people whose lives you're trying to save are the same ones who let that monster keep his job and lied to you about it. Our operation in

Ukraine is not just about retaliation anymore. It's also about tracking him down."

Yulia stares at me, and I see the torturous conflict in her gaze. She wants Kirill dead just as much as I do, but she doesn't want UUR agents to die in the process. I understand that on some level; she must've gotten to know many of them during her training, maybe even become friends with a few, so she doesn't want their deaths on her conscience.

Unfortunately for those agents, *my* conscience can handle their deaths just fine.

"So what do I tell Misha?" Yulia finally asks. Her voice is still hoarse, but the tears are drying on her face. "Is he supposed to sit tight and wait while you exterminate everyone in UUR? Train with the guards and hope his parents survive the purge?"

"What you tell him is up to you," I say, refusing to rise to her bait. "I'd be more diplomatic if I were in your shoes, but he's your brother and you know best. Now"—I use my grip on her arm to tug her closer—"where were we?"

Yulia looks like she's about to say something else, but I'm done with this discussion.

Wrapping my arms around her slender frame, I bend my head and slant my mouth across her lips.

CHAPTER FORTY

❖ YULIA ❖

Lucas's kiss holds an edge of anger, his lips and tongue punishing as he invades my mouth, and fear-tinged arousal heats my core, adding to my turmoil.

The man I love is killing my former colleagues, and it's all my fault. If I hadn't let Lucas break me that time, if he hadn't come after me, none of this would be happening. Rationally, I understand there were other factors at play—Obenko's ill-advised attack on Esguerra's plane, for one—but I still feel responsible for the current mess.

If my brother's adoptive family dies, it'll be on me.

It doesn't help that underneath the crushing press of guilt, I'm not entirely sorry. Somewhere along the way, a root of hatred had taken hold within me, and I didn't know it until Lucas brought up Kirill's name. I'd suppressed all thoughts of my former trainer, telling myself that I'd already gotten my revenge, but as soon as Lucas mentioned him, I realized the damage I inflicted wasn't enough.

I want Kirill dead, wiped off the face of the Earth— along with anyone who might be helping him.

Lucas deepens the kiss, his arms tightening around me, and my head falls back under the pressure of his mouth. His tongue explores me with a hunger that borders on brutality, his teeth tugging at my lower lip, and I moan helplessly, my hands moving up to clutch at his muscled shoulders as he backs me up against the kitchen wall, trapping me there. He's wearing jeans and a T-shirt, and I'm dressed too, but even through our layers of clothing, I can feel the heat of his large body and smell the clean musk of his skin. His erection is like a rock pressing into my stomach, and my nipples tighten, my body responding to his need.

"Fuck, Yulia, I want you," he mutters, raising his head, and I gasp as one of his big hands slides down my body and cups my sex through my shorts, palming it hard. The heel of his hand puts pressure on my clit, and moisture rushes to my core as he moves his palm in a semi-circle, the rough rhythm shockingly erotic.

"Yes." My heartbeat thunders in my ears, my muscles tensing with intensifying pleasure. "Oh God, yes . . ." I don't know what I'm saying; all I know is I want him—this man, this ruthless killer who's wrong for me in so many ways. I want him, and I fear him. I hate him, and I love him. The dichotomy of my emotions tears at me, slicing me into pieces, yet it all feels right too, like I'm supposed to be here, in his arms.

Like I belong with him.

He lowers his head to kiss me again, and I latch on to his mouth, responding with the same fierce need. My teeth sink into his lower lip until I taste blood, and it unleashes something violent inside me, a wildness I never knew was there. I'm trapped in his embrace, yet at that moment I feel free—free to rage, free to hurt him as I've been hurt. It feels like a chain snapping, and I revel in the sensation, my helplessness giving way to triumph as he tears his mouth away and I see the smear of blood on his lips. His broad chest heaves with labored breaths as he stares down at me, his pale eyes slitted with burning need, and the wildness inside me grows, crowding out fear and reason.

I want him, and I'm not going to deny myself.

Reaching up, I clasp Lucas's face with both hands and pull his head down, reclaiming his mouth. He's still palming me between my legs, the hard pressure of his hand keeping me on the edge, but it's not enough, and I bite his lip again, as desperate for his pain as I am for release.

He shudders in response, and with startling swiftness, spins me around, backing me up against the edge of the table. His arm sweeps out in a violent arc, and my pulse leaps as I hear the bowls shatter, the remnants of our dinner splattering on the floor. It almost jolts me out of my trance-like state, but he's already laying me on the table, and heat rushes through me again, centering in a pulsing ache between my thighs as he drags my shorts off my legs and yanks down the zipper of his jeans.

We're still kissing, our lips and tongues dueling with feral hunger, when he drives into me, his thick cock splitting me open. I gasp into his mouth, tensing at the shockwave of sensations. My flesh quivers around him, trying to adjust, but he doesn't stop, doesn't slow down. He just starts pounding into me, and I tear my mouth away, my breath coming in pained gasps as his thrusts drag me back and forth on the hard table. His possession is violent, overwhelming, yet I want more. More of his roughness, more of this dark, savage heat.

I want him to match the animal inside me, to hurt me as I'm hurting him.

My legs come up, wrapping around his hips, and I sink my teeth into the corded muscle of his neck, reveling in the taste of salt and man. His big body shudders, and he rasps out a curse, his pace picking up until he's all but drilling into me. My hands fist in his sweat-drenched shirt, and the tension inside me grows, the heat between my legs swelling and intensifying. It seems to be taking over all my senses, crowding out everything but the need to come.

"Lucas," I gasp, feeling the swell begin to crest. "Oh, fuck, Lucas!"

Impossibly, his thrusts pick up speed, and I'm hurled over the edge, the orgasm hitting me with massive force. The pleasure blasts through my nerve endings, so sharp it's almost painful, and I cry out, my muscles clenching and releasing in pulsing waves. My heart hammers uncontrollably as aftershocks ripple through my body, but Lucas is not done yet. Before I can so much as draw in a breath, he pulls out and flips me onto my stomach, bending me over the table.

"Is this what you want?" he bites out, driving into me again. Gripping my hair, he forces my upper body to arch off the table. "For me to fuck you? To use you and make you hurt?"

"Yes." Oh God, yes. His cock is thick and burning hot inside me, a threat and a promise all at once. I didn't know I wanted this, but I do. I want the pain he inflicts to be the only one in my mind, his touch the only one in my memory. It's sick and utterly illogical, but I want Lucas to hurt me so I can forget about Kirill.

"All right." My captor's voice is dark and strained. "Remember, you asked for this."

My pulse spikes, but he's already pulling my hair harder, making my neck bend at an impossible angle. I cry out, my hands flying up to grab at his wrist, but he ignores my flailing arms and thrusts two fingers of his free hand into my mouth, making me gag from the sudden assault. His fingers are faintly salty, and they feel huge and rough in my mouth, almost as big as a cock. He pushes them in so far that I gag again and spit up saliva—which is apparently what he's after.

Pulling his wet fingers out of my mouth, he uses his grip on my hair to push me down, flattening my face against the table.

"Wait, Lucas . . ." Panic explodes in my brain as he moves the hand from my mouth to my ass and starts working one finger into the tight ring of muscle. "I don't . . . this isn't . . ." I reach back blindly, my hands pushing at his hips, but I have no leverage in this position. I'm bent over the table with his cock deep inside me; even if he weren't built of solid muscle, there'd be little I could do.

"Shh . . . It's going to be okay." Lucas accompanies the words with a shallow thrust of his cock, and I suck in a breath as his finger presses deeper, the slick coating of my saliva easing the way. "You're going to be okay, baby." His hand releases my hair, his palm splaying on my upper back to keep me in place. "We've done this before, remember?"

It's true; he used his finger, and I enjoyed it on some level, but he wants to go further today. I can sense his hunger, and it terrifies me. I want to push away the bad memories, replace them with a hurt of my choosing, but this is too much, too close to my nightmares. I clench my buttocks, trying to keep him out, but the second finger is already pushing into me, making my flesh stretch and burn at the invasion.

"Wait, not like this . . ." Beyond the burn is a strange, uncomfortable fullness, a feeling of being overstuffed and overtaken. His cock flexes inside me, adding to the sensation, and my breathing turns shallow as sweat trickles down my back. "Please, Lucas . . ."

He ignores my begging, slowly working his slick fingers into my ass, and my body gives in to his inexorable advance, the muscles stretching because they have to. Panting, I lie with my face pressed against the hard surface of the table and feel his cock throb in my pussy. His fingers are all the way in now, and it *is* too much. My body wasn't made for this. Everything about this penetration feels wrong and unnatural, like the time when—

Lucas begins to thrust, distracting me from my thoughts, and I realize that somewhere along the way, my straining muscles relaxed slightly, the burn from the invasion lessening. He's not moving his fingers— he's just keeping them inside me—and with his cock pumping in and out in a slow, careful rhythm, the sensation isn't as uncomfortable as it was.

I close my eyes and try to steady my breathing. His fingers still feel too large, but there's no actual pain, and the realization calms me further, drawing my attention to the slowly gathering tension in my core. The thrusting motions of his cock are reigniting my arousal, and the invasive fullness in my ass doesn't seem to take away from that. In some perverse way, it's even adding to the intensity.

I may survive this after all.

"Yulia." Lucas's voice is hoarse as he withdraws almost all the way. "I'm going to fuck you hard now."

My heart lurches, all illusion of calm fleeing. "Wait—"

But it's too late. Before I can finish speaking, he rams his cock back in, pushing me into the edge of the table. I cry out, my hands sliding forward to brace myself, but he's already withdrawing and thrusting back in. The hard battering of his hips moves me on his fingers, and I cry out again, tensing at the overwhelming sensations. But he doesn't stop. He keeps thrusting, keeps fucking me, and the discomfort morphs into something else: a dark, throbbing heat that spreads through my whole body. My heart gallops in my chest, my breathing turns frantic, and I feel myself rocketing to the edge again, the dual invasion of my body intensifying all my senses. The hot musk of sex in the air, the quivering of my overstretched flesh, the restraining pressure of his big hand on my back—it all adds to my sensory overload, winding me tighter and tighter. My cries grow louder, transforming into screams, and then I shatter, exploding with a force that steals my breath and dims my vision. My muscles spasm, milking his cock and fingers, and I hear his raspy groan as he thrusts in one last time and stops, pulsing deep inside me in release.

Dazed and trembling, I lie there, unable to say or do anything as Lucas slowly pulls his fingers out and lifts his hand from my back. His cock is still inside me, but after a moment, he withdraws that too. Cool air washes over my heated flesh as he steps back, and I feel the slickness coating my folds—my own moisture combined with his seed.

"Hang on, baby," he murmurs, stepping away, and I hear the sink running.

A minute later, he returns, holding a wet paper towel. By then, I've recovered enough to push myself off the table and stand on shaking legs, and I take the towel from him, using it to mop at the wetness between my legs. Lucas watches me with hooded gaze, his jeans already zipped up, and a hot flush crawls through my hairline as I see my shorts on the floor, lying next to the mess of broken bowls and spilled food.

Swallowing, I ball the used paper towel in my hand and turn toward my shorts, but Lucas catches my arm.

"I've got it," he says, his pale eyes gleaming. "Go take a shower. I'll join you in a moment."

I don't argue, and a minute later, I'm standing under the hot spray, my mind mercifully blank. True to his word, Lucas joins me in a bit, and I close my eyes, leaning against him as he washes me from head to toe, taking care of me yet again. I'm glad he doesn't say anything or ask me any questions. I'm not sure I'll ever be able to articulate why I wanted something so dark from him ... why even now, after he pushed me far beyond my limits, I feel grateful for the experience.

When we're both clean, Lucas leads me out of the shower and wraps a towel around me before grabbing one for himself. He's still silent, his gaze oddly watchful, and finally, I feel the urge to speak.

"You didn't fuck me in the ass," I say, my hands twisting in the towel. "Why?"

"Because you weren't ready." He finishes drying himself and casually hangs up his towel, revealing his body in all its powerful masculinity. "Not to mention, we'd need some real lube for that. You're tight, and, well . , ." He glances down at his cock, which, even soft, is impressively sized.

"Right." I swallow the sudden lump of fear in my throat. "You're bigger than your two fingers."

"Yes, somewhat," he says drily, and I see a glimmer of amusement in his eyes.

For some reason, knowing he finds this funny makes me flush again. Turning, I step toward the door to exit the bathroom, but Lucas steps in front of me, his expression turning serious.

"Don't worry, beautiful," he murmurs, cupping my chin. His thumb brushes over my lower lip in a gentle caress. "Every part of you will be mine eventually. You're going to forget him, I promise you that."

I stare at him, equal parts startled and terrified by his perceptiveness, but Lucas is already lowering his hand and turning away.

"Come," he says, opening the door. "Let's go get dressed. We'll make something else for lunch."

He heads down the hallway, and I follow, my thoughts in disarray.

I'm not sure what I expected from my new captivity, but this—whatever this is—wasn't it.

PART IV: THE NEW CAPTIVITY

CHAPTER FORTY-ONE

❖ YULIA ❖

Over the next couple of weeks, Lucas and I go back to something resembling our old routine. With my strength rapidly returning, I take over the cooking and other domestic chores, and Lucas resumes his normal working schedule, returning home only in the evenings and for mealtimes. While he's gone, I read books and do body-weight exercises to stay fit, and when we're together, we discuss the books I've read. We also go on morning walks together. The main difference between now and before is the presence of my brother on the estate and that, technically, I'm allowed to walk around on my own.

I say "technically," because the first time I'm about to take advantage of that opportunity, Lucas cautions me to avoid Esguerra as much as possible.

"He won't do anything to you, but it's best if you don't draw his attention unnecessarily," Lucas says, and I read between the lines.

If it weren't for Lucas, Esguerra would gladly do as his wife threatened and flay every bit of flesh from my bones.

Given this, I rethink my idea of strolling over to the guards' barracks to chat with my brother. Instead, I request that Diego bring him over to Lucas's house. I'm not afraid for myself—I've been living on borrowed time since my capture in Moscow—but I can't bear the thought of anything happening to Misha. That possibility worries me so much that when Diego comes over, I surreptitiously pull the young guard aside and ask him to keep my brother away from his boss.

"From Esguerra?" Diego gives me a surprised look. "Why? He's doesn't care about Michael. He's seen the kid half a dozen times since your arrival, and he's never shown any interest in him."

That reassures me somewhat. On the training field, Esguerra looked at me with unmistakable hatred. If he feels differently about my brother—or, rather, is indifferent toward him—it's a good thing. Still, the core of my fear remains. Even if the arms dealer's animosity is reserved solely for me, I know what he's capable of. If Esguerra decides to hurt me, it won't matter to him that Misha is fourteen, or that he had nothing to do with the crash.

My brother could end up paying for my sins.

"Are you sure Misha is safer here than in Ukraine?" I press Lucas that evening. "Maybe if his parents moved to a different part of the country, or—"

"Ukraine is a battle zone right now," Lucas says bluntly. "We've got three dozen men on the ground there now, and more are getting sent in as we speak. I can't guarantee your brother won't get caught in the crossfire. Do you want to take that risk?"

"No, of course not." I chew the inside of my cheek, trying to block out mental images of the massacre that must be taking place. "But what about Misha's adoptive parents? They're probably worried sick about him—not to mention terrified, if they have any clue about what's going on."

"The best I can do is send them word that Misha's alive and well," Lucas says. "That, and remind our men that they're off-limits. But like I said, I can't make any guarantees. The situation is volatile, and since I'm not there to oversee the operation in person, the men have been given a lot of autonomy to carry out the mission as they see fit."

I swallow. "I understand . . . and thank you. Anything you can do to keep Misha's parents safe would be greatly appreciated," I say, and mean it. I may not be able to prevent Lucas and Esguerra from getting their vengeance, but if I can keep my brother's family out of harm's way, then I won't feel quite so conflicted about it—helpless and complicit all at once.

I'm not only sleeping with a monster; I'm in love with him.

And the monster knows it. He revels in it, making me admit my feelings almost every day. I don't know why Lucas gets such a kick out of it—I can't be the first woman to have fallen for him—but he definitely enjoys hearing the words from me. He forces me to scream them as he fucks me roughly, and to whisper them as he cradles me gently in his embrace. The constant juxtaposition of violent possessiveness and tender care confuses me, keeping me off-balance. I have no idea where my captor stands. One minute, I'm certain he views me as his sex toy, and the next, I find myself hoping it's something more.

I find myself dreaming that someday he may love me too.

It doesn't help that Lucas keeps doing things that make me feel like we're in a real relationship. Every time he learns about a food or drink I like, he surprises me by getting it for me. Over the past week, we've received deliveries of hard-to-find Russian candy, a box of ripe persimmons from Israel, five exotic varieties of Earl Grey tea, and freshly baked loaves of German rye bread. He's also ordered me a wider variety of clothes— some of which he allowed me to choose for myself online—and all kinds of toiletries and bath products, including my favorite peach-scented shampoo.

I'm so pampered it scares me.

And it's not just about the things Lucas buys for me. It's everything he does. If I so much as get a scratch, he bandages it for me. If my muscles ache after a workout, he gives me a full body rub. We've started watching TV together in the evenings, and he's gotten into the habit of stroking my hair or playing with my hand as I sit curled up next to him. It's an absentminded sort of affection, like petting a cat, but that doesn't lessen its impact on me. It's what I've been starving for, what I've wanted for so long. Every time my captor kisses me goodnight, every time he holds me close, the dry, empty fissures around my heart heal a bit, the pain of my losses fading.

With Lucas, the terrifying loneliness of the past eleven years seems like a distant memory.

What touches me most, however, is that Lucas understands my devotion to my brother and doesn't try to interfere with the rebuilding of our relationship. Despite Misha's continued antagonism toward him, he lets me invite my brother over as often as I want, and the three of us start having meals together—meals that often brim with awkward tension.

"Your brother doesn't like me much, does he?" Lucas says drily after our first joint lunch. "For a few moments there, I thought he was going to pull a Yulia and try to stab me with a fork."

"I'm sorry," I apologize, worried that he'd want Misha to stay away. "I'll talk to him. It's just that with his uncle and what happened in Ukraine—"

"It's okay, baby. I understand." Lucas's gaze softens unexpectedly. "He's still a kid, and he's been through a lot. He has every reason to hate me. I'm not going to hold it against him."

I blink. "You're not?"

"No. He'll come around. And if he doesn't . . . Well, he's your brother, so I'll deal."

My throat swells with emotion. "Thank you," I manage to say. "Really, Lucas, thank you for that and . . . and everything."

It's not lost on me that by hunting me down in Ukraine, Lucas most likely saved my life—and he certainly saved my sanity. I don't know if I could've survived a second assault from Kirill, so in a way, my recapture had also been my rescue.

"Of course," Lucas says, stepping toward me. The warmth in his gaze transforms into a familiar dark heat. "It's my pleasure, believe me."

And as he sweeps me up in his arms, I forget all about my worries—for the time being, at least.

* * *

"Are you in love with him?" Misha asks after we've been on the estate for almost six weeks. "Is he your boyfriend for real?"

"What?" I glance at my brother in surprise. We're walking in the forest to minimize the chances of running into Esguerra, and up until this moment, we were discussing utterly innocuous subjects: Misha's old school, his best friend Andrey, and the types of movies boys his age are into. This came out of nowhere. "Why do you ask?" I say cautiously.

Misha shrugs. "I don't know. In the beginning, I thought maybe you were playing him so it would be easier for us to get away, but the more I see you two together, the less that seems to be the case." He shoots me an indecipherable look. "Do you even want to leave?"

"Michael, I . . ." I take a breath, knowing I need to tread carefully. Our relationship has been going so well. Last week, I finally convinced Lucas to let me get online, and I showed Misha the pictures I'd uploaded to the cloud. He viewed them silently, with no accusations of lies or manipulations, and I thought we were finally making progress. The last thing I want is to push us back to our adversarial beginnings.

"Listen, Michael," I say finally, "I'm working on getting you back to your family. I told you, your parents were notified that you're okay, and as soon as things in Ukraine settle down a bit—"

"That's not what I'm asking." Misha stops and turns to face me. "Do you want to leave? If you had a chance to get away from him, would you take it?"

I stop too, struck by the question. In the last month, I haven't thought about escape at all. Even if I didn't have the trackers embedded under my skin, the fact that Lucas found me in Ukraine showed me there's nowhere I can run. Even if I somehow managed to escape again, Lucas would just come after me and bring me back.

That's not what Misha wants to know, though.

"No," I say quietly, holding my brother's gaze. "I wouldn't leave if I could."

He nods. "That's what I thought."

He resumes walking, and I hurry to catch up with his long strides. Misha seems to have grown another inch or two since we've been here, his shoulders broadening and filling out. I suspect when he's fully grown, he'll have Lucas's height and build. For now, though, he's still a boy—and I'm still his big sister.

"Michael, listen to me." I fall into step beside him. "Just because I don't want to leave doesn't mean I'm not working to make it happen for you. Please believe me. I'm doing everything I can to get you home."

"I know." He glances at me, his brow furrowed with a frown. "I just wish you'd come with me when I leave. A lot of people here hate you, you know."

"I know." I smile to chase away the stressed look on his face. "But don't worry about me. I'm going to be fine."

"Because you have *him*."

"Lucas? Yes." I've noticed that my brother doesn't like to refer to Lucas by his name, preferring to just say "he." "He'll keep me safe."

Misha is still frowning, so on impulse, I reach over and ruffle his hair playfully. "You know, this mop on your head is getting long. Want me to give you a haircut, or are you trying to grow a ponytail?"

"Eeww, no." Misha grimaces and reaches up with his hand. His fingers disappear in the thick blond strands. "Yeah, I guess I do need to cut it," he says grudgingly. "Are you good at giving haircuts?"

"I'm sure I'll manage." I grin at his dubious expression. "If I screw it up, we'll just ask Lucas to fix it—he gives himself a buzz cut every other week."

At the mention of Lucas, Misha tenses again, and his gaze slides away. "That's okay," he mutters, suddenly fascinated by an ant hill to our left. "I'm sure whatever you do will be fine."

I sigh but let it go. I can't force my brother to like Lucas. The brutal attack on the black site and Obenko's death left an indelible impression on his young psyche. Misha regards Lucas as the enemy, and rightly so.

If Lucas hadn't realized who Misha was, my brother would've been one of the casualties of that attack.

We walk without talking for a few minutes, but as we approach the edge of the forest, I touch Misha's arm, bringing him to a halt. "I'm sorry about what happened that day," I say when he turns to face me. "Truly, I am. If I could go back and change things, I would. The last thing I wanted was to endanger you or the others, believe me."

Misha stares at me, then says slowly, "It wasn't your fault . . . not really. I'm sorry I said that before. Besides, if they hadn't come—" He stops, his Adam's apple bobbing.

"What?"

"You probably would've been killed." His words are barely audible. Turning away, he continues walking, and I hurry after him, my stomach knotted tight.

"Who told you that, Michael?" Catching up with him, I grab his arm, bringing him to a stop again. "Why did you say that?"

"Because it's true." Misha's face is shadowed, his forearm tense in my grip. "I overheard Uncle Vasya talking about it with Kirill Ivanovich. I didn't want to believe it at first—I thought maybe I misunderstood, or took their words out of context—but the more I thought about it, the clearer it became. They were going to kill you and tell me you ran off with your lover." He draws in an unsteady breath. "They were going to lie, like they've lied about you all along."

"Oh, Michael . . ." I release his arm, my heart clenching at the pain in his eyes. I can't even fathom how agonizing this betrayal must be for him. Obenko had been my boss and mentor, but for my brother, he had been so much more. Misha must've fought so hard against this knowledge, seeking to deny the truth for as long as he could. "Maybe you did misunderstand," I say, unable to bear his distress. "Maybe it was—"

"No, don't. You've been saying this all along, and I was too stupid to believe you. And then when you showed me those pictures last week..." Shaking his head, Misha takes a step back. "I should've listened to you from the start. I just didn't want to believe what you were saying, you know?" His face contorts. "He was dead and—"

"And he was your uncle, a man you looked up to, and I was the sister who left you when you were three." I keep my voice soft and even. "You had no reason to believe me over him. I understand . . . and I understood then too." I inhale to ease the constriction in my throat. "And I'm sorry, Michael. I'm really, truly sorry that things worked out this way."

Misha's expression doesn't change. "You have nothing to be sorry for," he says, his voice strained. "Uncle Vasya—Obenko—is a liar, and I'm an idiot for believing him. Kent said—" He stops again, his face reddening for some reason.

"Lucas?" I stare at Misha blankly. "You talked to him?"

"Yesterday," Misha mumbles, and begins walking again. "When he took me back to the barracks after dinner."

"What did he say?" I ask, falling into step beside him. Misha doesn't respond, so I say more firmly, "What did he say, Michael?"

"He said Kirill Ivanovich hurt you when you were my age," he says reluctantly. "And that Obenko told you they took care of him and they didn't." He glances at me, his face now pale. "Is it true? Did he"—he stops, blocking my way—"do something to you?"

Oh God. The rush of blood to my brain almost makes me dizzy. My cheeks turn hot, then cold as rage fills my stomach. How dare Lucas tell this to a fourteen-year-old? I never wanted Misha to know about Kirill. From what I've been able to pry out of him, it seems my brother has suppressed most of what happened to him at the orphanage. He remembers that it was bad, but he doesn't know the extent of it. Something like this could bring back those horrible memories, and even if it doesn't, I don't want him exposed to that kind of ugliness. It's bad enough that Misha's uncle deceived him; now my brother is going to think the whole world is made up of awful people.

For a moment, I'm tempted to deny everything, but that would make me just one more person who's lied to Misha. "Yes," I say, my voice strained. "It's true. But I was a little older than you—fifteen—and they did keep him away from me after they learned what happened."

Misha's hands curl as I speak. "Are you making excuses for them?" His voice rises incredulously. "For these . . . these *monsters*? After everything they've done to you? I thought Kent was making it up so I'd hate him less, but he wasn't, was he? That's what the two of you were talking about back at the black site. I heard you, but there was so much going on I didn't really register it. Kirill hurt you, and I . . ." His face twists painfully. "Oh, fuck, I trained with the guy. I liked him."

"Mishen'ka . . ." Pushing my anger at Lucas aside, I reach out to touch Misha's shoulder, but he steps away, shaking his head.

"I'm such an idiot." Stumbling over a root, he catches himself on a tree and continues to back away, muttering bitterly, "I'm such a fucking idiot . . ."

"Michael." Pushing my concerns about his suppressed memories aside, I make my voice stern. "I don't want you to use that kind of language. Do you understand? You're not an idiot, and you're certainly not a fucking anything. There was no way you could've known this, just like you couldn't have known that Obenko was lying. Nothing about this situation is your fault."

Misha blinks. "But—"

"No buts." Wiping all emotion from my face, I come closer and stop in front of him. "I don't want to hear any more whining. What's done is done. It's in the past. This, here and now, is the present. We're here, and we're not going to look back. Yes, we've been through some bad things, and we've known some bad people, but we survived and we're stronger now." Softening my voice a little, I reach out and squeeze his hand. "Aren't we?"

"Yes," Misha whispers, his fingers tightening around mine. "We are."

"Good." I release his hand and step back. "Now let's go. Diego told me he might take you to shooting practice this afternoon, since you've been good and all. You don't want to be late for that."

I turn and begin walking, and Misha trails next to me, the bitterness on his face replaced by a look of bewilderment. I've never spoken to him like that before, and he doesn't know what to make of it.

Despite my simmering fury at Lucas, I smile as we approach his house.

I'm Misha's big sister, and it feels good to act like one.

CHAPTER FORTY-TWO

❖ LUCAS ❖

"How could you do this?"

The minute I walk through the front door, Yulia stalks toward me, all long legs and flowing blond hair. Her blue eyes are narrowed into slits, her nostrils all but breathing fire.

"Do what?" I ask, confused. I did receive a rather gruesome update from Ukraine this morning, but I don't see how Yulia could've found out about that. "What are you talking about?"

"Misha," she hisses, stopping in front of me. Her hands are clenched at her sides. "You told him about Kirill."

"Oh." I almost smile but think better of it. Yulia looks ready to deck me, and given her restored health, she might land a blow or two before I subdue her. Keeping my expression carefully neutral, I say in a reasonable tone, "Why shouldn't I have told him? He deserves to know the truth. You know that part of his anger is because he feels deceived, right? Nobody likes to be manipulated."

Yulia's teeth snap together. "He's fourteen. He's still a child. You don't tell children about brutal rape— especially children with his kind of background. Kirill was his trainer. Misha admired him—"

"Yes, exactly." I catch her wrists as a preemptive defense measure. "Your brother kept talking about the bastard and all the things he taught him. Do you think that was good for him? Healthy? How do you think Michael would've felt when he found out that you let him respect your rapist? And he would've found out, believe me. Truth has a way of coming out."

Yulia's wrists are stiff in my grasp, but she doesn't kick me or try to get away. I take it as a sign that I'm getting through to her and say, "Also, he's not a child. Not really. You know your brother already slept with a girl, right?"

"What?" Yulia's mouth drops open.

"Yes, he told Diego about it." I use her shock to pull her closer, molding her lower body against my hardening cock. "The trainees went out to a club a few months ago, and he hooked up with an older girl there. He's crazy proud of it, like any teenage boy would be."

Her throat works. "But—"

"Don't worry. He used protection. Diego asked."

And before Yulia can recover from that, I lower my head and kiss her, enjoying the way she struggles before melting against me.

It takes a long time before we sit down to dinner that evening, but I don't regret a minute of the delay.

* * *

As our new life together continues, I find myself increasingly obsessed with all things Yulia. Everything about her fascinates me: the way she hums under her breath when she's cooking, how she stretches in the morning, the purring moan that escapes her lips when I kiss her neck. Her body has filled out again, her sickly pallor fading, and one look at her golden beauty is all it takes to get me hard these days. I fuck her every chance I get, and it's not enough. I want her constantly, with a need that consumes me. Every time I take her, it's the best feeling ever, yet I'm still left craving more.

Sometimes I think I'll go to my grave wanting her.

If it were just a sexual itch, I might've been able to handle it. But my hunger runs deeper. I want to know everything about her, every tiny detail of her life. I don't like thinking of my past, so I've never had much interest in that of other people, but with Yulia, my curiosity knows no bounds.

"You know, you never told me your real name," I say as we're eating lunch one day. "Your last name, I mean."

"Oh." She blinks. "Why do you care about that?"

"Because I do." I put down my fork and stare at her intently. "You have no one to protect anymore, so please, tell me, baby."

She hesitates, then says, "It's Molotova. I was born Yulia Borisovna Molotova."

Molotova. I make a mental note of that. I haven't forgotten what she told me about the headmistress of her orphanage, and I intend to use this information to track the woman down. I debate disclosing this to Yulia, but I'm not sure how she'd react, so I decide to keep quiet for now.

Changing the topic, I ask, "Have you ever killed anyone? Not in a fight or as self-defense, but outright."

To my surprise, Yulia nods. "Yes, once," she murmurs, looking down at her plate.

"When?" I reach across the table to cover her slender hand with my palm. "How did it happen?"

"It was during training, as the last part of the program," she says, her gaze veiled as she looks up at me. "None of us were supposed to be assassins, but they wanted to make sure we'd be able to pull the trigger if it came to that."

"So what did they do? Have you kill someone?"

"In a way." She wets her lips. "They brought in a dying homeless man. He had Stage Four liver cancer. He only had a few days to live at best, and he was in terrible pain. They shot him full of drugs, and then, instead of a paper target, they strung him up. Our goal was to make a killing shot."

"So all of you shot at this one guy?"

"Yes." Yulia's fingers twitch under my palm. "We used marked bullets, and he was autopsied afterwards to see whose bullets hit the target. A couple of trainees couldn't bring themselves to shoot."

"But you could."

"Yes." She pulls her hand out of my grasp but doesn't look away. "The autopsy revealed that three bullets hit his heart."

"Was yours one of them?" I ask, leaning back.

"No." Her gaze is unflinching. "Mine was found in his brain."

* * *

That night, Yulia clings to me with a passion bordering on desperation, and I realize my questioning brought back some bad memories. I know I should leave her alone, let her live in the present the way she clearly wants to do, but the questions keep gnawing at me, and I finally give in.

"Have you ever slept with a man of your own initiative?" I ask as we lie tangled together after a long bout of sex. By all rights, I should be sinking into sleep, but my body hums with energy and my thoughts keep returning to this topic.

Yulia stiffens in my arms. Turning over, she pulls back to look at me. "What do you mean? I was only forced that one time—"

"I mean, did you ever date anyone who wasn't an assignment?" I say, placing my hand on her hip. "Go to bars, clubs? Hook up with a guy just for fun?" I'd intended the question to be a casual one, but as I say the words, I realize that Yulia with another man will never be a casual topic for me.

I want to commit murder at the mere thought that someone who wasn't me touched her.

Yulia's gaze lights with comprehension. "No," she says softly. "I never dated. It wouldn't have been fair to the guy."

"So there was a guy?" My jealousy sharpens. "Someone you wanted?"

"What?" To my relief, she seems startled by the notion. "No, there was no one. I just meant that I was always on assignment, so I would've been a terrible girlfriend."

"So not even a casual hook-up?" I press.

"No." She bites her lip. "I didn't see the point. I had classes and school assignments on top of my job, and I didn't have much free time."

"So you're telling me that other than your three assigned lovers and myself, you've never been with anyone else?"

Her face tightens. "You're forgetting Kirill."

"I'm not forgetting him." The fact that we still haven't found him or his body is like a festering splinter under my skin. Suppressing the flare of rage, I say evenly, "He was your assailant, not your lover."

"In that case, yes." Yulia's blue eyes are clear and guileless as she looks at me. "I've had four lovers, including you."

I stare at her, hardly able to believe my ears. My seductive spy—the beautiful girl who used her body to get information—has slept with fewer men than an average college student.

"What about you?" she parries, propping herself up on one elbow. "How many women have *you* slept with?" The look in her eyes is a mirror image of my earlier jealousy.

"Probably not as many as you think," I say, pleased by her possessiveness. "But definitely more than four. Like your brother, I started fairly young, and . . . well, I wasn't much of a relationship guy back then."

Her eyes narrow. "Really? And you are now?"

"I'm in a relationship with you, am I not?" I say, my cock stirring at the sight of her nipple peeking out from under the blanket. "So yeah, I'd say so."

Yulia opens her mouth to reply, but I'm already pulling the blanket away. Rolling on top of her, I push her legs apart with my knees and grip my cock, positioning it against her opening. She's slick from our earlier session, so I thrust in, invading her silky tightness with no preliminaries. She doesn't seem to mind, her arms and legs wrapping around me to hold me close, and I begin to fuck her in earnest, taking her hard and fast. It takes only a few minutes before my orgasm starts to build, and I force myself to slow down, wanting to prolong the moment.

"Tell me you love me," I demand, stroking deep into her body. "I want to hear you say it."

"I love you, Lucas," she breathes in my ear, her legs squeezing my hips. Her pussy is like a hot, slippery glove around my dick, and my balls pull tight against my body as I feel her spasms begin. We detonate together, and in that moment, I feel as if we're one, as if our ragged halves have fused, forming one unbroken whole. Our lungs work in tandem, our breaths intermingle, and when I raise my head and see Yulia looking at me, something hot and dense expands inside my chest.

"I'll always love you," she whispers, curving her hand around my cheek, and the feeling grows stronger, the dense heat spreading until it fills every hollow corner of my soul.

With Yulia, I feel complete, and I treasure the sensation.

CHAPTER FORTY-THREE

❖ YULIA ❖

In some bizarre way, it feels like Lucas and I are newlyweds, and this unusual period—this lengthy truce between us—is our honeymoon.

Part of it is definitely the sex. Far from fading with time, the attraction between us only burns hotter, the magnetic pull intensifying with each passing day. Our bodies are attuned to each other in ways I could've never imagined. A look, a breath, a touch, and the flames ignite. Neither one of us can get enough. As many times as Lucas reaches for me, I respond, my body craving his no matter how sore I get. His touch reduces me to someone I don't recognize, a primitive being of wants and needs. It's like I've been programmed to exist solely for his pleasure, to desire him in all ways. He pushes me past my limits, and I want more. Rough or gentle, my captor consumes me, my need for him tethering me tighter than any ropes.

Beyond the sex, however, there is a growing emotional intimacy between us. Every day, Lucas demands my love, and I give it, helpless to do anything else. It's not an equal exchange; Lucas never says the words back or gives me any indication of his feelings. However, after we have sex, he holds me close, as if afraid to let me stray to the other side of the bed, and I know those quiet, tender moments are as important to him as they are to me. They give me hope that one day, I might have more of him—that I might reach the man underneath the hard shell.

"You know, you never really told me how you ended up here . . . how you went from being a Navy SEAL to Esguerra's second-in-command," I murmur one night when we lie there like that, wrapped in each other so completely it's impossible to tell where one ends and the other one begins. Tracing a circle on his powerful chest with my finger, I say, "All I know is what I read in your file, and there was nothing that explained why you did it."

"Killed my commanding officer?" Lucas's voice doesn't betray any emotion, but his shoulder muscle flexes under my head. "Is that what you want to know? Why I killed the bastard?"

"Yes." I scoot back a little so I can look at him. In the dim light of the bedside lamp, my captor's face is as harsh as I've ever seen it. It doesn't deter me, though. "Why did you do it?" I ask softly.

"Because he killed my best friend." Cold, ancient anger creeps into Lucas's voice. "Jackson—my friend—caught Roberts selling weapons to the Taliban, and he was going to report him. But before he could, Roberts had him killed . . . made it look like an ambush by hostiles. I was there when it happened."

"Oh, Lucas, I'm so sorry . . ." I reach up to touch his face, but he intercepts my hand, catching it in a viselike grip.

"Don't." He glances at me, his eyes slitted. "It was in Afghanistan, a long time ago." His gaze returns to the ceiling, but he doesn't release my hand. Holding my fingers tightly, he says, "In any case, I survived. It took several days for me to return to the base, but I made it. And when I got there, I killed the bastard. I took his own gun and peppered him with bullets."

Of course he did. I stare at my captor with a mix of sadness and bitter understanding. Like me, he had been betrayed by someone he trusted, someone who was supposed to have had his back. I don't know what I would've done to Obenko had he lived, but it neither shocks nor appalls me that Lucas chose this brutal method of retaliation.

"So what happened then?" I prompt when Lucas remains silent, his gaze locked on the ceiling. "Were you arrested?"

"Yes." He still doesn't look at me."I was taken back to the States for a court martial. Roberts had friends in high places, and my allegations against him were swept under the rug faster than I could make a formal report."

"How did you escape then?"

Lucas finally turns to face me. "My parents," he says in a hard, flat voice. "They couldn't tolerate the embarrassment of having their son tried for murder, so they arranged for me to disappear. My father made a deal with me: he'd help me vanish in South America, and I'd never contact them again."

"They wanted you out of their lives?" I gape at him, unable to fathom any parent making such a deal. "Why? Because of the murder charge?"

"Because, according to my father, I'm a bad apple—'rotten to the core' is the way he put it."

"Oh, Lucas . . ." My heart shatters on his behalf. "Your father was wrong. You're not—"

"Not a bad man?" He quirks an eyebrow, a sardonic smile flitting across his face. "Come now, beautiful, you know what I am. My parents sent me to all the best schools, gave me every advantage they could, and what did I do? I threw it all away, joined the Navy so I could satisfy my urge to fight. That's pretty fucked up, no?

Can you really blame my parents for wanting to have nothing to do with me?"

"Yes, I can." I swallow, holding his gaze. "You were still their son. They should've stood by you."

"You don't understand." Lucas's eyes glint with ice. "They never wanted a son. I was to be their legacy. A perfect extension of them . . . a culmination of their ambitions. And I ruined all of that when I became a soldier. The murder charge was just the last straw. My father was right to offer me that deal. I didn't fit into their lives—I never had—and they certainly didn't fit into mine."

I bite the inside of my cheek, trying to hold back the tears stinging my eyes. I can picture Lucas as a volatile, restless boy constantly pushed and prodded to be something he didn't want to be. I can also see how his corporate lawyer parents must've been out of their depths trying to raise a child who was, at his core, a warrior—a boy who, by some strange quirk of genetics, was utterly unlike them.

Still, to tell their son that they never wanted to see him again . . .

"So you haven't spoken to them since then?" I ask, keeping a steady tone. "Not even once?"

"No." His gaze is pure steel. "Why would I?"

Why would he, indeed? To me, family is sacred, but my parents were very different from Lucas's family. I can't imagine Mom and Dad walking away from either me or Misha, no matter what path we chose to follow in life. They would've stood by us no matter what, just like I would stand by my brother.

And by Lucas, I realize with a sudden jolt of shock. In fact, I *am* standing by him, even as he and Esguerra lay waste to the organization I worked for. His father wasn't completely wrong—Lucas is not a nice guy, by any means—but that doesn't alter how I feel about him.

Maybe I'm rotten to the core as well, but somewhere along the way, my ruthless captor has become something like my family.

I push the startling revelation aside to focus on the rest of the story. "So how did you end up with Esguerra, then?" I ask, propping myself up on one elbow. "Did you just run into him somewhere in South America, and he hired you?"

"It was . . . a bit more complicated than that." The corners of Lucas's mouth twitch. "I was actually hired by a Mexican cartel to guard a shipment of weapons that they purchased from Esguerra. But when I showed up to do my job, I discovered that one of the cartel leaders had gotten greedy and decided to steal the shipment for himself, double-crossing Esguerra and his own people in the process. There was a nasty shootout, and at the end of it, Esguerra and I were among the few survivors, each of us pinned behind cover. He was running low on ammunition, and I had only a few bullets left, so instead of us continuing to try to kill each other, he offered to hire me on a permanent basis. Needless to say, I agreed." He chuckles darkly before adding, "Oh, and then I shot a guy who was sneaking up behind Esguerra to try to gut him. That sealed the deal, so to speak."

"Is that why you said Esguerra owes you?" I ask, remembering his long-ago words. "Because you saved his life that time?"

"No. That was just me doing my new job. Esguerra owes me for something else."

I look at him expectantly, and after a moment, Lucas sighs and says, "Esguerra was hurt last year in a warehouse explosion in Thailand. I carried him out and got him to a hospital, but he was in a coma for almost three months. I kept things together for him during that time, made sure the business didn't fall apart, his wife was safe, et cetera."

"I see." No wonder Lucas was confident that Esguerra would let him keep me. True loyalty had to be rarer than unicorns in the arms dealer's world. "And you weren't once tempted to take it all for yourself? Esguerra's business has to be worth billions."

"It is, but Esguerra pays me quite well, so what would be the point?" Lucas gives me a wry look. "Besides, I kind of like the guy. He used his contacts to take my name off the wanted lists after I started working for him. Not to mention, he doesn't pretend to be anything other than what he is, and that works for me."

Of course. I can see how that would be appealing after his commander's betrayal in Afghanistan. Still, many men in Lucas's position would've been blinded by greed, and that he wasn't speaks volumes about his character.

My captor may not be close to his family, but in his own way, he's as loyal as I am.

* * *

As our extended pseudo-honeymoon continues, I find myself with a strange problem: I have an excessive amount of free time. I have no assignments or classes, no real responsibilities of any kind. Initially, it had been nice; the illness and the traumatic events that preceded it had taken a lot out of me, leaving me exhausted mentally as well as physically. For several weeks, I'd been content to read, watch TV, spend time with Misha, and putter leisurely around the house, but as the weeks turned into months, I began itching to do more. I'd always been busy—first as a student, then as a trainee, and the last few years as an active spy on assignment. Free time had been a luxury I treasured, but now I'm awash in it and I don't like it.

To fill up the hours, I begin experimenting with new recipes. Lucas grants me access to the Internet—on a monitored computer, since he still doesn't trust me completely—and I find myself browsing various websites in search of new and interesting dishes. Lucas is all for my new hobby—he enjoys the results of it at every meal—and I gradually develop a kitchen repertoire that ranges from classic Russian dishes like *borscht* to exotic fusion cuisine that incorporates elements from Asian, French, and Latino cooking. I even come up with my own variations, like cilantro-curry sushi topped with pickled beets, Peking duck stuffed with apple-flavored cabbage, and arepas with Russian eggplant spread.

"Yulia, this is phenomenal," Lucas says when I make delicate pastries layered with shiitake mushrooms and Camembert cheese. "Seriously, this is better than any high-end restaurant. You should've been a chef."

"It really is amazing," my brother chimes in, devouring his fourth pastry. He's taken to eating lunch with us almost every day, and I suspect my cooking is a big reason for that. He's even willing to tolerate Lucas these days, though they're still far from being best buddies.

"Good. I'm glad you're enjoying it," I say, getting up to carry my plate to the sink. I'm full to bursting after two pastries, but Misha and Lucas seem to have infinite room in their stomachs. I conceal a grin as Lucas reaches for the second-to-last pastry and my brother instantly grabs the last one, stuffing it into his mouth like he's afraid it'll run away.

"Do you have any extra?" Misha asks after he chews and swallows. "Diego and Eduardo begged me to bring back some leftovers."

"What the hell?" Lucas pauses mid-bite to give Misha a glare. "They can make their own pastries. We won't have any leftovers."

"Actually, I made an extra batch just in case," I say, heading over to the oven. This is not the first time the two guards have begged for food through my brother, and I suspect it won't be the last. If Lucas allowed it, they'd come over to eat here every day, but since he doesn't, they find other ways to benefit from my new hobby. "Just tell them to eat the pastries before they cool completely. They won't be as good reheated in the microwave."

"Of course," Misha says as I put plastic wrap over the foil tray and hand it to him. "I'll give it to them right away."

Lucas observes us with an unhappy frown. "But what about—"

"I'll make more soon," I promise, grinning. "For dinner, I'm making enoki pasta with cashew sauce, and chocolate bread pudding with yuzu-raspberry topping. If you're still hungry after that, I'll make these pastries again, okay?"

Misha listens with clear envy before asking, "Do you think you'll have some bread pudding left if I come by after dinner? The guards invited me to a barbecue tonight, but I'll probably have some room for dessert . . ."

"Yes, of course." I beam at him. "I'll be sure to save some for you."

"Yeah, him and half the guards," Lucas mutters, getting up to wash his plate. "Next thing you know, we'll be feeding the whole compound."

I laugh, but before long, Diego and Eduardo start finding various excuses to stop by, often bringing a couple of their friends with them. I don't mind cooking larger portions—it's a fun challenge for me—but Lucas gets irritated, especially when our meals get interrupted by frequent visitors.

"This is not a fucking restaurant," he roars at Diego when the young guard "just happens to swing by" with six of his buddies at lunchtime. "Yulia cooks for me and her brother, got it? Now get the fuck out before I give you an extra shift."

The guards leave, dejected, but the next day, Eduardo comes by right before Lucas is due to return for lunch. "You wouldn't happen to have any of that shrimp salad left, would you?" he asks, keeping a wary eye on the front door. "Michael mentioned that you made some last night, and—"

"Sure." I suppress a grin. "But you better hurry. I think Lucas and Michael are almost here."

I give him a container of the leftover salad, and he thanks me before rushing out the door. The next day, Diego copies Eduardo's maneuver, stopping by a half hour before dinner, and I give him a whole extra cranberry-and-rice stuffed chicken I made for just such an occasion. He thanks me profusely, and for the next week, I surreptitiously feed the guards that way. On the following Monday, however, Lucas catches me in the act, and he's not pleased.

"What the fuck is this?" he snarls, stalking into the kitchen just as I'm giving a tray of freshly baked meat pies to Diego. Stopping next to us, he gives the guard a furious look. "I warned you—"

"Lucas, it's okay. I made enough for everyone," I assure him. "Really, it's fine. I don't mind cooking for them. I enjoy it."

"See? She's fine with it." Diego grins, snatching the tray out of my hands. "Thanks, princess. You're the best."

He sprints out of the kitchen, and Lucas turns toward me, jaw clenched. "What the fuck are you doing? It's not your job to feed the guards. They have a cafeteria in the barracks, you know."

"I know." Impulsively, I step toward him and lay my hand on his hard jaw, feeling the muscles working under the stubble-roughened skin. "It's okay, though. This is fun for me. I like it that the guards enjoy my cooking. It makes me feel . . ." I pause, searching for the right word.

"Useful?" Lucas says, his expression softening, and I nod, surprised that he pinpointed it so well.

He sighs and covers my hand with his before bringing my fingers to his mouth. Brushing his lips over my knuckles, he studies me, his expression now more troubled than angry. "Yulia, sweetheart . . . You are useful to *me*, okay? You don't need to feed every person on this estate to prove your worth."

I stare at him, my stomach inexplicably tight as he releases my hand. "What if I don't want to be useful just to you?" I whisper. "What if I need more than to warm your bed and take care of your house? You know I finished a university for real, right?" I can see Lucas's gaze darken as I speak, but I can't stop, my voice growing stronger with each word. "I have a degree in English Language and International Relations, and I was an excellent interpreter as well as a spy. For six years, I lived in one of the most cosmopolitan cities in the world and interacted with the highest-ranked officials in the Russian government. I was always going places, doing things, and now I barely step foot outside your house because I don't want Esguerra to remember that I exist." I stop to draw in a breath, and realize that a muscle is ticking in Lucas's jaw.

"Is that right?" he says, his voice deadly quiet. "You miss being a spy?"

I instantly curse my loose tongue. I should've known how Lucas would interpret my words. "No, of course not—"

"You miss fucking men on assignment?" He moves closer, backing me up against the kitchen counter.

My pulse spikes. "No, that's not what I—"

His hand grips my throat, tightening just enough to let me feel the steely strength in those fingers. Leaning in, he whispers in my ear, "Or is it that I'm not enough for you?" His breath heats my skin, making my arms erupt in goosebumps. "Do you need more variety, beautiful?"

"No," I choke out, my breathing turning shallow. A jealous Lucas is a terrifying thing. "That's not it at all. I just meant that—"

"You're mine," he growls, raising his head to pin me with an arctic stare. "I don't give a fuck what kind of life you led before. I caught you, tagged you, and you're fucking mine. No man will ever touch you again, and if I want to keep you in a fucking cage for the rest of your life, I will. Understand?"

His grip on my neck loosens, but my throat closes up, the pain like a tidal wave crashing through me. For weeks, I'd existed in a bubble of domestic bliss, playing house with a man who views me as nothing more than a possession, a glorified sex slave he "tagged" with the trackers. Any other woman would've fought tooth and nail for her freedom, but I embraced my captivity like I'd been born to it, letting myself imagine our messed-up relationship could someday turn into something real.

In my longing for my captor's love, I again built castles in the sand.

"I understand," I manage to whisper through numb lips. "I'm sorry."

Lucas releases me and steps back, his face still taut with anger, and I turn away, blindly reaching for some dishes to wash.

Our "honeymoon," such as it was, is over.

* * *

That night, Lucas doesn't come home until late, and Misha and I eat dinner by ourselves. I put on a happy mask for my brother, but I know he senses something off. It's a relief to usher him out of the house with a batch of leftovers for the guards; more than anything, I want to be alone to lick my wounds.

I'm already finishing my shower when Lucas returns. He enters the bathroom just as I'm stepping out of the stall, and without saying a word, he sweeps me up into his arms and carries me to the bedroom. His face is hard, his gaze shuttered as he walks, and the old unease slithers through me. I don't think he'll truly hurt me—physically, at least—but that doesn't lessen my anxiety. Lucas in this mood is unpredictable, and I'm barely keeping myself together as is. For a brief, insane moment, I consider fighting him, but instantly dismiss the idea. It's not like I stand a chance of actually winning. Besides, what would be the point of trying to resist? Like he said, I'm his to do with as he wants.

My life—and my brother's—is in his hands.

If I could cling to the numbness that encased me this afternoon, it would've been easier, but everything is sharp and bright in my mind, every sensation painfully vivid. I feel the heat of his skin through our clothes and the way his arm muscles flex as he places me on the bed; I see the pale glitter of his eyes and smell his warm male scent. He bends over me, and my body comes to life, a familiar heat brewing low in my stomach. My nipples peak, my breasts aching for his touch, and my sex grows slick as he kisses me, his tongue invading my mouth with rough, demanding strokes. His large hands catch my wrists, pinning them above my head, and I close my eyes, willingly sinking into the heated oblivion of lust. My hurt and anxiety dissipate, and animal instinct takes over. Moaning, I arch against Lucas, rubbing my hardened nipples against his T-shirt, and my insides clench as I feel the thick bulge in his jeans pressing against my naked hip.

Yes, take me, fuck me, make me forget . . . The erotic chant plays on a loop in my mind. For now, I don't need to worry about the future, about my life with a man who views me as his exclusive toy. I don't need to think about the fact that I may never be more than a vessel for his lust. I can just focus on his drugging kisses and the warm, heavy weight of his body on top of mine.

It's only when he transfers my wrists into one of his hands and rummages in the bedside drawer with the other that I resurface enough to feel a flicker of unease. Opening my eyes, I tear my lips away from his. "Lucas, what are you—"

He cuts me off with another deep, devouring kiss, and in the next moment, I have my answer. A cold metal touches my left wrist, and then I hear a click as the handcuff locks in place. Gasping, I turn my head to the side and try to twist my other wrist out of his grasp, but Lucas uses my motion to turn me over onto my side and drag my handcuffed arm toward the metal pole he'd installed by the bed during the early days of my captivity. Straddling me, he loops the handcuff around the pole and grabs my other wrist, cuffing it before I can put up any real resistance.

My unease transforms into real fear. I'm lying on my side, naked and with my wrists handcuffed to the pole—just like old times.

"Why are you doing this?" My voice turns high and thin as I turn my head to gaze at Lucas, who's now reaching for something else in the bedside drawer. "Lucas, don't, please." My hair is all over my face, interfering with my vision, and before I can shake it off, a soft dark cloth drops over my eyes.

"Shh," Lucas whispers, tying it around my head. "You're going to be fine, baby."

Fine? He just handcuffed and blindfolded me. My pulse drums in my ears, my arousal dampened by panic. "Lucas, please . . . What are you going to do?"

Still straddling me, he leans down, and I feel his warm breath on the side of my face. "Do you love me?" he murmurs. His lips brush the rim of my ear, his tongue tracing over the outer edge. "Do you love me, Yulia?"

I swallow thickly. "Yes. You know I do."

"Do you trust me?"

No. The truth almost slips out, but I clamp my lips shut just in time. I don't trust Lucas—I never have—but I'm certainly not about to admit it at the moment. I don't know the rules of this new game, and until I do, I'm not going to play along.

"I see," he murmurs, and I realize that my non-answer was an answer in itself. My heart rate speeds up further.

"Lucas, I—"

"It's okay." He bites my earlobe gently. "You don't have to lie." He moves off me, and I hear the sounds of clothes being removed, followed by that of the nightstand drawer being pulled out. I listen, straining, but I don't hear anything else, and a moment later, Lucas turns me so that I'm lying on my back, my handcuffed arms pulled to one side.

I'm about to ask again what he's planning to do, but he's already moving down my body and pushing my legs apart, his powerful hands pinning my thighs to the mattress.

The first touch of his tongue on my folds is startlingly soft, a caress rather than an assault. It both disorients and disarms me. I'd been prepared for something frightening and brutal, but the leisurely strokes of his tongue on my labia and at the rim of my opening are nothing of the sort. He licks me like he has all the time in the world, his lips and tongue toying with my sensitive flesh for what feels like hours before he gets anywhere near my pulsing clit. By then, I'm soaking wet and moaning his name, my hips moving uncontrollably as my arousal returns in full force. If it weren't for his hands holding down my thighs, I would've ground my sex against his mouth, forcibly taking the orgasm that shimmers just beyond my reach.

"Please, Lucas," I beg as his tongue circles my clit with maddeningly light strokes. "Just a little more, please . . ."

To my surprise, he obliges, latching on to my clit with a sucking pull that I feel all the way down to my toes. A choked cry escapes my throat as my inner muscles tighten, and then the orgasm washes over me, sweeping away everything but the devastating pleasure. I come so hard that I see flickers of light, my hips almost coming off the bed despite the restraining pressure of his hands. The pulsations continue for several long moments, and when it's all over, I'm left lying there, boneless and panting, wrung out by the sensations.

I know Lucas is not done with me yet, but I'm still startled when he flips me over onto my stomach, making the handcuffs clang against the metal pole. My arms are now stretched to the opposite side, and for the first time, the scary versatility of this kind of restraint dawns on me.

Lucas can do anything he wants to me, in any position, and I can't do anything to stop him.

He straddles my legs, immobilizing them against the bed, and fear prickles at me again, chasing away some of the post-orgasm endorphins. A second later, I feel something cool and wet trickle between my ass cheeks and realize my anxiety is justified.

Lucas poured some lube on me.

"Don't, please." I yank at the cuffs chaining me to the pole, my heartbeat skyrocketing. "Please . . . not like this."

"It's okay, beautiful." Ignoring my attempts to wriggle away, Lucas stuffs two thick pillows under my hips, propping me up so I'm almost on all fours. "I told you, you're going to be fine."

But I won't be. I know that from experience. He'll tear me, his cock too long and thick for my body to accept that way. He's played with my ass several times in recent weeks, using his fingers and a couple of small toys, but he's never pushed beyond that and I'd foolishly begun to hope that he wouldn't, that he'd respect my wishes in that regard. I should've known better, of course.

His lust knows no boundaries when it comes to me.

He leans over me, the heat of his body warming my chilled skin, and I realize I'm trembling, my back covered with a layer of cold sweat. His hand strokes the side of my hip, and I flinch before I can control my reaction, my muscles locking tight in anticipation of the pain to come.

"Yulia . . ." He gathers my hair to the side, moving it off my sweat-dampened back, and I feel his lips brush over my nape at the same time as his stiff cock presses against my leg. "I won't hurt you, baby, I promise."

Not hurt me? I want to scream that it's a lie, that he wouldn't restrain and blindfold me if he intended to make love to me sweetly, but I don't get a chance because at that moment, Lucas's fingers slip between my legs and find my clit. Pressing on it gently, he kisses my neck again, and to my shock, I feel a twinge of something that's not fear . . . a hot, tight pleasure that somehow coexists with my panic.

"I won't hurt you," he repeats, his words whisper soft as his lips trail over my shoulder, and some of my anxiety ebbs, melting away in the heat that's starting to pulse through me. By now, Lucas knows everything about my body, and he uses that knowledge without qualms, his fingers teasing out sensations that should've been beyond my reach.

The second orgasm catches me by surprise, and I pant into the mattress as waves of pleasure ripple through me. I haven't forgotten what awaits me, but it's hard to cling to fear when one's brain is swimming in endorphins. And Lucas is not done pleasuring me yet. His hand finds my pussy entrance, and one long finger pushes inside, unerringly locating my G-spot. Before long, the tension coils in my core again, and another orgasm, albeit a weaker one this time, rocks my body.

"No more, please," I moan when his finger withdraws from my spasming channel and circles my swollen clit. "I can't do it again."

"Yes, baby, you can." His teeth graze my neck, and then he whispers in my ear, "Again and again, as many times as it takes."

It takes two more orgasms, as it turns out. Or at least that's how many Lucas forces on me before my muscles turn to mush and I'm too exhausted to come again. By that point, I've stopped worrying about the dangerous slickness between my ass cheeks—I've stopped thinking, period. So when his fingers withdraw from my dripping-wet pussy and slide up between my cheeks, I just lie there, dazed and limp, barely reacting as two of those long fingers push into my ass, one after another, gliding in with almost no resistance.

"That's it, sweetheart. There's a good girl," Lucas croons as I remain relaxed, accepting his two fingers without clenching. It's still not my favorite sensation; the fullness feels odd and invasive, but there's no pain and I'm too drained to resist as he begins to fuck my ass with those fingers, pumping them in and out slowly. "Such a good girl . . ." The smooth, gliding rhythm is strangely hypnotic, making me feel like my mind is disconnected from my body. Dimly, I'm aware that I should be afraid, that I should be protesting this violation, but it doesn't seem worth the effort, particularly when Lucas's other hand presses gently on my clit again, coaxing a twinge of pleasure from my overstimulated flesh.

I'm so immersed in that disconnected state that it doesn't frighten me when his fingers withdraw and something smooth and thick presses against my back opening instead. My body remains limp and relaxed, even when I feel a massive, stretching pressure and hear Lucas groan under his breath, "Fuck, baby, you're tight . . ." The pressure intensifies, edging into pain, and it's only then that some of my fear returns, along with the urge to tighten against the intrusion.

"No, sweetheart, don't tense. Just breathe through it." The command comes in a low, strained voice, and I realize what this self-restraint is costing Lucas, how tightly he's reining himself in to avoid hurting me. Oddly, the knowledge calms me somewhat, and I take slow, deep breaths, trying to keep my muscles relaxed.

"Yes, that's it," he praises hoarsely, and I feel him begin to penetrate me, the broad head of his cock stretching the tight ring of muscle at my entrance. It burns, the urge to clamp down almost unbearable, but I continue to breathe evenly, and slowly, he advances, working his massive cock into me millimeter by millimeter.

When the head is all the way in, he pauses, stroking my hip soothingly, and after a few moments, I feel the stinging burn subside. I'm able to relax a bit more, and Lucas resumes his slow advance. As he pushes deeper into me, however, my calm flees. He's big, far too big.

My heartbeat picks up, my breathing turning shallow and frantic. The slickness of the lube reduces friction, but it doesn't alter his size, and my insides churn as Lucas forces more of himself into me, stretching me past my limits. Overwhelmed, I whimper into the mattress, and he kisses my nape, the tender gesture a stark contrast to the merciless invasion of my body.

"Just a little more," he murmurs, and I realize that I inadvertently tightened around him, trying to prevent him from going deeper. "You can take it, baby."

No, I can't, I want to protest, but all I can do is make an incoherent noise, something between a grunting moan and a whimper. I'm shaking and sweating, my hands clutching at the metal pole I'm handcuffed to. This is nothing like the horrific pain Kirill inflicted on me that day, but in its own way, it's just as agonizing. Lucas's slow, careful movements allow me to feel his length fully . . . to absorb the immense, overwhelming pressure forcing my insides apart. His cock seems to fill every part of me, violating and possessing me at the same time, taking me to a place where darkness and eroticism collide, twisting together in some perverse symphony.

"Fuck, Yulia, you feel amazing," Lucas groans, and I realize he's in me fully, his balls pressing against my sex. His hand is still between my legs, his fingers putting pressure on my clit, and I bite back a cry as he shifts inside me, my stomach roiling at the strange sensation. "You're tight . . . so fucking tight." He presses harder on my clit, two of his fingers catching it in a scissor-like grip, and sharp, unexpected pleasure jolts my core, making me gasp out loud.

"Yes, there it is, beautiful . . ." Lucas's voice brims with dark satisfaction. "You can do it. Come for me one more time." His fingers begin to move in that scissoring motion, and to my shock, my body tightens on a wave of heat. The extreme fullness inside me both hampers and enhances the sensations, the pulsing ache from my clit warring with the agony from my overstretched ass. His cock feels like a steel pipe inside me, but the way his fingers are touching me makes my insides cramp in a different, distinctly pleasurable way. I cry out, trembling at the impending rush of orgasm, and Lucas grips my clit harder, pinching it almost painfully.

"That's it, just like that, baby . . ." He pinches my clit again, and helplessly, I explode, my abused nerve endings electrified by his rough touch. My body spasms over and over again, clenching around his thick length, and I sob at the painful ecstasy, at the scorching wrongness of it all. The pleasure is dark and brutal, and when he begins to move inside me, the thrust and drag of his cock sends me spiraling higher, the foreign sensations enhanced by the blindfold and the cold steel around my wrists. I don't know how long it takes before Lucas comes, his hot seed flooding my raw insides, but by the time he withdraws from me and unlocks my handcuffs, all I can do is lie there, weak and shaking, my ass burning and my clit pulsing with residual aftershocks.

Silently, he draws me into his arms, and I cry against his chest, feeling both broken and freed.

The past with Kirill is officially behind me. Every part of me now belongs to Lucas, for better or for worse.

CHAPTER FORTY-FOUR

❖ YULIA ❖

At breakfast, Lucas is unusually quiet, his gaze trained on me thoughtfully, and I have to fight a blush every time I look up from my plate and see those pale eyes watching me. I want to ask him what he's thinking, but some bizarre shyness keeps me silent. It doesn't help that I'm sore, my every movement a reminder of what occurred between us. He didn't tear me like I feared, but I'm still very much aware that something large and thick had been inside me, taking me places I never knew I could go . . . making me feel things I never knew I could feel.

To expedite the meal, I make quick work of my mushroom-spinach quiche and get up to take my plate to the sink. When I return to the table to get Lucas's plate, he surprises me by catching my arm, his long fingers closing around my wrist in an unbreakable grip.

"Yulia." His eyes glint with something indefinable. "That was delicious, thank you."

"Oh." I blink. "You're welcome." I expect him to let go of my wrist at that point, but he continues holding it without saying anything else.

"Um, let me get your plate . . ." Awkwardly, I reach for it with my other hand, but he moves it to the side, out of my reach.

"I'll get it myself, don't worry. Yulia . . ." He inhales deeply. "Are you all right?"

"I'm fine." My face burns all the way to the roots of my hair, but I force myself not to avert my gaze like some blushing virgin. "Everything's fine."

"Good." His eyes darken. "I didn't want to hurt you."

"You didn't." I swallow. "Not much, at least."

Lucas studies me for a few more moments, then nods, seemingly satisfied. Releasing my wrist, he stands up and carries his plate to the sink. He washes it along with my plate, and I just stand there, unsure whether this odd conversation is over. Finally, I decide to leave the kitchen, but before I can walk out, Lucas wipes his hands on a paper towel and turns toward me.

In a few long strides, he closes the distance between us, stopping less than a foot in front of me. "Just so you know," he says quietly, "I'd never truly harm you. You *are* mine, but that doesn't mean I'd ever abuse you. Your happiness matters to me, Yulia. You can believe me or not, but it's the truth."

I open my mouth, then close it, unable to form a coherent sentence. This is the closest Lucas has ever come to telling me how he feels—and to acknowledging hurtful things said in the heat of jealousy. Yet there's no regret on his face, no real apology in his words. What he said last night is the absolute truth—in this relationship, I have all the rights of a slave—and he's not about to deny it. What he's promising, however, is to be a good owner, and strangely, I do find that reassuring. Last night—any night, really—he could've hurt me badly, but he didn't, and as I look at the hard man in front of me, I know with sudden certainty that he never will.

It may be stupid of me, but I trust my captor—in this, at least.

Before I can formulate how to tell him this, Lucas bends his head, kissing me on the mouth, and walks out of the kitchen, leaving me standing there dazed . . . and filled with new, fragile hope.

* * *

We don't discuss the issue of me cooking for the guards again, but a week later, I get a delivery of restaurant-grade kitchen equipment, everything from an enormous oven to huge pots and pans. Diego and

Eduardo spend two days remodeling the kitchen and installing everything, and when they're done, I have everything I need to cook for a small army.

And by the time the next week is through, that's exactly what I find myself doing. As soon as Lucas leaves for work, I get busy preparing for the madness that is lunch. Diego and Eduardo must've told the other guards that Lucas relented, and the kitchen teems with visitors from ten in the morning until late into the afternoon. And then the dinner rush begins. One day, seventy-nine guards stop by—I count, just to make sure I'm not exaggerating—and I realize I'm going to have to do something to manage the situation. Lucas is remarkably stoic about everything, putting up with the insane disruption of our routine without any complaints, but I'm sure he won't let this go on forever. And I myself miss having meals with just the two of us—or three, if Misha comes over. There's a huge difference between giving a few leftovers to the guards and running what is quickly becoming an all-day restaurant operation. By the time dinner is over, I'm exhausted to the point of passing out, and several times, I do pass out in the living room as we watch TV—a situation that usually results in Lucas carrying me to bed and fucking my brains out before letting me go back to sleep.

There's also another, more tricky concern.

"Lucas, are the guards defraying any of the food expenses?" I ask him one morning as I mix up batter for *blini*—Russian-style crepes. "Or is Esguerra paying for the ingredients?"

"No, and no," Lucas replies, watching me with a hooded stare from the table. I have no idea if he wants the crepes, or if it's my tiny shorts that have him intrigued, but there's a distinct look of hunger on his starkly masculine face.

Refusing to let it distract me, I put down the whisk on a paper towel and frown at Lucas. "No? But this is a lot of food—and some of the ingredients are really expensive."

"So what?" His gaze travels over my body, lingering on the sliver of stomach exposed by my tank top. "You're enjoying this, and we can afford it."

I tug down the shirt and wait for his eyes to meet mine again. "We?"

"Sure," Lucas says without blinking. "I told you, Esguerra pays me well, and I've accumulated a nice stash over the years."

"Right." I decide that he misspoke with that pronoun, and return to the topic at hand. "But that still doesn't mean you should pay out of pocket for everyone's food," I say. "I mean, we're talking hundreds of dollars a day."

Lucas shrugs. "All right. If you're worried, I'll tell the guards to start paying for their meals. Your food is certainly good enough for a high-end restaurant, so I think it's a good idea if you charged like one."

"Seriously?" I stare at him. "You want me to run a real restaurant?"

"Sweetheart, I don't know if you're aware of this, but you *are* running a real restaurant." Lucas gets up to walk over to me. His eyes gleam as he stops in front of me and says, "A very good restaurant, as evidenced by the fact that a third of the guards come by at least once a day. And the rest . . . Well, many are still stuck on the crash, but most who don't come simply can't—they have duties that prevent them from leaving their posts."

"Oh." I hadn't realized my food was that popular, though the seventy-nine visitors that one day should've given me a clue.

"Yes, oh." Lucas reaches out to brush a strand of hair off my forehead. "You've been having fun with this, so I haven't said anything, but now that we're talking about it, I think it's a good idea to make the fuckers pay, and pay well. That might weed out some of the cheaper bastards and reduce the workload for you."

"All right," I agree after a moment of deliberation. "If you think that would be okay, I'll try."

* * *

I follow Lucas's suggestion with trepidation, certain that no one in their right mind would want to pay for my cooking when they could eat in the cafeteria for free. The main reason I do it is because I don't want to bankrupt Lucas with my hobby. He's been beyond generous with me, but I can't ask him to subsidize everyone's meals forever. Also, I'm not exactly opposed to a reduced workload; as fun of a challenge as this has been, laboring in the kitchen for ten-plus hours a day is hard work. I'm so tired I'm having to wear concealer to hide my undereye circles, and I know if Lucas notices that, he might put a stop to the whole operation.

My health is still his top worry.

To my surprise, when I post the prices—genuine high-end restaurant prices, written in black marker on a sheet of paper pinned to the front door—nobody so much as voices a peep of protest. By the time the day is over, I make over six million Colombian pesos—nearly two thousand US dollars.

Stunned, I show the haul to Lucas. "They paid. Can you believe it? They actually paid."

"I can, unfortunately." He glowers at the pile of money on the table. "They're not as cheap as I'd hoped."

And so the madness continues. My business—and I have to think of it as such now—is very lucrative, but it's also exhausting. I do everything from the cooking to the serving to the cleaning. By the time another three weeks have gone by, I realize that if I'm going to operate as a restaurant, I'm going to need to either get help or limit the scope of what I'm doing.

"I think I'm going to serve only lunch," I say to Lucas as I scrub the pots and pans left over from dinner. "And if you don't mind, I'll put out a few tables in the back yard, make it into a sit-down cafe of sorts instead of giving everyone takeout. That way, if more people come than can be comfortably seated during open hours, they'll have to make a reservation for another day."

"That's an excellent idea," Lucas says, coming over to help me lift a heavy pan out of the sink. "For tonight, why don't you go to bed early? I'll finish up here and join you."

"No, that's okay, I can do it," I say, but he brushes me aside and goes to work scrubbing the remaining pots. Seeing that he has no intention of budging, I sigh and thank him before wearily trudging off to take a shower.

At this point, I'll take any help I can get.

* * *

The next day, I start implementing my ideas. At first, some guards grumble about being deprived of dinner, but when Lucas shows up and gives them a glacial stare, all the grumbling stops. By the time the week is over, I've successfully transitioned from a disorganized all-day takeout operation to a small and highly sought-after lunch cafe.

"I'm booked solid for the next three weeks," I tell Lucas in gleeful disbelief as we go on a morning walk—

our first in almost two weeks. "Seriously, I'm having to take reservations for the next month."

"Of course, what did you expect?" He gives me a warm smile. "I've always told you your cooking is amazing."

I grin, delighted at the praise. I suspect Lucas is more excited about the return of our private dinners than my cafe's popularity, but that doesn't change the fact that he's been incredibly supportive of my venture. I'm sure the profit the cafe makes doesn't hurt, but he was on board with everything even when my hobby was a financial drain.

"What have you been doing with the money?" I ask, wondering for the first time what happens to the pile of cash I give Lucas every night. "Do you deposit it somewhere? Invest it?"

"I put it into your account, of course. What else?"

"My account?" My eyebrows crawl up. "What do you mean, my account?"

"The account I opened for you in the Cayman Islands," Lucas says casually, as if that sort of thing is done every day. "Well, technically, it's in both of our names, as per the advice of my accountant, but you're the primary account holder."

"What?" I stop and frown at him, certain I must be misunderstanding something. "You've been depositing that money into an account for me? Why?"

"Because it's your money," he says, as if it's obvious. "You earned it, so what else would I do with it?"

"Um, keep it, seeing as I'm cooking with the ingredients you buy using equipment that you paid for?"

"Yes, but I'm not the one doing the actual cooking," Lucas says reasonably. "Besides, I do deduct food expenses before making the deposits. The money going into the account is pure business profit—*your* business profit."

My head spins as I stare at him. "But what do you expect me to do with that money? And how much money is there by now, anyway?"

"As of yesterday, there's a little over forty thousand dollars." He resumes walking, and I hurry after him, feeling like I've fallen through a rabbit hole. "As to what you want to do with it, it's up to you. If you want, I can ask my portfolio manager to invest it for you, or if you feel like playing the stock market yourself, you can do that too. Or just leave it sitting there until you have a better idea of what you want to do with it."

My Alice-in-Wonderland feeling intensifies. "I can play the stock market?"

"If that's what you want to do. Or you can leave it to the professionals—Winters, my portfolio manager, is quite good."

Right. Because everyone knows captives have access to topnotch portfolio managers. My mind races as I try to work through the implications of this. "Lucas, are you . . ." I glance at him cautiously. "Are you going to set me free?"

He stops and turns to face me, his casual demeanor gone without a trace. "What do you mean by that?" His pale eyes glint dangerously. "Are you saying you want to leave?"

"No, but"—I swallow, my pulse kicking up—"would you let me if I did?" Could Lucas have changed his mind about our relationship? Is it possible he's grown to care about me enough to give me this choice?

He steps toward me, his broad shoulders blocking out the sun streaming through the trees. "Never," he says with harsh finality. "You're not leaving me. You can do whatever you want, run a thousand restaurants, make millions if you feel like it, but you'll do it by my side. I'm not letting you go, Yulia—not now, not ever."

I stare up at him, my heart pounding with a contradictory mixture of dismay and elation. "Never? But what if you get tired of me?"

"That's not going to happen."

"You can't say that for sure—"

"Yes, I can." He steps even closer, forcing me to back up against a tree. Bracing his palms on the thick trunk behind me, he leans in, his eyes gleaming. "I've never wanted another woman the way I want you. You're like a fire under my skin. I want you every minute of every day. It doesn't matter how often we fuck; the moment I pull out, I want to be in you again, feeling your wet, silky heat, smelling you ... tasting you." He draws in a deep breath, his muscular chest expanding, and I feel my own breathing quicken as his hard pecs touch my peaked nipples. My palms press against the tree behind me, the rough bark digging into my skin. I'm caged by him, surrounded, the fire that he just talked about burning under my skin as well.

Involuntarily, my tongue comes out to moisten my lips, and I see Lucas's eyes darken.

"Yulia . . ." He presses his lower body against mine, and I feel the hard swell in his jeans. "I can't stop wanting you, no matter what I do," he says in a low, thick voice. "Every night, when I hold you, I think that maybe tomorrow will be the day when this obsession lessens, when I can go a few hours without thinking about you, without craving you like a fucking drug, but that's not what happens. I wake up just as addicted, and you know what, baby?"

"What?" I manage to whisper, my mouth dry and my pulse hammering. What Lucas is saying, the way he's looking at me . . .

"I kind of like it." He lowers his head until his mouth hovers less than a centimeter from mine. I can smell the bergamot of Earl Grey on his breath, see the darkness of his pupils and the blue-gray rings of irises surrounding them. "You give me something I didn't know I wanted, and I'm not about to let it slip away."

"What . . ." I inhale, prickles of heat racing up and down my spine. "What do I give you?"

"This." His lips ghost over mine, the tenderness of the kiss contrasting with the savage hunger I feel in him. "You. Whichever way I want." His mouth trails over my jaw, warm and soft on my skin, and I close my eyes, a moan escaping my lips as my head involuntarily tips back. I feel hot and dizzy, my body thrumming with a dark, pulsing heat that has nothing to do with the mid-morning sun beaming down on the rainforest canopy above us. I'm drunk on Lucas, high on whatever chemical cocktail my brain cooks up in his presence. He's not telling me anything I didn't already know—his sexual obsession with me has been obvious from the beginning—yet the needy part of me searches for a deeper meaning in his erotically charged words, tries to decipher them like a puzzle. Could this be his way of telling me he cares about me? That he loves me, even?

I open my eyes, fighting the drugged sensation so I can find the courage to ask, and then I hear it.

A woman's peal of laughter, followed by the sound of twigs snapping under someone's feet.

Lucas must've heard it too, because he releases me and spins around, keeping me protectively behind him.

A second later, a small, dark-haired girl sprints out from behind the trees, her tanned face glowing with a smile and her white sports bra soaked with sweat. Two steps behind her is a tall, darkly handsome man. He's wearing nothing but a pair of gray running shorts, his bronzed, muscular body gleaming with perspiration and his white teeth bared in a grin.

His blue eyes meet mine from behind the shelter of Lucas's body, and the heat inside me turns to ice.

It's Julian and Nora Esguerra.

They must've been out for a run.

Seeing us, they stop, breathing heavily. Their smiles disappear without a trace.

"Hey there," Lucas says calmly, seemingly oblivious to the tension crackling in the air. "How's your run?"

"Hot. Humid. You know, the usual," Esguerra responds in the same casual manner, but I see the hard set of his jaw as he steps forward to stand next to Nora. He towers over her petite frame, his biceps almost the same width as her slender waist. A ray of sunlight falls across his face, and I notice a faint white scar on his left cheekbone. It runs all the way to the top of his eyebrow, crossing his left eye.

His fake left eye, I remember with a cold shudder. He lost the real one after the plane crash I'd caused.

"Sorry, we didn't mean to interrupt," Nora says, her cool tone belying her apology. Her dark eyes travel from me to Lucas, then back to me as she adds, "It's my fault. We don't usually run this way, but I went off our usual path today."

Lucas's massive shoulders rise in a brief shrug. "It's your estate. You can go wherever you wish." His voice is still unruffled, but the muscles in his arms tighten, and when I glance at Esguerra, I see him staring at me, his gaze menacing in its intensity.

The ice inside me spreads all the way down to my toes. I'm not afraid for myself, but I can't bear the thought of endangering Lucas, who's standing in front of me like a human shield. He's ready to fight for me, I can feel it.

To protect me, he'll go up against Esguerra and die—if not in the fight itself, then afterwards, at the hands of two hundred guards presumably loyal to their boss.

"Lucas," I say quietly, curling my fingers around his wrist. "Come. We should go."

He doesn't move, and neither does Esguerra. The two men appear to be rooted in place, their powerful muscles bunched tight as they glare at each other. Lucas is a couple of centimeters taller and slightly thicker in the chest than Esguerra, but I have a feeling they'd be evenly matched in a fight. Violence is the language they speak; it's there in the scars on their bodies and the savagery in their eyes.

If the line of trust is crossed, only one of them will leave this forest alive.

Apparently reaching the same conclusion, Nora says softly, "Yes, Julian, we should go." Parroting my gesture, she wraps her slim fingers around her husband's broad wrist, her tiny hand appearing childlike next to his. Esguerra tenses further, and for a moment, I'm certain he'll twist out of her grasp, shaking her off with the ease of an adult pushing away a clinging toddler, but he doesn't.

"Yes," he says, making a visible effort to relax. "You're right. Let's go. I have some work to do."

Nora nods and drops her hand, turning away. "Race you!" she yells at Esguerra over her shoulder, and with one last glance in our direction, she sprints away, disappearing into the trees. Her husband follows, and a few moments later, we're alone again.

Lucas turns to face me. "Are you all right?" he asks quietly.

"Of course." I force a smile to my lips. "Why wouldn't I be?" Stepping to the left, I slip around him and hurry toward his house, unwilling to stay in the forest even a moment longer.

I no longer have any doubts about my future here.

The next time Esguerra sees me, blood will be spilled.

CHAPTER FORTY-FIVE

❖ LUCAS ❖

The moment we get home, Yulia excuses herself and disappears into the bathroom to take a shower before starting lunch preparations. I consider joining her there, but decide against it.

As much as I want to comfort her after what happened, there's something I must do first.

Half an hour later, I walk into Esguerra's office. He must've just showered and changed, because his hair is wet as he stands up to face me, his eyes hard and his jaw stiff with anger.

I don't bother beating around the bush. "She's mine," I say harshly, approaching his desk. "Which part of that was unclear?"

Esguerra's gaze hardens even more. "I didn't touch her."

"No, but you want to, don't you?" I put my fists on the desk and lean forward. "You want to make her pay for what happened."

"Yes—and so should you." He mirrors my aggressive stance, the wide desk between us the only barrier to the violence simmering in the air. "Almost four dozen of our men died, and she's walking around like nothing happened . . . running a fucking restaurant on *my* property." His words drip with barely restrained rage. "Do you know that a reservation at 'Yulia's cafe' is the hottest commodity on the estate these days? The guards treat those slots like they're fucking gold."

I straighten, glaring at him. "Yes, of course I know." It was only yesterday that I had to break up a fight between two guards—a fight that resulted from a card game where the prize was an eleven-thirty reservation slot on Friday.

"And you're letting this happen?" Rounding the desk with sharp strides, Esguerra stops in front of me, fists clenched. "This is *my* estate. I'm letting her live because I owe you, but I do not want to be reminded of her existence every day, do you understand me?"

"Perfectly." I meet his furious look with one of my own. "Which is why I'm leaving."

Esguerra goes still, the anger transforming into something colder. "Excuse me?"

"That's what I came here to discuss," I say, folding my arms across my chest. Pushing down the rage boiling in my gut, I say in a steady tone, "You will never forgive her, and I will never give her up, so the way I see it, we have two options. We can kill each other over this, or I can take her—and myself—out of the picture."

"You're quitting?"

"If that's what you want." I give him a level look. "We work well together, but it may be time to go our separate ways. I'll train my replacement before I go, of course. Thomas is an excellent pilot, so you'll be fine there, and Diego is smart and loyal; he'll make a good second-in-command for you. Or . . ." I let my voice trail off.

Esguerra's eyebrows snap together. "Or what?"

"Or we can figure out a way for us to work together without me living here." I pause, letting that sink in. "Before you decided to make this compound your permanent home, we went wherever the business took us. It was nice to settle down here—and certainly safer for you and Nora, given that situation with Al-Quadar—but you know as well as I do that we've had to give up a few lucrative opportunities because you wanted to limit travel."

His nostrils flare. "What exactly are you suggesting?"

"When you were in a coma, I ran the whole organization. I handled everything from suppliers to customers, and I got to know every aspect of the business. If you want—if you trust me enough—I can be more than the second-in-command working by your side. I can represent us internationally, do whatever is necessary to grow the business abroad."

All emotion fades from Esguerra's face. "You want to be my partner."

"You could call it that, though an executive operations manager might be a more accurate label. You'd have the final say on major decisions, but I would run the new ventures and keep an eye on our existing operations in person. I could set up base someplace central, like Europe or Dubai, and do as much travel as necessary to keep things running smoothly."

"You've thought this through."

"Yes. I've known for some time that this won't work long term."

"Because of *her*."

"Yes, because of Yulia." I hold his icy gaze. "I'm not about to let anything happen to her."

"And if I don't agree to this?"

"Your business, your choice," I say. "I like working with you, but I have other options. For one thing, I can go legit and open a security firm somewhere. If you don't want this, just say the word, and I'll be gone."

He stares at me, and I know what he's thinking. He can't let me leave—I know too much about the inner workings of his business—so he has two choices: kill me or agree to my proposition. I gaze back at him calmly, ready for either possibility. I know I'm taking a risk, pushing him like this, but I don't see any other way to resolve this situation. Yulia can't spend the rest of her life hiding in my house and trying not to draw Esguerra's attention. At some point, something's going to go wrong, and when it does, things are going to get ugly.

I have to take her away before that happens.

Just when I think Esguerra has decided my loyalty isn't worth it, he sighs and steps back, his hands uncurling at his sides. "Does she really mean that much to you?" There's weary resignation in his voice. "Can't you find another pretty blonde to fuck?

I raise my eyebrows. "Could you find another petite brunette?"

A humorless smile stretches across his face. "It's like that, huh?"

"She's my everything," I say without blinking. "So yes, I guess it's like that."

Esguerra looks at me, his smile fading. Then he says abruptly, "Ten percent of profits from the new ventures, plus the same salary—that's my offer."

"Seventy percent," I reply without missing a beat. "I'll be doing all the work, so it's only fair."

"Twenty percent."

"Sixty."

"Thirty."

"Fifty, and that's my final offer."

"Forty-five."

I shake my head, though I couldn't care less about those five percent. "Fifty percent," I repeat. If Esguerra is to respect me as a partner, I need to stand my ground. It'll make for a better working relationship longer term. "Take it or leave it."

He studies me coolly, then inclines his head. "All right. Fifty percent of the new ventures' profit."

"Deal." I extend my hand, and we shake on it. "I'll get the ball rolling, so we can be out of your hair soon," I say, releasing his hand and stepping back. "Just one more thing . . ."

Esguerra's mouth tightens. "What is it?"

"You know as well as I do that our line of work is dangerous, especially out there, beyond the compound," I say. "Given that, I need your promise that you won't *ever* come after Yulia or her family. No matter what happens to me."

Esguerra nods curtly. "You have my word."

* * *

That evening, Yulia is quiet and withdrawn, her gaze trained on her plate throughout most of the meal despite her brother's presence at our table. Several times, Michael tries to engage her in conversation, but after getting only monosyllabic responses, he gives up and quickly finishes his meal.

"What's up with her?" he mutters as I walk him to the guards' barracks while Yulia stays behind to clean up. "Is she mad at me or something?"

"It has nothing to do with you," I say. "She's just worried about something."

"What?" The boy shoots me an anxious glance. "Did something happen?"

"No." I smile reassuringly. I've grown to like Yulia's brother over the past few weeks, and I don't want him to worry either. "She thinks it has, but she's wrong."

The boy frowns in confusion. "So everything is fine?"

"Yes, Michael," I say as we approach the building. "Everything is fine, I promise."

He gives me a doubtful look, but when we stop in front of the entrance, he says gruffly, "Tell Yulia I said, 'Good night and stop worrying.' She's such a worrywart sometimes."

"She is, isn't she?" I grin at the kid. "And you tell Diego that I'm going to need to talk to him first thing tomorrow, okay?"

He nods and goes into the building, and I walk back home. When I get there, I find Yulia sitting in the lounge chair in the library, her nose buried in a book.

"Hey, beautiful," I say, crossing the room. "What are you reading?"

She looks up. "*Gone Girl.*" She puts down the book and stands up. "I should probably go shower. I'm tired."

"Yulia." I catch her wrist as she tries to walk past me. "We have to talk."

She hesitates, then says, "All right, let's talk. Lucas" She draws in an unsteady breath. "You know this can't go on forever. Sooner or later, you and Esguerra will come to blows because of me, and I can't bear that. If anything happened to you—" Her voice breaks. "You have to let me go."

"No." I pull her toward me, my gut clenching at the mere suggestion. "I'm not letting you go."

"You have to." Her gaze turns imploring. "It's the only way."

"No, baby." I move my hands up to clasp her upper arms. "There's another alternative. We're going to leave together."

"What?" Yulia's lips part in shock. "What do you mean?"

"I'm going to oversee the expansion of Esguerra's organization," I explain. "There will be quite a bit of travel involved, so we won't be living here. We'll set up base somewhere in Europe or the Middle East—you can help me figure out exactly where."

Her eyes are impossibly wide as she stares up at me. "You want to leave here? But it's your home. What about—"

"I've lived here less than two years," I say, amused. "Another place can be home just as easily. This is Esguerra's estate, not mine."

"But I thought you liked it here."

"I do—but I'll like it elsewhere too." Moving one hand to her chin, I tilt her face up. "Anywhere you are will be my home, beautiful."

She exhales shakily. "But—"

"No buts." I press my thumb to her soft lips. "I'm not sacrificing anything, believe me. I'll be Esguerra's fifty-percent partner on these new ventures, so if all goes well, we'll get filthy rich."

"We?" she whispers when I take my thumb away.

"Yes, you and me." And before she can ask, I add, "We'll take your brother back to his parents. Things are quieting down in Ukraine, so it's safe for him to return. We'll visit him as often as you want, of course, and if he wishes to stay with us, that's also an option."

"Lucas . . ." Her forehead creases in a frown. "Are you sure about this? If you're doing it for me—"

"I'm doing it for us." Lowering my hands, I cup her ass and pull her against me, my cock hardening as I feel her legs press against mine. Holding her gaze, I say, "I want to know that you're safe, that no one will ever be able to take you away from me. You'll have the best bodyguards money can buy, men who are loyal to me and me only. We'll build a fortress of our own, beautiful—a place where you won't have to fear anyone or anything."

Yulia's palms press against my chest. "A fortress?" Her eyes gleam with hope and a strange kind of unease.

"Yes." I tighten my grip on her ass, enjoying the feel of her firm flesh even through the thick material of her shorts. Forcing my mind off the lust pounding in my veins, I clarify, "Nothing as extreme as Esguerra's compound, but a safe place of our own. Nobody will be able to touch you there."

"Except you," she murmurs, her slender hands fisting in my shirt.

"Yes." My lips twist into a dark smile. "Except me." She'll never be safe from me, no matter where she goes or what she does. I will protect her from everyone else, but I will never set her free.

"When ..." She runs her tongue over her lips. "When are we leaving?"

"Soon," I say, my eyes following the movement of her tongue. "Maybe in a month or less."

And before my balls can explode, I reach for the zipper of her shorts and capture her lips in a deep, hungry kiss.

CHAPTER FORTY-SIX

❖ YULIA ❖

The next month zooms by in a flurry of work and departure preparations. I continue operating the cafe, figuring the extra money can't hurt, though I do stop ordering new food supplies and limit the menu as various products run out. The cafe keeps me busy, which is good because Lucas works nonstop, frequently putting in eighteen- and twenty-hour days. In a span of four weeks, he trains Diego to oversee the guards on the compound, sets up manufacturing facilities in Croatia, finds clients for the weapons that will be made at those facilities, and purchases a house on the Karpass Peninsula in Cyprus—a country we settled on as our home base due to its warm climate, strategic proximity to Europe and the Middle East, and relatively high percentage of population fluent in either English or Russian.

"The house is on a cliff overlooking a private beach," Lucas says when he shows me photos of the new property. "It has only five bedrooms, but there's an infinity pool, a balcony on the second floor, and a fully equipped gym in the basement. Oh, and I'm having them remodel the kitchen, so it'll be done exactly to your specifications."

"It's beautiful," I say, looking through each photo. Though "only" five bedrooms, the house is large and spacious, with an open floor plan and floor-to-ceiling windows facing the Mediterranean. And most importantly for Lucas, it's set on ten acres of land that he intends to fence in and protect via bodyguards, guard dogs, and a variety of surveillance drones.

We *will be* living in a fortress—albeit a gorgeous, beachfront one.

It seems so surreal that I often feel the urge to pinch myself. The life Lucas is planning for us is like nothing I could've imagined when Esguerra's men came to extract me from that Moscow prison. I'm still Lucas's prisoner—the faint white marks where the trackers went in are a daily reminder of that—but the lack of freedom bothers me less nowadays. Maybe it's the needy little girl within me, but Lucas's fierce, unapologetic possessiveness reassures me almost as much as it frightens me.

I belong to him, and there's a comforting stability in that.

Of course, even if I could leave Lucas, I wouldn't. With every kiss, with every caring gesture big and small, my captor ties me to him a little tighter, makes me love him a little more. And though he doesn't say the words back, I'm increasingly certain that he loves me too, as much as a man like him is capable of loving anyone. What we have together is not normal, but neither are we. My "normal" ended with my parents' crash, and Lucas's may never have existed in the first place. But as I'm fast discovering, I don't need normal. My ruthless mercenary is giving me everything I've ever wanted, and when I stop to think about it, I'm seized by equal parts joy and fear.

Things are going so well I'm terrified something will happen to snatch it all away.

"Is everything okay?" Misha asks during dinner one day. Lucas is working late again, so it's just the two of us for the third night in a row. "You look worried."

"Do I?" Pushing my mushroom risotto away, I make a conscious effort to relax the tense muscles in my forehead. "I'm sorry, Mishen'ka. I'm just thinking, that's all."

Misha frowns over his quickly emptying plate. "What about?"

"This, that . . . the transition," I say with a shrug. "Nothing in particular." I don't want to tell my teenage brother that the future, though bright and shiny, scares me to the point of nightmares every night, that a cold, hard fist seems to be permanently lodged inside my chest, squeezing my heart every time I think of how fragile and fleeting happiness can be. Pushing the dark thought aside, I smile at Misha and say, "What about you? Are you excited about going home?"

"Yes, of course." Misha's face brightens as he reaches for a second serving of the risotto. "Lucas let me speak to my parents yesterday. Mom was crying, but they were happy tears, you know? And Dad is already planning all the things we're going to do together."

"Oh, that's wonderful." The knowledge of my upcoming separation from my brother is like an acid burn on my heart, but the joy in his eyes makes it all worthwhile. "How are they?"

Lucas showed me the surveillance photos taken of Misha's parents, and I can now picture them in my mind. Natalia Rudenko, Obenko's sister and Misha's adoptive mother, is a slim, stylish brunette who resembles her brother, while Misha's father, Viktor, is plump and balding—a typical middle-aged engineer. He's almost ten years older than his forty-something wife, and he looks it, but he has a kind face, and in many of the pictures I've seen, he gazes at his wife with a worshipful smile.

"They're good," Misha says. "Same, you know." His expression turns somber as he adds, "Mom's been grieving for Uncle Vasya, but Dad said she's doing better now. They've always known that his job was dangerous, so what happened wasn't a huge surprise. It helped that Lucas contacted them back then and told them I'm okay."

"Right." Lucas's message explained that I, Misha's long-lost sister, had come out of a long-term undercover assignment to take Misha someplace safe for a while. "So what did they say about that?"

"Well, they had a million questions, as you would expect, but for the most part, they were just relieved I'm returning home and"—he gives me a slightly bashful look—"going back to school."

I smile, more than a little relieved myself. It seems that the recent events have cooled some of my brother's enthusiasm for nontraditional career paths—at least for a while. "Will you have to take any extra classes to catch up?" I ask. It's already October, so Misha has missed at least a few weeks of ninth grade.

"No, I don't think so," he says, chowing down on the risotto. "We covered most of the subjects taught in school during UUR training."

"Oh, yes, that's right." I'd almost forgotten that the reason why I'd been able to start college at sixteen was because the curriculum for trainees had included math, science, history, and language studies at levels far beyond those taught to kids that age. "So you're more than caught up."

Misha nods, reaching for a cup of water next to his plate. "Yeah, I should be fine." He gulps down the water, and I study him, noticing again the leaner, harder lines of his face. With every day that passes, my baby brother grows up a little more, maturing right in front of my eyes. Soon, he won't be a boy at all, just like he's no longer the toddler of my memories.

My throat grows tight as I think again about him leaving. "I'm going to miss you," I say, trying not to sound as choked up as I feel. "A lot."

Misha puts down his cup. "I'll miss you too, Yulia." His expression is even more somber than before. "You'll come to visit, though, won't you?"

"Of course." Unable to sit still, I get up, swallowing the tears stinging the back of my throat. "We'll be just a three-hour flight away. Practically next door." At least when we're not traveling all over Europe, Asia, and the Middle East, as Lucas warned me we will have to. Pushing that knowledge aside, I say with forced brightness, "And you'll come visit us. During summers, school holidays, and such."

"Yeah, that's going to be great." Finishing his plate, Misha gets up too. "I'll be the envy of all my friends, vacationing in Cyprus like that."

"That's right." I smile, though all I want to do is cry. "You'll be the most popular boy in school."

"Oh, I was anyway," he says with a total lack of modesty. "So it's all good."

I laugh and walk around the table to hug him. He lets me, and even hugs me back, his sinewy arms sturdy and strong. When I pull away and look at him, I realize my baby brother has grown another couple of inches in the last month and get all choked up again.

"Oh, come on," Misha mutters as the tears I've been holding back spill out. Pulling me into another hug, he pats my back awkwardly. "Don't cry. Come on, it's going to be fine. We'll see each other often, and we'll email and Skype . . ."

"I know." I pull away and smile at Misha, wiping the wetness on my cheeks with the back of my hand. "It's just that I keep remembering how little you were, and now you're growing up so fast, changing into this young man . . ." I sniffle. "I'm sorry. I'm just being silly."

"Well, you are a girl," he says, scratching the back of his neck. "You're allowed, I guess."

I burst out laughing at that chauvinistic statement, and for the rest of the meal, we don't discuss the separation again.

* * *

On the afternoon before our departure, I throw a big party in Lucas's back yard, inviting all of my cafe's customers and anyone else who wants to come. Using the remaining food supplies, I make a variety of hors d'oeuvres and, with Lucas, Eduardo, and Diego's help, set up a couple of barbecue stations where I grill steaks, burgers, and lamb chops. Manning the grills is hot, sweaty work, but I feel elated as guard after guard comes up to me to say goodbye and express his gratitude for the gourmet meals.

"We're going to miss you here," one of the guards says gruffly. "Seriously, your cafe was the best food I've eaten."

"Thank you." I beam at him, then turn to smile at another guard who says something similar to me in Spanish. Most of these men are ex-soldiers of some kind, tough, scarred killers armed to the teeth, and to have them thank me like this touches me tremendously.

Of course, most guards here today are new recruits or those who didn't have friends among the victims of the crash, but I don't let that bother me. I know I'll never be fully accepted at Esguerra's estate—that's why we're leaving, after all—and to have so many people express regret at my departure is a gift beyond anything I could've expected.

"You're one lucky son of a bitch," a red-haired guard says to Lucas as I put a piece of medium-rare steak on his plate. "Seriously, man. Your girl's the best."

"I know," Lucas says and wraps a possessive arm around my waist. "Now move along, O'Malley. You're holding up the line."

After all the barbecue is eaten and the last of the hors d'oeuvres disappear off the plates, the party starts to wind down. Lucas leaves to get on yet another call with new suppliers, and Diego, Eduardo, and Misha carry the empty platters inside and collect all the trash.

Exhausted, I go in to wash my hands, and when I come out, I see that all the guards are gone. Only one person is standing in the middle of Lucas's yard, her curvy figure clad in her usual black dress.

Stunned, I stare at the maid who helped me escape. "Rosa? What are you doing here?"

She casts a nervous glance at the house, where Misha and the two guards are still cleaning up, then says hesitantly, "Do you have a moment? I was hoping to talk to you alone."

I automatically scan her for weapons. Finding nothing suspicious, I say, "Okay, sure. Want to take a little walk?"

She nods and disappears into the trees. I follow, both curious and uneasy. I'm fairly certain she won't physically attack me, but I don't know what she's after and that makes me nervous. At the same time, I recall what Lucas told me about the events in Chicago, and sympathy tempers my wariness.

I may not know Rosa's motivations, but I certainly understand what she's been through.

When I catch up to Rosa, she stops and turns to face me. "Yulia, I . . ." She takes a breath. "I wanted to thank you for what you told Lucas. Nora said she spoke to you, but I wasn't sure if you'd do it or not."

"Well, Nora didn't leave me much choice," I say drily, recalling the petite girl's graphic threat. "But you're welcome. I assume you and Nora are both okay?"

Rosa nods, flushing. "Yes. I was under house arrest for a while, and I don't have access to those keys anymore, but Señor Esguerra reinstated my position in the main house a few weeks ago."

I smile, genuinely happy on her behalf. "Good, I'm glad. And I guess I should thank you for helping me that time. It was very nice of you—"

To my surprise, Rosa shakes her head. "It wasn't nice," she mutters. "It was stupid. *I* was stupid."

The smile dies on my lips. "What do you mean?"

Rosa's face is now dark red. "I had a crush on Lucas, and I thought that if you were gone . . ." Her hands twist in her skirt. "I'm sorry. I don't know what I was thinking. It was just that I wanted to believe that he was different. But then he was keeping you like that and—" She stops, pressing her lips together.

"And it was ruining the image you had of him," I say, finally beginning to understand. "You thought that if you let me go, you'd be doing something good while increasing your chances with the man you want." Seeing the stricken look on her face, I stop, then say gently, "Except he's not really the man you want, is he?"

"No." Her brown eyes darken. "He's not. He never was. I made up the man I wanted, and I pinned him on the nearest handsome face."

"Oh, Rosa . . ." Giving in to a sudden impulse, I step forward and give her hand a comforting squeeze. "Listen to me," I say softly. "You're going to find the right person for you, and he might not be whom you imagined, but you'll want him anyway, flaws and all. It won't be perfect, but it will be real, and you'll know it—you'll feel it. You'll both feel it."

She swallows thickly and pulls her hand away. "Is that what it's like for you and Lucas?"

"Yes," I say, and the truth of that sears through me. "It's not tender and pretty like I thought it would be. Some might even say it's ugly. But it's us. It's our reality, our version of perfect. And you will also have that one day—your own version of perfect. It might not be what you expect, or with whom you expect, but it *will* make you happy."

The girl's lips tremble for a second; then her face goes blank and she steps back. "You should go," she says, her hands once again playing with the skirt of her dress. "They'll be looking for you if you don't return soon."

"Right."

I'm about to turn and go back when Rosa says quietly, "Goodbye, Yulia. I wish you and Lucas all the best. I really do."

"Thank you—and the same to you," I say, but Rosa is already walking away, her black-clad figure melting into the greenery of the rainforest and disappearing out of sight.

CHAPTER FORTY-SEVEN

❖ LUCAS ❖

I expected Yulia and her brother to sleep on our flight to Ukraine, but they spend the entire time talking. Whenever I stick my head out of the pilot's cabin to check on them, they're deep in conversation, and I go back, not wanting to intrude on their sibling time.

I'll have Yulia to myself soon enough.

When we approach Ukrainian airspace, I make contact with our men on the ground. Last week, they finally tracked down the last three known UUR associates and eliminated them as per my orders. To my disappointment, none of them were harboring Kirill, which means Yulia's former trainer is either completely off the grid or, as Yulia thought, the fucker ended up expiring from his injuries and we just haven't found his body. The latter possibility brings me little joy—I wanted to kill the bastard with my own hands—but it's better than the alternative. The men also tracked down the headmistress of Yulia's orphanage. The woman was already in jail for child abuse and trafficking, so I had to settle for sending in an assassin who cornered her in a bathroom and demonstrated just how much her victims suffered. The video of her death—all three hours of it—was the highlight of my Wednesday last week. Someday, I might show it to Yulia, but for now, I've decided not to, to avoid bringing back bad memories for her.

"You've been cleared to land," Thomas reports when I get him on the phone. I smile, satisfied that the bribe campaign we've been conducting is proving so effective. Despite the bloody war we've waged against UUR, most of Ukrainian bureaucrats are more than willing to look the other way—especially since Yulia's former agency was strictly off the books.

Nobody cares about a few officially nonexistent spies when fat checks are in play.

When we land at the private airport, there's an armored SUV waiting for us, and we go straight to Michael's parents' place. Thomas and two other guards ride along, while a dozen more of our men follow in other cars. I'm not expecting any trouble, but it's always good to be cautious when in hostile territory.

Bribes or not, Ukraine has little love for anyone connected to the Esguerra organization.

"Are you sure my brother will be safe?" Yulia asked me last night, and I assured her that thanks to our hacking and subsequent destruction of UUR's files, it's all but impossible to connect the adoptive son of two civilians to her, and by extension, to me and Esguerra. Just in case, though, I personally hired two bodyguards to watch over Michael and his family over the next few months. I don't think he's in danger, but I know how much the kid means to Yulia. And, to be honest, he's grown on me too. Yulia would probably be upset to hear this, but there's something about Michael that reminds me of myself at that age.

Vasiliy Obenko hadn't been entirely wrong to recruit him; the boy would've made an excellent agent had he completed his training.

On the ride from the airport, Yulia and Michael are both silent, and I know they're thinking of the upcoming separation. Theoretically, I could've hired more men to ensure Michael's safety and let him go home earlier, but I wanted to give Yulia more time with her brother, and I'm glad I did. The boy has come a long way from the defiant, sullen teenager who'd been fed lies about his sister. The two siblings are now as close as any I've seen, and I know that makes Yulia happy—which makes me happy in return.

If I could turn back the clock and wipe away all the pain in her past, I'd do it in a heartbeat. But since I can't, I have to settle for making sure she never has to suffer again.

She's mine, and I'm going to take care of her for the rest of our lives.

* * *

Michael's parents live on the fifth floor of an apartment building on the outskirts of Kiev. The two bodyguards I hired greet us at the entrance to the building and report that all is quiet. I thank them and give them the rest of the day off before instructing Thomas and the others to wait downstairs. There's no elevator, so Yulia, Michael, and I take the stairs.

Yulia walks a couple of steps ahead of me. She's wearing flat boots and stylish skinny jeans—both are her recent online purchases—and I can't tear my eyes away from her shapely ass, which flexes with every step she climbs.

"Dude, keep a lid on it for at least a few more minutes," Michael mutters, climbing the stairs next to me, and I shoot him a grin, not the least bit embarrassed that he caught me lusting after his sister.

"Why?" I reply in a low voice. "Your sister is hot. You didn't know that?"

"Ugh." He grimaces in disgust, and Yulia gives us a suspicious look over her shoulder.

"What are you guys talking about?" she asks as we clear the third-floor landing.

"Nothing," Misha says quickly, his face turning red. "Just guy stuff."

"Uh-huh." She gives us an exasperated look but doesn't press further, and we clear the remaining two flights in silence. I'm glad we don't run into any neighbors, because I have my M16 with me.

After what happened in Chicago, I don't go anywhere without a weapon.

When we reach the fifth floor, Yulia stops in front of apartment 5A and rings the doorbell.

My first hint that something is wrong is the white face of the trim, dark-haired woman who opens the door. It's Natalia Rudenko, Michael's adoptive mother—I recognize her hazel eyes from the surveillance photos. Instead of smiling and stepping forward to embrace her son, she swings the door wide and steps back, her lipsticked mouth trembling.

Instantly, I see why.

Wrapped around her stomach and partially concealed by the apron she's wearing is a tangle of wires and a black box with a blinking light.

"Mama?" Michael says uncertainly, stepping forward, and I instinctively grab his arm, yanking him back as I step in front of Yulia, shielding her from the bomb. My pulse jumps with a blast of adrenaline, terror and rage swamping me in a toxic shockwave.

Yulia, Misha, and a bomb.

Motherfucking fuck.

"It's okay, let the boy in," an accented male voice drawls in English. "He's not any safer out there than in here. There's enough to blow this whole building."

I don't move, though every instinct screams for me to rush in and attack, to protect Yulia and her brother. Only the knowledge that doing so means certain death for them keeps me still.

Calling upon all my years of battle experience, I block out the hammering beat of fear and assess the situation.

In addition to the woman, there are two men standing in the hallway. One of them, a portly, middle-aged man, is wired the same way as Michael's mother. I recognize his terrified face too. It's Viktor Rudenko, Michael's adoptive father. But he's not the one who holds my attention.

It's the massively built man standing behind him, his thin lips curled in a snarl of a smile.

Kirill Ivanovich Luchenko, the man we've been hunting.

He found us instead.

CHAPTER FORTY-EIGHT

❖ YULIA ❖

I've never known terror this intense, this all-consuming. Lucas is a human wall in front of me, but I can see around his powerful body, and the surreal tableau makes my stomach drop to my feet.

Kirill is standing in the brightly lit hallway behind Misha's parents, who are wrapped in tangled wires. There's a gun in his right hand, and in his left, he's clutching something small and black.

A detonator, I realize with nauseating panic.

He's got his thumb on the detonator.

"Come on in," he says in English, looking at Lucas and Misha before focusing on me. A grotesque smile stretches his mouth as his gaze meets mine. "Make yourself at home. We're all one happy family here, aren't we?"

Lucas doesn't move a muscle, even when Misha tries to shove him aside, his young face contorted with the same terror that holds me paralyzed. I know what's going through my brother's mind; like me, he's probably seen this kind of detonator in explosives training.

It's UUR's version of a suicide vest, one designed to be used only in the most desperate of circumstances. Kirill doesn't need to press a button for the explosive to go off; he just needs to take his thumb *off* the button.

If his thumb slips—if he's shot, for instance—the bomb will be triggered.

Lucas must've realized this too, because he's not reaching for the M16 slung across his back.

"Let me through," my brother hisses when Lucas still doesn't budge. "It's my parents. Fucking let me through!"

This time, I'm the one to catch Misha's arm. "Don't," I say quietly, and he freezes in place. I don't know if my brother thinks I have a plan, or if it's the false calmness of my voice, but he stops shoving at Lucas and stands still, staring fixedly into the hallway.

"You don't want to come in?" Kirill says. "Fine, we can do it the hard way."

In a blur of motion, he lifts his right hand and fires. The shot is muffled—Kirill's gun has a silencer on it—but the screams that follow are unmistakable. I convulsively leap forward, terrified for Lucas, but he's still standing there, refusing to budge even as my brother renews his efforts to get into the apartment.

The bullet hit Misha's father in the leg, I realize as I peer around Misha's struggling figure. The older man is on the floor, screaming as he clutches his bleeding leg, and Misha's mother is kneeling next to him, weeping hysterically.

"The next bullet goes into his head," Kirill says, and Misha stills again. "And the one after that, into her brain." He waves the gun at the crying woman. "Oh, and if any of you try to run, I'm going to shoot both of them immediately, and the bombs will go off before you make it down a single flight of stairs." His smile widens as he takes in our expressions. "Like I said, come in and make yourself at home."

"Lucas, please," I whisper when he still doesn't move. Bile churns thickly in my throat. "Please, we have to do this. We can't let him kill them in front of Misha." I have no idea if Kirill is crazy enough to sacrifice himself by setting off the explosives, but I have no doubt he'll shoot Misha's parents without a second thought.

"You. Drop your weapon before you come in," Kirill says, gesturing at Lucas with the gun. "You don't want this to go off by mistake." He lifts his left hand—the one with the detonator—to illustrate exactly what he means.

Without saying a word, Lucas reaches for the strap of his M16 and drops the weapon on the floor. Then, just as silently, he steps into the hallway.

Misha and I follow. My brother's face is deathly pale, his eyes wild with fear. I have no doubt I look the same way. Terror is a hollow, icy pit in my stomach. When Kirill had captured me before, I'd been on my own, and I could escape into the dark corners of my mind. But there's no escape here, not when the only two people I love are in danger next to me—in danger *because* of me.

I know why Kirill is doing something so reckless and insane. He's after me. He wants to punish me for what I did to him, and he doesn't care who gets hurt in the process. Lucas is still in front of me, his body forming a shield between me and my former trainer, but he won't be able to save me.

We have the numbers advantage and men on the ground, but Kirill has his thumb on that detonator.

"Come here, bitch," my former trainer says, his gaze swinging toward me. His dark eyes glint with rage and something close to madness. "You're the one I want."

Ignoring the sickening terror twisting my insides, I step around my brother, pushing him behind me, but Lucas blocks my way.

"She's not going anywhere." His voice is lethal steel.

"No?" Kirill lifts his gun, pointing it at Viktor Rudenko's temple. The man freezes, his screams dying down, and Kirill's eyes cut back to me as Natalia's weeping grows in volume. "Don't make me repeat myself."

"Lucas, let me go." I try to squeeze past him, but the narrow hallway is stuffed with furniture, and I almost trip on a stool placed in front of a tall mirror. Chills of horror race up and down my spine as Kirill's jaw hardens at Lucas's uncompromising stance. Frantically, I grip Lucas's arm and try to push him aside. "Please, Lucas, let me through."

He ignores me. Every muscle in his body is locked tight, and when I glance at his face, the subzero fury in his pale eyes spikes my terror even more.

He's not going to listen to reason.

To protect me, he's going to let Misha's parents die—and get himself killed in the process.

"Why do you want her?" he asks Kirill, his tone incongruously calm. "You know you're going to die here today."

"Do I?" Kirill laughs, the sound oddly high pitched, and for the first time, I notice the changes in his appearance. His hair is now more gray than brown, his face is bloated, and the body that had always been hard muscle looks merely thick instead. It's as if he's aged ten years over the last few months. "And what makes you think I care?"

Lucas's expression doesn't change. "I know you don't. That's why you're here, aren't you? To go out in a blaze of glory rather than live like the pathetic half-man you've become?" Contempt seeps into his voice.

"You should've just come to us from the beginning. I could've made it so much simpler for you, put you out of your dickless misery that much sooner."

What is Lucas doing? My heart pounds in horror as I watch Kirill's face contort with rage and his right hand come up, the gun pointing straight at Lucas's chest.

It's as if Lucas is trying to get himself shot.

And in the next instant, I realize that's exactly what he's doing. My captor is hoping to sacrifice himself and buy us some time. To do what, I'm not sure. We're on the fifth floor of a walk-up building. Even if the guards on the ground heard the shot—unlikely, given the silencer Kirill is using—they'd never get here in time. And even if they did, there'd still be the matter of explosives.

Regardless, even if Lucas does have a plan, I can't let him do this.

In a split second, I come up with the only solution I can.

"Oh, yeah, that's right," I say loudly. Behind me, I hear Misha suck in a breath, but I ignore him. "I almost forgot that I shot your balls and cock off," I continue, imbuing my tone with as much derision as I can. "What's that like, huh? Must be rough not being able to rape fifteen-year-olds."

The fury that twists Kirill's features is demonic. His bloated face turns a blotchy purple, and the gun swings toward me. Lucas moves to block me from Kirill's view, but I jump to the other side, exposing myself again.

I'm the one my former trainer wants. If I can get him to kill me, there's a chance the others might walk away.

"Go ahead," I taunt the man, jumping from side to side to avoid Lucas's attempts to shield me. "Shoot me like the coward you are, like the miserable slug that you've become." The words spill out of my mouth faster and faster. "Just look at yourself. The famous Kirill Luchenko, never defeated in combat. And what happened to you? Got your dick blown away. I bet that must've hurt. I bet you can't take a piss without crying like a baby. I wouldn't know how that feels, of course, but—"

The shot rings out, the noise deafening despite the silencer. Something slams into me, and I go flying.

My last thought is a desperate hope that Misha and Lucas survive.

CHAPTER FORTY-NINE

❖ LUCAS ❖

Everything happens in an instant. The second the shot rings out, I'm already in motion, leaping at Kirill. I don't dare look back because if I see Yulia dead or dying, I'll lose the last shreds of my sanity, and I can't let that happen.

I have to save her brother.

We crash into the wall, and Kirill twists to protect the gun, but that's not what I'm after. With both hands, I grab his left fist and squeeze tight, forcing his fingers to remain closed and his thumb to stay on the detonator. At the same time, I pull back and slam into him again, twisting so that my shoulder hits his right arm. The gun clatters to the floor, but before I can celebrate my victory, he uses his bulk to push me back and smashes his right fist into my temple.

My vision goes dark for a second, my ears ringing, but I hang on to consciousness and force him back against the wall. The rage and grief boiling in my chest give me superhuman strength. *The motherfucker shot Yulia.* With a roar, I squeeze my fingers harder and hear his bones breaking. He bellows and swings his right fist at me, but I duck this time, keeping my hands locked around his left hand. Distantly, I'm aware that Michael's parents are scrambling to get out of the way, but I block out their panicked cries. The fight is happening with blurring speed; even a second of inattention could be fatal.

My ears ring and I taste blood as another blow connects with my jaw, but I move my leg in time to block Kirill's knee coming at my groin. Simultaneously, I jerk back to avoid a third blow and turn sideways to elbow him in the ribs. I hit him hard, but he doesn't even grunt this time. The bastard is built like a tank, and though his reflexes aren't as good as mine, he knows what he's doing. Under normal circumstances, it would've been a difficult fight, but with both of my hands squeezing his left fist, I'm at a severe disadvantage. I can't let go of his hand, however, because I'm certain he'll trigger that bomb.

At this point, all the fucker cares about is revenge, and he'll die to obtain it.

He raped Yulia at fifteen. He shot her.

The fury is like rocket fuel for my muscles. Spinning around, I slam the back of my head into his nose, crushing bone and cartilage, and before he can recover, I use my grip on his fist to swing him around and throw him against the opposite wall.

His eyes roll backward as his head hits the hard surface, but he manages to land a kick, his boot crashing straight into my kidney. My breath hisses out, my grip on his fist slackening for a moment, and he throws himself on the floor, dragging me along as I tighten my grip again. We collide and roll, and in the next moment I see what he was after.

The gun he dropped earlier.

He's grabbed it with his right hand, and he's aiming it straight at my head.

I see his finger start to tighten on the trigger, and things seem to slow. I register everything with vibrant clarity, as if my brain decided to take one last snapshot by sending my senses into overdrive. In that split second before I die, I see Kirill's victorious snarl, smell the rank sweat dripping down his face, and hear Michael's parents' screams at the back of the hallway. I also think of Yulia and how desperately I hope she survives.

I'd die a thousand deaths to keep her living.

The gun goes off with a deafening blast.

Only I don't die.

Instead, Kirill jerks with a scream, his right arm exploding into bloody bits. Stunned, I look up to see

Michael holding my M16. The boy is panting, his pale face streaked with sweat and blood, and in the next instant, he squeezes the trigger again, releasing a round of bullets into Kirill's right shoulder.

Howling, Kirill kicks out at Michael, and I refocus on my opponent.

It's time to finish this thing.

Keeping my fingers locked tightly around Kirill's left fist, I slam my forehead into his bleeding nose, again and again, reveling in the crunch as I hammer the bone fragments into his brain. This isn't how I wanted the bastard to go, but it'll have to do.

When he's lying there unmoving, his face a bloody mess, I look up at Michael, my head throbbing. "Shoot his left arm," I order hoarsely, and the kid gets it right away.

Without hesitation, he unleashes another volley on the dead man's upper arm. The bullets cut the bone clean through. All I have to do is yank on the fist, and the arm separates from the body.

Ignoring the blood gushing from the stump, I climb to my feet, holding the severed appendage by the fist wrapped around the detonator. My heart thumps in a hollow, uneven rhythm as I turn toward the entrance. Behind me, Michael's mother is sobbing and his father is groaning in pain, but I don't give a fuck.

All I care about is Yulia.

She's lying unmoving amidst shards of broken mirror, her body crumpled like a rag doll's. Her long blond hair covers her face, but there's blood everywhere, all over her slim frame.

The hollowness in my chest spreads.

No. Fuck, no.

She can't be dead. She can't be.

"Yulia," I whisper, sinking to my knees beside her. I feel like I'm suffocating, like my lungs are collapsing in my ribcage. "Yulia, sweetheart . . ."

She doesn't move.

Numbly, I tighten my left hand around Kirill's fist, pressing down on the thumb to secure the detonator inside, and with my right hand, I reach for her. My fingers are drenched with Kirill's blood, and as I brush aside her hair, I have a sudden horrible feeling that I'm polluting her with my touch, that I'm destroying something pure and beautiful . . . an angel who doesn't belong in my ugly world.

Her lashes are brown half-moons on her pale cheeks, her mouth slightly parted. It's as if she's sleeping, except there's blood.

So much fucking blood.

"Yulia . . ." My hand shakes as I touch her face, leaving bloody fingerprints on her porcelain skin. The hollowness inside me expands, my very bones creaking under the pressure of the emptiness within. I can't picture a life without her. Fuck, I can't picture a single week without her. In a few short months, she's become my entire world. If she's dead, if she's gone . . . My fingers graze the side of her neck, feeling for her pulse, and I freeze, a violent shudder rippling through me.

There is a beat. A faint, but unmistakable beat.

"Yulia!" I bend down, gathering her against me with my free arm. She's soft and warm, unmistakably alive. I feel the puffs of her breath on my neck, and my pulse roars with fierce joy.

She's alive.

My Yulia is alive.

For a moment, it's enough, but as my head clears, a new fear seizes me.

Why is she unconscious, and where did all the blood come from?

Lowering her to the floor, I frantically pat her down, looking for the bullet wound. She has numerous small cuts from the broken glass, and there's a bloody gash on the side of her head, but I don't see where the bullet went in.

"Is she okay?" Michael says, and I glance up to see him standing there. He's swaying on his feet, his face greenish white. For a moment, I think he's going to puke from the sight of the severed arm I'm still holding, but as I watch, he sinks to his knees next to me—or, more precisely, collapses to his knees.

Frowning, I start to reach for him and stop.

Blood is dribbling from under Michael's dark T-shirt.

"Misha?" Yulia croaks hoarsely, and I turn my head to see her eyelids open. As she focuses on us, horror crosses her face, and I know she's reached the same conclusion.

Her brother has been shot.

CHAPTER FIFTY

❖ YULIA ❖

In the next ten minutes, everything seems to happen at once. There's blood everywhere: on Misha, who lies down beside me, on Lucas, around Kirill's mangled body, and on the severed arm Lucas is holding. A couple of meters away, Misha's father is groaning in agony, his leg bleeding uncontrollably, and Misha's mother is weeping and rushing back and forth between her wounded husband and son. Lucas's men—who must've heard the unsilenced gunshots—burst in, weapons ready, and Lucas starts barking orders at them. Within a minute, he has two men working on disarming the explosives, and two more trying to stem Misha's and his father's bleeding. I try to get up to help, but every time I move, a wave of nausea hits me and I have to lie down, my skull throbbing where I split my head open on the mirror. My frantic questions go unanswered in the chaos, but by the time we're back in the armored SUV and speeding toward a hospital, I piece together what happened.

It wasn't a bullet that slammed into me. It was my brother. Misha knocked me out of the way, pushing me headfirst into the mirror that shattered. In the process, he took the bullet meant for me. According to Lucas, it went through the fleshy part of his shoulder, knocking him down on top of me. It's mostly Misha's blood that covers me, though I also bled from my head injury and the glass cutting into my skin.

"He'll be fine," Lucas says for the fifth time as I reach for Misha, who's passed out in the backseat next to me. "He lost a good amount of blood, but we stopped the bleeding and he'll be okay. He saved us all. If he hadn't gotten my M16—" He breaks off, but a chill streaks down my spine as I fill in the unspoken words.

We'd come within seconds of dying, all of us. In one fell swoop, I could've lost my brother and the man who's become my entire life.

My hand trembling, I squeeze Misha's palm, and then I reach for Lucas, who's sitting on the other side of me.

Only he doesn't let me hold his hand. The minute I touch him, Lucas pulls me into his lap, wrapping me tightly in his embrace, and buries his face in my hair. I can feel the shudders wracking his big body, and I can no longer restrain myself.

Clutching him with all my strength, I cry.

I just hold Lucas and cry.

* * *

A local hospital takes care of Misha's and Viktor's gunshot wounds and the gash on my head, and then we fly to Switzerland to recuperate at a private clinic Lucas has used before. Misha's parents come with us, not wanting to be separated from their son despite their fear of me and Lucas.

I do my best to reassure them that they're safe, but I know that to them, we're scary strangers from a violent world—a world that invaded their lives in the most brutal way. What Kirill did, the way he terrorized them, left scars that will never go away.

Before that awful day, they knew what Natalia's brother did for his country, but they didn't truly understand it.

"We woke up that morning, and he was there, holding a gun on us," Natalia sobs as she tells us what happened. "He tied Viktor up and strapped the bomb to me, and then he did the same thing to him. We thought he was a terrorist—we thought we were going to die—but then he started talking about you and how he was waiting for you, and that's when we realized what he was really after..." She breaks down in hysterics at that point, and Lucas has to call a nurse for a sedative to calm her down.

Viktor—Misha's adoptive father—is in a similar state, though he tries to put on a brave face for his wife. Whenever Natalia starts to cry, he comforts her, telling her that he's fine, but the nurses told me that he himself wakes up screaming from nightmares.

The bullet that entered Viktor's leg shattered his kneecap, and he may never again walk without a limp.

The only bright spot in the whole mess is that Misha's shoulder wound has indeed turned out to be as clean as Lucas said. My brother lost a lot of blood, but the doctors promised that he'll be back on his feet—albeit with an arm sling—within a week.

While we recuperate, Lucas's men tear apart Rudenkos' apartment to figure out how Kirill got in unseen, and what they find gives us all pause. It turns out that Misha's parents' new apartment—where they had been relocated after I returned—had originally been a UUR safe house. As such, it had a secret apartment concealed behind the living room wall—a place stocked with medical supplies, ammunition, and enough food to last for several months. It was there that Kirill must've gone to heal when he escaped from the black site. How he survived the trip and concealed his tracks will always be a mystery, but judging from the state of the apartment, he'd been hunkered down there the entire time we'd been searching for him.

Misha's parents swear they had no idea he was there, and after questioning them extensively, Lucas decides they're telling the truth.

Apparently, they heard noises in their living room several times, but chalked them up to strange acoustics of their new apartment building.

"I thought it was a ghost," Natalia Rudenko whispers, her eyes red and swollen in her pale face. "Viktor told me I was being an idiot, and I shut up. But I should've listened to my instincts. I'll never forgive myself for what happened."

Lucas starts to fire another question at her, but I stop him by laying my hand on his arm. The poor woman is in no state for further interrogation. "It's not your fault," I assure her gently. "Kirill was a seasoned agent. If he wanted to stay hidden, you didn't stand a chance."

"That's what Viktor said, but still, I should've known." Squeezing her eyes closed, she pinches the bridge of her nose with trembling fingers. "There were little clues, like our computer getting hacked that time, and a few things seeming to get moved on occasion . . ."

Secretly, I agree that she should've found those things suspicious—I certainly would have—but she's a civilian, and I'm not. Regular people aren't trained to look for those types of patterns, and even though Natalia wasn't a complete stranger to the shadowy world of intelligence organizations, she couldn't have imagined that a secret agent would be hiding in her apartment.

"The hacking of the computer must be how Kirill learned we were coming," Lucas says grimly, and I nod in agreement. I don't know if my former trainer used Rudenkos' apartment because it was the best hiding spot, or because he suspected I might return with Misha one day, but either way, he was well positioned to strike when we least expected it.

The guards were keeping watch for danger from the outside, but the enemy had been inside all along.

To my relief, Misha seems far less traumatized than his parents. I don't know if it's his UUR training or what he's already lived through during Lucas's attack on the black site, but my brother is recovering quickly in more ways than one. Far from being distraught and remorseful about his role in Kirill's death, Misha seems proud that he got to participate in the takedown of the man who hurt me and nearly killed his parents.

"I'm glad I got to shoot the bastard," he says fiercely when Lucas and I visit his bedside. "It's the least he deserved."

"You did well, kid," Lucas says, patting his uninjured shoulder. "Your hands didn't even shake when you shot off his arm."

I wince at the graphic imagery, but Misha just nods, accepting the praise as his due. He and Lucas appear to be on the same wavelength now, as if fighting Kirill together brought them closer. I like that development, but it does disturb me to see my fourteen-year-old brother being so casual about a man's gruesome death.

"And why should he be upset?" Lucas says when I mention my concern to him later that evening in our private hospital room. "He's old enough to understand that you have to do what's necessary if you want to survive and protect those you care about. The kid's growing up, and whether you want to admit it or not, he's not a delicate flower."

"Neither is he a remorseless killer—or at least he shouldn't be," I retort, but Lucas just sits down on the edge of the bed and picks up my hand. His gaze is hard and shuttered, but his grip is gentle. He's been this way, caring yet distant, ever since we got to this clinic, and no matter how much I try, I can't figure out why he does nothing more than cuddle me at night.

The doctors cleared me for sex the day before yesterday, but Lucas still hasn't touched me.

"Sweetheart," he murmurs, squeezing my hand lightly, "your brother is not like you. He never was, and never will be. It was his choice to join UUR, and whether you want to admit it or not, he belonged there more than you ever did."

The conviction in Lucas's voice distracts me from the puzzle of his behavior. Frowning, I say, "I don't think so. Misha probably imagined it would be glamorous, being a spy and all. I'm sure that's why he joined: so he could play at being James Bond. But when he saw what it was really like—"

"He still wanted it," Lucas says quietly. "Or wants it, I should say."

Struck, I stare at him. "What do you mean? He's going back to school."

"He is—but only to make you and his parents happy."

"What? How do you know that?"

Lucas sighs, his thumb stroking the inside of my palm. "He told me. Yesterday. He wants to come work for me when he's older, but for now, he thinks it's a good idea to finish civilian school so he could 'blend better into the general population.'" He pauses, then adds softly, "Those are his words, not mine."

"I see." Pulling my hand from his grasp, I get up, my temples throbbing with a headache that has nothing to do with the half-healed gash across my skull. I should be surprised, but I'm not. On some level, I already knew this.

Like Lucas, my brother is drawn to danger, and he'll eventually embrace this kind of life.

The pain creeps up on me; it's just a faint ache at first, but with every second, it grows stronger, welling up until it chokes me from within. My throat constricts, and I feel myself start to hyperventilate, frantically sucking in air to fill my stiff and empty lungs. A hoarse sob bubbles up, followed by another and another, and then Lucas is on his feet next to me, drawing me into his embrace as raw, ugly sounds tear from my throat. It feels like I'm cracking inside, like

I'm crumbling into bits. I try to stop, to control myself, but the sobs just keep on coming.

"Yulia, sweetheart, it's okay . . . Everything's going to be okay." Lucas's arms are around me, holding me tight, and the knowledge that he's here, that I'm no longer alone, opens the dam even more. The tears pour out, burning and cleansing at the same time, a toxic flood that destroys and renews at once.

I cry for my brother's future and our past, for all the lies and losses and betrayals. I cry for what might've been and what has come to pass, for the cruelty of fate and its incongruous mercy.

I cry because I can't stop, and because I know I don't have to.

I trust Lucas to hold me as I break, to lend me his strength when I need it most.

Somehow we end up back on the bed, with me curled in his arms as he rocks me on his lap, cradling me like I'm the most precious thing in his world. And still I cry. I cry until my throat is raw and torn, until my agony drowns in exhaustion. I'm only half-aware when Lucas lays me down and removes my clothes, and by the time he slides in beside me, I'm asleep.

Asleep and purged of all my fears.

* * *

I wake up to find Lucas sitting on the edge of the bed, watching me. Instantly, the recollection of last night comes to me, and I flush, remembering my inexplicable breakdown.

"I'm sorry," I mutter, clutching the blanket to my chest as I sit up. "I don't know what came over me."

Lucas doesn't move. "You have nothing to be sorry for, baby." Despite the reassuring words, his gaze is inscrutable, his expression still closed off and distant. "You were due for a good cry."

"Yes, well, I had one, that's for sure." Feeling embarrassed, I slide from under the blanket and grab a robe, then slip into the adjoining bathroom to take a quick shower and brush my teeth before the nurses make their morning rounds.

When I come out, I see Lucas still sitting on the bed, unmoving. The bruises on his face—the mementos of his fight with Kirill—are faded now, and with the morning light spilling across his hard, masculine features, he resembles a warrior's statue more than a living, breathing human being. Only his eyes belie that impression; sharp and clear, they track my every movement the way a big cat watches its prey.

My breath catches, and I find myself walking toward him, my legs carrying me to the bed almost against my will.

When I'm next to him, he curls his hand around my wrist, pulling me down to sit next to him.

"Lucas . . ." I stare at him, feeling strangely nervous. "What are you—"

"Shh." He presses two fingers against my lips, his touch incredibly gentle. His eyes burn into mine, and to my shock, I see a dark shadow of agony in his pale gaze. "I'm only going to say it once, and I want you to listen," he says quietly, lowering his hand. "I've deposited some money into your account—about two million to start. Later, I'll add more, but that should be enough to get you settled in the beginning. Of course, if you ever need anything, you and Michael can always come to me—"

"What?" I reel back, certain I misheard. "What are you talking about?"

"Let me finish." His jaw is rigid. "I will also provide you with a set of bodyguards," he continues, his voice growing more strained with each word. "Their job will be to protect you, but I expect you to be smart and not do anything to endanger yourself. If you have to fly somewhere, I'll send someone to take you, and I'll personally oversee the security perimeter around your new house. Also—"

"Lucas, what are you talking about?" Shaking, I jump to my feet. "Is this some kind of joke?"

"Of course not." He stands up, his muscles all but vibrating with tension. "You think this is easy for me? Fuck!" He spins around and starts to pace, his every movement filled with barely controlled violence.

Stunned, I watch him for a couple of moments; then the neurons in my brain start to fire. Stepping forward, I catch his arm, feeling the coiled strength within.

"Lucas, are you—" I swallow thickly. "Does this mean you're letting me leave?"

His eyes narrow dangerously. "What else would it fucking mean?"

My heart thuds heavily as I drop my hand. "But why? Is it this?" Self-consciously, I touch the narrow strip of shaved hair on my head, where the stitches from the gash are visible despite my best attempts to hide them. Like Lucas's, the bruises on my face are almost gone, but the scars from the broken glass are not. They're healing—the doctors assured me they'll be all but invisible one day—but for now, I'm far from beautiful, and it suddenly dawns on me that Lucas's distance may have a very obvious cause.

His desire for me has cooled.

"What?" Incredulity fills his voice as his eyes follow the movement of my hand. "Are *you* fucking joking? You think I don't want you because of this wound?"

"You didn't touch me last night." I know I sound like an insecure schoolgirl, but I can't help it. Lucas is a highly sexual man, and for him to forego a chance to fuck me . . .

"Of course I didn't touch you," he says through clenched teeth. "You're still healing, and I— Fuck." He twists as if to turn away again, but stops himself. Reaching over, he grips my arm. "Yulia . . . If I'd touched you, if I'd taken you again, I wouldn't have been able to do this, do you understand?" His voice roughens. "I'd keep you with me like the selfish bastard I am, and you'd never get a chance to leave."

All breath exits my lungs. "No, I don't understand. If you still want me, then why are you doing this?"

"Because you don't belong in this world ... *my* world. They forced you into this life, made you into someone you never wanted to become. When I saw you lying there, hurt and bleeding—" He breaks off, then says raggedly, "You should've never been in that kind of danger, never met men like Kirill and Obenko ..." He takes a deep breath. "Men like me."

I stare at him, a strange ache unfurling deep inside my chest. "Lucas, you're not—"

"Yes, I am." His hard mouth twists. "Let's not pretend. I'm like *them*—the men who hurt you and used you and manipulated you. You never had a choice about it all, and I didn't give you one either. I took you for my own because I wanted you, and I kept you because I couldn't picture a life without you. When you escaped, I would've torn the world apart looking for you, beautiful. I would've done anything to get you back."

A tingle ripples down my spine. "So why are you letting me go?" I whisper, my heart beating erratically. Could it be? Is Lucas—

"Because I can't bear to lose you," he says harshly. "When I saw you lying there, covered in blood, I thought you were dead. I thought he'd killed you." A visible shudder ripples over Lucas's skin before he steps closer, his hands moving up to grip my shoulders. Leaning in, he says with barely controlled fury, "What the fuck were you thinking anyway, taunting the bastard like that? You should've stayed quiet, let me—"

"Let you get shot?" Everything inside me recoils at the mere notion. "I would never. He was after me, not you or Misha—"

"So you tried to sacrifice yourself for us, like you've been doing for your brother all along? Did you really think there was a chance in hell I'd let you do that?" His fingers dig into my shoulders, but before I can so much as wince, his grip eases and his harsh expression softens. "Yulia," he whispers hoarsely, "don't you know that I'd take a thousand bullets, die a hundred deaths before I let anything hurt you?"

My pulse lurches. "Lucas . . ."

"You're my reason for existing now." His eyes glitter fiercely. "You're my everything. I want you in my bed, but I want you in my life even more. It's been that way from the very beginning. Even when I hated you, I loved you. If you were gone—"

"You love me?" My lungs seize as I latch on to those words. I'd suspected, hoped—I even told myself I knew—but up until he said it, I hadn't been certain. For Lucas to finally admit this . . .

"Of course I love you." His hands move up to frame my face, his big palms warm on my skin. Gazing down on me, he says roughly, "I've loved you from the moment I saw Diego carry you off that plane, thin and dirty and so gorgeous it made my chest hurt. I told myself it was only lust, pretended I could fuck you out of my system, but I ended up falling for you even more, wanting you more each day. Your loyalty, your bravery, your warmth—it was everything I never knew I needed. Before you came into my life, I didn't have anyone, didn't care about anyone, and I was fine that way. But when I met you . . ." He inhales. "Fuck, it was like I saw the sun for the first time. You made my world so much brighter, so much fuller . . ."

My throat is so tight I can barely speak. "So then why—"

"Because you were made for love and family, for pretty things and soft words." Pain laces his voice as he drops his hands. "You should've been adored by your parents and brother, worshipped by loving boyfriends and loyal friends, and instead—"

"And instead I fell for you." Reaching for him, I grip his powerful hand. Tears blur my eyes as I stare up at my ruthless captor, the man who's now *my* everything. "I fell in love with the man who saved me from Kirill and the Russian prison, who nursed me back to health and gave me my brother back. Lucas . . ." I curve my palm around his hard jaw. "You might be like them, but you've always given me more than you've taken. Always."

He stares at me, and I see the growing frustration on his face. "Yulia . . ." His voice is low and lethal. "If you're going to walk away, tell me now. I'm giving you this one chance, do you understand?"

"I do." A smile trembles on my lips as I lower my hand. "I understand."

His muscles coil, as though bracing for a blow. "And?"

"And I'm staying."

For a second, Lucas is still, as if frozen in disbelief, and then he's on me, his lips devouring me with a hunger that's both violent and tender. His hands roam over my body, his touch rough yet restrained, cognizant of my healing injuries. We tumble backward on the bed, our mouths fused together and our hands ripping at each other's clothes. Somewhere out there are nurses and doctors, my brother and his adoptive parents, the whole entire world, but here, in this private room, it's just us and the heat burning brighter with each moment.

"I love you," I gasp as Lucas thrusts into me, and he whispers the words back, his voice raspy and thick as he moves inside me, claiming me over and over again. We come together, our bodies shattering in perfect symphony, and as we lie tangled in the aftermath, Lucas holds my gaze. In his eyes are lust and possessiveness, hunger and need, and underneath it all, the warm tenderness of love.

In a few minutes, the nurses will come, and our little bubble will break. We'll work on healing and moving on, on building our new life and settling into our new home. For now, however, we don't need to worry about what the future holds.

What Lucas and I have together will never be pretty, but it's perfect.

Our own version of perfect.

BONUS EPILOGUE: NORA & JULIAN

Approximately 3 Years Later

SPOILER ALERT: If you haven't read the *Twist Me* trilogy, please stop and read that first. What follows is for those of you who loved Nora & Julian's story and asked for a glimpse of their future beyond the epilogue of *Hold Me (Twist Me #3)*. Oh, and it gives a peek at Lucas & Yulia's future too.

* * *

❖ JULIAN ❖

Nora's scream echoes off the walls, the tormented sound flaying me open. I lean against the door frame, shaking from the effort it takes to remain still and not attack the white-coated buzzards hovering over my wife. My shirt is soaked with sweat, and my hands flex convulsively at my sides, the urge to protect Nora battling with the knowledge that I'd only get in the doctors' way.

The baby is two weeks early, and I've never felt so fucking useless in my life.

"Do you want me to get you anything?" Lucas asks quietly, and I realize he came up from the hallway to stand next to me. "Water, coffee . . . a shot of vodka?" His expression is uncharacteristically sympathetic.

"I'm fine." My voice is like a rasp of sandpaper over wood, and I clear my throat before continuing. "They said it's not long now. That's why they've tapered off the epidural."

Lucas nods. "Right. I've been reading up on it."

"Oh?" The bizarre statement—and momentary absence of screams from Nora—awakens a twinge of curiosity. "Are you and Yulia . . .?"

"No, not yet, but Yulia's been talking about it ever since the wedding." He exhales audibly. "I was thinking it wouldn't be so bad, but now that I've seen this—"

"Julian!"

Nora's agonized cry cuts off whatever he was going to say next, and I forget about everything, all but leaping across the room in response to her call.

"Mr. Esguerra, please, you have to step back—"

"She needs me," I snarl at the doctor blocking my path. If he wasn't the best obstetrician in the Swiss clinic, he'd already be dead. Shoving the idiot aside, I step forward to grip Nora's trembling hand. Her palm is slippery with sweat, but her fingers curl around mine with startling strength, her knuckles turning white as her towering belly ripples with another contraction. Her small face is a twisted mask of pain, her eyes scrunched shut, and my chest heaves with helpless fury as another scream rips from her throat. I'd give anything to trade places with her, to take this pain from her, but I can't, and the knowledge shreds me into pieces.

"I'm here, baby." My voice is hoarse, my free hand unsteady as I reach over to brush the sweat-soaked hair off her forehead. "I'm here for you."

Nora opens her eyes, and my heart clenches as her gaze meets mine and she attempts a reassuring smile. "It's okay," she pants. "It'll be fine. I just need to—" But before she finishes speaking, her face contorts again, and I hear the doctors yelling, telling her to push, to bear down. Nora's hand tightens around mine with unbelievable force, her delicate fingers almost crushing the bones in my palm, and her whole body seems to go into a massive spasm, her head arching back with a scream that cuts me like a thousand knives. Her agony shatters me, ripping away all pretense at calm and reason. Red mist edges my vision, blood pounding loudly in my temples, and I know I won't be able to bear this much longer.

Holding Nora's hand, I turn and roar at the doctors, "Fucking help her! Now!"

But none of them are paying attention to me. All three doctors are clustered at the foot of the bed where a sheet is shielding Nora's lower body from view. I see one of them bending and then . . .

"There she is!" The doctor who blocked my path earlier straightens, holding something small, wriggling, and bloody. He turns away, working with quick, efficient movements, and in the next instant, an infant's cry pierces the air. It's weak and uncertain at first, but soon, it gains strength. The shock of that high-pitched, demanding sound is like a percussive wave from an explosion, stunning me into paralysis. When I finally manage to turn my head to look at Nora, I realize that her hand is limp in mine, her features no longer contorted in agony. She's crying instead, and laughing at the same time, and then she pulls her hand away and reaches for the baby the doctor is handing to her—the tiny, wriggling creature whose cries are growing in volume.

"Oh my God, Julian," she sobs as the doctor places the newborn into her arms and raises the bed to a half-sitting position. "Oh God, just look at her . . ." She cradles it against her chest, her hospital gown falling open to reveal one pregnancy-swollen breast, and as I gape in mute shock, the little thing begins to root at the breast, its pink mouth opening and closing several times before it latches on to Nora's nipple.

No, not *it*. She. Our daughter.

Nora and I have a daughter. One who's nursing at her breast like a pro.

My vision narrows, the sounds of the hospital fading away. A nuclear bomb could've gone off next to us, and I wouldn't have noticed. All I see, all I'm aware of is my beautiful, precious pet, her tangled hair falling forward in a dark cloud as she leans over the nursing baby. Mesmerized, I step closer, trying to make out all the details, and my pulse takes on a strangely audible beat. It's like I'm listening to someone else's heartbeat through a stethoscope. *Thu-thump.* A tiny fist kneads the softness of Nora's plump breast. *Thu-thump.* The little mouth works industriously, small cheeks hollowing out with every sucking motion. *Thu-thump.* The hair on the tiny head is dark and downy, as soft-looking as her lightly golden skin.

"What color are her eyes?" I whisper when I can speak, and Nora lets out a shaky laugh, glancing up at me.

"What color do you think?" Her face is glowing with tenderness. "Blue, like yours."

Like mine. The words sear through me. I don't really care about the color of her eyes—many babies' eyes change as they get older—but knowing that this tiny being is mine, that she's *my* daughter, takes my breath away. My hand shakes as I reach forward and gently touch one tiny foot, my fingers shockingly huge next to the baby's minuscule toes. It seems impossible that something so little can exist; she looks like a doll . . . a living, breathing human doll.

My Nora in miniature, only infinitely more vulnerable and fragile.

My chest constricts, and I yank my hand away, sudden irrational fear flooding my mind. Is it normal for a newborn to be so little? She *is* two weeks early. What if I hurt that tiny foot by touching it? Looking up, I pin the doctor with a deadly glare. "Is she—"

"She's healthy," the doctor reassures me with a smile. "A little on the small side at two-point-seven kilograms, but perfectly normal."

"She *is* perfect," Nora murmurs, gazing down at the baby with a love so consuming and absolute that my breath leaves my lungs again.

My wife. My child. My family.

My vision blurs for a moment, my eyes stinging, and I have to blink to clear away the watery veil. I haven't cried since I was a small child, but if I'm remembering the sensations correctly, this burning behind my eyes means I'm on the verge.

"Come here," Nora whispers, glancing up at me again, and I step closer, unable to help myself. Slowly, I lift my hand and stroke the baby's head with one finger, everything inside me going still as the baby releases Nora's nipple and blinks up at me. Nora had been right, I register in the split second before her tiny face scrunches up angrily.

She does have blue eyes.

Opening her mouth, my daughter lets out a bellow, and Nora laughs before helping the baby find her nipple again. Instantly, the little creature quiets, sucking industriously, and I lower my hand, staring at the wonder of it all.

"What do you want to call her?" I ask in a hushed tone as the baby continues to feed. Because of Nora's miscarriage three years ago, we agreed not to name the baby until she was actually here, but I suspect my pet has given it some thought on her own.

Sure enough, Nora looks up at me and smiles. "How about Elizabeth?"

A bittersweet ache squeezes my chest. "For Beth?"

"For Beth," Nora confirms. "But I think we can call her Liz—or Lizzy. Doesn't she look like a Lizzy?"

"She does." I brush my fingers across the downy head. "She very much does."

* * *

Nora and the baby fall asleep, both worn out by their ordeal, and I step out of the room to grab a bottle of water and stretch my legs. To my surprise, when I get to the end of the hallway, I see two blond heads bent together in the waiting area.

Lucas's wife—the Ukrainian girl who was involved in the crash—is with him.

As I approach, Yulia glances in my direction. Instantly, she leaps to her feet, her pale face turning even whiter. Lucas gets to his feet as well, stepping protectively in front of her.

I let out a sigh. I promised Lucas I won't hurt her, but he still doesn't trust me around her, even though Nora and I went to their wedding in Cyprus last year. I don't blame him for his overprotectiveness—usually, the mere sight of the former spy makes my blood pressure rise—but today, I'm not in the mood for conflict.

I'm too overjoyed to care about anything but Nora and our daughter.

Lizzy, I remind myself.

Nora and Lizzy.

My heart seizes. *I have a daughter named Lizzy.*

"Congratulations," Yulia says softly, gripping her husband's arm, and I realize she's talking to me. "Lucas and I are very happy for you."

To my surprise, I feel a weary smile tugging at my lips. "Thanks," I say, and mean it. I'll never forgive the girl for nearly killing me and endangering Nora as a result, but over the years, my fury at her has cooled to a tepid simmer. She makes Lucas happy, and Lucas makes me a lot of money on the new ventures, so I no longer fantasize about skinning her alive.

"How is Nora?" Lucas asks, sliding his arm around Yulia's slender waist and pulling her toward him. "She must be exhausted."

"She is. She fell asleep right after her video calls with her parents, Rosa, and Ana. They were all upset that they couldn't make it here in time, but they understood that the baby had her own timeline." Exhaling, I run a hand through my hair. "Nora is sleeping now, and so is Lizzy."

"Lizzy?" Yulia says, and I see her pretty face soften. "That's a beautiful name."

"Thanks. We like it." I love it, actually, but I'm not about to bond with Lucas's wife over baby names. Tolerance—as in, not killing her on the spot—is as far as I'm willing to go.

Turning my attention to Lucas, I say, "Thanks for flying out on such short notice and pulling the men off that Syria project. Things have been pretty quiet lately, but extra security never hurts." Especially where my wife and daughter are concerned. I picture Lizzy in danger, and my insides turn to dry ice.

I'm going to get the trackers on her as soon as the doctors allow it, and hire an extra dozen bodyguards to watch her at all times. If she so much as pricks her little finger, her security team will answer to me.

"No problem," Lucas says. "We were on our way to London anyway, for the opening of Yulia's new restaurant. Michael is already waiting for us there."

Ah, so that's why Yulia is here. I was wondering why Lucas brought her. If I recall correctly, this will be the fourth restaurant that Lucas's wife lends her brand and recipes to—an interesting business for a former spy.

"Anyways," Yulia says, giving me a wary look, "we didn't mean to hold you up. You probably have to return to Nora and the baby."

"I do," I say, not bothering to deny it. I'm still in a good mood, however, so I add, "If I don't see you again, good luck on your opening."

And without waiting for a reply, I continue heading down the hallway.

* * *

I'm giving Nora a foot rub—the only physical contact allowed for now—when the nurses bring the baby back for a feeding. Lizzy is screaming like a banshee, but the moment she's placed in Nora's arms, she goes quiet and begins to root for a nipple. I watch, mesmerized, as her tiny mouth finds its target, and she begins to suck. Nora croons to her, stroking her softly, and I just stare, unable to look away. My beautiful pet is a mother—the mother of my baby. I didn't think it was possible for me to feel more possessive of Nora, but I do. She belongs to me on a whole different level now, and seeing her like this brings out emotions I never thought myself capable of feeling. It's as if my whole life has been leading up to this—to my wife and child, to this terrifyingly incandescent joy.

"Do you want to hold her?" Nora murmurs when the baby releases her nipple, and I freeze, all my muscles locking tight. I've faced terrorists and drug lords, dealt with generals and heads of state, and I've never been this intimidated.

"Are you sure?" My voice comes out strained. "You don't think I might hurt her?"

"No." Nora's soft lips curve in a smile. "Here you go." Carefully, she hands me the baby, and I do my best to hold her the way Nora did, settling her in the crook of my arm while supporting her little head with my hand. Lizzy is unbelievably light, a tiny, warm bundle of sweet-smelling baby, and as I watch, she blinks at me again and closes her eyes.

"She's sleeping," I whisper in amazement. "Nora, she's sleeping in my arms."

"I know," Nora whispers, and I look up to see her smiling even as tears roll down her cheeks. "The two of you . . . God, I could've never imagined this."

"Me neither." Careful not to jostle Lizzy, I clasp Nora's delicate fingers in my free hand and bring them to my lips. Kissing her knuckles, I murmur, "I love you, baby, so much."

Nora's lips quiver in a smile. "And I love you, Julian."

We sit and watch our daughter sleeping, and I know it's just the beginning.

Our real story is about to unfold.

SNEAK PEEKS

Thank you for reading! If you would consider leaving a review, it would be greatly appreciated.

While *Claim Me* concludes Lucas & Yulia's story, I have many more books coming your way. If you'd like to be notified when the next book is out, please sign up for my new release email list at www.annazaires.com.

If you haven't read Nora & Julian's story, I encourage you to try *Twist Me*. All three books in that trilogy are now available.

Additionally, if you liked this book, you might enjoy Mia & Korum's story, another trilogy of mine that is already complete.

Finally, if you like audiobooks, please be sure to check out this series and our other books on Audible.com.

And now please turn the page for a little taste of *Twist Me*, *Close Liaisons*, and some of my other works.

EXCERPT FROM *TWIST ME*

Author's Note: *Twist Me* is a dark erotic trilogy about Nora and Julian Esguerra. All three books are now available.

* * *

Kidnapped. Taken to a private island.

I never thought this could happen to me. I never imagined one chance meeting on the eve of my eighteenth birthday could change my life so completely.

Now I belong to him. To Julian. To a man who is as ruthless as he is beautiful—a man whose touch makes me burn. A man whose tenderness I find more devastating than his cruelty.

My captor is an enigma. I don't know who he is or why he took me. There is a darkness inside him—a darkness that scares me even as it draws me in.

My name is Nora Leston, and this is my story.

* * *

It's evening now. With every minute that passes, I'm starting to get more and more anxious at the thought of seeing my captor again.

The novel that I've been reading can no longer hold my interest. I put it down and walk in circles around the room.

I am dressed in the clothes Beth had given me earlier. It's not what I would've chosen to wear, but it's better than a bathrobe. A sexy pair of white lacy panties and a matching bra for underwear. A pretty blue sundress that buttons in the front. Everything fits me suspiciously well. Has he been stalking me for a while? Learning everything about me, including my clothing size?

The thought makes me sick.

I am trying not to think about what's to come, but it's impossible. I don't know why I'm so sure he'll come to me tonight. It's possible he has an entire harem of women stashed away on this island, and he visits each one only once a week, like sultans used to do.

Yet somehow I know he'll be here soon. Last night had simply whetted his appetite. I know he's not done with me, not by a long shot.

Finally, the door opens.

He walks in like he owns the place. Which, of course, he does.

I am again struck by his masculine beauty. He could've been a model or a movie star, with a face like his. If there was any fairness in the world, he would've been short or had some other imperfection to offset that face.

But he doesn't. His body is tall and muscular, perfectly proportioned. I remember what it feels like to have him inside me, and I feel an unwelcome jolt of arousal.

He's again wearing jeans and a T-shirt. A gray one this time. He seems to favor simple clothing, and he's smart to do so. His looks don't need any enhancement.

He smiles at me. It's his fallen angel smile—dark and seductive at the same time. "Hello, Nora."

I don't know what to say to him, so I blurt out the first thing that pops into my head. "How long are you going to keep me here?"

He cocks his head slightly to the side. "Here in the room? Or on the island?"

"Both."

"Beth will show you around tomorrow, take you swimming if you'd like," he says, approaching me. "You won't be locked in, unless you do something foolish."

"Such as?" I ask, my heart pounding in my chest as he stops next to me and lifts his hand to stroke my hair.

"Trying to harm Beth or yourself." His voice is soft, his gaze hypnotic as he looks down at me. The way he's touching my hair is oddly relaxing.

I blink, trying to break his spell. "And what about on the island? How long will you keep me here?"

His hand caresses my face, curves around my cheek. I catch myself leaning into his touch, like a cat getting petted, and I immediately stiffen.

His lips curl into a knowing smile. The bastard knows the effect he has on me. "A long time, I hope," he says.

For some reason, I'm not surprised. He wouldn't have bothered bringing me all the way here if he just wanted to fuck me a few times. I'm terrified, but I'm not surprised.

I gather my courage and ask the next logical question. "Why did you kidnap me?"

The smile leaves his face. He doesn't answer, just looks at me with an inscrutable blue gaze.

I begin to shake. "Are you going to kill me?"

"No, Nora, I won't kill you."

His denial reassures me, although he could obviously be lying.

"Are you going to sell me?" I can barely get the words out. "Like to be a prostitute or something?"

"No," he says softly. "Never. You're mine and mine alone."

I feel a tiny bit calmer, but there is one more thing I have to know. "Are you going to hurt me?"

For a moment, he doesn't answer again. Something dark briefly flashes in his eyes. "Probably," he says quietly.

And then he leans down and kisses me, his warm lips soft and gentle on mine.

For a second, I stand there frozen, unresponsive. I believe him. I know he's telling the truth when he says he'll hurt me. There's something in him that scares me—that has scared me from the very beginning.

He's nothing like the boys I've gone on dates with. He's capable of anything.

And I'm completely at his mercy.

I think about trying to fight him again. That would be the normal thing to do in my situation. The brave thing to do.

And yet I don't do it.

I can feel the darkness inside him. There's something wrong with him. His outer beauty hides something monstrous underneath.

I don't want to unleash that darkness. I don't know what will happen if I do.

So I stand still in his embrace and let him kiss me. And when he picks me up again and takes me to bed, I don't try to resist in any way.

Instead, I close my eyes and give in to the sensations.

* * *

All three books in the *Twist Me* trilogy are now available. Please visit my website at www.annazaires.com to learn more and to sign up for my new release email list.

EXCERPT FROM *CLOSE LIAISONS*

Author's Note: *Close Liaisons* is the first book in my erotic sci-fi romance trilogy, the Krinar Chronicles. While not as dark as *Twist Me* and *Capture Me*, it does have some elements that readers of dark erotica may enjoy.

* * *

A dark and edgy romance that will appeal to fans of erotic and turbulent relationships . . .

In the near future, the Krinar rule the Earth. An advanced race from another galaxy, they are still a mystery to us—and we are completely at their mercy.

Shy and innocent, Mia Stalis is a college student in New York City who has led a very normal life. Like most people, she's never had any interactions with the invaders—until one fateful day in the park changes everything. Having caught Korum's eye, she must now contend with a powerful, dangerously seductive Krinar who wants to possess her and will stop at nothing to make her his own.

How far would you go to regain your freedom? How much would you sacrifice to help your people? What choice will you make when you begin to fall for your enemy?

* * *

Breathe, Mia, breathe. Somewhere in the back of her mind, a small rational voice kept repeating those words. That same oddly objective part of her noted his symmetric face structure, with golden skin stretched tightly over high cheekbones and a firm jaw. Pictures and videos of Ks that she'd seen had hardly done them justice. Standing no more than thirty feet away, the creature was simply stunning.

As she continued staring at him, still frozen in place, he straightened and began walking toward her. Or rather stalking toward her, she thought stupidly, as his every movement reminded her of a jungle cat sinuously approaching a gazelle. All the while, his eyes never left hers. As he approached, she could make out individual yellow flecks in his light golden eyes and the thick long lashes surrounding them.

She watched in horrified disbelief as he sat down on her bench, less than two feet away from her, and smiled, showing white even teeth. No fangs, she noted with some functioning part of her brain. Not even a hint of them. That used to be another myth about them, like their supposed abhorrence of the sun.

"What's your name?" The creature practically purred the question at her. His voice was low and smooth, completely unaccented. His nostrils flared slightly, as though inhaling her scent.

"Um . . ." Mia swallowed nervously. "M-Mia."

"Mia," he repeated slowly, seemingly savoring her name. "Mia what?"

"Mia Stalis." Oh crap, why did he want to know her name? Why was he here, talking to her? In general, what was he doing in Central Park, so far away from any of the K Centers? *Breathe, Mia, breathe.*

"Relax, Mia Stalis." His smile got wider, exposing a dimple in his left cheek. A dimple? Ks had dimples? "Have you never encountered one of us before?"

"No, I haven't." Mia exhaled sharply, realizing that she was holding her breath. She was proud that her voice didn't sound as shaky as she felt. Should she ask? Did she want to know?

She gathered her courage. "What, um—" Another swallow. "What do you want from me?"

"For now, conversation." He looked like he was about to laugh at her, those gold eyes crinkling slightly at the corners.

Strangely, that pissed her off enough to take the edge off her fear. If there was anything Mia hated, it was being laughed at. With her short, skinny stature and a general lack of social skills that came from an awkward teenage phase involving every girl's nightmare of braces, frizzy hair, and glasses, Mia had more than enough experience being the butt of someone's joke.

She lifted her chin belligerently. "Okay, then, what is *your* name?"

"It's Korum."

"Just Korum?"

"We don't really have last names, not the way you do. My full name is much longer, but you wouldn't be able to pronounce it if I told you."

Okay, that was interesting. She now remembered reading something like that in *The New York Times*. So far, so good. Her legs had nearly stopped shaking, and her breathing was returning to normal. Maybe, just maybe, she would get out of this alive. This conversation business seemed safe enough, although the way he kept staring at her with those unblinking yellowish eyes was unnerving. She decided to keep him talking.

"What are you doing here, Korum?"

"I just told you, making conversation with you, Mia." His voice again held a hint of laughter.

Frustrated, Mia blew out her breath. "I meant, what are you doing here in Central Park? In New York City in general?"

He smiled again, cocking his head slightly to the side. "Maybe I'm hoping to meet a pretty curly-haired girl."

Okay, enough was enough. He was clearly toying with her. Now that she could think a little again, she realized that they were in the middle of Central Park, in full view of about a gazillion spectators. She surreptitiously glanced around to confirm that. Yep, sure enough, although people were obviously steering clear of her bench and its otherworldly occupant, there were a number of brave souls staring their way from farther up the path. A couple were even cautiously filming them with their wristwatch cameras. If the K tried anything with her, it would be on YouTube in the blink of an eye, and he had to know it. Of course, he may or may not care about that.

Still, going on the assumption that since she'd never come across any videos of K assaults on college students in the middle of Central Park, she was relatively safe, Mia cautiously reached for her laptop and lifted it to stuff it back into her backpack.

"Let me help you with that, Mia—"

And before she could blink, she felt him take her heavy laptop from her suddenly boneless fingers, gently brushing against her knuckles in the process. A sensation similar to a mild electric shock shot through Mia at his touch, leaving her nerve endings tingling in its wake.

Reaching for her backpack, he carefully put away the laptop in a smooth, sinuous motion. "There you go, all better now."

Oh God, he had touched her. Maybe her theory about the safety of public locations was bogus. She felt her breathing speeding up again, and her heart rate was probably well into the anaerobic zone at this point.

"I have to go now . . . Bye!"

How she managed to squeeze out those words without hyperventilating, she would never know. Grabbing the strap of the backpack he'd just put down, she jumped to her feet, noting somewhere in the back of her mind that her earlier paralysis seemed to be gone.

"Bye, Mia. I will see you later." His softly mocking voice carried in the clear spring air as she took off, nearly running in her haste to get away.

* * *

If you'd like to find out more, please visit my website at www.annazaires.com. All three books in the Krinar Chronicles trilogy are now available.

EXCERPT FROM *THE THOUGHT READERS* BY DIMA ZALES

Author's Note: If you'd like to try something different—and especially if you enjoy urban fantasy and science fiction—you might want to check out *The Thought Readers*, the first book in the *Mind Dimensions* series that I'm collaborating on with Dima Zales, my husband. But be warned, there is not much romance or sex in this one. Instead of sex, there's mind reading. The book is now available at most retailers.

* * *

Everyone thinks I'm a genius.

Everyone is wrong.

Sure, I finished Harvard at eighteen and now make crazy money at a hedge fund. But that's not because I'm unusually smart or hard-working.

It's because I cheat.

You see, I have a unique ability. I can go outside time into my own personal version of reality—the place I call "the Quiet"—where I can explore my surroundings while the rest of the world stands still.

I thought I was the only one who could do this—until I met *her*.

My name is Darren, and this is how I learned that I'm a Reader.

* * *

Sometimes I think I'm crazy. I'm sitting at a casino table in Atlantic City, and everyone around me is motionless. I call this the *Quiet*, as though giving it a name makes it seem more real—as though giving it a name changes the fact that all the players around me are frozen like statues, and I'm walking among them, looking at the cards they've been dealt.

The problem with the theory of my being crazy is that when I 'unfreeze' the world, as I just have, the cards the players turn over are the same ones I just saw in the Quiet. If I were crazy, wouldn't these cards be different? Unless I'm so far gone that I'm imagining the cards on the table, too.

But then I also win. If that's a delusion—if the pile of chips on my side of the table is a delusion—then I might as well question everything. Maybe my name isn't even Darren.

No. I can't think that way. If I'm really that confused, I don't want to snap out of it—because if I do, I'll probably wake up in a mental hospital.

Besides, I love my life, crazy and all.

My shrink thinks the Quiet is an inventive way I describe the 'inner workings of my genius.' Now that sounds crazy to me. She also might want me, but that's beside the point. Suffice it to say, she's as far as it gets from my datable age range, which is currently right around twenty-four. Still young, still hot, but done with school and pretty much beyond the clubbing phase. I hate clubbing, almost as much as I hated studying. In any case, my shrink's explanation doesn't work, as it doesn't account for the way I know things even a genius wouldn't know—like the exact value and suit of the other players' cards.

I watch as the dealer begins a new round. Besides me, there are three players at the table: Grandma, the Cowboy, and the Professional, as I call them. I feel that now almost-imperceptible fear that accompanies the phasing. That's what I call the process: phasing into the Quiet. Worrying about my sanity has always facilitated phasing; fear seems helpful in this process.

I phase in, and everything gets quiet. Hence the name for this state.

It's eerie to me, even now. Outside the Quiet, this casino is very loud: drunk people talking, slot machines, ringing of wins, music—the only place louder is a club or a concert. And yet, right at this moment, I could probably hear a pin drop. It's like I've gone deaf to the chaos that surrounds me.

Having so many frozen people around adds to the strangeness of it all. Here is a waitress stopped mid-step, carrying a tray with drinks. There is a woman about to pull a slot machine lever. At my own table, the dealer's hand is raised, the last card he dealt hanging unnaturally in midair. I walk up to him from the side of the table and reach for it. It's a king, meant for the Professional. Once I let the card go, it falls on the table rather than continuing to float as before—but I know full well that it will be back in the air, in the exact position it was when I grabbed it, when I phase out.

The Professional looks like someone who makes money playing poker, or at least the way I always imagined someone like that might look. Scruffy, shades on, a little sketchy-looking. He's been doing an excellent job with the poker face—basically not twitching a single muscle throughout the game. His face is so expressionless that I wonder if he might've gotten Botox to help maintain such a stony countenance. His hand is on the table, protectively covering the cards dealt to him.

I move his limp hand away. It feels normal. Well, in a manner of speaking. The hand is sweaty and hairy, so moving it aside is unpleasant and is admittedly an abnormal thing to do. The normal part is that the hand is warm, rather than cold. When I was a kid, I expected people to feel cold in the Quiet, like stone statues.

With the Professional's hand moved away, I pick up his cards. Combined with the king that was hanging in the air, he has a nice high pair. Good to know.

I walk over to Grandma. She's already holding her cards, and she has fanned them nicely for me. I'm able to avoid touching her wrinkled, spotted hands. This is a relief, as I've recently become conflicted about touching people—or, more specifically, women—in the Quiet. If I had to, I would rationalize touching Grandma's hand as harmless, or at least not creepy, but it's better to avoid it if possible.

In any case, she has a low pair. I feel bad for her. She's been losing a lot tonight. Her chips are dwindling. Her losses are due, at least partially, to the fact that she has a terrible poker face. Even before looking at her cards, I knew they wouldn't be good because I could tell she was disappointed as soon as her hand was dealt. I also caught a gleeful gleam in her eyes a few rounds ago when she had a winning three of a kind.

This whole game of poker is, to a large degree, an exercise in reading people—something I really want to get better at. At my job, I've been told I'm great at reading people. I'm not, though; I'm just good at using the Quiet to make it seem like I am. I do want to learn how to read people for real, though. It would be nice to know what everyone is thinking.

What I don't care that much about in this poker game is money. I do well enough financially to not have to depend on hitting it big gambling. I don't care if I win or lose, though quintupling my money back at the blackjack table was fun. This whole trip has been more about going gambling because I finally can, being twenty-one and all. I was never into fake IDs, so this is an actual milestone for me.

Leaving Grandma alone, I move on to the next player—the Cowboy. I can't resist taking off his straw hat and trying it on. I wonder if it's possible for me to get lice this way. Since I've never been able to bring back any inanimate objects from the Quiet, nor otherwise affect the real world in any lasting way, I figure I won't be able to get any living critters to come back with me, either.

Dropping the hat, I look at his cards. He has a pair of aces—a better hand than the Professional. Maybe the Cowboy is a professional, too. He has a good poker face, as far as I can tell. It'll be interesting to watch those two in this round.

Next, I walk up to the deck and look at the top cards, memorizing them. I'm not leaving anything to chance.

When my task in the Quiet is complete, I walk back to myself. Oh, yes, did I mention that I see myself sitting there, frozen like the rest of them? That's the weirdest part. It's like having an out-of-body experience.

Approaching my frozen self, I look at him. I usually avoid doing this, as it's too unsettling. No amount of looking in the mirror—or seeing videos of yourself on YouTube—can prepare you for viewing your own three-dimensional body up close. It's not something anyone is meant to experience. Well, aside from identical twins, I guess.

It's hard to believe that this person is me. He looks more like some random guy. Well, maybe a bit better than that. I do find this guy interesting. He looks cool. He looks smart. I think women would probably consider him good-looking, though I know that's not a modest thing to think.

It's not like I'm an expert at gauging how attractive a guy is, but some things are common sense. I can tell when a dude is ugly, and this frozen me is not. I also know that generally, being good-looking requires a symmetrical face, and the statue of me has that. A strong jaw doesn't hurt, either. Check. Having broad shoulders is a positive, and being tall really helps. All covered. I have blue eyes—that seems to be a plus. Girls have told me they like my eyes, though right now, on the frozen me, the eyes look creepy—glassy. They look like the eyes of a lifeless wax figure.

Realizing that I'm dwelling on this subject way too long, I shake my head. I can just picture my shrink analyzing this moment. Who would imagine admiring themselves like this as part of their mental illness? I can just picture her scribbling down *Narcissist*, underlining it for emphasis.

Enough. I need to leave the Quiet. Raising my hand, I touch my frozen self on the forehead, and I hear noise again as I phase out.

Everything is back to normal.

The card that I looked at a moment before—the king that I left on the table—is in the air again, and from there it follows the trajectory it was always meant to, landing near the Professional's hands. Grandma is still eyeing her fanned cards in disappointment, and the Cowboy has his hat on again, though I took it off him in the Quiet. Everything is exactly as it was.

On some level, my brain never ceases to be surprised at the discontinuity of the experience in the Quiet and outside it. As humans, we're hardwired to question reality when such things happen. When I was trying to outwit my shrink early on in my therapy, I once read an entire psychology textbook during our session. She, of course, didn't notice it, as I did it in the Quiet. The book talked about how babies as young as two months old are surprised if they see something out of the ordinary, like gravity appearing to work backwards. It's no wonder my brain has trouble adapting. Until I was ten, the world behaved normally, but everything has been weird since then, to put it mildly.

Glancing down, I realize I'm holding three of a kind. Next time, I'll look at my cards before phasing. If I have something this strong, I might take my chances and play fair.

The game unfolds predictably because I know everybody's cards. At the end, Grandma gets up. She's clearly lost enough money.

And that's when I see the girl for the first time.

She's hot. My friend Bert at work claims that I have a 'type,' but I reject that idea. I don't like to think of myself as shallow or predictable. But I might actually be a bit of both, because this girl fits Bert's description of my type to a T. And my reaction is extreme interest, to say the least.

Large blue eyes. Well-defined cheekbones on a slender face, with a hint of something exotic. Long, shapely legs, like those of a dancer. Dark wavy hair in a ponytail—a hairstyle that I like. And without bangs— even better. I hate bangs—not sure why girls do that to themselves. Though lack of bangs is not, strictly speaking, in Bert's description of my type, it probably should be.

I continue staring at her. With her high heels and tight skirt, she's overdressed for this place. Or maybe I'm underdressed in my jeans and t-shirt. Either way, I don't care. I have to try to talk to her.

I debate phasing into the Quiet and approaching her, so I can do something creepy like stare at her up close, or maybe even snoop in her pockets. Anything to help me when I talk to her.

I decide against it, which is probably the first time that's ever happened.

I know that my reasoning for breaking my usual habit—if you can even call it that—is strange. I picture the following chain of events: she agrees to date me, we go out for a while, we get serious, and because of the deep connection we have, I come clean about the Quiet. She learns I did something creepy and has a fit, then dumps me. It's ridiculous to think this, of course, considering that we haven't even spoken yet. Talk about jumping the gun. She might have an IQ below seventy, or the personality of a piece of wood. There can be twenty different reasons why I wouldn't want to date her. And besides, it's not all up to me. She might tell me to go fuck myself as soon as I try to talk to her.

Still, working at a hedge fund has taught me to hedge. As crazy as that reasoning is, I stick with my decision not to phase because I know it's the gentlemanly thing to do. In keeping with this unusually chivalrous me, I also decide not to cheat at this round of poker.

As the cards are dealt again, I reflect on how good it feels to have done the honorable thing—even without anyone knowing. Maybe I should try to respect people's privacy more often. As soon as I think this, I mentally snort. *Yeah, right.* I have to be realistic. I wouldn't be where I am today if I'd followed that advice. In fact, if I made a habit of respecting people's privacy, I would lose my job within days—and with it, a lot of the comforts I've become accustomed to.

Copying the Professional's move, I cover my cards with my hand as soon as I receive them. I'm about to sneak a peek at what I was dealt when something unusual happens.

The world goes quiet, just like it does when I phase in . . . but I did nothing this time.

And at that moment, I see *her*—the girl sitting across the table from me, the girl I was just thinking about. She's standing next to me, pulling her hand away from mine. Or, strictly speaking, from my frozen self's hand—as I'm standing a little to the side looking at her.

She's also still sitting in front of me at the table, a frozen statue like all the others.

My mind goes into overdrive as my heartbeat jumps. I don't even consider the possibility of that second girl being a twin sister or something like that. I know it's her. She's doing what I did just a few minutes ago. She's walking in the Quiet. The world around us is frozen, but we are not.

A horrified look crosses her face as she realizes the same thing. Before I can react, she lunges across the table and touches her own forehead.

The world becomes normal again.

She stares at me from across the table, shocked, her eyes huge and her face pale. Her hands tremble as she rises to her feet. Without so much as a word, she turns and begins walking away, then breaks into a run a couple of seconds later.

Getting over my own shock, I get up and run after her. It's not exactly smooth. If she notices a guy she doesn't know running after her, dating will be the last thing on her mind. But I'm beyond that now. She's the only person I've met who can do what I do. She's proof that I'm not insane. She might have what I want most in the world.

She might have answers.

* * *

If you'd like to learn more about our fantasy and science fiction books, please visit Dima Zales's website at www.dimazales.com and sign up for his new release email list. You can also connect with him on Facebook, Google Plus, Twitter, and Goodreads.

ABOUT THE AUTHOR

Anna Zaires is a *New York Times, USA Today,* and #1 international bestselling author of sci-fi romance and contemporary dark erotic romance. She fell in love with books at the age of five, when her grandmother taught her to read. Since then, she has always lived partially in a fantasy world where the only limits were those of her imagination. Currently residing in Florida, Anna is happily married to Dima Zales (a science fiction and fantasy author) and closely collaborates with him on all their works.

To learn more, please visit www.annazaires.com.

16651071R00258

Printed in Great Britain
by Amazon